A Catalog
of Such Stuff
as Dreams Are
Made On

weatherhead books on asia

Weatherhead Books on Asia
Weatherhead East Asian Institute, Columbia University
For a list of titles in the series, see page 325.

A Catalog
of Such Stuff
as Dreams Are
Made On

Translated by Bonnie S. McDougall
and Anders Hansson

Dung Kai-cheung

Columbia University Press
New York

Columbia University Press wishes to express its appreciation for assistance given by the Pushkin Fund in the publication of this book.
This publication has been supported by the Richard W. Weatherhead Publication Fund of the Weatherhead East Asian Institute, Columbia University.

Columbia University Press
Publishers Since 1893
New York   Chichester, West Sussex
cup.columbia.edu
A Catalog of Stuff as Dreams Are Made On © Dung Kai-Cheung 2011
English edition © Columbia University Press 2022
Originally published in Complex Chinese by Linking Publishing Co., Ltd. in Taiwan
Published by arrangement with Linking Publishing Co., Ltd., through Ailbert Cultural Company Limited
Cantonese Love Stories by Dung Kai-cheung
Text Copyright © Dung Kai-cheung
First published by Penguin Books Australia 2017
Reprinted by permission of Penguin Random House Australia Pty Ltd
Library of Congress Cataloging-in-Publication Data
Names: Dong, Qizhang, 1967– author. | McDougall, Bonnie S., 1941– translator. | Hansson, Anders, 1944– translator.
Title: A catalog of such stuff as dreams are made on / Dung Kai-cheung ; translated by Bonnie S. McDougall and Anders Hansson.
Other titles: Menghua lu. English
Description: English edition. | New York : Columbia University Press, 2022. | Series: Weatherhead books on Asia
Identifiers: LCCN 2021045284 (print) | LCCN 2021045285 (ebook) | ISBN 9780231205429 (hardback ; acid-free paper) | ISBN 9780231205436 (trade paperback ; acid-free paper) | ISBN 9780231555999 (ebook)
Subjects: LCSH: Dong, Qizhang, 1967—Translations into English. | Hong Kong (China)—Fiction. | LCGFT: Short stories.
Classification: LCC PL2936.3.O54 M4613 2022 (print) | LCC PL2936.3.O54 (ebook) | DDC 895.13/52—dc23/eng/20211203
LC record available at https://lccn.loc.gov/2021045284
LC ebook record available at https://lccn.loc.gov/2021045285

Columbia University Press books are printed on permanent and durable acid-free paper.
Printed in the United States of America
Cover design: Julia Kushnirsky
Cover image: Chihoi

For Torkel

Contents

CONTENTS

Author's Preface

The Mask

It may seem frivolous to say that the mask is currently in vogue, yet it is true that the prolonged necessity of wearing masks to protect us from infection has also made the mask a major item in our daily outfits. In addition to its practical function, it is all too natural for some to choose the right mask in order to look good in it, just as one chooses a nice pair of glasses or earrings. For us in Hong Kong, another kind of mask had been the emblem of our experience the year before the pandemic hit—the gas mask.

It would not be possible to write another book like *A Catalog of Such Stuff as Dreams Are Made On* given the current state of affairs. When the stories in this book were written twenty-two years ago, I selected new topics from local entertainment and fashion magazines every week from 1998 to 1999, letting my imagination run free in associations triggered by names, forms, usages, characteristics, promotional slogans, or popular comments.

The original Chinese title of the present book literally means "a record of dreams of prosperity," with allusions to the records of city life written in the Southern Song dynasty. After the Northern Song was destroyed by invaders from the north in 1127, the court moved to a new capital in the south. The intellectual elite who retreated with the government were deeply nostalgic about the material and cultural wealth of the old capital, Kaifeng. The most famous of the many accounts of the old capital's lively commercial activities and entertainments was *Dreams of Prosperity in the Eastern Capital (Dongjing menghua lu)* by Meng Yuanlao. A prevailing sense of the dreamlike quality and transitory nature of the good life permeates these works. The form of the *Catalog* is a reinvention of the Song records. For a full understanding of the book's original intentions, an anonymous collector and chronicler has to be presupposed.

I prefer to use the expression "sketches" instead of short stories for this book because of the speed with which they were written, the broad strokes that were employed, and their apparent incompleteness. The brevity of the form does not prevent it from compressing whole life stories or relatively long time spans, as the narratives move swiftly between general summaries and particular elaborations. For this reason, the sketches may not fit in with the usual expectations of flash fiction (although they may seem to belong in that category). From a broader perspective, all life is but a single flash.

Twenty-five of the ninety-nine stories in the present book were published as *Cantonese Love Stories* in 2017 by Penguin China for its Hong Kong Specials series, commemorating the twentieth anniversary of the retrocession. The title "love stories" is deliberately misleading, mainly justified on the grounds of its reference to a collection of local ballads translated by Cecil Clementi, a former governor of Hong Kong and lover of poetry, and entitled *Cantonese Love Songs*. The label "Cantonese" stands out unashamedly not just as a description but also a statement about the cultural and linguistic belongingness of the work. In short, although basically the text of the *Catalog* is comprehensible to Chinese readers, the use of local colloquial expressions and other linguistic and nonlinguistic factors give it a strong Cantonese flavor.

A book on objects in vogue seems destined to suffer the same fate as its subject matter. In its 2011 Chinese edition, I wrote jokingly about an aesthetic of obsolescence. More seriously, this process can be described as making obsolescence itself an aesthetic value, by means of which we may attempt to save things from oblivion. There is only one way to prevent the present from becoming obsolete: that is, when it leaves the impermanent ebb and flow of current affairs and enters the realm of history. Only then is the mask no longer a symbol of fear but a revelation of truth. It takes more than words to write this history.

Dung Kai-cheung

Translators' Note

Many of the sketches in this book are headed by introductory notes that comment on commercial and cultural phenomena in Hong Kong current in the years 1998 and 1999. Some of the notes explain the use of puns and wordplay in general, especially the author's dexterity in creating names with several levels of meaning. Formal names (surnames and personal names) have in most cases been transliterated with Latin letters as they would appear on an individual's Hong Kong ID card. Many Hong Kong people also adopt an English first name, and a small number of these may appear bizarre. Nicknames are in some cases translated; otherwise, explanations or Cantonese romanizations are provided. It is common in Cantonese for personal names to be prefixed by "Ah" among family and friends, and this usage is maintained; "Siu," meaning young, may also be included as part of a name. Where two people in a single sketch have names with different Chinese characters but identical pronunciation, an unconventional spelling for one of them is provided.

Some expressions that occur in the sketches are common in Hong Kong but have no close English equivalents. A *ch'a-ch'aan-t'ing* (tea cafeteria/restaurant) serves cheap Western-style food adjusted to Hong Kong taste as well as standard Chinese dishes. These places typically serve Hong Kong–style milk tea, so the expression "tea café" has been adopted for the translation. Other expressions are in a form of English used throughout Hong Kong (or sometimes borrowed from other languages) but not necessarily understood outside Asia; for instance, the expression "office lady," or "OL," is originally Japanese (ōeru) and refers to young female office workers who mostly perform simple routine tasks. VCDs are video compact discs; this digital video format remained popular in Hong Kong even after the introduction of DVDs.

The sketches "Red Wing," "Aprons," "Adidas," "Depsea Water," "The Duffel Coat," "Burberrys Blue Label," and "Made in Hong Kong" were first jointly translated by Bonnie McDougall and students in the MA program in translation studies at the University of Sydney in 2012, 2013, and 2014.

We are most grateful to Dung Kai-cheung for his patient assistance: he has carefully read our translation, spotted mistakes, and helped solve problems. The responsibility for any remaining errors is ours.

AH & BMcD

A Catalog
of Such Stuff
as Dreams Are
Made On

1

AGNÈS B.

The first time Ka Tsai took the train to his office, he saw a young woman with an Agnès b. bag hanging from her left shoulder, standing on the platform with her back toward him. The previous evening, Ka Tsai had fallen out with his girlfriend, Amy, and had gone off to drown his sorrows. When he drove his car home, he'd mounted the pavement, and the door on the left side had been torn off. The car had to go in for a big repair job, but fortunately no pedestrians had been hurt, and there weren't any police on the road. It was just that his neck was a little twisted and a bit sore.

That day the young woman was standing right at the edge of the railway platform, her back to Ka Tsai, gazing toward the vanishing point of the railway line in the distance. Her hair, which wasn't long, was tied on either side into two short plaits, revealing the vertebrae of her delicate white neck. She was wearing a simple, Jean Seberg–type blue-and-white striped long-sleeved T-shirt and a pair of jeans. Her shoulders were pulled back, her shoulder blades drawn in tightly, and her thin arms were held at an angle on each side with her hands slightly open. Her slender buttocks were high slung, and you could imagine her breasts sticking out in front. Ka Tsai, holding a heavy briefcase in his left hand, stared in the direction of the young woman. The whole stretch of the railway line in front of her curved to the left. There was something a little odd about her back, something somehow unbalanced about the way she stood, that made Ka Tsai keep glancing at her, and it looked as if he was about to lean out over the platform and fall onto the tracks. Then the train came up along the platform from behind, and Ka Tsai hastily ran up to the first carriage.

At first Ka Tsai thought it was because of the Agnès b. hanging from the young woman's left shoulder. It was a trapezium-shaped Agnès b. tote bag, dark blue with a white zipper, in the traditional travel-bag style much liked by young women, not the ordinary kind of middle-class product preferred by office ladies. The bag was medium-sized, although it looked swollen, as if something had been stuffed inside. There were no empty seats in the carriage. The young woman stood in front of the door on the other side, gazing outside, her hands pressed against the glass pane. Ka Tsai stood behind her, his eyes fixed on the strands of hair parted in the middle at the back of her head and on her smooth neck, which began to be a little unsymmetrical. Ka Tsai finally discovered that the young woman's backbone actually inclined toward the left.

After this, Ka Tsai punctually took that train every day, but he was never able to look directly at Agnès b.'s face; all he could see was the skewed view from behind, and the Agnès b. bag that was held ever more tightly against her left side. Ka Tsai of course didn't know her name, and just thought of her as Agnès b. Occasionally he thought about speaking to Agnès b. but never managed to find a pretext. On his way to and from work, he became addicted to looking at her back, and in the end he didn't even try to patch up his disagreement with Amy, both sides continuing their cold war. Ka Tsai could not stop himself from imagining Agnès b.'s naked body, but he limited himself to her back; he often imagined tracing her curved spine with his finger, joint by joint.

Later, when Ka Tsai's car was repaired, he ended up selling it and continued taking the train every day. One day someone jumped on the rail at the train station in front, and the trains came to a standstill. When it became clear that service could not be restored within a short period of time, the people on the platform began to stream out, until only Ka Tsai and Agnès b., who had been standing up at the top of the platform, were left.

Turning her head to look at the people leaving, Agnès b. said in a low voice, "You don't remember me?"

Ka Tsai gave a start, thinking he had misheard, and tried hard to identify her.

"My mother took me to your clinic," Agnès b. continued. "It was four years ago, I was fourteen. You told me to take off my clothes and bend over so you could examine me. You pressed your hands up and down my back and said my spine was curved. It was congenital, and it was already too late to do anything. If I had been a child, there could still have been time to correct it; now the only thing to do is to exercise more. When I get old, my muscles and bones will degenerate. I will experience back pain, and it may influence my heart and lung functions. If it's serious, there may be pressure on the nerves and paralysis of the limbs; it's hard to say."

Ka Tsai wanted to tell her that he was not a doctor but an accountant, but in the end he said vaguely, "Your present condition looks fine, no need to worry."

Agnès b. laughed. In a voice that could have been either a child's or a grown woman's, she said, "At that time your fingers were cold." As she finished speaking, she stepped toward the station exit, her left hand holding high the Agnès b. bag and swinging it gracefully in the air as if there weren't anything inside.

2
—

CUTIE PUNK

Shibuya is a busy district in Tokyo, known for its fashion
shops and nightlife. Takeshita Street in Harajuku has many
youth-oriented shops and eateries with the latest fads. Miriam Yeung is a popular Hong Kong singer and actress. Massive Attack is a British "trip hop" band.

In the summer of 1998, when Ah Pat went with Siu Pei on a pil-
grimage to Japan, nothing came of the plan to visit Kyoto's Kiyo-
mizu Temple, the Hakone hot springs, or even the Meiji Shrine
in Tokyo, all of which had been on Ah Pat's itinerary. For five
days and nights, Siu Pei had been hanging out in the sacred sites
of Harajuku's Takeshita Street and elsewhere in Shibuya, slipping back and forth between them, so that by the time they were
about to leave, she'd caught just a single glimpse of the Tokyo
Tower as they traveled past it. Nevertheless, Siu Pei returned
home fully satisfied, not only because both her suitcases were
packed full with the spoils of the trip but also because she had
at last discovered a style that was entirely her own.

On the flight home, Siu Pei had made a major change in her
appearance, her old spaghetti-strap floral dresses abandoned in
their Shinjuku hotel room. What she was wearing for the return
trip was a pink cutie top, plastic armbands in multiple colors, a
necklace made of plastic beads that looked like candies, and an
adjustable ring with flowers around it on her finger; in addition,

she had a punk leopard-spot scarf, a tiger-striped waist bag, a variety of broad and narrow leather straps, studs, and chunky metal bracelets. Stretching out one arm, Ah Pat steered Siu Pei on their way out through customs. Apprehensive of being hit on the head by an elbow, he managed to dodge Siu Pei's flailing arms as she waved to her sister, who'd come to meet them.

Ah Pat, who was five years older than Siu Pei, had got himself a tutoring job just after going to university, his pupil a girl in year three of secondary school. Arriving for the first time at the girl's home on the twentieth floor of her building, he encountered her throwing a Hello Kitty out of the window in a fit of bad temper. After Ah Pat had gone downstairs to pick up the Hello Kitty, the girl looked up at him, pouting, and then bursting into a grin. "I'm Siu Pei," she said. "Who are you?"

From then on Ah Pat began adapting to the ups and downs in Siu Pei's behavior. Once when a teacher had punished her at school, Siu Pei let off steam to Ah Pat at home afterward, and when Ah Pat said the teacher hadn't been unreasonable, Siu Pei banged her maths textbook on his head. Ah Pat didn't say anything but sat down on a sofa until the time was up and he left. On his next visit, Siu Pei had bought a mango pancake and offered it to him. As he bit into it, his heart melted. Seeing Siu Pei licking her lips, he passed over the other half to her. "This is for you!"

Overjoyed, Siu Pei gulped it down in one mouthful.

In the course of a few years, Siu Pei and Ah Pat split up and got together again several times, but in the end they stayed together. When Ah Pat found a job after graduation, his disposition became ever more stable, unaffected by even the most earth-shattering events. Siu Pei, on the other hand, vacillated, not knowing what she wanted to do. Going out to karaoke with her friends in the evening, she might sing Miriam Yeung songs, but then, upon returning home in the middle of the night, she might listen to Massive Attack on her own. At times she would spend the whole night at a rave with no thought of her school-work, but at other times she was afraid of not being accepted to university and studied throughout the night. That's why Siu Pei eventually felt Cutie Punk was where she belonged and where she wanted to stay forever if possible, ignoring all other trends. So even into late autumn she persisted in wearing sleeveless tops to demonstrate her chosen path.

Ever since she'd discovered Cutie Punk, Siu Pei's complicated temperament began to be less abrasive, as if the two opposing elements inside her were being reconciled. One day she suddenly had a brain wave when she and Ah Pat were going out to a buffet restaurant, covering her left arm in plastic cutie ornaments and her right arm in metallic punk. Afterward, when Ah Pat drove them to the seaside to take in the fresh air, he took the opportunity to suggest that they should get married after she'd graduated from university. Moved to tears, she knew Ah Pat truly loved her and that she'd never find another man in the whole world who was so kind to her. On the other hand, she had a strong aversion to the idea of marriage, seeing it as simply stripping away her freedom.

"You really want to marry me?" she exclaimed. "You're so good!"

"If I got married though," she followed up with hardly a pause, "would other people actually still want to go out with me for a good time? You're so stupid!"

Switching from one thing to another without any logic, they began quarreling. Siu Pei squared off against Ah Pat, striking him ferociously on the head with her right hand while stroking his face in a sweet and loving manner with her left hand. Not sure from one moment to the next whether he was suffering or feeling pleasure, Ah Pat fought as hard as he could to remove all the Cutie Punk accessories that Siu Pei was wearing.

After a gray, gloomy winter, summer days were coming back and the Cutie Punk trend was no more. Siu Pei received her report card: two Bs and two Cs, so going to university wasn't a problem. Back at home, she brought out all last year's plastic and metal ornaments, amounting to a few dozen altogether, and put them on her smooth bare arms as she sat in the sunshine in front of her twentieth-floor window, thinking back on the past eighteen years of her life and the summer that had truly belonged to her. The telephone rang: it was Ah Pat asking about her exam results. For no reason Siu Pei burst into tears, as the silvery metal and magical colors covering her body glittered in the light.

3

MAGPAPER

Magpaper was a magazine for young people first published as a supplement to the newspaper *Hong Kong Daily News* (until June 1997) and later reappearing as a weekly magazine. Contents included fashion, Hong Kong literature, cinema, music, comics, and social issues, e.g., homosexuality. *Over Time* was a Japanese television drama from 1999. Sorimachi Takashi is a Japanese actor and singer who played the main role in the 1998 television adaptation of the manga *Great Teacher Onizuka*. Esumi Makiko is a Japanese model, actress, and writer who also appeared in *GTO*. Jan Lamb is a Hong Kong DJ, singer, presenter, actor, director, DVD-cover designer, etc. Lai Tat Tat Wing is a Hong Kong artist known for his comics. *Love Generation* is a Japanese television serial from 1997 that included characters called Kimura Takuya and Matsu Takako. The British film *Melody* (1971) is the story of a young boy and girl who fall in love. It was tremendously popular in Japan and Hong Kong.

To Yiu Yiu, the winter of 1998–99 was a blank. Pleated skirts, gray suede shoes, Blue Label bags, *Over Time*, Sorimachi Takashi and Esumi Makiko—she was totally ignorant of them all. Instead she browsed through *Magpaper* every day, picking up one issue after another as if it were still a regularly published weekly.

On 10 October 1997, Yiu Yiu had noticed a new magazine with Jan Lamb on the cover at a newspaper stall. At the top, MAG was printed in large letters, with "Inaugural Issue" immediately above it. She bought a copy to have a look and was immediately struck by the sensation that this was it! She devoured it avidly on her way to class in the minibus, nearly forgetting to tell the driver where she was getting off. In the student canteen at lunchtime, she had reached the "Fellows" page when a boy sat down next to her, also with a copy of *Magpaper* in his hand. They exchanged secret glances, like long-lost relatives. He was Ah Ngon.

Yiu Yiu realized instinctively that Ah Ngon looked just like someone who had walked straight out of the pages of *Magpaper*, strongly resembling the new-era fashion models on the cover and inside pages. They were slim youths with drooping eyelids, lean bodies, and expressionless faces, coolly seductive, but once they smiled and flashed their teeth, they couldn't disguise their lack of worldliness; they were enchanting.

Ah Ngon had become a *Magpaper* fan before Yiu Yiu, reading it every day at the time it was still a newspaper supplement. When later on it became a weekly with a Chinese title meaning something like "new aspirations," he was even keener. Every week, as if by silent agreement, the two of them met in the canteen with their copies of *Magpaper* and a lot to talk about. There were the many and diverse new music terms, such as hardcore, gothic, ambient, techno, and grunge; there were large spectacles that were either flashy or cool; tight colorful shirts, bell-bottom trousers, and heroin-chic makeup; the very forthright gay-and-lesbian page; poetry and fiction replete with blood and disease; criticism that openly stated its intention; and Lai Tat Tat Wing's comics . . . Furthermore, it was the season of *Love Generation* and the winter when Kimura Takuya and Matsu Takako were all conquering.

When *Magpaper* became a fortnightly on 6 March 1998, Yiu Yiu had a feeling of foreboding. That day she didn't see Ah Ngon and sat disappointed on her own, eating her shiny red sweet-and-sour pork with rice. As she approached her bus stop after class in the evening, she saw Ah Ngon in the distance, standing with another skinny male student, both of them looking down reading an issue of *Magpaper*. With their faces stuck close together, pointing at this and that, their backs toward the sunset, they were like the two children in the film *Melody*. Yiu Yiu felt a tightness in the pit of her stomach and lowered her head to let her long hair shield her face as she hurriedly skirted their long shadows.

Magpaper subsequently ceased publication, the 1 May 1998 issue being the last. Yiu Yiu did not turn up for that year's final examinations; nobody knew why. Some said she had a sudden attack of amnesia, some even claiming that she was in a vegetative state. Ah Ngon, however, was unaware of this. He narrowly got his degree and actually managed to become a model.

Yiu Yiu knew nothing about Ah Ngon being a model. Coming back home from hospital to recuperate in October that year, she began leafing through *Magpaper*, getting through one issue per week as if she were reliving the past year. That took more than six months, coming to an abrupt end on 1 May 1999. It was only then that she suddenly recalled that she'd written a poem in April the previous year and submitted it to *Magpaper*, but in the end it was received too late for publication. Not the slightest notion of the contents of the poem, or even the topic, remained in her mind.

4
—

HELLO KITTY

When Tsui Kit Yuk moved up to primary school, the school regulations required her to adopt an English name. Her mother entered Kitty in the class book, saying that Kit Yuk's eyes were pointed, like a kitten's. After Tsui Kit Yuk had grown up, she didn't much look like a cat, nor was her temperament anything like a cat's. Nevertheless, whenever she had a birthday or celebration, her friends would give her Hello Kitty gifts. Everyone knew that Tsui Kit Yuk was a Hello Kitty fan.

In fact, Tsui Kit Yuk was not a particularly great admirer of Hello Kitty, nor was she particularly antagonistic toward it. It was just that when she'd come third in her fourth year of primary school, her mother had bought her a Hello Kitty water canteen as a reward. Afterward, her friends, not actually knowing why, began to give her Hello Kitty presents. To avoid being unpleasant to her friends, Tsui Kit Yuk went along with this, saying she liked Hello Kitty. Everyone felt more than ever that it was convenient having Kit Yuk as a friend.

Like the Hello Kitty presents she got over the years, Tsui Kit Yuk's friends kept accumulating; her old schoolmates from primary school, high school, and university kept in touch and would meet at arranged times. Actually, Tsui Kit Yuk was not particularly active in these arrangements, nor a brilliant conversationalist, but her old schoolmates first of all remembered Tsui Kit Yuk, and then, remembering her, agreed to get together.

Tsui Kit Yuk had studied accountancy at university, and her friends had joked that in the future she would get a job at the Sanrio Company that made Hello Kitty giftware, but she refused to comment. After graduating, she entered one of the "Big Six" audit firms, packed away her Hello Kitty pencil case and phone cover, and went to the office wearing a business suit. During the first training week, a young man wearing a sapphire-blue shirt with a gold tie hailed her in the corridor.

"Hi, Kitty, I'm Stephen in K division, same as you."

They shook hands.

Stephen was already a senior member of the team, and afterward Tsui Kit Yuk accompanied him many times on business trips, where he patiently guided her. Stephen wasn't talkative, his personality being quite a contrast to his eye-catching ties. "Hi, Kitty," he would greet her every morning, and then bury his head in his work. It wasn't until a year later that he and Tsui Kit Yuk began dating. When Tsui Kit Yuk and Stephen applied for seven days' vacation leave to go traveling in Japan, her friends were full of noisy admiration. They found it inexplicable, however, that Tsui Kit Yuk didn't visit Hello Kitty Land and Tokyo Disneyland. When she was pressed to say where she had been, Tsui Kit Yuk felt a little embarrassed. What she remembered was steam curling upward in the Hakone Hot Springs district, and long, relaxed days with the two of them just being together without saying a word.

Hello Kitty not only seemed immortal but also strove hard to become stronger and stronger. The gift industry suddenly expanded. Apart from the traditional fancy stationery, they were promoting Hello Kitty toasters, radios, TVs, cameras, mobile phones, vacuum cleaners, electric fans, credit cards, cotton-padded quilts, household furniture, notebook computers, cars and hundreds of other things. There were also teddy bears, chickens, puppies, and cats, cats, and more cats, all dressed up as Hello Kitty. People who adored them claimed that Hello Kitty was a unique gift, one that, lacking a mouth, was beyond the world of sentient beings. On the other hand, those opposed said Hello Kitty was wooden and without expression.

When it so happened that Tsui Kit Yuk and Stephen split up, her good friends competed to buy the most recent Hello Kitty products for her on the pretext of wishing her a happy birthday in advance but actually to cheer her up. Sitting in a restaurant, Tsui Kit Yuk opened the presents one by one to a chorus of admiring comments, while she repeatedly expressed her gratitude. After the meal, Tsui Kit Yuk went to the ladies, where she touched up her makeup in front of the mirror, but the more lipstick she applied, the messier it got. She took a paper tissue and violently wiped her lips, almost wiping away her mouth.

That evening, before she went to bed, Tsui Kit Yuk put lipstick on all 126 Hello Kitties in her bedroom. Afterward she dreamt that she was in the Hakone inn; it was barely light outside, the Tsui Kit Yuk in the mirror on her dressing table was putting on lipstick, and a strange man was fast asleep on the *tatami*. The more lipstick she put on, the messier it got, so she took a tissue and wiped it off, and her mouth was gone.

Tsui Kit Yuk woke up in alarm. The sky was between light and dark. Each of the Hello Kitties that surrounded her lacked a mouth.

5

TANK TOPS

JUPAS stands for Joint University Programmes Admissions System.

Lau See Nga's female classmates at university privately held a low opinion of her, claiming that she flirted with the male students and even professors. On the other hand, every single one of Lau See Nga's male classmates flattered her extravagantly, keen to exchange a few words with her or to sit next to her in class. Whether they loathed or adored her, all the students had their eyes fixed on the tank tops that Lau See Nga almost invariably wore.

Lau See Nga was crazy about tank tops, and her entire wardrobe was full of tops in different styles and colors. At times even she found it amazing that this brief, simple garment could be matched in such endless variety. Nor were they just for when it was blazing hot; she would wear a top under her blouse or jacket in the cool of autumn, while in the depths of winter, coat and jumper would come off whenever she stepped inside a heated room to reveal her usual skimpy top.

In fact, Lau See Nga wasn't overly fussy about what she wore, hardly bothered about makeup, and let her shoulder-length hair hang straight down. A pair of glasses with thin black frames perched on the bridge of her delicate nose, but they actually enhanced her graceful features. She was not talkative and gave the impression of not making an effort to listen to what people were saying, as if her heart wasn't in it, so everyone regarded her as indifferent and unapproachable; this only exacerbated the difference in attitudes of the male and female students.

When Lau See Nga was in a Band 4 secondary school studying for the Advanced-Level Examination, not a single student in her class was successful. The class took this painful experience to heart, and twelve students decided to study on their own to take the examination again, forming a Winners' Club to support and encourage each other. Lau See Nga initially had no intention of re-sitting the exam but then changed her mind. On weekdays she worked in a video-rental shop and at weekends she went to a tea café managed by the family of one of the club members to take part in an economics tutoring class. The tutor, whose name was Kwok, was a married man in his early thirties; he was a teacher in their old school who had previously taught them for one year. At first Mr. Kwok was reluctant to start teaching them again, but after asking who would be taking part, he finally agreed and even declined to charge them for it. The result was that four of them passed the exam the following year, three failed, and the other five had dropped out. Lau See Nga was accepted by the Department of Business Administration. It was then she began wearing tank tops, never appearing without them.

Toward the end of term in her second year of university, an elderly professor kept demanding that Lau See Nga revise her term paper. He made her come to see him about it every afternoon, and these sessions would drag on until late at night. As a result, Lau See Nga succeeded in coming at the head of her class that year.

When the university swimming team were training during the summer vacation that same year, every single one of the male swimmers repeatedly glanced toward Lau See Nga where she was sitting in the spectators' seats, reading a book, while the younger lads exerted extraordinary efforts with every stroke. When the training session was over, a swimmer from the Engineering Department called Chan Hing Yin pushed forward, climbed up the stone steps, and stood towering in front of Lau See Nga.

"Let's go!" he said.

Lau See Nga raised her head, looked at him through the clear lenses of her glasses, stood up, and, holding her book against her valiant chest, walked away at his side without saying a word, his strong dark arm wrapped around her soft white shoulder. The onlookers swooned in grief and envy. From then on, Chan Hing Yin walked with a spring in his step, his spirit elated. There was just one thing he couldn't understand, and no matter how many times he turned it over in his mind, it still bothered him. When he and Lau See Nga made love for the first time, while staying in a holiday flat on Cheung Chau, why wasn't she willing to take off the only thing left on her: the tank top?

After the JUPAS list of successful candidates had been announced, the members of the Winners' Club invited Mr. Kwok out for dim sum to thank him for his efforts. After the meal was over and the others dispersed, Lau See Nga and Mr. Kwok were left standing side by side at the bus stop. Wave after wave of hot August air engulfed them until she could smell the sweat from his body. Mr. Kwok was talking about his newly born son when he suddenly stopped.

"I have felt all along that you would make a good wife," he said, "and I can certainly picture your appearance when you get married in a few years' time."

Lau See Nga couldn't help finding this funny. "And what will I look like then?"

"It will be like you are now, won't it? Wearing a tank top, that's how it will be."

Mr. Kwok's bus arrived, and Lau See Nga waved goodbye in front of the bus stop. Her slender arm gleamed in the sunlight, stinging Mr. Kwok's eyes so much that he could hardly keep them open.

6
—
SENA'S PIANO II

Long Vacations is a Japanese television drama series from 1996. The main characters are jobless or struggling to find a permanent job. Sena Hidetoshi, played by Kimura Takuya, is a pianist who takes part in competitions. Hayama Minami, played by Yamaguchi Tomoko, is a penniless model who comes to stay in Sena's home. One of Sena's students is played by Hirosue Ryōko. "Prism of the Wind" ("Kaze no purizumu" 風のプリズム) is a song from 1997 performed by Hirosue Ryōko. In the music video of the song, she rides a bike through the streets wearing an open checked shirt, yellow T-shirt, and cream trousers. She rides into a building, through a corridor, and then imagines herself changing into a black dress and standing barefoot on stage, singing under a spotlight.

After her Certificate of Education exam, Ka Yan didn't want to look for a summer job right away but stayed at home unemployed, watching pirated VCDs of Japanese shows that her friend Siu Tsing had lent her. After listening to the piano tune that Sena plays to Minami in *Long Vacations*, she decided to learn the piano.

Her mother had made up her mind when her daughter was only little that she had no musical talent. They had bought a small toy piano for five-year-old Ka Yan, who stepped on it so all the keys fell out. However, Ka Yan thought it was just a pretext for her mother, who was too stingy to pay the steep fees for piano lessons. So, Ka Yan resolved to earn money for lessons herself and got work at a convenience store.

Ka Yan lived in a public-housing estate in Fan Ling, and the music center was in Sheung Shui, so she only needed five minutes to get there on her bike. She had lessons on Monday mornings and rented a practice room with a piano from Tuesday to Saturday. The piano teacher was a young fellow in his early twenties, who looked like a Community Youth Club member. There was nothing musician-like about him from any angle, although he always assumed an air of frustrated talent. When he enquired about the kind of music Ka Yan would like to learn, she asked if he watched Japanese TV shows, such as the one where Kimura Takuya is playing to Yamaguchi Tomoko. The young fellow frowned and snorted, saying he hadn't seen it. Furthermore, he didn't teach popular music.

They started off with learning some off-putting tunes, so boring that they made Ka Yan feel nervous, but in the face of her young teacher's haughty attitude, she became utterly determined, forcing herself to persevere in her exercises until in the end there was some progress. Throughout summer, except for time spent at work, all she did was practice the piano, going back and forth on her bike between Fan Ling and Sheung Shui. Once after class, the young fellow said Ka Yan's progress had been pretty good and she could move on to *First Lessons in Bach*. Had she heard of Bach, he wanted to know. Ka Yan turned away and grimaced.

For their next lesson, the young fellow brought out a CD.

"This is Glenn Gould playing Bach," he said. "In *Long Vacations*, when Hirosue Ryōko was leaving, Kimura Takuya gave her a CD saying it was by his favorite pianist. This is it. The way that show's written was not too bad at all actually."

After her lesson, Ka Yan for the first time left together with her teacher. Getting on her bike, she could hear him mumbling behind her, "You're really like Hirosue Ryōko, you play just as ferociously."

She turned her head around toward him and smiled, swaying on her bike as she rode off. Back home that evening after work, she eagerly put on the CD and spent the rest of the night listening to it. Her mother scolded her for having gone crazy playing the piano, but Ka Yan didn't hear her; she just knew her heart was beating up and down, high and low.

After the exam results were released, her school admitted Ka Yan into secondary six. On receiving her report card, she went to Sheung Shui to practice the piano. She ran into her teacher on the way, so she stopped and got off her bike. Each of them looked around to the left and right.

"Have you seen 'Prism of the Wind'?" he asked casually. Ka Yan didn't understand. "It's an MTV video with Hirosue Ryōko; she looks just like you."

With school vacation coming to an end, Ka Yan had been planning to save money to buy a piano. She wanted to ask her teacher for his opinion, but the music center staff told her Mr. Lam had resigned. When she'd left to go home on her bike, the wind grew much stronger, so that her open checked shirt flew up, and it seemed that even the bright yellow T-shirt she wore underneath it, her cream trousers, and her canvas shoes were buffeted. When she'd gone halfway, it seemed as if the light in the sky had suddenly been switched off. It began to rain heavily, water dripping from her eyelashes. The school was on her way back home, so she turned off toward it for shelter.

The school buildings were unusually deserted, but the glass doors of the assembly hall were unlocked, so she pushed them open and went in. Evenly lined-up rows of seats filled the room. As she walked up to the stage, the sound of the rain outside seemed further and further away. At center stage stood a grand piano. A few black evening dresses with spaghetti straps were hanging behind the stage. Ka Yan changed into one of them but didn't put her shoes back on, walking barefoot out on the stage. Before she sat down at the piano, a spotlight suddenly came on. Ka Yan swiftly played all of Bach's *Goldberg Variations* to the empty hall. From below the stage came applause. It was her young teacher sitting right in the middle of the empty seats. Ka Yan stood up and took a bow. Then her teacher went up on stage and played the tune Sena had played to Minami.

When the music came to an end, the spotlight went out and all sank into darkness. Only the distant sound of the rain remained, pitter-patter, pitter-patter.

7

IXUS

Satō Yasue is a Japanese actress and model. She won an award for her role in *Bounce Ko Gals*, a film from 1997 about school-girls engaging in "compensated dating" with older men. She also appeared as a model in *non-no* and other fashion magazines. Sakai Noriko is a Japanese singer and actress who appeared in a commercial for Canon's IXUS cameras on Hong Kong television.

Ponila's original name had been Paulina, but as a child she often had her hair tied into a little ponytail, so others began to call her Ponila. As her hair grew longer, her ponytail became far from little, but people still called her Little Ponila.

Ponila wasn't little anymore either, and her friends said she looked like *non-no*'s popular model Satō Yasue with her long arms and legs, but Ponila didn't think that was anything special. Later on, when she went to see *Bounce Ko Gals*, she discovered that Raku in the film was actually played by Satō Yasue, whose face in close-up showed masses of freckles. For Ponila it was like suddenly finding a long-lost relative.

After the film was over, Ponila rushed out to buy a camera, telling the shop assistant she wanted a light one that she could carry with her at any time, something like the one advertised by Sakai Noriko. The shop assistant nodded, crossing his forefingers as they did in the commercial.

"IXUS?" he said. "Size of a cigarette packet—smallest one in the world—inbuilt flash—with zoom and panorama. Not expensive, you'll get change from 2,000 dollars. Uses APS film, it's smaller than 135 film and it comes in a cartridge. You can expose the film first, then pick out the photos to be enlarged, and there are three image formats . . ."

Ponila just nodded; it was all the same to her.

Ponila had been a waitress for some time, switching from one restaurant to another, and she had friends everywhere. Girls got along well with Ponila. They felt she was a bit silly but not stupid, and had rather peculiar tastes but didn't scare anyone; you couldn't depend on her, but it was easy enough to get along with her. Boys also liked Ponila. She didn't lose her temper when they teased her, and she gave them a cheerful smile when they praised her. However, when it came to a proper relationship, they thought Ponila didn't take it seriously. Some of the boys had gone out with her, taking her to the cinema, going swimming, having a Valentine's Day dinner, but she always found it easy to put these things behind her and not mention them again.

After buying the IXUS, she wore it around her neck all day long, like a piece of jewelry, and as it rested right on her cleavage, no one could deny it was sexy. The girls said it was very "in," while the boys poked fun at her for dressing up as Sakai Noriko. However, gradually the boys began to feel quite uncomfortable because Ponila was always taking candid shots of them. For the most part they responded with spirit, swearing at her as they chased her off. They wanted to rip out the negatives, but Ponila only had to break into a smile and let the camera fall down on her chest to make the boys tongue-tied. Many of them were used to getting up to mischief, but once they noticed Ponila picking up her camera, the mood changed completely, and the other girls sided with Ponila, telling the boys they were being mean-spirited. Whenever anyone asked her why she only took photos of boys, Ponila would laugh without answering.

It was generally acknowledged that Siu On was the only boy who could put up with Ponila's eccentricities, talking and laughing cheerfully in front of her lens. Privately, however, he told her, "I don't mind you taking photos of me, but it would be fairer if I could also take photos of you." As a result they agreed to go to Cheung Chau on the weekend. The temperature reached thirty-four degrees that day, the sunrays turning the beach into a dazzling white expanse. As expected, Siu On had brought a complete set of supplementary equipment and a Nikon F4 plus three lenses for different distances, all of which he carried in two bags. Ponila's hands, however, were empty, with only the IXUS hanging from her neck. She hadn't brought a swimsuit and was wearing an orange floral sundress. As Siu On kept snapping away on his camera, she playfully ran down the beach into the waves, getting much of her dress wet. When he asked why she wasn't taking pictures, she simply shook her head and energetically kicked up spray.

They had their evening meal at an open-air restaurant next to the ferry pier. Seeing the stalls along the road soliciting guests for holiday flats, they exchanged glances and then went up to one of them. The room they got was tiny, and the old air conditioner made the room smell musty. Ponila had got sunburnt so her face, arms, and legs were scarlet, but when she took off her clothes, the rest of her body turned out to be very white, the cold and silvery metal of the IXUS intermittently gleaming between her breasts and occasionally hitting Siu On on the head. Afterward, when both of them were breathing heavily, there was suddenly a flash and the faint sound of the shutter. Turning over, Siu On saw Ponila holding the camera and without quite knowing why stretched his arm across her, tore away the camera, and threw it on the floor. Leaning toward the side of the bed, all red limbs and white body, Ponila sat there staring blankly ahead. Having no idea what to do next, Siu On eventually sighed deeply before getting off the bed and picking up the little camera. The camera body had broken apart and the film cartridge door had flown off, but there was no film roll inside. Puzzled, Siu On looked at Ponila, but she had lowered her eyes, and her long hair, loosely held together in a ponytail with an orange hairband, hung over her bare bosom.

8
—

GIRL SPECIMENS

Girl Specimens (Shaonü biaoben 少女標本) was a pop band formed in Taiwan in 1998. The Japanese fashion magazine *non-no* is directed at young women.

Candy wasn't keen on eating sweets, but whenever she passed a snack shop, she would buy some super-soft Japanese jelly sweets in funny packets, or chewing gum, or something else. Some unopened packets sank down among the jumble of odds and ends at the bottom of her rucksack or were left behind somewhere. No one really knew too much about Candy's affairs, since she switched to a new job more or less every couple of months, all of them involving selling trendy gadgets, clothes, and trinkets at shopping centers. Whenever she was beginning to get on close terms with those around her, she'd disappear.

Although no one had any clear understanding of where Candy was headed, they didn't find her easy to forget. Every so often, they would see Candy, draped in whatever took her fancy, in the top stories on street fashion in the weekly magazines. At one time she adopted a typical student outfit consisting of a short-sleeved blouse and a checked pleated short skirt in red, green, and black, together with large red platform boots and a big rose scarf around her neck. Her long black hair was divided along the middle, with three red hairpins at each temple and an absolutely straight part. One week she caused a sensation, by popular choice the winner of the grand prize, a Discman.

For a short period, Candy was selling crystal and silverware at the Island Beverley Shopping Center in Causeway Bay. Late in the morning one day before the crowds arrived, she was leafing through an issue of *non-no* and feeling thoroughly bored, when she heard a clicking sound. Raising her head, she saw a man standing outside the shop window with his face half hidden behind a camera. She paid no attention but looked down again and carried on reading about the hottest updates on fashion. Afterward, Cat from the shop next door told Candy the man was Fred, a photographer at a weekly, who specialized in taking pictures of girls. The ones who caught his eye might make it as cover girls, and it was also said he had lots of affairs with girls in his private life. Sucking a super-sour lime candy, Candy fixed her eyes on a corner of her scarf.

Fred actually did come back a couple of days later and, without saying a word, placed a large rolled-up object on the glass counter. Candy, chewing gum, looked at him suspiciously. Picking up the roll, she slowly unfolded it. It turned out to be a full-sized cinema poster in a warm yellow glow with a girl's cold sharp face. Candy couldn't help looking up and smiling, and Fred smiled back.

Candy let Fred take pictures of her, all of them outdoors, in parks, old market stalls, the bar district, and University Hall. She didn't pose in the usual contrived way that pretty girls did for photographs but didn't deliberately try to look weird either. Wearing matching clothes and accessories, she fooled around in front of the camera as if it were playtime at kindergarten, often giving way to uncontrollable giggling. Even Fred hadn't tried to encourage her to act with so much abandon, his hands shaking as he shot new material. As soon as the photos were ready, he'd study them for ages, but his gaze was never able to reach the depths of the girl's eyes.

Two months later, Fred finally asked Candy up to his home, a small open-plan flat that served for his photography, cooking, and sleeping. The walls were covered with enlarged pictures of Candy, looking like prototype settings for a film. She sat down by Fred's computer while he made green tea with honey and lemon for her. The monitor in front of her was displaying a Girl Specimens screen saver with the four female singers from Taiwan. Known as Versions 1, 2, 3, and 4, they were Yuki, Pace, Sin-Chet, and Cheer. When Candy moved the mouse, pictures of herself appeared, row after row filling the screen all the way down to the end of the document. Closing the CANDY file, she saw there were at least a few dozen old files: ALICE, AMY, ANNIE, AUBREY . . . all the way to WINNIE and YOKO. Opening some at random, she found that all of them were of charming young girls. There were also notes with detailed information about each individual, records of meetings and contacts, even copies of love letters. She sat there, transfixed, until the screen saver appeared again.

Fred came over and placed the honey-lemon tea before her. Candy sipped the tea and then suddenly pounced on Fred. They fell down on the floor locked in each other's arms.

Waking up the following morning, Fred discovered he was alone in bed. The photos on the walls had turned into blank sheets of paper, the CANDY file was gone from the computer, and there was no trace of Candy even among the negatives. All that remained was half a packet of plum candy and a pile of wrappers on the table.

9
CHE

Che was called Che because of something that had happened a year earlier, when people used to call her Ah Chi. The year 1997 was the thirtieth anniversary of the death of the legendary Latin American revolutionary Che Guevara, prompting a Che fever all over the world. The idol of the left-wing student upheavals of the 1960s was again being worshipped as he appeared in black-and-white photos, with a beard and a guerrilla beret. Che T-shirts, watches, jewelry, and souvenirs were on sale in great quantities. Ah Chi bought herself a Che T-shirt in communist red that she wore inside her coat throughout the winter, putting it back on again as soon as it was washed, so that everyone became used to seeing the bearded face on her chest. From then on she referred to herself as Che.

Ah Chi had bought her Che T-shirt together with her boyfriend Ah Kin, one for each of them. Ah Kin said the beardie cut a terrific figure. To the envy of their mates, the couple dashed around like lightning on a motorbike, with bangles up to their shoulders and their long, windswept hair dyed a golden yellow. One of Ah Kin's sworn brothers, Baldie, gave Ah Chi a call one evening and asked her out for karaoke. After drinking heavily, he cornered her as the rest of his band of villains fought to be the first to get at her. The following day Ah Kin took his gang into Baldie's territory and, without wasting words, went on the rampage, bashing heads till the blood flowed. A month afterward, as Ah Chi was waiting for Ah Kin in East Tsim Sha Tsui at midnight, she saw him come toward her on his bike very slowly. He stopped before her and pulled off his jacket. Something was stuck into his side and, looking closely, she saw a knife handle. Against the red T-shirt the blood was hardly visible, no more than a dark patch. Then he slid down to the ground from his motorbike.

Ah Chi left home after Ah Kin's death. She didn't take anything with her, only the clothes she was wearing. At the street corner she ran into her father, who was coming home from an all-night mah-jongg game. When she didn't speak, he asked where she was going.

"Nowhere in particular."

"How long for?"

"Don't know."

Che tied her long hair into a bunch of pigtails, tilted a beret on her head, mounted Ah Kin's motorbike, and began her slow, aimless journey. She fantasized about riding the bike on her own across mainland China, all the way to the Middle East or India, but ended up at a building where a friend of hers lived. After this, Che roamed around at random, spending the nights in friends' places.

Ah Kin's uncle was usually sitting on a miscellaneous collection of knickknacks, silverware, glassware, watches, pirated CDs, famous-brand smuggled goods, and suchlike. Che asked him for some goods to peddle in the street, where, if she was lucky, she could manage to pocket over a thousand dollars; otherwise, when her array of merchandise didn't earn enough for a meal, she went hungry. With a bike, Che had an advantage in being highly mobile. As soon as she stopped, she transacted her business, and if circumstances weren't right, she slipped away. It happened only once that she was arrested by the Hawker Control Team, and then she was all tears as she pleaded for herself. The avuncular officer had probably never caught a young girl hawker and felt it inappropriate to apply the full force of the law, so in the end she was let go.

Che also came across Baldie once more. She was on her motorbike and spotted him sitting on the railing outside a cinema, waiting for someone. As she rode past, she had no weapon to hand, so she simply knocked him on the back of his head with her helmet and sped away.

When summer came again, Che's Che T-shirt had become extremely worn and tattered. There was an article in a magazine that said a Cuban restaurant was opening in Central District and that they would respectfully put up a portrait of Che Guevara in a most tasteful style. Che believed that Che was actually Cuban. One day while she was displaying her wares in a pedestrian subway in Central, she came across a group of demonstrators protesting against employers cutting wages and then dismissing workers. Taking part in the demonstration was a university student from a social-work department who was studying the workers' movement through practical experience. When he saw Che selling bracelets, he pointed at her T-shirt and shouted, "Long live Che!" Toward evening, the student came back, walking to and fro as if he were looking for somebody. She had already packed up her merchandise and was standing to one side smoking a cigarette, and when she saw the student looking rather foolish, she called out to him.

Che and the student met up a few times and would take her motorbike to get back to his residential hall. While he sat behind with his arms around her waist, she was in front, steering the bike, furtively shedding tears. Once she took him for a walk along the Temple Street night market, and he let himself be hooked by a fortune-teller and relieved of some cash. The fortune-teller, who also had a line in physiognomy, was all smiles. "Two for the price of one!" he offered, taking a look at Che as well. Then, startled, he explained, "Young lady, you were a man, a great hero, in your previous incarnation. You were not Chinese but a native of

Argentina, and you had noble ambitions in human affairs. How regrettable that you passed away in the flower of your youth."

The student found this ridiculous. He was sure the man was a conman peddling superstition, so he teased Che by addressing her as "old boy." Che felt troubled at heart and looked down at the picture on her chest as she walked in front of him, immersed in her own thoughts.

10

PASTÉIS DE NATA

Andrew Stow, nicknamed Lord Stow in Macao, was an Englishman who opened a bakery on Coloane Island, south of urban Macao. It became famous for its Portuguese egg tarts, called *pastéis de nata* in Portuguese.

There were those who said Pui Pui's left eye was gray and others who said it wasn't. When Pui Pui was little, her classmates often teased her, saying that she was a witch because her nose was long and crooked. However, after she had grown up, it didn't seem so prominent.

Before Pui Pui had finished middle school, she got a job selling cakes, but it wasn't in the cake shop where she worked that she tasted Portuguese egg tarts for the first time. At that time, egg tarts baked according to the special recipe of Lord Stow's Bakery in Macao had just been introduced, and that night, after she had eaten one of Lord Stow's egg tarts, Pui Pui had a strange dream. She was riding an enormous boatlike egg tart, which took her to a quiet, faraway little island. Everything on the island—houses, trees, hills—was yellow, like egg yolk, and it all had the same spots of burnt color on the surface as on the Portuguese egg tarts. There was an old woman on the beach who had gray eyes and gray hair, and she was holding a large spoon like an oar, digging in the yellow sand. The old woman looked at Pui Pui and said, "So you've come back at last!"

At first Pui Pui didn't take this seriously, but then she noticed that whenever she had eaten a Portuguese egg tart, she would have the dream, and each time it was exactly the same. The cake shop where she worked had sent a baker to taste Lord Stow's egg tarts, and he had learnt to imitate them. Then they began producing Portuguese egg tarts themselves. Pui Pui ate one surreptitiously, but she didn't have a dream that night and supposed that she just worried too easily. The following day, however, she had one of Lord Stow's egg tarts and had the same dream as before. She knew then that her own shop wasn't making authentic egg tarts, but nobody believed her when she told them about it.

Even Pui Pui's boyfriend, Siu San, wouldn't believe her. He could gobble up five or six of the egg tarts without having weird dreams. Pui Pui herself was actually eating more and more of them, up to a dozen a day, and spent more money on them than on other food. At night she lay in bed and had the same dream over and over again, but even after ten such dreams it was still the same, nothing new happening; it just felt more and more stifling. When she woke up, she wanted to tell Siu San, but he pretended to be sound asleep, although he was actually silently cursing Lord Stow.

Later, Pui Pui said she wanted to go to Macao to find Lord Stow's. Siu San was actually a bit jealous but ended up coming along. After they arrived, Pui Pui preferred to walk around at random, so they strolled along the Praia Grande, ending up at the A-Ma Temple. Along the way they passed the grand old Hotel Bela Vista, and Pui Pui wanted to go in and have a cup of coffee, but Siu San suspected it would be too expensive just to look inside. Eventually they got to Coloane Island and found Lord Stow's Bakery, where Pui Pui bought four dozen Portuguese egg tarts, almost emptying the shop, but in the end they didn't find the place in her dream.

After dark they returned to a cheap hotel in the city center. Pui Pui asked Siu San to have a look at her left eye and say if he thought there was anything special about it. Siu San became impatient, shrugged, took his wallet, and went off to the Lisboa to make a killing or be killed at the gambling tables. Pui Pui had actually been about to tell Siu San that she had been born in Macao, where her father had been a junket operator at a casino. One evening he offended somebody and had his throat cut in the street. Pui Pui's mother abandoned her and fled. At the time, Pui Pui was only five, and an uncle had taken her away from Macao. She had never returned afterward and had told no one about the past.

Sitting alone in the hotel room, Pui Pui watched *Healing Hands* on television, leafed through an entire issue of *Next Magazine*, and ate forty-seven Portuguese egg tarts, and it was not yet half past ten. Then she packed her things, including the remaining egg tart, and walked out of the hotel. She caught a taxi to the ferry pier and bought a ticket from a tout for the last ferry of the evening.

On board, the man sitting next to Pui Pui was reading the *Ming Pao* newspaper, which had the news about the Portuguese novelist José Saramago being awarded the Nobel Prize in Literature. Saramago's works included *Baltasar and Blimunda*, *The Year of the Death of Ricardo Reis*, *The Stone Raft*, *The Gospel According to Jesus Christ*, and *Blindness*.

Pui Pui fished out the last of the Portuguese egg tarts from her bag and was about to put it into her mouth when the man next to her asked what those pastries were called. "*Pastéis de nata*," she replied, off the top of her head.

11

PHOTO STICKERS

Photo-sticker booths or photo-sticker machines are popular in East Asia. A booth can accommodate more than one person. Money is inserted and pictures are taken. People can then customize them in different ways, changing backgrounds, colors, lighting, retouching, etc. *Love Generation* was a Japanese TV serial that was broadcast in 1997. Two of the characters were played by Matsu Takako 松隆子 and Fujiwara Norika 藤原紀香. These two women are friends but have complicated lives involving love triangles. In Cantonese, their names are pronounced Chung Lung-Tsz and Tang-Yuen Kei-Heung.

The name Kei-Heung had been bestowed on her by her best friend, Lung-Tsz, and Lung-Tsz's name had in turn been given to her by Kei-Heung. At the time they'd been watching *Love Generation* together. Kei-Heung said that Lung-Tsz had a round face like the actor Lung-Tsz, so Lung-Tsz replied, "If I'm Lung-Tsz, then you have to be Kei-Heung!" Kei-Heung only had a supporting role in the TV series, but since Kei-Heung thought she was prettier than Lung-Tsz, she didn't mind.

It was Lung-Tsz who took Kei-Heung to the Magic Photo Sticker Booth. Kei-Heung was an expert on photo stickers, claiming that she had tried out all the photo-sticker machines in the city, so it was odd that she hadn't heard about the Magic Photo Sticker Booth.

Kei-Heung at first thought the Magic Sticker was just a gimmick. It was a booth set up especially for couples; they just had to enter their birth dates and the machine would perform an automatic divination. On the basis of the progression of astrological signs, it would then draw up a star chart showing the couple's compatibility and print it on to the photo stickers. The idea was that if the lovers stuck the photos on each other's personal belongings, they would never be separated.

Kei-Heung hadn't gone so far as to believe in this kind of nonsense, but she still felt it was quite interesting. Unable to resist the temptation of the new machine, she dragged her boyfriend Ah Ping for a set of photos. Although Ah Ping found it childish, he forced a smile to his face as they were photographed. Out of the set of twenty photo stickers, Kei-Heung stuck one on Ah Ping's wallet, with others going to her own purse, her mobile phone, her makeup box, her notebook, and her bedside mirror at home. She gave one to Lung-Tsz as a present and carefully tucked away the remaining thirteen.

The better part of a year passed, and events happened to turn out in unexpected ways. Lung-Tsz kept losing her temper with her boyfriend Siu Chit, who complained to Kei-Heung and asked her to act as an intermediary. As time passed, however, he developed a strong attachment to Kei-Heung. After struggling with conflicting feelings about this, Kei-Heung began to think that she and Siu Chit made quite a good match after all. He was openhearted and playful, not as solemn as Ah Ping. Eventually she suggested to Ah Ping that they should split up. Ah Ping was dead set against this, however, and kept pestering her, waiting every day outside her home and beseeching her tearfully to make up again. It got so bad that Kei-Heung moved temporarily to Siu Chit's home. The situation remained like this for two or three months.

After a while, Kei-Heung remembered the magic photo stickers. Although she also thought they were absurd, she still tore them off her purse, mobile phone, makeup box, notebook, and mirror, and burnt the thirteen she had stored away. She couldn't very well ask Lung-Tsz to return the one she had, but Kei-Heung worked out that Lung-Tsz would sooner or later come across it and, her temper being what it was, destroy it. The only one remaining would be the one in Ah Ping's hands.

Kei-Heung finally invited Ah Ping to meet her at a restaurant. Ah Ping was convinced this would be a turning point, so he carried on at length, analyzing the situation. He even said Siu Chit was not a trustworthy person. Kei-Heung didn't utter a word, but when Ah Ping went to the lavatory, she seized the opportunity to look for his wallet and hastily ripped off the photo sticker. In a short while Ah Ping was back. He sat down and said, "I think maybe we should just split up."

Siu Chit lived with Kei-Heung for six months but in the end returned to Lung-Tsz. While they were together, Kei-Heung and Siu Chit never went to a photo-sticker booth.

12

FOOTBALL KITS

Not counting her gym clothes at secondary-school PE classes, Lam Oh had worn a sports outfit only twice in her life, and in both cases it was a football kit. It was at the time of the World Cup, when a weekly magazine had a special issue about football shirts and wanted a girl for a photo session, and so the model agency sent Lam Oh. Never having considered herself the athletic type, she had no idea why she'd been picked.

After three years as a model, Lam Oh saw herself as being out of luck. Apart from never having made it big on the catwalk, she hadn't even wangled a spot on a magazine cover. At best she'd been in fashion photos on the inside pages and more commonly in the completely pointless demonstration or design photos in the magazines. When the tournament started, she didn't even get to be a World Cup girl in the backdrops to the television football coverage—all she managed was a minor special on football kit. She couldn't see that she was in any way inferior to the others. Her figure and appearance were pleasing, but how could she deal with the fact that the world wasn't exactly lacking in above-average beauty? It was like being no more than ordinary. In any case, this year's World Cup made Lam Oh feel even more lost than ever.

When she arrived at the studio on the day of the shoot, she learned that a football fan was going to be in the photos as well. Once they were finished with the studio photography, they went to the fan's home to take more pictures in addition to an interview. In low spirits, Lam Oh changed into various football shirts, shorts, and socks, all very loose-fitting and garish, more suitable for monkeys than people. It was not in the least bit to her liking. At the World Cup four years earlier, Lam Oh had gone to her boyfriend Ah Chai's home to watch the final with him. His family were on a trip abroad, and Ah Chai had turned down invitations from his other football mates, so it was the first time the two of them were on their own in the same room late at night. Something was inevitably to be expected. However, the football got in the way, and they had barely got intimate before they felt obliged to pause. The match began, Ah Chai supporting Brazil and Lam Oh Italy. To start with, they only pretended to be diametrically opposed, not imagining it might develop further, but for no good reason their language became hostile, and a cold war broke out. The result was victory for Brazil in a penalty shoot-out, but Lam Oh stubbornly refused to admit it, and Ah Chai said she was being unreasonable, claiming expertise she didn't have. What should have been a wonderful evening somehow went sour as they angrily voiced a whole series of everyday grudges. After Lam Oh had flung the door open and departed in a temper, she roamed the streets on her own in the early morning hours, vowing never to watch football again. Later on, she found herself a young man who was completely ignorant about football, thinking he was a better match for her. She split up with Ah Chai but in the end didn't stay long with the other man either.

It turned out that the focus of the photo shoot was a young woman. She was short, didn't look like the sporty type, and when she put on a football shirt, it looked rather like the robes of a church choir. She was extremely energetic and enthusiastic, her eyes shining with passion for football, so Lam Oh responded in a professional manner, jumping and laughing. Their arrival at the young woman's home was a real eye-opener for Lam Oh and made her reflect that this fan was a hundred times more fervent than Ah Chai had been. Piles of football books, magazines, and videotapes served as her table and chairs, the wallpaper was posters of star players, and her wardrobe was filled with well over a hundred football kits. While she was being interviewed as she displayed her treasures, Lam Oh, who had until then been weary of football, was actually beginning to feel admiration, something she hadn't thought conceivable. Just before Lam Oh left, the young woman presented her with a Brazilian national football shirt that had Ronaldo's autograph on it. She said she'd got him to sign it by making a special trip to a football stadium when she was traveling in Europe.

Back at home, Lam Oh kept wondering why the young woman had given away this precious object so lightly. She couldn't figure it out, and not knowing what to do with it, she just hung it up in front of her bed. She didn't watch a single one of the subsequent World Cup matches, nor did she think it was much fun to go out, since all the bars had turned into venues for live broadcasts of the competition. Instead she stayed at home every night, buried her head under the covers, and got a lot of sleep. After her shower one evening, she couldn't find her pajamas, so she took the Brazilian football shirt hanging by the bed and put it on. She fell asleep but suddenly woke up at midnight to hear the next-door neighbors making a racket. As if sleepwalking, she turned on her television only to realize it was the final between Brazil and France. To her surprise, the longer she watched, the more awake she felt, her heart thumping with excitement. When she saw Brazil concede a third goal, she hardly noticed that her tears had wet a big patch on the front of her shirt. She stretched out her hand to the phone on a side table and dialed Ah Chai's number from four years earlier.

Ah Chai answered, his voice sluggish. "Are you on your own?"

"Mm," she replied. "How about you?"

"I'm also on my own," he said.

Lam Oh wept without making a sound. "Ah Chai, Brazil lost, I'm so sorry, Brazil lost!"

13

RED WING

Red Wing shoes are made in the United States by a footwear company known for their heavy-duty work shoes and sports shoes. Little Twin Stars are a pair of angel-like characters created by Sanrio, the Japanese company responsible for Hello Kitty.

It was only when Tam Chi Wing started wearing her pair of Red Wing shoes that she understood how she could run out of a world.

Tam Chi Wing's first memory of running away was at the age of five. They were in a shopping mall when she reached for a Little Twin Stars hairband, but her mother wouldn't buy it for her. So she grabbed it, turned around, and ran. Her mother chased right after her, and the chase went on and on, but the mall was very big and it seemed as if it were impossible to get out.

However, her most dramatic long-distance run was at the age of ten. At the time, her parents were going through a crisis in their marriage and were constantly quarreling. One time, Tam Chi Wing cried so hard she got a beating. Suddenly, she pulled open the metal front door and ran out, racing wildly along the endless corridors of the public-housing estate. As she ran, she lost her flip-flops but didn't care, and it was only when she reached her grandma's house seven blocks away that she felt the pain as she looked down at her feet, covered in blood. As it turned out, her parents didn't file for divorce after her run, although they didn't become reconciled either; instead there was a perpetual coolness.

After that, Tam Chi Wing no longer regarded running as anything special. Her only way of dealing with problems was running. If she forgot to bring her homework or couldn't answer questions on the classroom quiz, she would push her desk away and rush out of the room. Even her teacher couldn't stop her. More often, Tam Chi Wing ran in order to get far away from her classmates. She had small, sharp eyes that seemed like thorns when she looked at someone, and eventually this was seen as some kind of crime that aroused the others' resentment. They liked to pull her hair during class or throw chalk at her, and they cheered when she ran away. Tam Chi Wing rushed to and fro all day long, so she could almost never stop to have a proper talk with anyone.

One time after a PE session, some girls stole the skirt of her school uniform. Tam Chi Wing questioned them in a low voice but stuttered so badly she couldn't go on, so she rushed out of the changing room and collided with Kwong Kin Sang, a boy from the class next door. Kwong Kin Sang picked himself up and chased after her. The next day after school, a few of the girls in her class waylaid her near the school, tied up her hands and feet with rope, pulled off her shoes and socks, and burned her heels with a cigarette butt. They called her names for running so hard and warned her not to get so close to Kwong Kin Sang in the future. Tam Chi Wing limped home, but the next day she pulled on her long stockings and went to school as usual.

When she wasn't running, Tam Chi Wing spent almost all her time in shopping malls. There was no need to run in that world, where no one knew her, disturbed her, or paid any attention to her. She could truly wander around alone, letting her eyes linger on the range of attractive merchandise. Once she had saved up enough money, she would bring something home, where it became a part of her, and she didn't have to ask her mother or anyone else for permission. After her feet had healed, Tam Chi Wing bought a pair of trendy Red Wing boots, red with white soles and square-cut toes. As she put them on, it seemed she could walk into the lively (if lonely) world of Japanese pop stars Kimura Takuya and Puffy.

Returning to the housing estate, she saw Kwong Kin Sang sitting on the side of the flowerbed at the foot of the building. The moment their eyes met, Tam Chi Wing turned and fled. Kwong Kin Sang started chasing her, shouting "Don't get me wrong! Don't be scared! Please just stop and talk!"

Soon he fell behind, short of breath, and lost sight of her. Tam Chi Wing, wearing her Red Wings, jumped over the area railings in a burst of energy and ran onto a pedestrian flyover that was under construction. She ran faster and faster, higher than the flyover, the road, the ground, and the human world, into a country where no one could catch up with her.

14

EAT AS MUCH AS YOU LIKE

SMAP×SMAP is a Japanese television show. In one part of the show, SMAP regulars cook food for celebrity guests.

When Ah Kei's love affair came to an end after three years, she discarded her handbags and long skirts and went to Mong Kok, where she had her long hair cut and bought a few of the currently popular T-shirts with Japanese words on them, attracted (not knowing what the words meant) by their apparent meaninglessness. The boutique also sold books on fortune-telling and horoscopes. The shopkeeper was a young woman with a patterned scarf around her head and lots of colorful bangles around her arms. Scanning the expression on Ah Kei's face, she asked if she'd just gone through an emotional upset. Ah Kei was at first rather startled, but considering that she still wasn't getting enough sleep at night, it could have been expected. Casually she picked up three T-shirts with the Japanese phrases ōwaribiki (big discount), muryō nyūjō (free admission), and tabe-hōdai (eat as much as you like).

"When it's a matter of emotions, it can be difficult to get a good reading," the shopkeeper said. "You should be careful so people don't take advantage of you, miss." Ah Kei just smiled as she paid and left.

I haven't got a boyfriend, I've got no chance of getting married, and my youth is slipping by; I've even quit my job, she thought to herself. *What have I got to lose?*

Ah Kei and Ah Sun had got to know each other when they were working in a fashion chain store. They were colleagues for three years and in a relationship for three years, during which time Ah Sun was promoted to store manager and Ah Kei to deputy manager. Everyone thought it was a match made in heaven. Thinking about it afterward, she wondered, in what respect was Ah Sun really superior to other people? Or was it just like her way of choosing clothes—anything that fits looks good?

Ah Kei now gave Siu Fai a phone call and set a time for them to meet. Two years earlier, Siu Fai had given Ah Kei's younger brother extra lessons after school. It was before Siu Fai went to university, when he was a big simpleminded boy, but he was cheery and strong and had shown extreme patience with her brother. From time to time, Ah Kei had finished work and was at home during the evening lessons, wearing her flimsy housecoat and stretching out her legs on the couch while she watched television. Without meaning to, Siu Fai found his gaze beginning to stray. Once Siu Fai brought two cinema tickets and surreptitiously handed them to her brother to pass on to Ah Kei. She actually turned up at the cinema, but when they had watched the film and came out, for her that counted as fulfilling any obligation.

"It's true that you and I are about the same age," she said, "but I've started work before you, and to me you've always been like a younger brother, so I don't think it's very appropriate for us to go out together." Afterward, when Siu Fai passed the university entrance examination, he stopped coaching Ah Kei's brother.

When she met Siu Fai again, he was much more self-assured, very suntanned, and he spoke forcefully. They went out for a meal twice, talking mainly about Siu Fai's university life. Ah Kei felt that he was getting more and more imposing, while she appeared more and more insignificant, and she dared not ask if he had a girlfriend or not. At midsummer, his university department arranged a camp on Cheung Chau. Ah Kei was reluctant to go inside the camp quarters to look for Siu Fai. Emerging at his leisure, Siu Fai led her down the hill, rented a holiday flat, and told her to wait for him there. Late that night, Siu Fai actually did slip in, condoms at the ready, and pulled off her T-shirt with the Japanese phrase *ōwaribiki*.

"You're the first girl I fancied," he said when it was over. "I've never been able to shake off the impression you made. But I think at last I can. You got it right, what you said before: it's not appropriate."

Ah Kei had never imagined that this time it would actually be even worse than breaking up with Ah Sun. It was simply unbearable, and she felt like giving up altogether. On impulse she went out for drinks with a former boss who had once pursued her, and afterward they ended up in bed together. When she woke up the next day, he was nowhere to be seen, and her T-shirt with the words *muryō nyūjō* was lying on the floor. He didn't even pay for the hotel room.

She went home and had a bath, feeling confused and upset. With an empty stomach, she went out and wandered along the streets. Happening to pass a newly opened sushi bar, she went in. She was the only customer in the place, and the food had not yet come onto the sushi train. Standing at the other end of the loop was a young cook who looked a bit like Kimura Takuya dressed as a chef in the TV show SMAP×SMAP. He was holding a ball of rice between his fingers and staring at her chest.

"Miss, do you know what *tabe-hōdai* means?" he mumbled. Ah Kei shook her head.

"In some restaurants in Japan you can eat as much as you like within a certain time for a fixed price." As he finished speaking, he pretended to pop the rice ball into his mouth. Ah Kei looked at him, feeling baffled, and rested her chin in her hand.

"That's very reasonable!" she said.

"Sure!" He bared his teeth in a grin. "That's what I think too, extremely reasonable!"

15

A BATHING APE

Lee Lai Shan and Sam Wong are two well-known windsurfers who are married to each other. Lee is an Olympic gold
medalist. She was born on Cheung Chau. A Bathing Ape is a
Japanese clothing brand, now owned by Hong Kong interests,
with international distribution. Its trademark is the head of
a big ape.

The day Yuen Hong Kwong arrived on Cheung Chau, he bought
a bunch of bananas at a fruit stall across from the pier, walked
to the shop at Tung Wan Beach, pulled open the roll-up door,
and placed his things on the table. He then stepped inside to
unpack and tidy up. When he came out again, he discovered that
one banana was missing. He looked up and saw a skinny little
girl walking slowly on the beach, peeling a banana.

"You stupid little bitch," he yelled, chasing after her. "Stealing other people's bananas!"

Unfazed, the girl stared at him with wide-open eyes and
pointed her half-peeled banana at the image of an ape-man on
the front of his T-shirt. "You're a fake," she giggled.

In the afternoon the next day, Yuen Hong Kwong saw the girl
walking back and forth along the beach, pushing her toes into
the sand and pulling them out again. Summer vacation had just
come to an end, leaving only a few people playing on the beach,
along with the girl's silhouette.

As the girl passed the shop front, Yuen Hong Kwong took out a can of Coke from the fridge. "Have a drink?" he offered gruffly.

The girl stretched her hand out for the can. "Why have you come here?" she asked.

"Lost my job," he answered. "Used to work in a restaurant. The economy's no good, everyone's down to eating shit. There's no one to help, so I couldn't pay my bills—a grown man, thirty-five years old, and I can't get a job. My aunt's husband had this shop, but he went back to the mainland for medical treatment, so I came here to take care of the business. It's just a temporary job."

It wasn't clear if the girl was listening or not. She sipped some Coke. "You've got a lousy temper," she remarked.

Yuen Hong Kwong gave her a ferocious look. "Sure, my classmates used to call me King Kong."

The girl was called Siu Yuen. She lived on the island and went to the island's middle school. Her skin was deeply tanned, the whites of her eyes and her teeth were both very white, and her hair was as soft as a newborn baby's. She spent every afternoon by herself on the beach in shorts and a loose white T-shirt, but no one ever saw her getting into the water. The shop wasn't doing any business, and Yuen Hong Kwong was getting bored stiff. He looked up and down the beach, and when he caught sight of Siu Yuen's delicate body, he was seized by a violent emotion for no apparent reason; it was as if youth itself was a crime. Siu Yuen said her little brother suffered from premature ageing; after turning ten, he was like an old man. Their mother didn't want him to mix with people, so they had moved to the Outlying Islands and had been living both on Peng Chau and Lantau. "All along we've been waiting for him to die," Siu Yuen said.

Yuen Hong Kwong hadn't seen her mother or brother. He knew she lived at Tung Tai and had walked over there to take a look, but all he saw was that the light in the second-floor window went out quite early at night.

Later on, Yuen Hong Kwong took the ferry to town to see his girlfriend, and along the way he bought an original A Bathing Ape T-shirt. Wearing it on his return to Cheung Chau, he grabbed a bunch of bananas and ran to the beach to show off to Siu Yuen. He squatted down next to her and peered at the windsurfers out at sea.

"I just used to play around," he muttered to himself. "If I'd gone on training, maybe I could have competed against Sam Wong."

"Why not against Lee Lai Shan?" asked Siu Yuen.

"Lee Lai Shan is a woman."

"Why don't you apply to be a policeman?" Siu Yuen asked again.

"I'm too old," he said.

"Then how about joining the triads?"

"Don't know how to get in with them."

"So you're trading in fake goods?"

He exploded with anger. "This one's the real thing!" he shouted. "It cost over a thousand dollars!"

Siu Yuen stood up and wiped the sand off her legs. "You don't have a clue what I'm talking about. The ape-men will soon make an attack on Earth. They're going to land on this beach. The Earth people haven't got much time left. When the time comes, they'll take me with them." She turned around, grabbed the bunch of bananas, and walked away.

Siu Yuen didn't talk to Yuen Hong Kwong over the next few days. For his part, turning his back on the shop, Yuen Hong Kwong spent his days immersed in the water, swimming. He got so tanned his skin turned coal black. When he noticed Siu Yuen on the beach, he'd become more vigorous, pummeling the water. One day his girlfriend came to Cheung Chau to look for him. Wearing a white skirt, she sat in front of the shop with no customers, watching him for a long time until he came out of the water.

"You still haven't been able to find a proper job, so we won't see each other again," she said.

After she'd left, Yuen Hong Kwong went to a food stall by the ferry pier for a beer and continued drinking until evening. Then, his eyes burning, he staggered over to the house where Siu Yuen was living. He climbed up a big tree next to the building and jumped in through a window. Inside it was pitch-black and he couldn't see Siu Yuen's mother or the spooky old-man brother; there was only a glimmer of light and the sound of splashing water from the crack between the bathroom door and the doorframe. Yuen Hong Kwong kicked open the door and entered. He saw moldy banana peels all over the floor and Siu Yuen lying in a tub filled with water the color of red wine, her bleeding hand holding a half-peeled banana. Weak but still alive, she smiled at him.

"Are you a fake? Or have you come to take me away from Earth?"

16

HYSTERIC GLAMOUR

Hysteric Glamour is a Japanese designer label. Hung Cha Fong
was a chain of small cafés serving Taiwan-style bubble tea,
among other things.

Sha Sha and Ma Nga appeared to be two people who would not
possibly get along with one another, but this is the kind of thing
that might happen with them: Sha Sha asks Ma Nga to go out
and see a movie with her. When they meet, Ma Nga is eating an
orange ice lolly and points at the front of the Hysteric Glamour
top that Sha Sha is wearing, and by an odd coincidence there is
an orange stain on it.

   When people first met Sha Sha, they would think she was
pretty: her face was plump, her skin milky white, and her bosom
ample. After they had spent some time with her, however, they
would get irritated at her stupidity. In fact, Sha Sha was not at
all stupid, it was just that she lacked self-confidence. She particularly detested her own exaggerated figure, feeling that her
breasts bounced around as if she was some kind of brainless
pinup.

   Sha Sha had dated five boys and each time had ended up
being rejected. The most recent case had been in her second year
of university; Lap Kei, the boyfriend, was one year ahead of her.
His subject being psychology, he was in the habit of analyzing
Sha Sha's personality type. He said women were emotionalized

animals, and that was particularly true of Sha Sha, who was close to being neurotic. One day, when Sha Sha had caught a cold and gone in to Mong Kok to see a doctor, she ran into Lap Kei in a Hung Cha Fong café, where he was chatting and joking with a woman. Sha Sha immediately went on the offensive, while Lap Kei didn't quite know what to do, and the woman just stared at her with an innocent grin as if it had nothing to do with her. Sha Sha sobbed her eyes out in front of everyone, utterly abandoning any thought of self-restraint. All she could see was the brief top the woman was wearing, with an image of a gorgeous long-haired woman and the word "glamour."

Lap Kei took the opportunity created by the scene she'd caused to dump her. She wept for five nights, but on the sixth day she seemed to have cried herself out. After class, she bumped into the woman wearing the top. The woman smiled at her, and as they stepped on the train, she started to talk.

"I came here to find Ah Kei. I told him off for being too beastly to you. I've got no time for people like that." Sha Sha was stunned. When they stopped at Sha Tin, the woman pulled Sha Sha off the train.

"Come on," she cried out, "let's get something to eat and we can forget about him." She carried on running, her white HG top flashing past.

The woman was Ma Nga, and she was four years older than Sha Sha. She was co-owner of a small fashion boutique in Mong Kok. Her waist was slender, her bosom no more than average, but her manner was bright and lively. Her clothes seemed to float around her body, allowing it to breathe and making her look very sexy. She was rather much given to giggling, but she was not empty-headed, and she was quite fearless. That same day, she asked Sha Sha to come and visit her shop, where she made her try on some new clothes, turning her this way and that, all the while telling her how her heart actually belonged to someone else and that she was saving herself for her boyfriend, who was studying in Japan. As Sha Sha listened, she couldn't help sobbing, making a large wet patch on her chest.

"Foolish child," Ma Nga said as she pulled off her Hysteric Glamour, handing it to Sha Sha to change into. "Here's your battle dress. I guarantee that from now on it will make you ever victorious. You don't believe me? Just wait and see: I know!" Then she whirled round, her hair flying out in all directions, and struck a martial pose. They looked at each other and burst out laughing.

When Sha Sha wore Ma Nga's Hysteric Glamour, it was so extremely tight that it drew lots of attention, but that didn't really worry her and she held her head high as she strode through campus. When she ran into Lap Kei, she didn't avoid him but walked straight ahead. Afterward she felt her heart beating hard, but, no longer hindered by infatuation, she broke into a smile.

One day when there was a touch of autumn on campus, Sha Sha was wearing a hooded jacket over her HG top. Walking downhill toward the canteen, she somehow felt that her chest was cold. There was a large patch that was wet as if from tears. Otherwise, she felt fresh and free from sweat on her body. Suddenly she had a bad feeling and pulled out her mobile phone to give Ma Nga a ring. At the other end, Ma Nga's voice was choked with sobs, and Sha Sha couldn't hear a word she was saying. She ran all the way to the station, rushed to Ma Nga's shop in Mong Kok, and found Ma Nga there holding a letter between her fingers. She looked up, her face wet with tears, and squeezed out a smile.

"Sha Sha, he doesn't want me anymore."

For the first time Sha Sha knew how brightly tears could glisten.

17

WINDOWS 98

The bedroom windows of Chan Sze Hang and Ho Mei Yam were opposite each other but far apart, and neither one ever noticed the existence of the other in daily life. However, they had for some time actually belonged to the same women's organization. They'd become acquainted on its website and exchanged emails for a while, talking about their feelings and worries. As Chan Sze Hang and Ho Mei Yam sent messages to each other, they were amazed to find out that they had both begun to use computers in 1995, that their computers had been installed by their boyfriends, and that they had both split up with those boyfriends in 1995 and had had no other romantic relationships for three years.

Chan Sze Hang only knew that Ho Mei Yam was doing business promotion, but she didn't know that through her work Ho Mei Yam had recently got to know a man called Sam, who was doing computer animation, and that for the first time in three years she was feeling distracted. Ho Mei Yam thought she had recovered from the wound of three years earlier and that her mind was tranquil, but after she had seen Sam working on the demo for a commercial on his computer, she returned home to find herself feeling a pain in her stomach every time she booted up her PC and heard the Windows 95 start-up tones. Her thoughts were too confused, and she wasn't in the right frame of mind to reply to Chan Sze Hang's messages.

Ho Mei Yam only knew that Chan Sze Hang worked at a real estate agency, and that the pressure of work was immense, especially in the market conditions of the past few months. However, she had no idea that Chan Sze Hang had recently shown a flat to a young university professor, and the man had actually become quite interested in her and asked her out for dinner. Chan Sze Hang knew that she no longer counted as young and that opportunities were becoming scarce, but she was worried that she might invite scorn for not being as well educated. When she thought of how she'd been rejected three years earlier, Chan Sze Hang's normally fearless attitude at work turned into a sense of inferiority, to the point that she wouldn't even touch the computer that her former boyfriend had set up.

Sam had invited Ho Mei Yam out a number of times, but she had said no each time. Preferring to avoid complications, she would wait for the workday to be over so she could forget about him. One evening she was obliged to turn on the computer to write something, and in passing she looked to see if there was any email from Chan Sze Hang. She was taken aback when she opened Outlook Express to discover the inbox full of messages from Sam. With her heart thumping, she read on until she was halfway through. She felt dizzy. Unexpectedly, he explained that before he hadn't understood how to value feelings and had been blaming himself for three years. Now he was hoping that he could make a new beginning with Ho Mei Yam.

The more Chan Sze Hang began to take to the young professor, the more worried she became, but in the end she took the initiative to meet him. Learning that he was teaching computer engineering, Chan Sze Hang couldn't help feeling her heart sink. He kept rambling on about computer software, asking Chan Sze Hang if she had installed Windows 98.

"Will you help me?" she asked, gritting her teeth.

To find something related to computers to talk about, Chan Sze Hang had walked at random around a computer mall that day. As it happened, she ran into her boyfriend of three years earlier, who was out shopping with a woman wearing a gray trouser suit. Startled, Chan Sze Hang made a quick escape. After Ho Mei Yam and Sam had finished buying equipment, they went back to her home to let Sam do the installation. When Sam came into her bedroom, he pointed toward a distant spot outside the window.

"My old girlfriend lives right across from here."

Ho Mei Yam gazed blankly in that direction but saw only a large number of densely spaced windows.

The professor went up to Chan Sze Hang's flat. They made some small talk and the mood was a bit weird, but suddenly there was action. After it was over, his mobile phone rang and he left hastily without a word. Only a CD with Windows 98 was left behind. After Sam had finished with the installation on Ho Mei Yam's computer, he asked her to come and start up Windows 98. She'd received new emails. At the top there was a new message from Sam. What he said was very simple, but Ho Mei Yam couldn't contain herself. She got up in the middle of the night to email Chan Sze Hang, with whom she had been out of touch for some time.

> *Sze Hang*: When I opened my window this evening, I
> hadn't expected to see the moon in the sky.
> Mei Yam.

In the middle of the night, Chan Sze Hang got out of bed in a daze, picked up the Windows 98 disk from the table, and inserted it into the computer's CD drive. She waited for thirty minutes until the installation was finished and then attempted to restart, but the computer failed to start up. She tried a dozen times, but it was always the same; the more she tried, the more infuriated she became. Striking wildly at the machine, she cried until the whole keyboard was wet with tears.

18
—

NON — NO

The Japanese fashion magazine *non-no* is directed at young adult women. Younger girls read *Seventeen* or *Zipper*.

When she turned eighteen, Nora felt the magazines *Seventeen* and *Zipper* weren't right for her anymore, so she only read *non-no*, embarking on a bland period in her life, with nothing too flowery or pretentious. Nora didn't know Japanese but always carried an issue of *non-no*. People who got to know her later called her Non-No, but she called herself No-No or Don't-Don't. Some malicious people called her No-Glow because her skin was rather dark and she rarely looked cheerful, but some sex-obsessed boys gave her the nickname Hole-in-One.

In addition to *non-no*, Nora's handbag also contained a pair of scissors and a roll of sticky tape. Whenever she was sitting down, she would leaf through a copy of *non-no*, cut out pictures of clothes and young models, and stick them wherever she liked, sometimes to the windows inside train carriages or on restaurant menus, or sometimes postboxes, ATMs, display windows, lift doors, public telephones, and even people's backs. Sometimes she just cut out pictures of dresses; at other times it would be the whole model or just part of her, and she would also put other clothing onto these cutouts.

Nora couldn't actually be considered obsessed with shopping for clothes, but in the summer of the year when she turned nineteen, she stuck to wearing *non-no*–style tank tops, embroidered with flowers but otherwise nothing fancy. When she met her old friends, they claimed she had gone conservative, not like the girl of old who dared to shock and offend; now she couldn't follow the trends and be a "cutie." It was just "No-No" and "Don't-Don't," and looking as if she'd had enough fun and turned her mind to virtuous living. Nora bowed her head, cut something out of *non-no*, stuck it over a friend's mouth, and then, for once, broke out laughing. When they asked if she had gone out with any boys recently, she stood up all of a sudden, shedding scraps of paper on the floor.

When Nora worked at a hairdresser's for six months, there was no lack of boys pursuing her, but she kept her distance, so they sensibly backed off of their own accord. Her job was to do the shampooing, and she never bothered to learn how to cut hair or do anything else; she didn't care about acquiring any professional skills and was satisfied with shampooing. During quiet periods, she would leaf through *non-no* and cut out pictures of people. When she was washing men's hair, some customers took the chance to stroke her hand, or, feeling itchy, might ask for something extra, but Nora would splash foam into their eyes. The boss told her off, of course, but he got used to her behavior and even put up with her pasting cutouts all over the shop.

The boss's name was Ray. He was in his early thirties and had a full head of long hair. Once, pointing at the hairstyling page in the issue of *non-no* that Nora was looking at, he said, "Let me give you a haircut like that!"

Nora sat down stiffly in front of the mirror, the cape was placed on her shoulders, the scissors went snip-snip next to her ears, the fingers holding the scissors brushed every so often against her face, and clumps of hair tumbled to the floor. When Ray was only halfway through, she began to shake all over. He got such a shock that he dropped the scissors. He asked what was the matter, but she just said she felt cold.

He didn't continue with the haircut, and the next day Nora cut out the picture of the hairstyle from *non-no*, stuck it onto a photo of herself, and showed it to Ray.

"You see how weird it looks! It doesn't suit me."

Ray said the proportions weren't right.

"Then how about me cutting your hair?" she asked.

"Sure," Ray answered rashly.

Nora bought a few copies of *Men's non-no* and cut out some male headshots from the pages. She said it was practice. Ray rolled his eyes and didn't think she would follow through, but he didn't raise the matter again. A fortnight passed. One day when they were opening up the shop, Nora asked Ray if he really wanted to let her cut his hair. He thought it was just a casual remark and said, "Sure," as before, but he was taken aback when she reached for the scissors and got started. A few strands of hair drifted into the air. Ray put his arms around his head, fled the shop, and tramped around in the neighborhood for a while. When he returned, Nora was gone. In front of the mirror was an envelope. He opened it and found pictures of women's bodies and fashionable clothes, cut into tiny pieces and stuffed inside. There was also a picture of Nora's face, but no hair or neck, just her face.

19

KONJAK JELLIES

Okashiland is a chain of shops in Hong Kong that sells Japanese sweets and snacks. O Camp (Orientation Camp) is an obligatory induction for new university students.

When Wan Hoi Ka graduated from university, she stayed in the Department of Business Administration as an administrator. Even though she thought she hadn't seen much of the world, she was content with a steady, peaceful life as a high-level office lady. In her spare time, she and her colleagues sampled the full range of snacks at Okashiland while swapping opinions on Japanese television shows.

Before graduation, Wan Hoi Ka had imagined that her life would come to an end at that point. By unhappy chance, Lai Wai Man, the boyfriend she had been seeing for three years, told her over the phone before final exams that he was in love with someone else, and that person was none other than her roommate in the student hostel, Shi Hau Ling. Wan Hoi Ka thought he was teasing her. After playfully scolding him, she hung up and went out with Shi Hau Ling for a late-evening snack. As they were having fruit-salad sago pudding, tears began dripping, pit-a-pat, from Shi Hau Ling's eyes, and her head drooped lower and lower as her bowl filled with tears. Only then did Wan Hoi Ka suddenly wake up, as if from a dream.

With some difficulty, Wan Hoi Ka managed to graduate with a lower second, but the head of department had seen that she always completed her assignments, expressed herself well, and was familiar with departmental affairs, so he asked her to take up the vacant position of administrative assistant. Her classmates commented that this hardly matched the aspirations of the Wan Hoi Ka they had known as a stalwart of the student association in the department, but she appeared to treat it as something not worth making a fuss about; it was just a job.

After starting work, Wan Hoi Ka underwent two big transformations. The first one was dressing as an office lady with light makeup, wearing a trouser suit, and having lunch in the staff canteen. Her second change was losing weight, but that had nothing to do with her job. She went to work punctually at nine, got off at five, and didn't have a heavy workload. Wan Hoi Ka thought it was because she was eating konjak. Konjak, also known as "devil's tongue," is a taro-type root vegetable. It is frozen into a jellylike consistency and is said to contain plenty of fiber and have a fat-reducing effect. Packaged in little plastic cups with fruit juice, it had become a high-quality snack and been fashionable for a while in Japan and Taiwan.

Wan Hoi Ka, who'd kept her full figure after losing her boyfriend, started to shed pounds after beginning to eat konjak jellies, and her acquaintances thought they saw the magical effect of the devil's tongue. They also took to eating it and soon everyone was asking for some of hers. Wan Hoi Ka had been sampling konjak all over town and knew all the sweet, sour, and bitter varieties available: the heart-shaped jellies were the most satisfying but also the dearest. Most popular were lychee-flavored konjak jellies in *nata de coco*. Her office colleagues got together to order them, deputing Wan Hoi Ka to handle it. When they had made the purchase, they had ten cartons with over two thousand servings.

One day, when Wan Hoi Ka had been busy and was late for lunch, she thought she might as well go to the student canteen. As she sat by herself amid the hubbub made by the students, she had an illusion of being back in the days before her graduation. She absentmindedly ate the daily special as if no time had passed since she was there last, took out two konjak jellies for dessert, tore off the wrapper of one of them, and put the plastic cup to her lips. As she was about to suck the jelly and fruit juice into her mouth, someone rather brashly called out, "Hey, miss!"

She hastily looked up, her mouth full of juice and soft jelly, and saw a male student who appeared familiar. In a moment she remembered: his name was Ricky, he was a third-year student in the Philosophy Department, and she had got to know him in O Camp, where she had been his "group mother."

"A girl eating konjak jellies, very sexy," he remarked.

Afterward, Ricky often went to see Wan Hoi Ka at the Department of Business Administration, talking about what he had just been up to and gossiping about this and that. Once he brought a packet of heart-shaped jellies, saying they were leftovers from his classmates. Wan Hoi Ka put the transparent heart-shaped jellies to her lips. In a daze, she sucked at them; it was as if her heart had also turned to jelly.

Before the academic year was over, Wan Hoi Ka had twice had lunch with Ricky, squeezing into the crowd in the canteen and chatting loudly. When she took off her jacket, revealing her tank top, she looked just like a pretty young undergraduate. Ricky wore a T-shirt and jeans, as always, and went on and on about Foucault's theory of prisons and its relationship to the modern school system. They even had a minor debate about the concepts of management theory, and Wan Hoi Ka felt her spirits rise as she discovered that her brain had not yet become useless.

Later she heard that Ricky had gone to teach in a middle school after graduation. Wan Hoi Kai continued to lose weight, until she looked like a wire coat hanger when she was wearing a tank top. People began to worry about her and told her to give up eating konjak. The jellies seemed to become more tasteless the more she ate, but Wan Hoi Ka went on eating them, one after the other.

20

MEBIUS

Beach Boys was a Japanese television comedy series. One of the principal characters was a salaryman played by Takenouchi Yutaka.

Mei-bei's reason for buying a Sharp Mebius notebook PC was perhaps just its resemblance to her own name. Only later did she find out that it actually referred to the famous Möbius band: a long strip of paper with one end twisted halfway and joined to the other end so as to form a band with a single side that is neither inner nor outer.

That afternoon in Mong Kok, when Mei-bei had just purchased her Mebius, she sat down in a shopping mall tearoom and pulled it out, too impatient to wait. Before starting up the sleek, impossibly thin, silvery machine, she'd just left it on the table so she could sit and admire it. When she finally pulled up the display screen, she noticed, at a table diagonally across from her, a man who was using a laptop. At a glance she recognized that his machine was a Sony Vaio.

Mei-bei had always felt such behavior as sitting in a café and writing was really utterly affected and ridiculous, but the next day she came back anyway, carrying her Mebius, and sat down in the same tearoom. It was as if the ultrathin Mebius was a window leading to the unknown. To buy the machine, she'd spent half her savings from two years' work as a journalist. At her

weekly magazine, she'd been writing texts about trendy products, until one day she suddenly went to the news editor and
resigned. She said she wanted to write something that truly
belonged to herself, and had even worked out both plot and characters already. There was no special reason for all this, it was
just that she'd had enough of materialism and had decided to
do something that involved emotions. Mei-bei's fingers began
tapping, and the screen wallpaper appeared, with the Mebius
logo in the form of a figure 8 against sky and clouds. As she
started up Chinese Word, she noticed the man again. He had his
back turned toward her and was hitting the keys noisily.

The chief male character in Mei-bei's novel was called
Lau Wa Sang. He was a very knowledgeable up-and-coming
author who despised the world and scorned vulgarity, his heart
set on writing a monumental masterpiece. The main female
character was called Wai and worked as a salesgirl in a fashion
store. Very much into the latest trends, she always dressed
from head to foot in fake brands, not knowing or not caring
about what was genuine and what was not. She was the object
of Lau Wa Sang's desire. One day, Lau Wa Sang woke up and
discovered Wai had gone missing, so he set out on a full day's
search. In different places along the way, coming across various
current fads and recalling time spent together with Wai, he
discovered that, beneath his own contempt and misunder-
standing, he had actually fallen deeply in love with her.

For three consecutive afternoons, Mei-bei came across Vaio
man in the tearoom. He always sat in front of her to the left,
wearing a business suit, his manner being somewhat reminis-
cent of the white-collar worker played by Takenouchi Yutaka in
Beach Boys. All the time he was using English-language Power-
Point, so she thought he was preparing a presentation for work.
The more Mei-bei typed, the more her mind wandered, and she
kept stealing glances at Vaio, while her novel was stuck at the
beginning, where Lau Wa Sang had woken up, letting his mind

wander while he lay in bed. On the fourth day, Mei-bei's Mebius hadn't been sufficiently charged, and she saw no point in being annoyed when it suddenly went to sleep. She was therefore watching the man's Vaio when his machine also ran out of power: it was as if it were in response to her own. The two of them foolishly sipped some tea, feeling rather bored. Suddenly the man tore off a strip of paper from his notepad, twisted it into the shape of a figure 8, held the ends together with a paper clip, wrote "Hi! Mebius!" on one side of it, turned around, and threw it on Mei-bei's table. Mei-bei suspiciously held up the loop of paper between her fingers to have a look. Suddenly realizing what it was, she picked up her pen and wrote on the other side: "Vaio, how are you!" Then she tossed it back.

On the fifth day, Vaio picked up his teacup and laptop and stepped over to Mei-bei, who invited him to sit down. The computers were placed next to each other so that they looked like a loving couple. They asked about each other's work just for the sake of exchanging a few words.

"Actually, it's not necessary for me to use my computer here," said Vaio.

Mei-bei approved. "Of course! It's absolutely unnecessary!" she said as if in a dream. "But why do you keep coming here day after day?"

"Perhaps because I'd bought a portable computer!" he said, resting his chin on his hand. They thought what he said was rather funny and grinned at each other.

Back home, Mei-bei dragged her sentimental novel to the recycle bin and created a new document. A new idea had occurred to her: she would write stories about the popular consumer goods that she was most familiar with, love stories happening because of Prada, Hello Kitty, photo stickers, and bucket hats. Why not? However, first she had to write about Mebius and Vaio, imagining their happy encounter the next afternoon.

21
—

COMBAT TROUSERS

To just about everyone, it was really unimaginable that Che Siu Man would wear the popular kind of twill combat trousers with outside pockets on the thighs. The impression she gave was that of a good girl who was diligent in her studies. Her parents were in fact very strict in disciplining her, and her school results were always excellent. She had one year until the Certificate of Education examination.

Che Siu Man normally wore an ordinary T-shirt and jeans and was so wholesome that it was almost inhuman, but in Ah Ngat's eyes she was sweeter and lovelier than any of the stylish girls he'd played around with. Ah Ngat hadn't finished fifth year of middle school and was doing odd jobs such as delivering newspapers and take-out food, helping with removals, or taking on some slightly shady deals, but, in short, didn't go so far as breaking the law to commit real crimes. At times in the afternoon, he would sit in front of a tea café reading comics, and when it happened that Che Siu Man passed by after school, he would cast sidelong glances at her. Eventually he coaxed her into talking by inviting her to have a soft drink. She didn't actually refuse but sat down on a stool. After finishing her drink, she left.

It was in the summer of that year that Che Siu Man suddenly appeared in her combat trousers. They were olive green and very wide, making her legs appear clumsy, even though they were actually slender and pretty. Every day Ah Ngat waited for her to walk past and would ask where she was going. It would be either the tutorial school or the library, or else she was on her way home to do some revision.

"Let's go swimming!" Ah Ngat once said, knowing very well there was no chance Che Siu Man would agree but thinking to himself that only a swimsuit or short skirt would do justice to her shapely figure. Che Siu Man was very careful to spend only as much time sitting with Ah Ngat as was needed for a single soft drink, so Ah Ngat never knew whether he qualified as Che Siu Man's friend or not. Nothing came of these encounters, of course.

One day Che Siu Man did something unprecedented: she told Ah Ngat a secret about herself. She said she had been in the British armed forces in a previous life, dying in action in the War of Resistance against Japan. Thinking she was just having a laugh, Ah Ngat said he himself had been in the Japanese Imperial Army in a previous life. He was taken aback when Che Siu Man gave him a loud smack on the face.

"You simply have no idea of suffering!" she said harshly. She ran away as fast as she could in her combat trousers, while Ah Ngat followed her with his eyes, rubbing his cheek that was still smarting from the slap. He was baffled.

Later on, when Che Siu Man talked a second time about her previous existence, Ah Ngat had learnt to behave himself and dared not say anything rash. She said she'd been a British officer's wife, her husband had died in action, but she had clung on to life to cherish his memory. Speechless, Ah Ngat watched her hands tightly gripping a textbook; he began to feel anxious.

One day Che Siu Man had dark rings under her eyes, as if she hadn't slept all night. "I'm going to see him," she told Ah Ngat.

Feeling worried, Ah Ngat waited for her when she came out from her tutorial. He accompanied her on the MTR to Central, where they changed to a bus for Stanley, finally arriving at Stanley Military Cemetery.

The moon was full, white and silvery, and Ah Ngat had a clear view of Che Siu Man as she knelt in front of a headstone and pulled out a gleaming little knife. With no pause for reflection, he leapt at her. In the confusion, it wasn't certain who caused the injury, but there was blood all over Che Siu Man's trousers. Suddenly Ah Ngat undid her trousers as they rolled back and forth on the grass. Being the stronger, he eventually pulled them off and ran to a hillside in the distance, where he pulled out a cigarette lighter, set fire to the trousers, and burnt them. When he returned, he found Che Siu Man lying on the grave crying, her body curled into a ball and twitching. Taking a deep breath, he bent down and pulled her up in his arms. As they walked along, they encountered a policeman. Ah Ngat's shirt was wrapped around Che Siu Man so that it looked like a skirt, leaving Ah Ngat in his white vest. They managed to get past without having to make up any excuses.

After that, Che Siu Man didn't go back to the tutorial classes and was less serious about her studies. Ah Ngat stopped taking things easy and signed up for a course at a technical school with the intention of becoming an electrician. Before summer was over, they went swimming together, getting so sunburnt that their skin peeled.

22

—

PUTTY

Puffy (aka Puffy AmiYumi) is a Japanese pop group consisting of two young women called Ami and Yumi. They frequently appear in similar outfits. *With Love* is a Japanese television serial from 1998.

People who met them for the first time couldn't tell Ah Win and Ah Wen apart, and even friends who knew them well might also make mistakes if they weren't paying attention. There were also times when the two of them went out of their way to be mischievous, so that the one who clearly was Win said she was Wen, but if you called her Wen, she played the part of Win. Some people simply said WinWen, so they would never make a mistake telling who was who, and, after Puffy became a big act, some just called them Puffy. They accepted this.

In fact, Ah Win and Ah Wen were not completely alike to start off with, differing slightly in height and weight. However, both had big eyes, round faces, and, in addition, the same hairstyles, makeup, and way of dressing. They were like clones in their manners and speech, so gradually they became indistinguishable.

The girls had got to know each other in form three in secondary school. They attended a Catholic school, where they sat next to each other, and their real names were Winnie and Wendy. One day Ah Win had plaited her hair into pigtails, and Ah Wen imitated her as a joke. When their teacher called their names, she actually got them mixed up, and the girls found it very amusing. From then on, they often dressed up in the same way for the fun of confusing classmates and teachers. In form four, they were placed in different classes and were deeply disconsolate at being torn apart. During breaks, at lunchtime, and after school, they were inseparable, consoling each other for the pain of separation. Classmates who were taking world history called them WWII.

Ah Win and Ah Wen used to get good marks, but just before the Certificate of Education examination in form five, they were discovered by one of the nuns hiding in a toilet cubicle and subjected to strict questioning. They maintained that they had just been there to have a quick look at a comics magazine for girls, but the school authorities were convinced there was more to it than that and suspended them for two weeks. It was also decided without appeal that they could not go on to sixth form in that school. As a result, Ah Win's and Ah Wen's exam results were a complete mess, and, with no regrets whatsoever, the pair of them bade farewell to school life.

The more alike Ah Win and Ah Wen became, the more they distanced themselves from other people. Normally they were high-spirited and fun to be with, but afterward no one was able to work out what they had said, let alone having any real understanding of them. They moved away from home and shared a flat, sleeping and washing themselves together, and even when they got jobs as sales assistants, it was in the same shop. When it came to making friends, the two of them stuck together; if anyone didn't like Ah Win, Ah Wen wouldn't have anything to do with them either, and vice versa.

Ah Win and Ah Wen often joked that when they got married, they would share the same husband. Boys felt intimidated when they heard that, and quite a few who had pursued them beat the retreat. The boys said there was simply no way of prizing them apart: if you asked one out, both would invariably come, and so cinema tickets, presents, and sweet compliments would have to be doubled in quantity. Would-be suitors couldn't take it. Because of all this, some concluded that Ah Win and Ah Wen were actually lesbians, and going out with boys was just a smoke screen.

Two of their young male coworkers didn't believe the gossip and agreed to attack separately, each locking onto one of the girls. To start with, the boys were quite good-natured about it, but slowly that turned into exasperation and confusion; they felt like ending it but couldn't. One day the four of them agreed to go and watch a VCD of *With Love* in the girls' home. Saying he was going to buy beer, one of the boys dragged Ah Win along to the nearest supermarket, but once they were in the car, he drove up a distant hillside. When Ah Win threatened to jump out of the vehicle, he paid no attention. In the meantime, Ah Wen and the other boy went home and opened a bottle of red wine. Drinking as they waited, their faces and ears turning red, they went on to kiss and cuddle each other, with Ah Wen half yielding, half pushing him back. In the car up on the hill, Ah Win, in a daze, also let the boy kiss her, but nothing more than that. Suddenly, for no apparent reason, she screamed in pain, put a hand to her belly, pushed open the car door, and dived out. Following her, the boy saw her sink to the ground after only a few steps. A spot of blood had appeared below her waist. He stood there horrified.

23
—

SONY DV

DV is a digital video format. The Sony Handycam DCR-TRV9
was a mini-DV camcorder released in 1998. The Japanese film
A Lost Paradise (*Shitsurakuen* 失楽園) from 1997 is about a
fifty-four-year-old married magazine editor and a thirty-
seven-year-old married typesetter who commit suicide after
having an affair. The two main characters are played by
Hashimoto Kōji and Kuroki Hitomi. Ozawa Madoka is a Japanese adult-video actress. Films rated level three in Hong Kong
are only for persons aged eighteen and above.

Lau Wai Sum had one of those figures that make it difficult to
guess a person's age. Nowhere on her body was there any sur-
plus flesh, and her soft pink skin was like a schoolgirl's. However, she wore her hair at medium length, with an even fringe
across her face, small, black-framed glasses, and often tight
clothes with high-heeled strap sandals, like a fashion-conscious
secretary.

Lau Wai Sum didn't actually pay too much attention to the
way other people rated her looks, but she'd been unable to dis-
miss Lam Wai Pong's first comment about her: "Your style is so
middle-class."

Lau Wai Sum's school results had all along been middling.
When she sat the university entrance exam, she actually had a
good chance of doing well, but on the day of the English exam,

she unfortunately ran a high fever. As she was overcome by diz-
ziness, the mass of people crowded like ants in the examination
hall seemed to emit a kind of fuzzy glow, and she passed out,
having completed less than half of the exam paper. As a result,
she failed two subjects. Suddenly losing heart and simply looking
for any job, she joined a small-scale public relations company.
She'd originally applied for a position as an ordinary office
worker, but when she showed herself efficient and careful, got
along well with her coworkers, and also had proper and correct
manners, her superiors promoted her to be a trainee public-
relations officer. However, they told her to dress up a bit—she
couldn't always look like a high school graduate.

Lau Wai Sum had never let anyone know there was something slightly wrong with her eyes. Whenever she looked at
people, her eyes always had a glow about them, an aftereffect of
the fever she'd had that time. She'd been for a couple of eye
examinations, but they failed to identify the problem. Wearing
polarized sunglasses didn't help either, and so, as time passed,
she came to regard her condition as normal. When she happened to read a magazine article about heat-sensitive photos of
New Age–type human-body aura, she suddenly became aware
that the body glow she'd been seeing varied in strength. From
then on, she was able to spot when colleagues had a fever or
were upset, or when men were sexually aroused.

Lau Wai Sum was also aware there hadn't been any sexual
impulse behind it when Lam Wai Pong had said her style was
middle-class. A few days after they'd moved in together, she
asked him about that initial remark, but he hadn't got the slightest recollection of it. When she pressed him, he came up with a
few explanations.

"Perhaps it was because I felt you were like those young
women professionals whose clothes, expressions, conversations, actions are all so perfectly clean and tidy." Unsure
whether she was satisfied or not, Lau Wai Sum held her tongue.

When they were first living together, Lam Wai Pong was quite passionate about Lau Wai Sum. She was quite sure about this but still dared not examine it too closely. Making love was always in the evening, Lau Wai Sum insisting that the light was turned off and also closing her eyes; otherwise, all became blindingly white. Initially thinking she was shy, Lam Wai Pong didn't mind but was gentle and considerate with her. Later on, however, he asked, "Why is it you're so timid?" Then he brought home a few pirated VCDs with erotic films for them to enjoy together at home in order to foster desire, but they found that *A Lost Paradise* with Kuroki Hitomi and Hashimoto Kōji embracing each other in secret was much too restrained. As for a level-three VCD with Ozawa Madoka, it just got left at the side of the videodisc player.

Lam Wai Pong had held a job as computer programmer, and they'd got to know each other when he installed a new system for Lau Wai Sum's company. They dated for six months, lived together for a year and a half, and then he went to study in the United States, changing his field to business administration.

"If you go now, then we split up. Isn't there truly any way you can stay?" Lau Wai Sum had asked him earnestly. He had nothing to say in reply.

Lau Wai Sum went out and bought a Sony DCR-TRV9 digital camcorder after reading about it in the papers. It had an infrared mode with the capability of taking photos at night within a three-meter range. When rumors circulated in the market that it could see through clothing, the price had immediately shot up, eventually reaching fourteen thousand dollars. People who took the camcorders outside were regarded as Peeping Toms, and women fell over each other to evade them. So staff at the video-equipment shop cast sidelong glances at Lau Wai Sum.

Lau Wai Sum concealed the camcorder in a stuffed toy facing their bed. The night before Lam Wai Pong's departure, she made love to him for the last time. It was as if she'd changed into a different person, astounding him to such a degree that he nearly felt impelled to change his plans. When he left, he actually couldn't help shedding tears, not at all understanding why he did so.

The following evening, Lau Wai Sum mustered enough courage to watch the recorded video. For the first time she clearly saw two naked bodies without any glow around them as they moved with abandon. She wept for a while; the defect in her eyes had disappeared.

24
—
APRONS

The first time Ah Tsin saw Pointy Pearl was at the university's Christmas dance. The girls had dressed up as young society beauties in ball gowns with plunging necklines and low backs, all except Pointy Pearl, who wore a short red apron with a huge bow at the back. Ah Tsin thought she was the sexiest girl there, even though she was wearing a blouse and long skirt under the apron.

Afterward he often bumped into the apron girl on campus, and every time she was wearing a different apron. Some were long, others short; some were checked, others single colors; some were brightly colored, others plain. Once, when he was visiting a classmate's room, he saw Pointy Pearl dragging a large suitcase upstairs. Halfway up, her suitcase sprang open, spilling aprons all over the stairs. Ah Tsin went up to help her gather them. They felt like underwear as he clutched them in his hands, and his heart beat a little faster. As a joke, he asked if she were studying cooking.

"I get them by mail order from Japanese fashion magazines," replied Pointy Pearl, adding, "I loathe cooking."

During Ah Chin's first year at university, the boys in his dormitory would see the girl in a blue-checked apron climb up the long slope at dusk every day, carrying a food container to wait for Ah Chin under the banyan tree outside the dormitory. Later, they found out that she was known as Brighteyes, that the two had been in the same class in high school, that they had been dating for two years, and that she used to cook for Ah Chin while they were preparing for the university entrance exam. In the end, Ah Chin passed the exam but Brighteyes didn't make it through. The apron had been a present from Ah Chin, but it had become badly stained over the years. When Ah Chin noticed that she wore it every time she came to his room, he was cross with her for it being so grubby, but Brighteyes just said she'd been careless.

Pointy Pearl's mother was a professional chef who had published books, appeared on TV shows, and ran a food-and-drink business. Pointy Pearl's parents got divorced when she was twelve, but although she lived with her mother afterward, she never got to taste her mother's cooking again. Instead, she'd have instant noodles alone at home every night after school, and her greatest pleasure was to wear one of her mother's aprons to bed. Although Ah Tsin was well aware that Pointy Pearl detested kitchens, he borrowed a village house that a friend was renting and prepared a kitchen full of ingredients for her to show off her culinary skills. Pointy Pearl insisted on not cooking, and for a while neither of them gave way. Finally, she went into the kitchen, reduced the foodstuffs to a pile of charcoal, swept away the dishes, and sat down at the table, bursting into tears. Deeply distraught, and saying over and over again that it was all his fault, Ah Tsin collapsed into a fit of crying. Pointy Pearl untied her food-stained cream apron, and, with empty stomachs, the two of them did what lovers do.

The boys in Ah Chin's class were at first very envious of him, but when they noticed that he'd stopped going to the banyan tree for his meals, they gradually avoided mentioning it. Brighteyes still came to the dormitory every day, and she would pound on the door if he hid in his room. His neighbors found this unbearable, so they would urge him to open up. Once Brighteyes had gone inside, she would stay for a long time, and sometimes the others could hear tears and quarrels. Eventually Ah Chin took to avoiding her altogether, and she stopped looking for him. She would sit and wait outside the dormitory entrance until daybreak, holding the food container, but Ah Chin never came back. When the other boys came out to go to class in the morning, they would see that Brighteyes had cried so hard that her apron was soaked in tears. Someone said that Ah Chin was going to another girl's dormitory, but no one dared to tell Brighteyes. Some time afterward, the word spread that Brighteyes had taken her own life.

The relationship between Ah Tsin and Pointy Pearl remained the same as before, although she never thought it would last forever. One night she sneaked into Ah Tsin's room and made love to him wearing only a short, blue-checked apron. The pair gripped each other in an almost deathly embrace. Early the next morning, she tiptoed outside. Another girl, also wearing an apron, brushed past her in the dimly lit hall, and then she heard someone knocking on a door behind her. It seemed to be Ah Tsin's room. Outside it was a bright spring morning. Pointy Pearl took a deep breath and stretched, looking at the distant hills as she stood under the banyan tree. Turning around, she saw the girl walking out. There was a large dark patch on the bib of her apron.

"Oh, it's soiled!" Pointy Pearl exclaimed, not able to tell what it was.

The girl nodded. "I can't wash it off," she replied.

Pointy Pearl took off the apron she was wearing, handed it over to the girl and said, "Here, I have lots more." The girl changed aprons and smiled at Pointy Pearl.

The two aprons were actually the same.

25

AIR JURDAN

Air Jordan is a brand of shoes and athletic clothing designed, owned, and produced by Nike's Jordan brand subsidiary. The shoes, informally referred to in the plural as Jordans or simply Js, were first produced for Michael Jordan in 1984 and released for public consumption in 1985.

Mei Sui and Tun Wing had fallen in love because of basketball, but they had never played together, up until the time when they were reluctantly pitted against each other. Mei Sui and Tun Wing had matriculated at university at the same time, both had been picked for the university teams in their first year, both had become team captains in their second year, and both had led their teams to the championship in the universities' joint basketball competition. The only difference between them was the difference between the girls' section and the boys' section. Tun Wing was 180 centimeters tall, which wasn't remarkable among the boys, whereas, at 180 centimeters, Mei Sui stood out among the girls like a crane among hens. Mei Sui's hands and feet were long and slender, and her soft hair, stretched to make it twice as straight, hung loose down to her waist. However, she scooped it up into a bun when she played, leaving several fine hairs to stray enticingly down her smooth white neck. Because she was so tall, boys who were a little shorter hung back; fortunately, there was Tun Wing, an almost perfect match.

When Mei Sui was in high school, she liked playing basket-ball, but her mother, complaining that she was getting taller and taller, blamed her height on basketball and strictly forbade her to play for a time. With strong encouragement from the school's physical education teacher, however, Mei Sui became an excellent player, and in the end her mother was left with nothing to say. Miss Chow, the PE teacher, was a young woman of a sunny disposition who had just begun to teach, having previously made a name for herself on school ball courts. As Mei Sui broke through to reach the basket and throw in the ball, feeling Miss Chow's concentrated gaze urging her on, her body was filled with an irre-pressible energy. Two years later, Miss Chow moved to a new job, but Mei Sui remained committed to basketball.

From the time she got to know Tun Wing on the university team, Mei Sui would come to watch him, whether he was com-peting formally or informally. People who didn't know about her took her for one of the cheerleaders who came to cheer on their boyfriends at the court. After watching him, she practiced on her own, gradually feeling some improvement in the way she handled the ball. When Mei Sui competed, however, Tun Wing never came to watch, just as there weren't any of the boyfriends of the girl players watching from the side; the spectators were just a few male students who came to check out the girls. Although Mei Sui's skills were outstanding, she nevertheless felt a sense of loss.

It was only natural, even inevitable, that Tun Wing and Mei Sui began dating. As far as inviting her to a meal or to watch a movie, giving her small presents at her birthday parties, accom-panying her to the doctor's, and keeping her company when she revised for exams, Tun Wing put in an adequate amount of effort. When Mei Sui said that the red-and-white Nike Air Jor-dans that he wore looked very good, he immediately gave her a pair exactly the same, costing 2,500 dollars. When she said they were too expensive, he replied, "Let's treat my fee for giving private lessons this month as volunteer work." When the others saw the lovers' matching Air Jordans, they regarded them as an ideal couple in reality as well as in name. Mei Sui, nevertheless, felt that the shoes were very heavy and made walking difficult.

As the summer holidays approached, people were bored and at a loss for something fun to do. One idea for an activity to beat the midsummer heat was to make Tun Wing and Mei Sui compete to see who was the better basketball player. Tun Wing and Mei Sui both looked unhappy at this but couldn't think of a reason to refuse. At first they intended just to treat it as a joke, but oddly enough, once they got started, their competitive spirit mysteriously stiffened. They agreed to compete in two rounds: first shooting the ball from fixed points, then a ten-minute competition between the two of them. In the first round, shooting the ball from further and further away, Mei Sui got ahead by two points, but when they got to the three-point line, she lost a ball. This had the crowd in an uproar, and she lost that round twelve to thirteen.

As soon as the second round started, Mei Sui went on the attack, and Tun Wing found himself caught unprepared. The two pairs of Air Jordans flashed to and fro under the basket. Then Mei Sui leapt up to the basket, but the ball rebounded off the board. As her feet hit the ground, her Air Jordans suddenly burst apart with a loud crack, and the soles came off. The crowd was stunned, but Mei Sui just ran to the side of the court, took off her shoes, and returned to play barefooted. Tun Wing was too late to call a halt; Mei Sui already had the ball and was attacking. They were like two fancy windup toys, automatically jumping and hopping about, not yielding an inch in their life-or-death battle. Mei Sui reversed the score and won by thirteen to twelve, but the spectators felt it had all somehow gone wrong; they dared not applaud but made excuses and drifted away, leaving the two behind. Dripping with sweat, they would not look at each other.

"What the hell did you think you were doing?" Tun Wing muttered as he turned and left.

Mei Sui, one hand rolling up her long hair that had worked its way loose, picked up her Air Jordans with her other hand and limped away, her ankles and the soles of her feet painful.

26

ICQ

ICQ is an instant-messaging computer program, most widely used from the late 1990s to the early 2000s.

There was a period when a fairly large number of people on ICQ knew Pie Chart. Some of them had quite frequent contact, such as Jon, Ricky, Betty B., Big Foot, Jacque, Mini, Hello Hello, Xiao, and Cherie; all of them had asked the question: Who actually are you, Pie Chart?

Pie Chart's answer was never the same from one day to the next. It might be, for instance: "Today I'm 40% Ricky, 27% Mini, 15% Xiao, 13% Vivian, 9% Diana, 5% Little Wave . . ." The answers were all along this line, depending on whoever was taking part that day. Having very broad interests, Pie Chart was able to rattle on about any subject under heaven, so that other people were often keen to involve Pie Chart in their chats. Pie Chart did not refuse such overtures and, while online, would respond to any approach. That made some feel Pie Chart was a bit excessive.

Among them, Jon and Betty B. got along particularly well with Pie Chart. Jon often told Pie Chart about his own feelings, and Pie Chart would reply earnestly, without knowing whether they were genuine or false, sometimes spending an entire evening online with Jon and continuing on until dawn.

"Can you belong to me 100%?" Jon later asked.

"You're being a bit silly," Pie Chart answered. "How could there be 100% of Pie Chart?"

"Then how much of you is yourself?" Jon persisted.

Pie Chart paused for a moment before responding. "Pie Chart has no self."

Someone who had assumed the name Bar Chart once angrily rebuked Pie Chart: "You are quite shameless."

"ICQ has too many time wasters," Betty B. said, offering comfort.

"What about us then?" Pie Chart replied.

Betty B. mentioned she'd recently been jilted but was fortunate to have Pie Chart as a companion—otherwise she wouldn't have known how to get through the long nights.

"I just like sharing," was all Pie Chart said.

Betty B. spoke of many private matters concerning herself: her family, which boy at school had a crush on her, how as a child she'd encountered a man in the park who'd molested her and pulled down her pants, and how she was quite keen to go to bed with a certain male teacher . . . Then she went on to ask Pie Chart personal questions about love and sex. When Pie Chart held forth on an extravagant variety of suggestions, she became inordinately excited.

Pie Chart, however, suddenly spoke up. "But you mustn't ever make any idiotic suggestions such as us meeting face to face."

"Don't imagine I live near you," Pie Chart also told Jon once. "That's just the sort of coincidence you find in television shows." Subsequently, Pie Chart vanished from ICQ.

Jon passed the university entrance exam and took a job in a pizza parlor for the summer vacation. A girl there, Ah Pai, seemed capable and experienced, had solid buttocks and round arms, and could easily carry six pizzas at the same time. Once when they were preparing a salad together, Jon casually asked, "Have you been on ICQ?"

Ah Pai turned around. "What Q did you say?" she asked.

Jon paused, stirring a bowl of pineapple pieces over and over again. Ah Pai was a good person, willing to help others, hard-working and with a forthright streak, while in her roughness there was also something delicate. After work, she would often find an excuse to wait for Jon and go for a leisurely stroll with him. As they wandered along the streets until late at night, it was almost inevitable that they fell in love. Ah Pai loosened her hair, which she kept tied in a ponytail at work. It was very long, and when it brushed against Jon's face as they walked, he suddenly asked Ah Pai if she knew Pie Chart.

Ah Pai opened her eyes wide. "Pie Chart? I didn't even get a pass in maths at school."

27
—

THE COLORED SUNGLASSES

The first time Zhou Heng came to Wong Hau Yam's flat to repair the intercom, she thought he was twenty-two or twenty-three. He was dressed simply in a dark green bomber jacket, with a tattered tool bag on his back and his untidy hair stuck to his forehead. However, on the bridge of his nose sat a pair of fashionable yellow-tinted sunglasses with heavy black frames, which she found rather unexpected. As he came in, Zhou Heng took off his shoes, bending down to put them neatly next to each other before taking apart the intercom next to the door. He pointed out to Wong Hau Yam how the button had become too distant from its point of contact, but it could be fixed by prizing it a little closer. When he'd finished and was picking up his tools, Wong Hau Yam asked him why he was wearing glasses like these.

"You should know, they're trendy," he said.

A few days later, Wong Hau Yam again asked the estate management office to send someone to fix the intercom. When the doorbell rang on Friday morning, the man with the yellow sunglasses was standing outside again.

"The contact points are too far apart again," Zhou Heng remarked as he examined it. Wong Hau Yam was standing to the side with her legs crossed, watching him.

"Do you lot only come here on Fridays?" she asked.

"I'm definitely here on Fridays," Zhou Heng replied matter-of-factly.

The following Friday, Zhou Heng again received instructions to go to Miss Wong's flat, 10C in block 2, to repair the intercom. That day Wong Hau Yam had just washed her hair and was absorbed in playing the theme tune of a Japanese television show on her piano. On the back, where her hair hung down, her white T-shirt had a large wet patch, making it see-through. Zhou Heng was wearing the glasses that looked like industrial wear. He remained silent while he was working, but just as he was about to leave, he spoke up.

"Are you giving piano lessons, Miss Wong?" he asked.

"Just for the time being," Wong Hau Yam said languidly. "It's six months since I got my master's degree and I haven't been able to find a job so far. I was studying linguistics." Probably thinking he wouldn't understand, she broke off.

A week later, Zhou Heng arrived at Wong Hau Yam's home for the fourth time but didn't utter a word, as if he were there for the first time. He became aware that Wong Hau Yam's home was in some disorder, with piano scores all over the place. The problem with the intercom was the same as before, and when he'd finished, he said he'd go downstairs to test it for her. Wong Hau Yam turned on her television and switched to the channel for the closed-circuit view of the lobby. When she saw Zhou Heng press the button downstairs, the intercom buzzed. She answered and said to Zhou Heng, "Can you come up again?" Zhou Heng didn't know which way to look, and in close-up on the screen his glasses appeared particularly incongruous.

After asking Zhou Heng to sit down, Wong Hau Yam had gone to the kitchen to fetch something to drink when she suddenly heard the piano. Returning, she found Zhou Heng playing Chopin's Nocturne in E-flat Major. He looked quite embarrassed after he'd finished.

"On the mainland I was selected for special education when I was four, and so I studied the piano for six years, but by the time I was eleven, we'd ended up here and I couldn't keep on with it. Also, we hadn't any money, so I didn't continue playing; instead I qualified as a mechanic." With a self-mocking smile still on his lips, he took off his weird glasses to wipe his eyes, stood up to say goodbye, and carefully put on his shoes. Carrying two glasses of orange juice, Wong Hau Yam followed him with her eyes as he left.

"You've been doing it on purpose!" she said to his back.

Zhou Heng turned around, his yellow sunglasses back in place. "Your piano needs tuning," he said.

Another three days passed and the intercom developed a genuine fault. Wong Hau Yam made an appointment for repairs with the management office. On Thursday evening, a research student from the graduate school gave her a phone call to find out if she would be interested in helping with a large-scale research project, and asked if she could see him the next morning. He also wanted to know if she would be free for lunch. Thinking it over for a moment, she said that would be fine.

When she got home on Friday evening, Wong Hau Yam discovered Zhou Heng's yellow sunglasses stuck into the grill of her security door. As soon as she was inside, the intercom sounded—so it had been mended. However, when she picked up, there was no answer. Hurriedly she turned on the closed-circuit television, but there was not a soul to be seen at the lobby entrance. Feeling exhausted, Wong Hau Yam let herself fall back on her couch. She put on the sunglasses and, in the blurred yellow light, saw Zhou Heng from behind as he sat at the piano playing Chopin. Early the next morning, Wong Hau Yam called the management company and asked for Zhou Heng. However, the staff member who answered said the company's human resources had been reorganized and Zhou Heng had been dismissed a full two weeks earlier.

28
—

SEIKO LUKIA

Lukia is one of Seiko's ranges of watches. G-shocks are shock-resistant sports watches made by Casio. Esumi Makiko is a Japanese model and actress who appeared in Hong Kong advertising for Citizen XC watches. Matsu Takako is a Japanese actress and pop star who appeared in advertising for Seiko Lukia. Orientation Camp is an obligatory induction for new university students.

When Flower of Science was admitted to university and moved away from home into a student hostel, she initially found it rather difficult to adjust to her fellow students' completely irregular lifestyle, one that turned night into day. What Flower herself didn't know, when she bought herself a present in the form of a Seiko LK, was the kind of connection this might have with student life. It was just that she felt that ever since she'd started wearing the watch, time had begun to pass particularly slowly, and she wasn't sure whether it was the Seiko LK that had changed the rhythm of her life or whether she'd at last found a timepiece that fitted that rhythm.

Flower, who'd studied science ever since year four of secondary school, was called "the flower of the science class" by her classmates. The boys were always chasing her, but Flower didn't take it seriously, saying it was just because not many girls were doing science. Later there was a rumor that Flower had never actually dated anyone, which meant there was nothing to support her nickname, but it didn't bother her, as she'd become used to it. When her new acquaintances at university asked how she'd got her name, she just said she liked doing flower arrangements.

There were actually a rather large number of pot plants—asparagus fern, golden pothos, ivy—in Flower's room. She often stared intently at the leaves, hoping to see for herself how they slowly grew, but there was no difference even after a long while. In the opposite case, however, if she didn't look at them one evening, they would have grown a section taller by the next morning. From that she concluded time must be something entirely different for plants, and she believed the feeling imparted by the Seiko LK was the plant-life sense that she had all along imagined.

Arty, whom she'd met at Orientation Camp, had from the outset been determined to date Flower of Science. The first time he asked her out for a meal, he had a present for her. He explained that it was the kind of Citizen XC watch that was being advertised by the actress Esumi Makiko, but Flower said it was too expensive for her to accept, and also she'd just bought herself a watch. Arty secretly regretted having been too late, but on seeing the Seiko LK on Flower's wrist, he felt enlightened: "So the one you'd go for is Matsu Takako." Flower, however, didn't understand what he meant.

Flower was quite friendly to Arty, and they were never short of things to talk about. However, when he was with her, Arty always sensed some kind of incompatibility, something he couldn't immediately explain. It could have been that she walked a bit slowly, ate her food in an unhurried way, and also spoke quite placidly. Nevertheless, once he began thinking about actually sorting out these trivialities, even he found it ridiculous. On one occasion Arty attempted to explain his muddled impressions to Flower.

"Perhaps the reason is we don't live in the same time," she said. Arty, who was reading arts, thought she was provoking an argument with her bagful of science books, so he went straight back, found an introduction to Einstein's theory of relativity, and subjected it to intense scrutiny. The next time they met, he'd only gained the most rudimentary understanding of it.

"Let's enter your time then!" he said.

It was a bizarre afternoon. While it seemed nothing at all happened, it also seemed everything changed all at once. One of Flower's classes had been canceled at the last moment, and she was sitting by the swimming pool relaxing with a book. Feeling a sudden urge to see Arty, she called his mobile. He skipped a class to come be with her, but while she had a smile on her lips, she had little to say. In the pool, two male students were swimming in rather slow freestyle: a sweep with the arms, a kick, a sweep with the arms, a kick. The late-autumn sunlight descended like fine dust, but the water was certainly very cold, and the swimmers must have been freezing. Flower had never experienced such a glorious afternoon and hoped Arty too was able to feel the same way: it seemed to her that as long as life had light, wind, sound, and companionship, nothing else was needed.

Arty suddenly stood up, brushed off his trousers, and pointed at his G-Shock watch. "Let's go!" he said. "It's past six and already dark! I've asked my classmates to work on our project this evening." The Seiko LK on Flower's wrist showed half past three, the silver watchband reflecting flashes of sunlight. She raised her head and saw that Arty had walked off into the distance, his figure neither growing nor diminishing in size.

Afterward, Flower happened to see Arty on the university grounds as he was running for the school bus, pulling a young woman along with him. Looking at her Seiko LK and seeing there was plenty of time, Flower felt in no hurry and slowly walked on, letting the bus drive off.

29
—

MY MELODY

My Melody is a little girl rabbit created by the Sanrio company in Japan and is mainly popular in Asian countries. She wears a red or pink hood covering her ears. Fukada Kyōko is a Japanese actress and singer.

Everybody knew May Mei liked My Melody. It helped that no one could possibly overlook the obvious fact that My Melody and May Mei had one characteristic in common, although they kindly pretended that was not the case.

May Mei's classmates in primary school, who were insensitive to other children's feelings, had occasionally poked fun at her because of her harelip. Other than that, her blemish had never caused her any particular worry. It's not clear if it was prompted by this congenital flaw, but once she had gone on to secondary school, May Mei doubled her efforts in her studies as well as in her kind treatment of others. The other girls in her class were prettier than May Mei, thanks to her lip, and so no one felt jealous or wary of her; and if in some respect they were not as good as May Mei, they felt less envy thanks to her lip. As a result, May Mei actually became the best liked and respected girl in her class and was often elected monitor and student rep.

May Mei's skin was milky white, her fine loose hair was brownish like the soft fur of a small animal, and her round eyes resembled translucent lychees. Apart from her lip, she did in fact deserve to be called a lovely young girl, so by the time she'd turned fifteen, May Mei had no lack of suitors.

Immediately after May Mei's birth, her mother had fallen into a depression. A scar remained after an operation on the lip, so May Mei's mother saw it as confirmation that her daughter was not destined for happiness. However, contrary to what might be expected, as time passed, she ceased being concerned about her daughter's self-esteem. In year three of primary school, May Mei began clamoring for My Melody stationary.

This made her mother tell her off for being freaky. "Isn't it enough the way people make fun of you?" she asked.

By the time May Mei was old enough to understand the way things are, she always thought it odd that for some strange reason her mother regarded rabbits as taboo.

May Mei learnt to use makeup very early, especially using brightening creams to conceal the scar on her lip. Sometimes she applied powder before going to school, and since her teachers were aware of the situation, they turned a blind eye. When her exam results were not good enough to go on to higher education, she responded to an ad for a sales assistant at a department-store cosmetics counter. While the quality of her skin was absolutely beyond reproach, the scar on her lip was another matter. In the end, only a small skincare-and-beauty parlor was willing to employ her. Putting all her energy into learning the trade, she advanced to become a specialist in bridal makeup. Customer response was quite good, and the business flourished.

Very early one morning, May Mei braided her hair into two plaits with colorful ribbons and put on a white blouse that she was fond of, its sleeves loosely rolled up and the top two buttons left undone. Tugging her hard-backed cosmetics case, she moved over to the train window as she sped toward the home of that day's bride. A man with a nylon briefcase dangling from his shoulder suddenly came over to her.

"Do you do bridal makeup, miss?" he asked.

As far as love was concerned, May Mei felt she had nothing to complain about except that she'd never had the pleasure of being kissed. Among her three boyfriends, who had been quite nice to her, Ah Hon had been particularly considerate. They'd reached the stage where they were affectionate enough to hug each other, but he wouldn't kiss her on the lips. She still thought that had nothing to do with them splitting up.

The man she encountered on the train was called Ah Chi. Later on, when May Mei had handled the makeup for Ah Chi's bride, he invited her out after the wedding, saying he wanted to present her with some of the wedding photographs. They also had a meal together, chatting freely with each other. When Ah Chi drove her back, he forced a kiss on her. That night, May Mei's lip burst open so that it bled all over her pillow. Three days later, when Ah Chi went to May Mei's beauty company, he noticed a gauze bandage on her lip, without understanding what had happened.

"I don't know why," he offered in apology, "but when I first ran into you on the train that day, I felt an urge to kiss you on the lips." Handing her a plush My Melody doll, he said something about Fukada Kyōko also playing with My Melody toys.

May Mei pulled lightly at the red cap that encased My Melody's ears. Her eyes reddened and she spoke through tightened lips. "You know, even in primary school I often suspected there weren't actually any long ears underneath My Melody's mysterious hood, and in fact she basically wasn't a rabbit."

30

SNOOPY

McDonald's launched a marketing campaign in Hong Kong in
autumn 1998, giving out Snoopy figures in twenty-eight different national costumes, including a Hong Kong Snoopy in
a fisherman's garb. A new Snoopy was released every day. In
October 1998, there were scuffles among the vast numbers of
people who lined up to get the little plastic toys.

Ho Chi was not in fact particularly fond of Snoopy, but ever since
she'd asked the boys first for one Snoopy and then for a follow-
up, it seemed that gradually she'd got to like them, and Snoopy
presents had piled up at home. Demanding more and more, she'd
gone through several boys and turned down even more.

Ho Chi's latest boyfriend, Lok Man, had given her three
three-foot-tall stuffed Snoopy toys. They were lined up on the
couch in the living room, leaving no space for her family. Ho Chi
was thus quite confident in commanding Lok Man to queue at
McDonald's to collect a Snoopy, and it came as a surprise when
he suddenly spoke up.

"I've had enough, young lady. Just leave me alone!"

After falling out with Lok Man, Ho Chi didn't feel anything
in particular, apart from initially being angry. When she got up
the next morning, she gritted her teeth and decided to wait in
line herself. The queue outside McDonald's was very long, so she
stood there all morning before finally collecting her first Snoopy,

together with a Happy Meal. She did actually have a feeling of successful self-reliance and accomplishment. Starting from the next day, she persisted for a total of twenty-eight days in succession, eating twenty-eight hamburgers, drinking twenty-eight Coca-Colas, and acquiring Snoopy figures in the national dress of twenty-eight countries. By the time she was halfway through this ordeal, she'd become dulled, hardly conscious of pain but still refusing to give up. With great difficulty, she persevered to the final day, intending to look up Lok Man with the twenty-eight toys to show him what she'd done. On the way, however, she saw a rubbish bin in the street stuffed with uneaten hamburgers. All of a sudden, she was overcome by a sense of extreme futility and sadness.

In the end she gave Tai Fung a ring to suggest a meeting. Tai Fung had dated Ho Chi in the past but had retreated when she'd begun to see another boy in secret. He'd still often talked to her on the phone afterward, but they hadn't met face-to-face. When Tai Fung invited her for dinner at a small restaurant, she was delighted. Seeing that they were offering freshly made clay-pot mutton, she placed her order. In the October weather, they ate until they were sweating, spitting out a big pile of skin and bones. After the meal, they went for a walk down the street and passed a McDonald's.

"That mutton pot we had a little while ago was really a big con," Tai Fung said. "Pretty damn awful, like eating tough dog meat."

When Ho Chi heard this, she squatted down by the curb and threw up, alarming the passersby, who gave her a wide berth. She went on vomiting for what seemed like an eternity.

After she'd stopped, Tai Fung helped Ho Chi walk to his place. She was utterly exhausted from throwing up and let him lay her down on a couch. Her eyelids just half-open, she could see a jigsaw puzzle hanging on the opposite wall, a picture of Snoopy that had a piece missing in one of his eyes. When she'd been doing that puzzle together with Tai Fung three years earlier, she'd lost her temper because of the missing piece and thrown the whole jigsaw at Tai Fung's head, so that the pieces scattered all over him and the floor. She'd never imagined that he'd complete it again on his own. Her eyes reddened.

"I'm pretty disgusting, aren't I?" she asked.

Tai Fung didn't speak, or if he did, she didn't hear him. Then she curled up on the couch and fell asleep. Tai Fung, not sure what might actually be the matter, sat by her side throughout the night, watching over her. When he saw her face regain color, he felt relieved and happy, but it wasn't until dawn that he went to his bedroom for a brief sleep.

When he woke up, Ho Chi was not to be found in the living room, but he heard sounds from the kitchen. Opening the door, he saw Ho Chi wearing an apron and cooking something. He laughed at her.

"Is the princess learning how to make breakfast?"

She turned to him with a gentle wifely smile, revealing what was boiling in a pot.

"Absolutely! I'm making clay-pot dog meat."

The steaming pot was full of plastic Snoopies rattling against one another.

31
—
PANATELLAS

The Hong Kong School Drama Festival encourages primary
and secondary schools to develop drama as a regular cocur-
ricular activity. Events are organized in three phases: training, school performance, and public performance.

Everyone called her Panatella after the long, thin cigars, or Tella
for short. At the age of fourteen, when her friends were learning
to smoke Marlboros, Tella had already begun to smoke cigars.
Big cigars could easily come to two to three hundred dollars
apiece, and she couldn't afford them, but at least she could
smoke panatellas, which were also rather slender and suitable
for girls. She hadn't expected that cigars would become trendy
four or five years later among the younger generation, and people who had got to know her only recently assumed she was
just fitting in.

Tella was in the school's drama society in fourth form, and
by sixth form she was frequently present at performances. At
any post-performance discussion, she was sure to offer opinions
that made good sense, so, little by little, people in the field came
to recognize her, but nobody knew what kind of acting she might
have done herself or what kind of work she might have done
backstage. They just remembered Tella's posture when they
were sitting in a circle rating everyone and debating among
themselves. Posing with her thin cigar between her middle and

ring fingers and her elegant long matches made her look too grown-up but at the same time charming.

Some people regarded Tella as weird. While she had an innocent, beautiful face and a slightly plump figure that made her look devastatingly young, she also made a show of having much experience and being well-connected, although she had never done any proper work. When asked, she said no one had asked her to perform, but that she was in negotiations, or busy with coursework at university at the moment, or even contemplating writing art criticism.

There were lots of other rumors about Tella. Some people said you just had to offer her cigars and she'd go to bed with you, smoking and having sex, spending as much time on one as on the other. A senior member of a big drama troupe revealed to his friends in private that on one occasion, when he had been chatting with some of the younger people in the theater world, he had asked Tella after the meeting broke up if she wanted to try his cigars at home. The outcome was that she chose a nine-inch-long Presidente, and they engaged in amorous battle for a full two hours. Another man, a young director, declared that he'd also hooked up with Tella. He'd invited her to smoke a Churchill cigar, and they shared an hour of passion. Then there was an up-and-coming actor who was highly esteemed as having great potential. After a fair bit of drink, he claimed to have taken Tella home and given her a Corona. Alternately clamping her teeth on it and crying out for all of forty-five minutes, she ended up with tobacco ash all over her body as well as the floor. Finally, there was a student working on set construction who bragged to his mates that he had got fifteen minutes of joy behind the scenes with Tella in exchange for a tiny little cheap cigar.

In her fifth year of primary school, Tella had moved to Canada, but by the time she was fourteen, her parents divorced and she moved back on her own. She brought nothing with her except a box of Cohiba cigars that her father had left behind. From then on, she lived alone in her mother's old property, continuing her school studies without any money problems. When she was in sixth form and her school took part in the Drama Festival, she played the role of Lolita in a revised dramatization of Nabokov's work. When she brazenly smoked a big cigar on stage, the teachers stopped the performance halfway through, and she was lucky to escape with a warning and no demerit on her record.

Once, after a one-person show, a bunch of people went out for karaoke and good-natured gossip. The only one not taking part in the conversation was Tella, who was smoking one of her panatellas. After the up-and-coming actor had finished two beers (which was more than was good for him and made his eyes turn red), he suddenly stretched out his hand and snatched the half-smoked cigar in Tella's hand. "You stupid girl, aping others, smoking crap!" he yelled.

Tella in turn grabbed his glass and threw it on the floor, so that glass splinters and splashes of beer flew in all directions. Everyone was dumbstruck. Tella pulled out another cigar, cut it, and struck one of her long matches to light it. She pulled ferociously on her panatella, the black pupils of her eyes shooting sparks.

32

SECONDHAND CLOTHES

Since she was little, Chiu Yi Lan had usually taken over her elder sister's old clothes. Apart from the fact that the family was poor, this was also due to her mother's partiality. Soon after Chiu Yi Lan's birth, her father had abandoned his family for a new lover. Consequently, her mother looked on Chiu Yi Lan as a burden; she also claimed she brought bad luck and became more disagreeable the more you looked at her. Chiu Yi Lan was not very lively by nature but appeared bitter and miserable, and people took against her at first sight. Her sister was the opposite: clever, cute, and sensitive to other people's thoughts and feelings. It was no wonder their mother favored her.

Until she turned fifteen, Chiu Yi Lan had never worn new clothes. Whether they were school uniforms, everyday clothes, or even pajamas and underwear, all were hand-me-downs that her sister had worn. That was how it had always been, and Chiu Yi Lan found nothing the matter with it but saw it as the way things should be. Also, her sister was only two years older, and when Chiu Yi Lan was fourteen, her sister had started to work in her spare time, earning some cash. She only wore her new clothes once or twice before passing them on to Chiu Yi Lan, mostly long before they were outmoded. As a result, Chiu Yi Lan began to look less wretched.

It wasn't that Chiu Yi Lan hadn't tried buying clothes for herself. In the first year of secondary school, she'd taken a fancy to a denim dungaree dress, so, after secretly selling some of her sister's treasured trading cards of film stars, plus her compensation for doing her classmates' homework, she bought herself new clothes for the first time. The weird thing was that as soon as she put on the new dress, she felt so terribly itchy all over that she couldn't get it off fast enough. After a day or two, she wore it again, but it was still itchy. She tried it on five times, but it was just the same. Suspecting something wrong with the material, she handed it to her sister, who wore it for a day out in town without the slightest problem. From then on, Chiu Yi Lan knew she couldn't wear brand-new clothing: it had been proven beyond doubt.

When Chiu Yi Lan first acquired a taste for choosing her own clothing, it was entirely based on what was offered in a secondhand clothes shop. Originally Chiu Yi Lan had no idea that she was destined to encounter such a thing as popular vintage fashion, and when it first came to her attention, it didn't occur to her that she might try it out. It was only strolling through the shopping center on her own one day that she came across a shop filled with piles of college-look sweatshirts. As usual, she picked up and put down garments, asking about prices, styles, and sizes just as a comforting way to pass the time. She was about to turn around to leave, but the boy in the shop, who was wearing an old T-shirt and jeans with holes in them, kept pestering her. He pursued her from the third to the first level of the mall, holding a hooded red sweatshirt with the words UTAH UNIVERSITY, and eloquently repeated that it would set off her beauty incredibly well. While she found him annoying, Chiu Yi Lan also thought the whole thing funny, and so she bought it. At home she tossed it aside and wouldn't put it on. Going in and out, she pretended not to see it, but after taking a shower, she finally did try it on: it was actually soft as silk. For the first time, Chiu Yi Lan felt the pleasure of fabric rubbing against her skin.

The next day, Chiu Yi Lan went to the vintage clothes shop in the shopping center dressed in her red sweatshirt to look for the boy in the shop. Facing each other, both secretly smiled before saying a word. Chiu Yi Lan not only bought quite a few secondhand garments from the shop, she put on a complete cowgirl outfit. Soon she was also helping out in the shop. The boy's name was Garrett, and he had been crazy about collecting old things since childhood. He and a friend had pooled their resources to start up the enterprise, and now he often made trips to Japan to make purchases in that mecca of vintage fashion. He was joint owner.

Chiu Yi Lan seemed to have changed beyond recognition, being solicitous to customers, chatting with them, and smiling. She had begun to love looking at herself in the mirror and walked purposefully with long strides. When her mother told her off for being besotted and buying rubbish, she answered back for the first time in her life: "It's much better than the rubbish you see fit to hand down to me!" With that, she picked up whatever secondhand clothes she had and walked out. When she gave Garrett a call, he immediately rushed to meet her.

They arrived at Garrett's home, which looked just like a big pile of junk with comics, Japanese magazines, shoeboxes, vinyl records, jeans, and denim shirts piled up to the ceiling. A broken couch was partly covered with the stuff, and even the bed was only half-free of it. Garrett led Chiu Yi Lan into the piles of junk. Climbing and crawling in and out, they played hunting for treasure, snatching old things from their childhood years from the jaws of death, so excited that they screamed with laughter. As they stumbled along, they pulled off their clothes and had clumsy sex. Once they were done, Chiu Yi Lan felt itchy all over, just as she'd felt as a child. When she asked Garrett, he said it was the first time ever for him.

"I've never loved a girl like this," he added.

33

TELETUBBIES

Since childhood, Ah Po had been able to receive broadcast radio waves. All she had to do was close her eyes, and a television program being broadcast at that moment would be reflected on her retinas, just like the picture generated by a cathode-ray tube on a screen. So even though Ah Po rarely watched television, she knew the programs like the palm of her hand. At first her family and classmates wouldn't believe this was happening and suspected Ah Po of secretly reading the advance summaries in the television weekly or of having heard about them, but some time later, when there was a direct sports broadcast, Ah Po could tell the state of play and the outcome of the match without watching it. Ah Po was also able to report instantly to friends and family when there was breaking news of an accident, and so everyone around her was absolutely astounded and began to believe in Ah Po's uncanny ability.

However, Ah Po's extraordinary powers could not be employed completely at will. Often a broadcast would start up without warning, but at other times she was unable to receive anything at all, no matter how hard she tried. Because she was often receiving television broadcasts while she was studying or even sitting exams, Ah Po was unable to concentrate, so her school results were highly variable. At times, when people were chatting with her in a perfectly ordinary way, or when everyone was in high spirits, Ah Po might all of a sudden sink into a confused state, like someone religious experiencing a vision. As a result, little by little, her family and friends' attitude to her remarkable ability turned from curiosity and excitement to intolerance and annoyance. After a while they didn't even treat it as anything special but left her talking to herself in a dream.

Ah Po's only recourse was to make new friends, creating new amazement and fascination, but her ability to tell what she saw was deteriorating, as her words could never keep up with the speed and color of the television images. Her boyfriend, Ka Ming, disliked the way she would get the names of players and teams mixed up when she related direct broadcasts of football matches, while her girl friends disliked the way her descriptions of drama series did not arouse enough emotion. They also rather felt watching television on their own was much better. As a result, even Ah Po herself no longer cared much about receiving programs, but the electromagnetic waves were like a nightmare that couldn't be whisked away—they could attack at any time. As she became more and more incoherent, it was basically impossible for her to have a normal conversation or social life. All she could do was hide in the closed world of television.

Early one morning, Ah Po was lazing around in bed half-asleep when all at once she began receiving a program on an English-language channel. Four babyish Teletubbies were scampering about in a grassy place called Teletubbyland. The biggest one was colored purple and called Tinky Winky, the next one was the green Dipsy, the third one the yellow Laa-Laa, and the smallest one the red Po. The Teletubbies each had an antenna on the tops of their heads and a television screen on their chubby bellies that could show snippets from broadcasts. Ah Po got out of bed thinking she was dreaming. It was only when she looked at the TV program that she realized it was a British children's program, translated into Chinese as the *Antenna Toddlers*.

Afterward, Ah Po found Teletubby dolls for two hundred dollars in a Kalm's gift store, so she bought a Po and went home. When you pressed her belly, she could say things in Cantonese like "Faster, faster!" People told Ah Po that a set of pocket-sized fakes could be bought for just over seventy dollars, and girls started going around with them hanging from their bags. Ka Ming, on the other hand, was entirely hostile to them. Watching an episode, he simply found it idiotic: a bunch of freaks running about, over and over again, impossible to hear what they were saying—so boring that it hurt. He said they ought to call them the "Crossed-Wires Toddlers." He also told Ah Po excitedly that there was a big anti-Teletubbies Internet alliance that accused them of hallucinogenic-drug use, homosexuality, and being an evil force poisoning children. They executed the Teletubbies on the Internet, where they were drawn and quartered.

Ah Po closed her eyes for a long time. "We'd better split up," she said then.

Ka Ming was flabbergasted. "Are you serious or is this some kind of joke? You're splitting up with me because of the Teletubbies? You really are . . . such a . . . such an . . . idiot!"

Ah Po kept on playing extracts from the Teletubbies in her head, listening to them shouting "Again! Again!" in their childish voices when they had finished watching a broadcast and wanted to do it all over again. Feeling so lonely, so lonely, she sobbed silently.

34

HA KAM SHING

Ha Kam Shing 夏金城 is a singer and songwriter who produced
his own music. He adopted the English name Summer Gold
City (a literal translation of his Chinese name) and is associated with the street market on Temple Street in Kowloon. He
released a record in 1980 and three CDs, in 1998, 1999, and
2000, all under his own label. Kaneshiro Takeshi 金城武 is a
Taiwanese Japanese actor and singer. Kaneshiro means "gold
city" and is written with the same characters that are pronounced *kam shing* in Cantonese.

The remarkable Ha Kam Shing was actually an ordinary sort of
bloke. Eighteen years ago, he sold the two taxis he had been running and spent nearly all his money producing a record with his
own songs. Tuneless, with crude lyrics, they appealed directly
to the hearts of the urban working class, becoming for a while a
popular talking point. Ha Kam Shing staged a comeback eighteen years later. He had more to say, satirizing the shortcom-
ings of the day, and so he recorded a new CD, spending more
than he had and not even able to afford the jewel cases. It was
the same year that Siu Ling turned eighteen.

Siu Ling didn't remember Ha Kam Shing. She also didn't
know how she had got her own name, although she had a
clear memory of her mother calling her Pretty Girl. However, her mother had died when Siu Ling was two years old,

so after a while Siu Ling couldn't be sure. At home it was as if she hadn't got a name. Her father and brothers just yelled "stupid girl." Later on, her schoolmates also somehow began to call her Pretty Girl. Because of all this, Siu Ling came to be more and more confused about what she could recall of her mother.

Her father said her mother had been mentally ill and had killed herself jumping off their building. Since childhood, Siu Ling suffered from a fear of heights and often had nightmares about falling from high places. Her father was not at home most of the time, and when he did return, he would beat her two brothers. In the middle of the night, he crept into Siu Ling's bed, saying he felt so lonely without Mummy and telling Siu Ling to comfort Daddy in Mummy's stead. Then he pulled off her pajamas. Sometimes, when Siu Ling would not comply, he threatened to throw her out of the window so that she would fall down on the street and be with her mother.

Siu Ling left home when she was thirteen, stayed with boyfriends and had relationships with a lot of boys but didn't trust them and wasn't serious about any of them. Helping people sell pirated copies of CDs in the streets, she might earn a pittance so she could buy herself something to wear. If she didn't have enough for a famous brand, she would get a knockoff, vowing that she would look pretty even if it was fake. Counterfeit discs then invaded the shopping centers, where they were sold openly; Siu Ling was also quite pleased with this, and now at least she didn't have to run away from the cops. Later on, there was a big clampdown on shops selling pirated VCDs, so Siu Ling switched to a job as a shop assistant, selling genuine goods; it counted as being reformed.

One day a boy wearing sunglasses that looked like yellow diver's goggles asked Siu Ling if they had Ha Kam Shing. Not understanding, she said roughly, "Eh? Ha Kam Shing? We've got Kaneshiro Takeshi!"

"You don't even know about such a cult figure as Ha Kam Shing!" the boy said indignantly. "How can you be in this business?"

Siu Ling was not about to show any weakness. "Is this some kind of a trick? It's your idea of a pickup? Why don't you get lost!"

The boss had noticed what was going on and quickly stepped in. "Yes, yes, yes, we have both his old and new recordings." Afterward, Siu Ling got a reprimand.

After work, Siu Ling came across the goggles boy on the MTR and, deliberately squeezing her way to his side, asked where he was going. The boy was actually a bit scared of her and said something vague. When they arrived at his station, he slunk out, but Siu Ling was hot on his heels and said that he must have taken a fancy to her. As she carried on pursuing him, he cursed her rather ineffectively and hurried rather ineffectively. Not wanting her to follow him home, he walked around in circles, but Siu Ling was having fun and wasn't getting tired. Eventually the boy conceded defeat and invited Siu Ling to have an ice cream as a peace offering.

As they sat on a railing eating ice cream, Siu Ling snatched the boy's earphones and started up his Discman. It was playing a man who was singing so off-key that she burst out laughing.

"That's Ha Kam Shing's songs from eighteen years ago," the boy said. "The first one's called 'For the Sake of Pretty Girl.'"

"What?" Suddenly a strange feeling came over her.

On the disc was also a track called "Ma Siu Ling": "Where are you, Ma Siu Ling? I hope you escape, Ma Siu Ling . . ." To Siu Ling it was as if she had heard that voice, in that far distant place. Then came the song "Before and After Marriage": "Before we were married, he was so good to me, going out for meals he was never late . . . After we were married, he said I had no brains, washing and cooking was what he wanted me to do. His temper is filthy, abusing me and yet demanding that I work . . . With bitterness in my heart, I have nowhere to seek help . . ."

Darkness fell before Siu Ling's eyes. All she could see was one scene: the cheap rented room, looking down from the window on the fifteenth floor, and the body falling down.

Siu Ling suddenly fell off the railing, insensible to the world. Half-startled and half-doubtful, the boy said, "Hey, don't play games!"

35

NOKIA 8810

The Motorola PCN600 was popular in the early 1990s, before being superseded by the smaller Motorola StarTAC. The Nokia 8810 was released in 1998. It is a slider-style mobile phone, the first with an internal antenna, and it was regarded as a luxury item at the time.

The reason Lo Ting Fong came to be known as Motolo, and later on as Mololo, was probably because of her habit of always carrying her Motorola PCN600 mobile phone with her.

It was Mololo's habit never to disclose her actual location to anyone she talked to on the phone. At times she claimed to be out running in the park even though it was clear she was lazing in bed at home; that she was having a meal with friends in Tsuen Wan when she'd gone to Sheung Wan to see her doctor; or that she was swimming in the pool when she was at work. No one ever had any way of knowing where Mololo was heading, and there was never a trace of her in the places where people thought they would find her, but she might suddenly appear at the most unexpected moment. Those who could adjust to this became her friends, eventually seeing nothing weird about it.

Nevertheless, her friends had no idea whether Mololo's habit had originated with the popularity of mobile phones and were completely ignorant about Mololo as she'd been previously. Mololo was doing promotional work for a mobile-network service provider; she'd changed companies twice but not her line of work. Usually it was a matter of going from place to place to push for sales, part of a team touring the big shopping centers of Hong Kong, Kowloon, and the New Territories, almost as if they were hawking mobiles along the streets: the cheapest, fastest delivery, no monthly charge, no connection charge, free handset, free bonus points, now doing a great special-discount promotion, and so on and so forth.

Once, when Mololo was doing a promotion in New Town Plaza in Shatin, a man wearing a black leather coat came up to her and picked out one of her Motorola StarTACs. When he asked for her name, she pointed at his new mobile, saying "Motorola." Turning toward him, she picked up a receipt, wrote a mobile phone number on the back, and handed it to him. Before she'd finished work the following day, her mobile rang.

"It's Ben," the caller said. "I'd like to ask Motorola out for dinner."

Ben quickly learnt about Mololo's phone habit. She'd already lost a couple of boyfriends because of it, but it didn't bother her and she didn't change. Ben knew about that too. He was working on computer page layouts for a graphic design company, and at times, when he was bored, he would call Mololo to play a game of tracking her on the phone. He never got fed up with guessing, and she always enjoyed giving him hints, although in the end he never figured out what was true and what was false. Once when he gave Mololo a call while he was working at night, she told him she was taking a bath, provoking lecherous thoughts in him, but when he emerged from his office, she was waiting for him by the roadside, giving him such a fright that he jumped.

In great excitement one evening that summer, Ben showed Mololo a just-released Nokia 8810. It was the smallest-size GSM-standard mobile phone in the world, with shiny metallic plating and an internal antenna. The price was 7,380 dollars for official

NOKIA 8810

imports, while the asking price for parallel imports was between 10,000 and 20,000 dollars, and there were only 300 of them in the entire city. Mololo found it strange that he hadn't asked her.

"I got it through a friend," he said.

As she played with Ben's new treasure, she saw there were two sets of fingerprints, thick ones and slender ones, on the device's surface. It was so shiny that images could be seen on it as in a mirror. Ben said that once new stock arrived, he would give one to her, since girls could use it as a mirror to apply makeup. She shook her head, and, wiping the phone clean with the hem of her skirt, looked at her own reflection. Then she imprinted her own fingertips and lips before handing it back. After they'd eaten, Ben said he'd go home to do some urgent designs that were due the next day.

Mololo didn't go home but wandered aimlessly in the streets. She called Ben's home number and the phone rang for a long time with no answer. She called his mobile and left a message, then called again, altogether five times before Ben finally replied. She asked where he was.

"At home, don't you know," he said.

"No one was answering your home number."

"I'd switched calls to my mobile, of course."

"There was no answer on your mobile either."

"I was in the toilet."

"Can't you take calls there on your mobile?"

"How would I know it was you calling—and I hadn't got it with me."

"Where are you really?"

"Don't pick a fight over nothing."

Mololo hung up. Ben then called her back a dozen times but got no answer.

In the middle of the night, just as Ben had opened his door back at home, his mobile rang. It was Mololo, so he asked where she was.

"Here," she said.

Hurriedly turning on the light, Ben noticed a lip mark below his ear on his own reflection on the Nokia. He wiped the surface a couple of times and looked at the reflection again, but it was still there. Taking a closer look, he discovered the mark was actually on his own face, two blazing red smudges, strangely moist and itchy.

36
—

CΛMOUTLΛGΣ

Having parted with Ka Fai after two years of dating, Siu Chit was feeling at a loss the whole day. Wandering aimlessly in the streets, she came across a shop window showing her reflection wearing a white gauze dress, and she felt tired of being someone who'd always been fond of wearing white. As she entered the shop, she resolutely made up her mind to buy a camouflage outfit. Standing in front of the mirror, she didn't recognize herself.

Ka Fai liked to wear red, which made him seem rather flamboyant among the other boys, but fortunately he was big and tall, and there was nothing effeminate about him. In the beginning, he had often come to eat at the fast-food place where Siu Chit was working. Every day she looked forward to the red color appearing, as if waiting for the sun to rise. After a while, Ka Fai began to joke and chat with Siu Chit and her friend and colleague Fong Fong, and when Fong Fong switched to another job, Ka Fai invited Siu Chit out and they began dating. Only later did Siu Chit realize that Ka Fai had just used her to get close to Fong Fong, but by then it was already too late.

People said Siu Chit changed when she started to wear camouflage clothes, no longer the open, innocent girl she'd been in the past. At work, wearing the shop uniform, she didn't actually seem much different, but after work, taking the offensive in her camouflage combat gear, she overcame many male bastions. The young men who kept company with Siu Chit changed as quickly as patterns in a kaleidoscope. All who encountered her were dazzled, unable to tear their eyes away from the skimpy camouflage tank top hugging her body, set off by the loose denim pants around her hips and the purse dangling on her buttocks in a way that strikingly exaggerated their curve. From the way that she clung to the arms of the men at her side, it seemed they were able to imagine her supple body weight.

Fong Fong had been Siu Chit's only close friend, but after they broke up, no one presumed to say they understood Siu Chit, although everyone spoke with conviction of her recent situation. Some said they had seen Siu Chit having a meal in a hotel with Mr. Blue, who'd been wearing a golden-yellow tie set off by a sapphire-blue shirt and looked like a real estate manager who earned his living by being a smooth talker. Others said they had seen Siu Chit strolling with Mr. Brown in a Causeway Bay shopping mall. Looking honest and reliable from the way he combed his short hair, Mr. Brown wore a brown polo shirt and had been following after Siu Chit, carrying big and small parcels. Still others said they had seen Siu Chit embracing and kissing Mr. Orange at a dancehall or had seen her snuggling up to Mr. Green on a ferry to the Outlying Islands. However, regardless of whether it was Mr. Blue, Brown, Orange, or Green—or Mr. Yellow, Violet, Purple, White, or Black—none had been able to get any benefit from Siu Chit's body: they were just scattered pieces in a kaleidoscope.

That's how it was until Siu Chit encountered Mr. Gray. Superficially, he didn't look as if he stood out in any way, apart from the fact that he always wore dark gray. Every day Mr. Gray went to Siu Chit's fast-food place, sat down quietly in a corner, and concentrated on eating with his face turned down. Siu Chit had begun to feel fed up with all those males who had been pursuing her, and, getting off work early one day, she walked over to Mr. Gray to find out what might be his good points. Giving short answers to short questions, Mr. Gray was anything but forth-coming, but he aroused a wild ambition in Siu Chit. To start with, Mr. Gray seemingly couldn't stand being bothered, but later on he clearly made an effort to be together with Siu Chit and went along with her every wish—even though there were no signs of him doing it with enthusiasm, and he hardly ever looked directly at her. This only had the effect of making Siu Chit exasperated and impatient, so she concentrated her firepower in a ferocious attack. Mr. Gray was powerless to resist.

One evening in an empty train carriage, he said to Siu Chit, "I was abandoned by the girlfriend I had been dating for five years. I don't believe in love anymore." Hearing that, Siu Chit's tears flowed freely as she leaned on Mr. Gray, her face on his shoulder. After the train had arrived at the final station, Siu Chit went up to Mr. Gray's home, where she spent the night.

Afterward, Mr. Gray disappeared without a trace. Siu Chit had been in a confused state that evening and couldn't recall with certainty where he lived. She only remembered what Mr. Gray had once said: "Aren't you particularly conspicuous wearing camouflage in the concrete jungle? Shouldn't camou-flage in a big city be gray!"

37

LE COUPLE

Le Couple was a husband-and-wife Japanese duo. "Song of the Sunny Spot" was on their fifth single, issued in 1997. The Rise Shopping Mall has many fashion designers' shops and is not far from Hong Kong Polytechnic University, which has a well-regarded design school; Vivienne Tam is one of its graduates.

After Ah Kong had left, Pam began to make jumpsuits for a man and a woman, which didn't only have matching styles but constituted single garments to be worn by two people. They were cut from the same piece of cloth, not needing needle and thread, buttons, straps, or anything else to connect the parts, sleeve joined to sleeve, trouser leg to trouser leg. Two people had to wear it at the same time, getting up together and sitting down together, inseparable.

Pam's greatest ambition was to study fashion design, and her idol was Vivienne Tam, but she had sat the entrance exam for a design course a few times without success. Then she'd borrowed money from her sister to set up her own shop in the Rise Shopping Mall. While mainly selling Japanese goods, she had a special sales counter for her own designs, which were exclusively menswear. Aware of her limits, Pam practiced her basic skills day after day, cutting and stitching, as well as leafing through fashion magazines until the pages fell out. When occasionally a customer took a liking to her creations and bought one or two shirts, Pam would be overjoyed and invite her colleagues in the mall out for a big meal, spending all her money without bothering about the cost.

The first time Ah Kong turned up, he looked down at heel. Picking and choosing, he rummaged through the pile of Pam's handmade garments, spending a long time trying them on. He took a fancy to an Elvis Presley–style sapphire-blue outfit with pearls and sequins, saying it would be his battle dress for the band's gig that evening.

Suddenly he shook his head and sighed deeply. "It's a shame it's too expensive. I'm so broke I've worn holes in my trousers, so forget about it."

He was about to leave when Pam's heart softened.

"I could lend it to you, but then you'll have to work as a model for me."

Ah Kong grinned and made a gesture signaling OK.

In this way, Ah Kong became Pam's moving advertisement, attracting attention as he patrolled the shopping mall dressed in her men's fashions. He didn't receive any wages for selling her merchandise, the agreement being that he was allowed to wear the clothes. Whenever Pam came up with a new invention, the experiments took shape on Ah Kong's body. He didn't demur but was happy to take on even the weirdest shapes and appearances. With his sharp eyes, tousled hair, and free and easy manner, anything looked convincing on him. Gradually Pam and Ah Kong gained a certain reputation: her new clothes made it to a weekly magazine. Some people went crazy about them, while others pooh-poohed them, regarding their success as no more than a fluke.

Pam and Ah Kong became an ideal couple, wearing matching clothing and setting each other off splendidly. Ah Kong moved into Pam's home, his only personal belonging being a drum kit. He'd play his drums until he was tired, then fall fast asleep on the couch, his face flushed like a small child's. One evening, peeling an orange, Pam sat by his side, eating and enjoying the softened expression on Ah Kong's face as he slept. She was listening on her record player to Le Couple's "Song of the Sunny Spot," one of her favorites. Ah Kong suddenly woke up, saying he couldn't stand it, he couldn't stand that kind of sweet, soft voice, he was so terrified, absolutely terrified of that warm tone. Pam cradled his head, but Ah Kong shivered and mumbled to himself.

There was nothing unforeseen about Ah Kong leaving, and Pam had more or less been waiting for that day. Others, however, felt it was incredible: in their opinion there was no other couple in the world better matched. Ah Kong didn't even take his old drums with him but disappeared with no word of goodbye. Subsequently, Pam began to wear the jumpsuits herself, naming them Couple Wear, and the shop gradually came to offer nothing else for sale. The weekly magazine wrote about it once, claiming it was the most "in" kind of clothing for lovers. However, it soon became clear this was far from the case, with few people showing any interest in her goods and not a single garment being sold. Her friends tried to persuade Pam to make some ordinary clothes, but she paid no attention. Some customers asked for her jumpsuits to be cut in two, but she refused. As a result, her shop's business suffered a disastrous downturn, and, owing three months' rent, she was faced with bankruptcy.

The last day before closing down her business, Pam was tidying up in her shop and about to throw out her entire stock of Couple Wear (there were several dozen left), when a man and a woman with nose rings peeked inside and entered the shop, asking if it was all right to take a look. After taking a long time to make their choice, they bought a jet-black jumpsuit that hung together at the shoulders and put it on before leaving in high spirits. Pam followed them with her gaze as they walked away and their silhouettes merged into one. She narrowed her eyes as if dazzled by the sunlight.

"Thank you," she said in a low voice.

Pam had made up her mind. Next year she would sit the exam for the design school again.

38

BUCKET HATS

Urusei Yatsura is a Japanese manga featuring alien invaders but also a farcical love story. The Japanese horned beetle (*Allomyrina dichotoma*) is also known as the Japanese rhinoceros beetle.

The Yau Yau that other people got to know at the bar always wore a bucket hat, but her hat was never the same from day to day. She wore each hat once only and never again, not taking it off even for a moment.

Yau Yau's bucket hats had the happy effect of dazzling others into believing her hats were of every possible color and every possible material: cotton, hemp, velvet, silk, knitwear, wool, nylon, synthetic materials, plastic—everything there was. People said getting hold of so many bucket hats must keep Yau Yau constantly on the run; however, her obsession had quickly become known all over town, so a considerable number were gifts from others. Her coworkers and regular customers at the bar called Yau Yau the queen, or the star, of bucket hats. However, her rapid change of hats meant there was actually nobody who was definitely sure whether the bucket hats were truly never worn more than once.

Yau Yau was wearing a bucket hat on the day she applied for her job. Seeing that she appeared bright and quick-witted, the boss had employed her, and she started work right away. When he told her to take off her hat, Yau Yau said she'd cut her hair recently and done it badly: it looked so terrible that she couldn't face people without the hat. The boss accepted that, little expecting that from then on there would always be a hat on her head. However, the name of the bar itself was "Slow Boat," named after Haruki Murakami's story "A Slow Boat to China," so it could be said there was a connection, since a bucket hat is known as a "fisherman's hat" in Cantonese. Without meaning to, Yau Yau became a living signboard.

The bar was in a university neighborhood, and most patrons were students or teachers. There were no troublemakers among them, but that didn't mean that the customers showed little interest in the girl. Yau Yau became the focus of their attention: many of them said they had come to admire her bucket hats, although their actual purpose was to look at Yau Yau herself. Quite a few of the younger male students also arrived wearing bucket hats of their own, but it just looked as if they were being copycats or else had an ulterior motive. Absolutely no one else achieved Yau Yau's fusion of the individual and the hat.

Yau Yau had nothing at all against going out with those who pursued her, but her treatment of the men was exactly the same as her treatment of the bucket hats: she only went out with each one once and never again. Furthermore, she was utterly impartial, treating teachers and students the same, with no discrimination, so that no one had an advantage. As a result many of the men thought Yau Yau was a woman of easy virtue. Jealous and resentful, they left in anger, although new customers constantly replaced the old ones at the bar. Others understood what was going on and would rather observe it at a distance, content to gossip and joke. It could still be thought of as one of life's pleasures.

Yau Yau offered a great many explanations for always wearing her bucket hats. One was that her hair had been badly dyed, another that it had been burnt when her father maltreated her, yet another that her natural head shape was freakish and could not be shown in public. She also claimed that she'd had extremely dangerous brain surgery, which had left a great scar; that she had not a single hair actually growing on her head, and so the hair showing under the hat was false; that she was a devil woman with the number 666 on top of her head; that she was an alien Teletubby with an antenna on top of her head; that she was an Urusei Yatsura girl with horns on her head; that she was a unicorn spirit; and so forth.

Later on, when Yau Yau was suddenly no longer around, many opinions were offered, including the following: a postgraduate student of entomology had asked Yau Yau out once, but she refused whenever he tried again. As unrequited love turned into mania, he hid in a dark spot in the early morning hours one day, waiting for Yau Yau to get off work. According to the postgrad's own account, he had dashed out to seize Yau Yau in his arms, and in the disarray her red bucket hat was pulled off. Yau Yau disappeared, and all that could be seen was a red Japanese horned beetle flying out of the hat.

39

IMAC

With Love is a Japanese television serial from 1998. Hasegawa Takashi is a music composer who is going through bad times and doesn't believe in love. Murakami Amane is a bank employee who is always being criticized by her boss. They barely know each other, even though they work in the same building. One day, Takashi accidentally emails his works to Amane. Eventually they get acquainted through the Internet, without revealing their true identities.

That weekend Mei-ling happened to be passing through the mall when she bought an iMac on a sudden impulse.

Mei-ling had arranged to meet Ka-kei, her good friend of many years, in the coffee shop on the third floor for a chat. Arriving fifteen minutes early, she was wandering around when she paused in front of a mobile promotion stall featuring an Apple computer, its body a transparent icy blue.

"The iMac is 40 percent faster than the Intel Pentium II," the salesman called out. "It's so fast to get online and dead easy to use, even the little kids know how. Have you gone online yet, miss?" Mei-ling shook her head and was about to walk away, but the salesman persisted.

"Do you know, miss, how to send email and check websites? Have you watched the show *With Love*? About a bank employee, Murakami Amane, emailing Hasegawa, a composer!"

No one would have believed it, but within fifteen minutes, Mei-ling (who was completely ignorant about famous-brand appliances) had decided to buy a computer and straight away signed up to go online. Later, gazing at the fruit-gummy–colored iMac in her bedroom, even Mei-ling found it hard to believe. Even more unimaginable, after she'd completed a simple installation procedure including the power cable, keyboard, mouse, and modem, she finally opened her email reader to find two new messages waiting for her. One was a welcome message from the telecommunications firm; the other was from the address evol-htiw@apple.com. The sender's name was "i" and it read simply, in English, "we meet at last."

Mei-ling thought it must be from the boy promoting Apple computers at the mall. At the time he'd been wearing a vibrant red-and-white T-shirt and black jeans; his face was narrow, his hair short, and his voice soft but strong. His smile was neither too silly nor too knowing. When he asked her for her login ID to go online, she'd thought it over and then wrote "htiwevol" on the form. The boy took the paper, tilted his face, and smiled. Next he asked her what kind of work she did. She answered that she was a bank teller.

"No, really? What a coincidence!" he exclaimed, half in disbelief. When it was all completed and he'd handed over the receipt, he pointed at the name badge on his chest.

"My name's Ivan, get in touch with me if you've got any questions, Miss Murakami Amane." Mei-ling stood there blankly, not understanding.

Afterward, Mei-ling continued to receive email from "i," all written in English in the form of greetings such as "hello," "welcome," "it's a pleasure," "enjoy yourself," "make yourself at home," "home again," "nice to see you," "nice to talk," "do you like it," lacking more substantial content. Mei-ling was at first startled and pleased, but she gradually came to find it irritating; it felt like an intrusion. She put the messages in the Trash without answering them. She was even thinking of making a complaint against the salesman. Mei-ling's passion for going online was only momentary, however, and before long she stopped bothering. The iMac sank to the status of an ornament. She spent every evening at home watching television dramas and gossiping with friends on the phone.

One weekend, Mei-ling made another date to meet Ka-kei at the coffee shop. Going through the main hall, she saw the mobile promotion stall was no longer there: there was just an empty space. It had all happened only two months ago. Mei-ling suddenly felt a loss, for no apparent reason.

She asked Ka-kei if she could borrow her VCDs with the Japanese TV serial *With Love* and went home and watched twelve episodes at a sitting, becoming ever more excited. She quickly went online, but there was no new mail. When she tried to retrieve her old messages, by a stroke of luck they hadn't all been deleted. She immediately sent a long and very forthright message to i's address, asking if he was Ivan and could they meet. A return message came straight away. Mei-ling stared at the iMac, icy cold and yet soft and gentle. On the screen was the line "it's i and i am here."

40

ROLEX DAYTONA

The Rolex Daytona was associated with race-car drivers. It was produced in limited quantities and very expensive. *Just a Little More Time, Oh Lord* is a Japanese television drama series from 1998 dealing with HIV infection, starring Kaneshiro Takeshi. Sorimachi Takashi is a Japanese actor, singer, and fashion model. Puffy is a Japanese pop group consisting of two young women, who often appear in similar outfits. During the Asian financial crisis of 1997, the Hang Seng Index took a heavy fall in October. The Hong Kong economy continued to be in a bad state until the following year, when the Hong Kong Monetary Authority raised interest rates and the government bought large amounts of shares on the stock market.

Ip Tze Chan never noticed the passage of time, even though she possessed twenty-eight watches. As far as she was concerned, the function of a wristwatch was no different from that of earrings and necklaces. However, it was only after she'd turned seventeen that it occurred to her that she'd never owned a genuinely precious watch. Those twenty-eight watches were at best just playthings.

Ever since watching *Just a Little More Time, Oh Lord* on television, Ip Tze Chan and her good friend Ah Kiu had dreamt day and night of saving enough money to buy a Rolex Daytona chronograph such as the one worn by Kaneshiro Takeshi in the television show. Unfortunately, it was too expensive at tens of thousands of dollars, and since Japanese-style "compensated dating" was still unknown locally, making fast money was just too unbearable. The only way out was to get a substitute in the form of a Seiko chronograph for no more than a few hundred dollars. However, a different watch was a different watch; it was as if even the time it showed was not the same. Occasionally Ip Tze Chan hoped subconsciously that heaven would bestow a different time on her, so when she encountered Kai Chi, it nearly made her believe in God for real.

Ip Tze Chan got to know Kai Chi at a rave. Throughout the evening, he'd been sitting to one side smoking and didn't get up for a single dance. Before the party was over, he turned to Ip Tze Chan, who was sitting next to him. "Let's go!" he said. "I'll give you a lift."

Ip Tze Chan looked at him, thought for a moment, and left with him. What she hadn't at all expected was that the boy's car was a BMW. It was already midnight, but Kai Chi said it was still early and why not go for a spin. Before long, the car was speeding along the Tsing Ma Bridge. Pointing at the Daytona on Kai Chi's wrist, Ip Tze Chan shouted in the wind: "Sorimachi Takashi and Puffy wear those."

"Is that so?" he replied.

The second time they met, Kai Chi gave Ip Tze Chan a Daytona as a present and afterward drove his BMW to her school every day to meet her after class. Her classmates and teachers were stunned speechless. When she asked Kai Chi what he was doing, he said he hadn't finished his degree at a Canadian university but had come back to help his father with his business. At first overwhelmed by such pampering, Ip Tze Chan accompanied Kai Chi everywhere, having fun and feeling that life had never been so exhilarating. However, she always found the Daytona very heavy on her wrist and was still not used to it, even after wearing it for a whole month: it was like having an artificial limb. Once when Kai Chi took her for a ride in the BMW to Lantau, he stopped by a hillside and leant forward to kiss her. As he unbuttoned her top, his Daytona watch began to press against the middle of her chest, frigid and hard, just like her heart. After they had made love, Kai Chi asked if there was anything she wanted to buy. Suddenly holding back the tears in her eyes, Ip Tze Chan pushed open the car door and dashed out, breaking into a run and running until at last she reached a bus stop. She traveled back to town on her own.

Once Ip Tze Chan refused to see Kai Chi, her Daytona stopped. Kai Chi tried to get in touch a few times, but as he had no idea what had really happened, nothing came of it. Ip Tze Chan handed in her Daytona to a couple of watch shops, but none was able to repair it. Even so, she kept wearing it day after day, at school and after school, and never put on any of her other twenty-eight watches. When Ah Kiu asked her out, she refused. Ip Tze Chan felt she was someone who had lost time.

Six months had passed before Ip Tze Chan and Kai Chi met again. By chance they had happened to go to the same fast-food restaurant, and, coming face-to-face, they were at first silent.

"Your watch has stopped, but you're still wearing it?" Kai Chi said after a while.

"What about your watch then?" was Ip Tze Chan's counterquestion.

"I sold it."

She hadn't expected that and was alarmed. "You sold it?"

"Sure!" Kai Chi said with a bitter smile. "The stock market crashed. Dad's company closed down, it went bankrupt. In our family we daren't even take a taxi now."

"So what are your plans?" she wanted to know.

"I've been thinking of going back to university," he said, "but I've got no money."

Ip Tze Chan thought it over and then got up, pulling Kai Chi with her and heading straight to the nearest watch shop. When she took off her Daytona and asked what price she could get for it, the proprietor treated it as a great treasure, saying it was tremendously well regarded by everyone and worth a hundred thousand. Ip Tze Chan was about to explain, but then she caught sight of one of the Daytona's hands moving. Holding it to her ear, she could also hear it going ticktock, ticktock.

41

VIVA JAPANESE TV DRAMA

Beach Boys was a Japanese television comedy series. One of
the female characters is named Izumi Makoto 和泉真琴. The
Chinese characters for Makoto are pronounced Chan Kam in
Cantonese. *GTO* stands for *Great Teacher Onizuka* and is the
name of a Japanese manga and its television adaptation.
Kaneshiro Takeshi played the main role in the Japanese television drama *Just a Little More Time, Oh Lord*. Sorimachi
Takashi is an actor and singer who played the role of Onizuka
Eikichi in *GTO*; My Little Lover is a pop band; Kudō Shizuka
is a pop singer; Le Couple was a husband-and-wife Japanese
band; Cagnet is an American pop and R&B group that recorded
theme tunes for Japanese television shows.

After Ngoi Kam had watched the Japanese television series
Beach Boys, she thought of changing her name to Chan Kam,
after the leading female character, but dared not say anything
to her parents about it, so in the end she didn't. The spring season of Japanese soap operas receded and the summer season
arrived in a great wave. Having just begun watching *GTO* when
she graduated from university, Ngoi Kam for a while fancied
becoming a teacher of problem children just like Eikichi Onizuka,
but by the time Kaneshiro Takeshi's *Just a Little More Time, Oh
Lord* began showing, she still hadn't found a job.

Ngoi Kam's boyfriend, Chi Kwong, had graduated the year before her and was doing telecom business promotion. With market demand continuously strong and his company having just started to get on the right track, he was quite busy and rarely able to go out with Ngoi Kam. Seeing her spending time at home unemployed, he would often make subtle comments to the effect that she made no serious efforts to find a job but just watched Japanese soap operas, her head filled with daydreams. Ngoi Kam didn't know what to do other than send off a large number of job applications, ninety of them altogether, but each one sank like a stone in the sea. Postage, envelopes, paper, and photos of herself came to a substantial sum.

One day, after a job interview, she passed a record shop. Deciding to cheer herself up, she went in and asked if they had any Japanese music. The young male shop assistant asked what kind of Japanese music she usually listened to, but Ngoi Kam didn't immediately know what to say. Picking up a CD in front of him, the boy said it was a new order and explained to her it was shakuhachi, the oldest and most traditional Japanese music. He put it on right away, and it was exactly like the harrowing sound of a bamboo flute in a Japanese horror movie, frightening Ngoi Kam.

"What I was looking for . . . ," she said, "something like the theme tunes of Japanese TV shows."

Looking rather disappointed, the boy took her to another part of the shop and picked up a CD case. On the cover were the buttocks of a couple of men wearing traditional Japanese-style thongs.

"This one with the bums has got everything you could want," he said. "It's a hot item. We've been selling loads of them lately."

This set of CDs, *Viva Japanese TV Drama*, simply enraptured Ngoi Kam: Sorimachi Takashi, My Little Lover, Kudō Shizuka, Le Couple, Cagnet—it had everyone and everything! Ngoi Kam listened right through until deep into the night. As disc two reached the end, she was about to switch off her player, but then the eerie sound of a flute was heard, rather like the kind of music the boy in the record shop had played. Hearing it late at night made her hair stand on end. She leafed through all the information inside the CD case but found nothing about any track of this kind.

The next day, Ngoi Kam took the CDs back to the shop. As it happened, the weird thing was being played over the loudspeakers again. As soon as the boy saw her, he became quite exultant. "You've come just at the right time, today I happen to have brought in a shakuhachi!" Right away he picked up an object from behind the counter that looked as if it were cut off from a piece of bamboo. "This is it. I've been learning to play it for two years."

The boy's name was Antiquarius. He had been to a shakuhachi performance for the first time two years earlier and immediately fallen in love with the instrument's delicate lyrical sound, so he had sought out a Japanese master musician, asking to become his disciple. Now he worked in the record shop in the daytime and practiced after work for three hours every day. Ngoi Kam was absolutely amazed and actually bought a shakuhachi CD. She asked Antiquarius if he had watched Japanese TV dramas, but he said he had never watched any.

Afterward, Ngoi Kam often went to the record shop to listen to Antiquarius holding forth on traditional Japanese music and the shakuhachi; she felt he was simply not of this world. When he asked her to go to a concert performed by himself and some Japanese expatriates, Ngoi Kam was pleasantly surprised. The audience was all Japanese, and there appeared to be none of his friends or family—she was his only personal friend present. In that unfamiliar musical environment, she suddenly felt very, very close to Antiquarius, as if his breath passing through his instrument was infusing her own body. She made a decision to tell Antiquarius a secret once the performance was over. However, by the time it had finished, Antiquarius asked Ngoi Kam to leave on her own, since he wanted to spend a little more time with his Japanese companions.

Not long after that, Antiquarius told her he was going to Japan to study the shakuhachi. His words and manner made his excitement and anticipation quite obvious, and so he didn't notice Ngoi Kam's gloomy silence. Just before his departure, she gave him her own *Viva Japanese TV Drama* CDs as a present.

"I hope you won't find this too awful to listen to," she said, "but I haven't got anything better to give you as a keepsake."

"Not at all, not at all!" Antiquarius smirked.

In the end, Ngoi Kam found a job as a kindergarten teacher. At home she often put on shakuhachi music, but it drove her family and Chi Kwong mad. They accused her of being so besotted with Japanese things that she'd taken leave of her senses. Ngoi Kam, however, seemed only to hear the ethereal sound coming from a far distance.

42

POLAROIDS

The Polaroid SX-70 was an advanced instant camera in the
1970s that retained its popularity. The Polaroid Xiao is an
instant pocket camera released in the late 1990s. Nakayama
Miho is a Japanese singer and actress who played dual roles
in the 1995 film *Love Letters*.

The reason people remembered Noi Noi was her Polaroid camera and the instant photos of herself that she had left behind.
Other than that, there was no trace of her.

Noi Noi's Polaroid phase may have started with *Love Letters*
two years earlier, because sharp-eyed people noticed that the
Polaroid Noi Noi was first using was the same style as the SX-70
used by Nakayama Miho in the film. However, more recently,
some were saying that Noi Noi had now switched to the newly
released pocket-sized Polaroid Xiao, a toylike little plastic box
that took pictures the size of a photo sticker; torn off in a strip,
they resembled a bookmark. Somebody even said that on a trip
to Japan they had seen Noi Noi in a Tokyo gift shop buying no
less than four cameras at one go, along with thirty rolls of film.

People who possessed photos that Noi Noi had taken of herself had got to know her at raves.

"Why don't you take me somewhere I've never been before!"
Noi Noi would say in the middle of the night when they stopped
dancing. For most of the boys, that was a rather difficult task,

because no one could think of a good place to go where Noi Noi hadn't already been. As a result, they took her to places like the apron of the old airport, a closed-down railway station, a bus depot, and a broadcast-station recording studio. Others couldn't think of any place, even though they scratched their heads until it hurt, and so Noi Noi would smile, wave goodbye, and leave.

Each time, Noi Noi took a picture of herself at the location, gave it to her companion, and then never saw him again. At times they might encounter a girl at a dance hall who looked like Noi Noi, but she always told them they were wrong. Actually, it also often happened that those boys, as luck would have it, ran into each other and found out their counterparts had also known Noi Noi. They brought out their photos for comparison, recounting their memories of her as well as exchanging rumors, like a little secret clique. However, the Noi Noi in their stories was always a little different, and the Noi Noi in the photos was even more ambiguous and confusing. The only thing that was constant was that all of them bragged in detail about making love to Noi Noi.

Rumor had it that the last boy to have been with Noi Noi was a student in the Design Department called Kit Sze. That evening, Noi Noi wore a blue scarf around her head and a short dress with an orange floral pattern over thin, wide-legged denim trousers. She put her usual question to Kit Sze, who'd come there by himself to dance.

"Come with me," he said without the slightest hesitation.

They arrived at a disused warehouse of the Government Supplies Department on Oil Street, North Point, where they climbed a low wall and jumped in. Taking Noi Noi by the hand, Kit Sze pulled her across an empty space. To her surprise, she felt a bit nervous, treading unsteadily one step at a time. He softly opened a warehouse door and they sidled inside, feeling their way in the dark up a flight of stairs to the first floor. A big window let in a dim light, so that Noi Noi could faintly distinguish a large, empty warehouse room that was partly in shadow. Kit Sze directed her where to stand and then walked over on his own to the far end, where it looked as if he was swallowed by the darkness. Noi Noi suddenly felt a bit frightened.

"Hey!" she called in a loud voice. "Where are you?"

Then the light came on from the far end. Noi Noi saw in front of her a display of various objects, among them paintings, writing, and other things. Kit Sze came over to her, pointing at one of the objects.

"That one's my work. This is a private showroom."

It was a huge canvas with a portrait of a girl. Looking at it closely, one could see that it was made up of more than a thousand small photos assembled like brickwork. The photos were all of the same girl as in the big picture, just developed in lighter and darker shades.

"Does it look like you?" Kit Sze asked.

"Who is she?" asked Noi Noi.

"Someone I like," Kit Sze answered.

As Noi Noi stared intently at the face hanging on the wall, her eyes became moist. Quietly pulling out her Xiao, she turned to Kit Sze. "Then I'll take one more, all right?" she said. Kit Sze nodded.

Stretching out her arms, Noi Noi pointed the lens at herself, the flash went off, and the photo was taken. After a short while, she tore off the picture and pushed the small piece of paper into Kit Sze's breast pocket.

"My original reason was just that I hoped people would remember me," she said. "There was nothing else I wanted."

43
—

LOVEGETY STATION

The original Lovegety was a small computerized matchmaking tool sold in Japan and Hong Kong in the late 1990s. When two people carrying a male and a female version came near each other, the devices would beep and flash. The Lovegety Station was an advanced version of the photo-sticker booths generating flash cards with varied designs and layouts, often as a cover of a pop magazine, so that the person taking a photo might look like a film star.

The first time Fantasia came to the Lovegety Station to have her picture taken, Realman stuck out his head from his shop selling action figures, his eyes following her white, delicate arms encircled by numerous metal-chain and leather bracelets; there was also a bruise on her left shoulder. The impression was so clear and precise that afterward it actually made Realman doubt whether there had truly been such a moment.

Realman had never tried out the Lovegety Station, although he knew it was a variety of the previously popular photo-sticker booths where you could have a flash-card photo taken in many different modes, for instance appearing as a pop idol on a magazine cover.

Fantasia generally came in the less busy periods, her arms swinging as she swept by like lightning. As she flashed past before Realman's eyes, his heart felt as if shaken by a thunderclap, and for a moment he went numb. Stationing himself against the wall outside his shop entrance, he waited for her to come out. He gazed at her as she stood by the machine, waiting for the pictures to emerge, her handbag slipping down until she pulled it up to her shoulder with her index finger—all of it fascinated him. Fantasia knew he was watching her and when she left she held up the photos in front of his face for a moment. "Seen enough?" she said.

Realman stared blankly for a moment before recovering and followed her to introduce himself: "I'm Realman. Made up the name myself."

"My name's Fantasia," she said glancing at him.

It seemed to Realman that she was intentionally poking fun at him, so he thought he might just as well go along with it. "We're meant for each other," he said.

That counted as Realman having broken the ice with Fantasia, and from then on, they would exchange a few words every time they met. Once he asked why she had so many photo cards done.

"I want to be a film star, of course!"

"When are you going to give me a photo?" he asked again.

"I'm going to break your heart!" she replied.

Some time later, one evening when the mall had almost closed down, Fantasia came rushing in, clickety-clack, clickety-clack, and disappeared into the booth for a long time. Summoning up his courage, Realman walked up and quietly pulled open the curtain to investigate. He discovered Fantasia sitting motionless to one side, with raw patches at the corners of her mouth and eyes. He asked if anyone had been mistreating her.

"It's my little brother," she said. "He likes the cards, so I have them done for him, but he's never satisfied."

Hearing this, Realman felt quite bewildered. He was thinking of giving Fantasia a hand but then dared not touch her. After a little while, Fantasia composed herself and put a coin into the slot as usual to have a photo taken, but she pulled out a better-looking one from her bag. "For you," she said to Realman.

After a couple of days, Fantasia returned to find Realman's shop window plastered with copies of her small photo. She immediately stepped inside and tore off every single one. Realman didn't take offense.

"I'm a fan of yours!" he argued.

"Aren't you being a bit stupid?" Fantasia said.

"You're the one that's stupid!" he retorted. "You play at being a star for some brother of yours! Is he an idiot? Getting his sister to do this sort of thing! Doesn't he know it's painful? And then he hits you!"

For a moment Fantasia had nothing to say. "Please don't slander my brother," she said in a downcast but firm voice. "This is the way we want it."

When Fantasia came to the Lovegety Station for the last time, Realman was very regretful about what had happened the previous time. However, he also felt it was really impossible to reason with Fantasia, and that he had been wronged, so he hid in his shop. After listening to her sobbing for a long time, he suddenly got up and dashed outside. Pulling the curtain aside, he saw Fantasia curled up on the floor. She was wiping her tears with her wrists red and swollen in a way that didn't seem to match the thick metal bracelets on her arms. Her bag was open, and a few dozen cards were scattered on the floor, all of them pictures of herself. Realman squatted down. He had intended to say, "Actually there's no brother, is there!" but what he came out with turned into, "Your brother won't need these ones, will he?" Fantasia nodded and cried. Realman gave her a hug.

Afterward, Realman went to the Lovegety Station on his own and had a photo card taken. He selected a film-star magazine cover as background and ROMANCE in capital letters as a caption before entering the names Realman and Fantasia. When the card came out, it had him in a pose embracing Fantasia. He then understood Fantasia—although it came a little too late.

44

—

PRADA

Suki remembered very clearly spending three thousand dollars on her Prada briefcase. At noon that day, Nelson had been waiting for her downstairs at her office building, and they went to a nearby cafeteria for a sandwich. Amid the crowd of people having lunch, he suggested they separate. Suki remained unexpectedly calm, holding her sandwich in both hands and taking bites out of it as breadcrumbs scattered over the table. After work the same day, Suki went for a stroll in the same shopping mall the cafeteria was in, circling the mall again and again until almost all the shops had closed. Then, for no particular reason, she bought the Prada briefcase.

Since then, Suki had gone alone to the cafeteria for a sandwich every evening after work. Although she'd moved out to live by herself after she'd graduated from university, it was only during this time that Suki became aware of what it meant to be "a single person." It wasn't that she couldn't see friends or go back home, it was just that she had to find ways to allow herself to be a single person and not have to justify herself to others.

The first person to mention the Prada was her old classmate Fanny. That evening, Suki had gone to the cafeteria as usual for her sandwich, lined up and taken her food, but when she reached the counter to pay, she discovered there wasn't enough change in her purse (she'd just bought a ticket to a concert). Embarrassed, she was giving an explanation to the lad at the cash register, but he put a finger to his lips. "You're only short ten dollars," he said softly. "Let me treat you!" He waved his hand for her to move on. Not quite knowing what to do, Suki picked up her tray and looked for somewhere to sit. When she glanced back at him, he looked as if nothing had happened. However, it was then that she bumped into Fanny at the cafeteria.

Fanny, who was still working as a journalist and was wearing T-shirt and jeans, went into raptures when she saw Suki all dressed up in a white suit. Then she saw her Prada. "Is that for real or a knockoff?" she asked.

"It's genuine," Suki replied.

"Of course," Fanny immediately responded, "you always dress so smartly, no way you'd be seen with a fake. How's it going with Nelson? When are you two going to tie the knot?"

Suki and Nelson had started dating during their first year at university. They met every day and every night, hardly ever doubting that in the future they would find jobs, get married, and have children. It didn't occur to them that it would all change within a year after graduation, when they began work at different companies. When she thought about it, Suki didn't see it as a massive tragedy but would give a bitter smile. At one point the lad at the cafeteria noticed she was smiling; when he asked her about it, her face crimsoned. Whenever he made a sandwich for Suki, he was sure to come up with an extra ingredient, like surreptitiously adding some smoked salmon. She would eat it with relish despite feeling rather anxious about him doing this. When she tried to give him back the ten dollars, he refused absolutely, protesting that this opportunity to invite a beautiful girl to a meal had made him very happy. Suki, who wondered if she was at least three or four years older than him, felt embarrassed by this flattery, which even she found a little unseemly.

Suki was asked three more times whether the Prada was genuine or fake. Once was when she happened to run into an office colleague and her boyfriend; another time was with another former classmate. This friend, who was a teacher, was carrying an identical Prada, which she said was a fake. When they compared it with Suki's Prada, they were astonished to discover that neither of them could tell the difference. Finally there was the time when she went home for dinner, and her mother (aside from urging her to look for a boyfriend) asked her where she'd bought the fake Prada. When she said it was genuine, her mother scolded her for being so stupid, sighing that her daughter was not as careful as she was about money matters.

Suki never imagined she and this young man would ever amount to anything, but when she didn't see him in the cafeteria one evening, she became conscious of a sense of loss. Feeling impelled to ask one of the others behind the counter, she learned that he'd got another job. Although she'd been hungry, Suki lost her appetite and left half of her sandwich. As she was walking out of the cafeteria, she saw the young man waiting for her.

"Would you care to join me for something to drink?" he asked.

Suki lowered her head and thought for just a moment. "All right, where should we go?"

The young man was wearing a trendy T-shirt and jeans. Walking alongside Suki, who was wearing a gray suit, he looked like her younger brother. He stretched out his hand to take the briefcase. "Let me carry this." When Suki tactfully declined, he countered, "Don't be afraid of me damaging your famous-brand bag!"

Suki felt this was actually quite funny, and, pretending to be cool and collected, allowed him to press the Prada to his chest. "Take it, it's just a fake. I got it in Shenzhen for under two hundred dollars."

45
—

STARTAC

The StarTAC was a clamshell mobile phone made by Motorola, first released in 1996. The Leonid meteor shower, which looks as if it comes from the constellation Leo, peaks in November every year; Leonid intensity increased in 1998 and 1999.

The girl who often came into the shop to get a new case for her mobile phone became known as Stargirl because the phone she kept bringing in was her StarTAC mobile. Stanley Lau, who specialized in fitting phone cases, thus acquired the nickname Starman Lau. Showing no sign of being bothered, he just remarked he couldn't reach the stars but only touch a little stardust. Nevertheless, he couldn't help feeling a bit confused, and, without consciously meaning to, he started to gaze up at the sky at night.

The first time Stargirl appeared, dressed all in black, she put down a black StarTAC on the desk, asking Stanley Lau if he could give it a new case. He asked what kind she wanted: transparent, soft colors, metallic, psychedelic?

"It doesn't matter," she said.

"Let's go for ice blue then!" he said, right away taking the StarTAC apart, and in less than ten minutes he'd replaced the outer case with a transparent blue model. The girl held the mobile in her white palm.

"It won't dissolve, will it?" she said to herself.

After that, Stargirl came almost every week to have her case changed, and Stanley Lau's colleague at the shop, Ah Sum, urged him to take action: "This sort of girl, if she's known you for three-four days, she's sure to dump her boyfriend for you. Grab your chance, don't let it slip!" Stanley Lau just shrugged.

Stargirl had six different transparent cases in a row. One day, when she wore a powder-blue dress of knitted wool, her body seeming so tall and thin that it might dissolve into powder at a touch, Stanley Lau said it might be best to switch to a powdery color. As usual, she had no opinion of her own, and in the end he couldn't help asking her why she didn't just get a new mobile.

"I can't possibly change the phone," she said.

"Well then, why do you go on changing the case over and over again?" he asked.

"Well, it's just the outer shell, isn't it," she said. Stanley Lau was thoroughly bewildered.

After going through powder-blue and camouflage patterns, Stanley Lau gave Stargirl's StarTAC a Hello Kitty case.

"What's your mobile number?" he asked in a way that was both meaningful and casual. She didn't answer, but it seemed the rims of her eyes were getting a bit red, or perhaps they only reflected the strawberry–ice cream color of her top.

The next time Stargirl came in, she was wearing black, just as she had been the first time. Stanley Lau proposed fitting a case with a flashing light. As the procedure was taking some time, he advised her to return later to pick it up, but she refused.

"Are you waiting for someone to call?" he asked. Her eyes flashed like shooting stars, and at that moment Stanley Lau's own phone rang. He didn't answer, however, but just glanced at the screen. Once the girl was gone, Stanley Lau tapped Ah Sum on the shoulder and told him he was leaving early. An ambiguous smile appeared on Ah Sum's face.

Stanley Lau followed Stargirl to Tai Po. It was already getting dark as the girl stood on the stone bridge over the river, still grasping her mobile phone. Hiding behind a banyan tree on the riverbank, Stanley Lau pulled out his own phone and dialed a number. Over on the bridge, the girl's phone flashed a red light. Quickly answering, she said hello in a voice full of longing, which suddenly turned into anger: "Who are you?"

"I'm the man who fixes phones."

"How do you know my number?"

"I used your mobile to call myself and then checked the number that was displayed."

"What do you want with me?"

"Oh, nothing. I was just worried about you. I'm actually not far from where you are." When the girl looked around, Stanley Lau became anxious and searched for something to say. "I believe the Leonid meteor shower is supposed to occur tonight. It's once every thirty-three years."

The girl looked up to the sky, remaining silent for some time; all he could see from a distance was the blinking red light next to her face.

"Who is it then that you've been waiting for?" he asked.

The voice on the mobile sounded as if coming from outer space. "It doesn't matter now. Before, only he knew my number, so as soon as the phone rang, it had to be him. It never occurred to me it would turn out differently, that there wouldn't be any more . . ."

The choking sobs at the other end made Stanley Lau want to try to defend himself, but then he saw Stargirl raise her arm high and pitch it forward. A soft red point flew out, describing a line through the air before vanishing into the inky black river. Stanley Lau immediately ran toward her as fast as he could, but already there was no one left on the bridge. Lifting his head, he saw the sky was oppressively powder pink, with not a single star visible, let alone a shooting star.

46

—

COLORS

Fukada Kyōko is a Japanese actress and singer who played a
leading role in the television drama *Just a Little More Time,
Oh Lord* in 1998. The photo book *Colors* from the same year
featured Fukada at age sixteen posing in her school uniform
and swimsuits. Sakai Noriko and Tomosaka Rie are Japanese
actresses and singers. Tomosaka's photo book *Feel,* where she
poses in skimpy dresses, bikinis, and underwear, was also
published in 1998.

Ever since Longlegs had seen the photo book *Colors,* featuring
Fukada Kyōko, at Peng Mun's home, she couldn't distinguish colors anymore. She went to a number of ophthalmologists, but
they were unable to diagnose the problem. When she looked at
the world around her, it was like a black-and-white film. As it happened, gray was the fashionable color that autumn and winter,
but she couldn't tell whether it was a stroke of good luck or of
irony.

Peng Mun had first been a great fan of Sakai Noriko, in the
way a young boy might be fond of his sister, but then he bought
Tomosaka Rie's erotic photo book *Feel.* At nineteen, she was
closer to him in age. After watching *Just a Little More Time, Oh
Lord,* he suddenly took offense at Tomosaka for being too
immoral and instead became infatuated with Fukada Kyōko's
pure character. Fukada's fame exploded, and at the age of sixteen she used this momentum to issue her first and last photo

book. This set boys like Peng Mun on fire, and they worshipped at her altar. As for Longlegs, it wasn't that she didn't admire Kyōko. They were the same age, but Kyōko had become the idol of vast numbers of people, so Longlegs, a bit envious, felt inferior. Their similarity in age troubled her in particular, as if Kyōko were a classmate who'd grabbed the limelight, making Peng Mun's obsession doubly disagreeable.

Peng Mun was one year ahead of Longlegs, and while they weren't at the same school, both were in Grade B at the inter-school sports meet. On the day they met, she was taking part in track-and-field events, coming first in the one-hundred-meter sprint after doing her utmost. Crossing the finishing line, she tumbled over, and a boy who was warming up beside the track immediately stepped forward to give her a hand. In all the time Longlegs and Peng Mun spent together, that was certainly the most memorable moment. She often felt it had been like a scene in a romantic play, but afterward it seemed to lack a solid foundation, and, thinking about it later, she experienced a sense of loss. After she'd begun dating Peng Mun, Longlegs gave up running, afraid that more such exercise would make her legs too thick. She was also careful to let Peng Mun shine alone in track and field.

The day she came across a copy of *Colors* on Peng Mun's desk, it was startling, even though she'd been mentally prepared for some time. As she furtively leafed through it, she had the upsetting sensation that she was spying, but when she thought of Peng Mun's eyes scanning that spread-eagled youthful body every evening, her mood turned to jealousy and anger. Fukada Kyōko's thighs were not any thinner than hers, and her most impressive skill was only crying tearfully in front of the camera, thought Longlegs. As Peng Mun came back to his study, she threw down the photo book with an air of indifference. "They call it *Colors*, so why are the photos all black and white?"

Since losing the ability to see colors, Longlegs began to feel there was nothing that was right for her about Peng Mun, and his feelings for her seemed to be fading too. Thinking of being shut out from Peng Mun's world of sensuality, she grasped him ever closer, not letting him go; she wanted him to be with her every day; when they went out, she wanted him to take the lead.

At first, Peng Mun actually felt quite worried about her behavior, but over time he began to find it annoying. "You're not even blind, you know, so what's with this pathetic act?"

On this, Longlegs burst into tears. Her face puckered, and she said she never wanted to see him again. Peng Mun did in fact disappear, leaving Longlegs to sit alone every day looking out through the window at the dark-gray skies. When her thoughts turned to her imagined enemy, Fukada Kyōko, she was overcome by resentment.

So Longlegs went back to school, even joining the school sports team again. Even though unable to distinguish color, Longlegs slowly realized there were different shades in the black, white, and gray world too. At times she distinguished between colors on the basis of tones of gray and found she wasn't wrong. At the interschool track-and-field events in spring the following year, Longlegs again won the hundred meters' race. As she crossed the finishing line, she spotted Peng Mun walking toward her and got into such a panic she couldn't stop running. Seeing what was happening, Peng Mun chased after her, and so they ran, one after the other, a whole lap until they dropped exhausted. They sat on the grass to catch their breaths.

"Why did your school change to gray pants?" Peng Mun said, panting heavily.

Looking at herself, knowing well that her school's athletic attire was red, Longlegs couldn't stop herself from laughing so hard that she had tears in her eyes. Getting up, she got started on Peng Mun, slapping him. "When I cry or when Fukada Kyōko cries—who's the prettier one? Tell me!" she demanded.

"It's you of course! It's you of course!" said Peng Mun, dodging her.

47
—

BEATMANIA

Beatmania is a Japanese rhythm video game released in 1997, played mainly in arcades. The game controls consist of five keys resembling the layout on a piano. A turntable to the right of the five keys is turned, or "scratched."

The first time Hip Ho played *Beatmania*, she suddenly realized the reason for her problem with Mainway. It was Mainway who had taken Hip Ho to a video-game arcade. In the big crush of onlookers around a *HipHopMania* game, Mainway was responding to the beat of the music while hitting five black-and-white keys and scratching a turntable looking like a black vinyl record, reaching a score of over 70,000. He told Hip Ho to have a go, but once she stepped up, crash bang, she reached over 100,000. Mainway's expression changed completely. It was a great loss of face, and for the rest of the evening he said nothing. However, this wasn't what was on Hip Ho's mind.

From then on, Hip Ho went to the arcade every evening after work to scratch the turntable; she beat everyone, no rival in sight. While she was playing, her entire body seemed to vibrate to the rhythm, her feet moving fast, slow, fast, slow, over and over again. Back home she lay on her bed, her heartbeat irregular, as if a black man were dancing frenetically inside her chest. Hip Ho then decided she might as well buy a controller and *Beatmania* software for her PlayStation at home. She went from

2nd-Mix to 3rd-Mix, losing herself in striving for perfection and paying no attention to Mainway when he was at home. Feeling it necessary to stand up to her, he played the theme tune from *Titanic* at maximum volume on the hi-fi. With speakers at war with each other, the windows in the flat came close to shattering. All of a sudden reaching the limit of her patience, Hip Ho threw the controller, smashing it into the hi-fi. Céline Dion's long-winded song came to an abrupt stop. When she walked out, Hip Ho didn't take anything with her except for the *Beatmania*. As they parted, she had this to say to Mainway: "Our ways of life are different: yours is a life of melody, mine one of beat. At times they coincide, but it also happens that they are completely incompatible." Her words left him completely bewildered.

After their separation, Hip Ho temporarily moved back to her old home. Her mom gave her a hard time, saying she had told her long ago that nothing good would come out of cohabiting, and went on to nag Hip Ho for being a grown-up woman of twenty with no family, no property of her own, her school results poor, and her life a complete mess. However, Hip Ho kept to herself, beating time and ignoring her mother. Later she bought herself a handheld game console with *Beatmania*, carrying it with her everywhere. At work she would hide in a quiet corner to play it. The level of difficulty had become of secondary importance as rhythm was now the main thing. Little by little, Hip Ho's movements and actions, no matter what, somehow acquired a certain beat. Since she detested having the beat interrupted, she would chew rhythmically when she had lunch with her colleagues, unwilling to take part in the conversation. When she was out shopping with her friends, she found them too casual and disorderly, walking and stopping erratically. Serving food in the Japanese restaurant where she was employed, her hips would sway this way and that, in time with her quick and slow steps. Reciting the menu to customers, she sounded like a rapper:

Miss! You want *black*-pepper *beef* with *coff*-ee!
Sir! You want *set*-menu *eel* with *milk* tea!

What Hip Ho couldn't understand was that the more she adjusted her own life to the beat, the more she appeared to be out of sync with the rest of the world. She had no way of adapting to the turgid pace of other people's lives, and no one else had any way of accurately grasping the rhythm of her body and mind. Hip Ho believed it would only be in the game arcade that she would be able to find her soulmate. However, while a few boys were fierce *Beatmania* players and also interested in Hip Ho, they weren't sure about the right thing to do and expressed their romantic feelings either too late or too early.

One evening, a sturdy young man called Dreggsie walked over to Hip Ho to compete with her. Hip Ho stayed calm and controlled under pressure, and the screen continuously flashed "Great!" "Great!" "Great!," while the man got "Poor!" "Poor!" "Poor!" all the time. He lost without even reaching 20,000 and left to an immediate uproar from the people queuing up. Rather to her own surprise, Hip Ho left with Dreggsie for a drink soon after, got drunk, and ended up in his home, carelessly humming the *Beatmania* beat at the same time as they were making love. As Dreggsie's body throbbed again and again, Hip Ho all of a sudden realized he was the man she was looking for! Hip Ho turned over so she was on top of Dreggsie and asked what kind of job he had. He was a bartender, he answered.

"Then I'll train as a bartender too," she said.

When Dreggsie wanted to know why she was called Hip Ho, she took his hands and placed them on her buttocks as she began swaying energetically, while the springs of the mattress sounded a hip-ho, hip-ho beat.

48
—

ADIDAS

Tripper felt that she'd finally be able to find Skinny again the day she found the Adidas jacket among his old things that her mother was sorting out. It was a tight, old-fashioned, light-blue tracksuit top with a zip, and it had three stripes down the sleeves from shoulder to cuff. When Tripper was little, her father had given Skinny a slap, claiming that he'd killed his goldfish. To his surprise, Skinny had struck back, and the two of them fought until the blood flowed. In reality, the goldfish had died after eating the eraser shreds that Tripper had dumped into the fish tank, but Tripper saw Skinny as protecting her.

There was a tiny bloodstain on the breast of the Adidas. Tripper believed that it was Skinny's, and gave it a lick to make certain. Skinny (whose looks lived up to his name) was eight years older than Tripper and sixteen when he left home. She was now eighteen, and the Adidas fitted her perfectly. After Skinny had left, her father left home as well, and her mother was out at work all day long. Since then, Tripper had often had a fantasy that there was a person called Fatty who assaulted her when she was taking a shower or sleeping, and she'd cry out for Skinny to save her.

Tripper put on the Adidas. Facing the mirror, she arranged her hair in two small pigtails, as she'd done when she was a child. She made straight for the bus, changed to a suburban train, and then transferred to the MTR, as sure of the way as a migrating bird. At the shopping mall, she stopped in front of a small shop selling uncensored pornographic discs. The skinny lad touting for business in front of the shop eyed her. "Hey, babe, you're hotter than them in the VCDs!"

"I'm your sister," said Tripper.

His jaw dropped, and he looked her up and down. "What the hell are you doing here?"

"Can you do three things for me?" Tripper asked.

Tripper dragged Skinny to a congee-and-noodle place and ordered two bowls of clay-pot rice with sausage and spare ribs. Skinny didn't ask why she was doing this but lowered his head and concentrated on eating. He spat the bones out all over the table. Tripper ate half of her meal and pushed the bowl over to Skinny. He picked his teeth. "Okay, talk! What d'you want me to do for you? Revenge or a loan?"

"Just eat. Dad used to smack me when I couldn't finish my meals, but you used to help me out when he wasn't looking," said Tripper.

Skinny grabbed half the sausage from her bowl. "I was just being greedy," he replied, licking his fingers.

Two days later, Tripper put the Adidas on again and went to the shop to find Skinny. However, she was told that he wasn't selling porn any more. Tripper bit her lip and wandered slowly along the streets. After some time, she saw him jump down from a truck in front of a garage. "Why are you avoiding me?" she asked him, right in his face.

"I've got real work to do, young lady, delivering the goods," said Skinny. Pulling him along, Tripper walked toward a shop selling trinkets and toys. Pointing at the My Melody in the display window, she said, "Take this for me."

As Skinny fished in his pocket, Tripper said, "I mean take, not buy. Don't you remember? We didn't have any money when we were kids, and you stole one exactly like this for me." Skinny wasn't pleased.

"How the hell do you remember everything!" he said, going into the shop.

After another couple of days had passed, Tripper went to the garage wearing the Adidas, but the roller door was down. An hour later, she made an appearance at Skinny's flat in Yau Ma Tei. Skinny almost exploded when he opened the door. "How the hell do you always manage to find me?"

"It's the Adidas," she replied.

Skinny paid her no attention but busied himself packing his things.

"Where are you going?" she asked.

He told her that the last time he'd helped smuggle petrol for the garage and it was confiscated by customs, he had cleared off right away, and now the boss laid all the blame on him.

Tripper grabbed him. "There's still one more thing."

"What?" yelled Skinny.

Tripper raised her face toward him. "Kiss me."

Skinny paused. Suddenly he hugged her, gave her a kiss, and unzipped her Adidas. She wasn't wearing anything underneath. Skinny stopped, tilted his head, and smiled wryly. "You think I'm a triad? Your skinny brother's just a no-hoper!" He picked up his bags and fled.

Tripper fell back on the sagging couch. Spread across the tea table were empty beer cans and a receipt for fifty-five dollars from the toy shop. Tripper tugged at the hem of the Adidas to zip it up, but the zipper broke immediately, and there was no way to zip it up again.

49
—

GUCCI

In the 1998 television adaptation of the Japanese manga *GTO* (*Great Teacher Onizuka*), the character Fuyutsuki Azusa was played by the actress Matsushima Nanako 松嶋菜菜子. The character 菜 ("greens") in her name is pronounced *na* in Japanese and *choi* in Cantonese.

The first day that Miss Choi-sam taught, she was wearing the Gucci watch. The students immediately created an uproar, making her jump, and afterward she was always on her guard about dressing up. Whether it was by good fortune or bad, she wasn't sure, but as soon as she'd graduated, she'd started at this rather famous girls' school, where the teachers' ages tended to be quite advanced. Every single one of them was like her mother at home; every day they instructed her as if she were a child, and it was very irritating. Also, there were no decent male colleagues. The students were nevertheless quite bright, but excessively diligent and hardworking, so the pressure was heavy. The worst nuisance was that they were more skillful than she was at buying famous brands.

After school on her first day, as she returned home, Miss Choi-sam discovered there was no way to take off her Gucci. The watchband, which was in the form of a silver ring, wasn't long enough to adjust, the clasp wouldn't open (it was too stiff to move), and she was afraid that prying it open might damage the watch. In the end, the result was that she washed herself with a plastic bag over her left hand and afterward went to sleep still wearing the watch. She hadn't expected, though, that the succeeding days would be the same, and it continued for such a long time that it was as if the watch became part of her body. By then it hardly mattered, and in any case no one knew. The Gucci even became Miss Choi-sam's trademark.

Nevertheless, her students still enjoyed calling her Miss Choi-sam, or Miss Cabbage Heart, since her real name was Choy Sam Yi. When she first became aware of this nickname, she was angry for several days, under the impression that cabbages sounded very low-class. Later, a student explained that she resembled a Japanese star in the TV adaptation of the comic GTO, whose name included the Chinese character for "greens," so eventually she calmed down.

Less than a month after she began teaching, a replacement maths teacher came to the school: a man called Chan Chi Ching, fairly young, with regular features. All the students and the unmarried female teachers eyed him greedily. Miss Choi-sam was no different from the other teachers, but after a short, simple conversation, she felt he was dull and unsociable, and her interest dropped sharply. When finally the week was over and Friday came around, the colleague she had originally agreed to go out with suddenly had something else to do. With nothing in particular to occupy her and feeling bored, Miss Choi-sam went by herself to a coffee shop near the school for afternoon tea. Sitting alone in front of the window, she looked at the sunshine flashing on the Gucci watchband, but after a while her eyes began to hurt, so she fished out a handkerchief to wipe them. Suddenly she heard someone ask, "Are you all right, Miss Choi-sam?" Looking up, she saw Chan Chi Ching.

"How did you know that?" she asked.

"The students call you that," he said. Her anger assuaged, she let the conversation lapse.

"I've long thought that you are very like Miss Fuyutsuki."

When she heard this, her anger completely evaporated. Pleased and surprised, she said, "Do you watch *GTO* too?"

Miss Choi-sam would never have guessed that Chan Chi Ching had a column in the newspaper reviewing popular culture. She also learnt that he had been an editor in the newspaper world for several years and had published a collection of fiction. When she asked him why he had come to teach, he admitted it was a kind of temporary escape, as he wanted to get away for a while from his previous social circles. When he in turn asked her the same question, she found herself unable to give a reason: it would have sounded too false or unambitious. She discovered she lacked the ability to decide what to do.

Miss Choi-sam and Chan Chi Ching had lunch together a few times. Once he asked her for the time; she rubbed her wrist, hesitated for a while, and then stretched her arm across the table toward him. Chan Chi Ching looked at it bashfully but didn't touch her. "You look very slender," he said suddenly, "but in fact you don't have thin bones, it's just that you're tall and so people don't see it."

Miss Choi-sam realized that he wasn't actually looking at the time but was talking about her figure. She couldn't get angry and just blushed.

Afterward, she would often run into Chan Chi Ching and then walk away, and as she walked away, she thought of running into him. This went on until the day when Chan Chi Ching left without saying goodbye. Miss Choi-sam spent the rest of the day feeling troubled. She went to her English lesson and told the students to occupy themselves with revision while she rested her chin on her hands and gazed into the distance. She didn't know how it happened, but the watchband clasp suddenly sprang open. She grasped her wrist, feeling very agitated, not even daring to look at the students. She bent her head and fastened the clasp again. During the break, she went to the school office and asked for Chan Chi Ching's address. That evening she went to look for him.

As Chan Chi Ching opened the door, Miss Choi-sam thrust her left hand toward him. "Help me," she said.

"How?" he answered.

"Undo this," she said.

Chan Chi Ching doubtfully got to work, pushing and pulling it, and finally took off the Gucci. However, he kept holding on to Miss Choi-sam's bare wrist, as if he could feel that her pulse was beating too violently. Miss Choi-sam bit her lip. "Help me," she said again.

Chan Chi Ching, confused, took a step backward, but his hands gripped hers more tightly.

50
YAHOO!

Ya-ho was known as Ya-ho because she was so easygoing. Whatever people said to her, she always answered *ya ho* in Cantonese, meaning "yeah, okay" or "yeah, sure," and she would never say no to anyone who asked for help with anything. As a result, she got along very well with everyone and knew people all over the place. People looking to make friends would go to her.

Ya-ho had been class rep from the beginning of secondary school. She was in charge of liaison and organized get-togethers after graduation, with a talent for tracking down old classmates who had been out of touch for several years. If you asked her for news of someone or other, it always turned out she knew all about them, and so she became the news network among her circle of friends.

Ya-ho was very good at matchmaking, but it also gave rise to a lot of fuss and bother. Needless to say, when her friends asked for help in finding suitable partners, it became Ya-ho's task to pass on notes to express their feelings. If difficulties arose in others' relationships, it was up to Ya-ho to step in and mediate. Even during breakups, they wanted Ya-ho's assistance in dealing with the fallout. Rushing about on behalf of her friends, Ya-ho felt exhausted at times, but seeing a friend find the one their heart belonged to in the boundless sea of humanity invariably roused her spirits.

One day, when Ya-ho was on the MTR, going home after work, Wing Yin gave her a call on her mobile asking her out. He was a former colleague from the time when she had been doing promotions for a telecom company. It was as if Ya-ho had all along been waiting for this moment, but she decided to go home first anyway, to change clothes. Ya-ho was short and slightly plump, but her hair was good and her face attractive, so she seemed on the whole a suitable prospect. Meeting Wing Yin at a McDonald's, she put her newly bought cow-spot handbag on the table, but Wing Yin's mind was focused on the girl he had been yearning for day and night, and it was quite clear to Ya-ho that that's how it would have to be.

When Ya-ho and Wing Yin were colleagues, they had often gone out to concerts together with her old classmate Mei Nei. Later Wing Yin often asked how Mei Nei was doing, but, after mulling it over, he took no further steps. Now he finally spoke out after some hesitation and was not in the least surprised when Ya-ho right away gave Mei Nei a call. The three of them went to see a film. They talked and laughed, but it didn't seem that anything else would happen. Wing Yin got in touch with Ya-ho again a couple of days later. This one really lacks courage, she thought to herself. However, she didn't feel annoyed, and it was even with a sense of hope that she arranged for them to meet with Mei Nei on Sunday to go bike riding. That's how it continued a number of times, always the three of them together, Wing Yin having even less courage to face Mei Nei on his own and Mei Nei's attitude ambiguous. While Ya-ho was the one who made arrangements, she didn't make any special efforts to push things further. Whenever Ya-ho wasn't busy, she would give Wing Yin a call to chat about Mei Nei until late at night, both of them endlessly wasting their energy on that topic.

One evening, when Ya-ho for some reason had been unable to get through to Wing Yin, she was sitting at home staring into space. Deciding to get on the Internet to while away the time, she was browsing Yahoo!, and then, without quite knowing why, she typed "love" in the search panel, and as she pressed the Enter key, she felt as if suspended in a void. The search turned up so many sites related to love that she was dazzled. Opening a few at random, she found them boring, and suddenly she felt quite depressed. She wanted to quit, but Yahoo! would just reload, and she found no way of quitting. At first irritated, Ya-ho then became scared, and at that point her mobile phone suddenly rang. It was Wing Yin.

Wing Yin asked to see her by the harborside. Ya-ho hastened there in a tense mood, but, crossing the road, she stumbled and fell, scraping her elbow. Wing Yin didn't ask about her arm but told her right away that he had bared his heart to Mei Nei. Ya-ho had never experienced such alarm—it was as if she was about to suffocate—and quickly asked, "And so? And so?" Wing Yin shook his head. Making a great show of rage, he turned his face to the harbor and howled: "Yaa . . . wooh!"

It seemed to Ya-ho as she was listening to him that he was calling her, and she involuntarily covered her ears with her hands. She wanted to turn and run away, but her feet wouldn't obey her, and slowly she sank to the ground.

51
—

FUJIFILM DIGITAL CAMERA

Siu Shue had resisted photography ever since childhood, and what she found particularly irritating were the swarms of people gathering in parks at the weekends, and girls wearing heavy makeup striking flirtatious poses in front of the lenses. Nonetheless, three photos were hidden away in Siu Shue's notebook.

The most recent one had been taken by Siu Shue's boyfriend, Tsung Yin, with his newly purchased Fujifilm digital camera FinePix-MX700. He said it had 1.5 million pixels, but Siu Shue could only see two people. That day was the first time Tsung Yin and Siu Shue had met since becoming lovers. They were wandering in the park and he'd given her a bunch of flowers, when he suddenly pulled out the delicate little digital camera. It was no use her shaking her head and waving her hands. As she yielded with some reluctance, he snapped several photos of them together. Afterward, Siu Shue saw something odd about herself in the pictures: as a result of the soft focus, her woolen jumper was shocking pink, her face scarlet, and her lips crimson. She'd had nowhere to put the flowers, and Tsung Yin rested his arm conventionally around her shoulders. She recalled that she'd worn dark blue that day and no makeup.

The oldest photo was one her father had taken of her as a child, when she would have been about four or five. At that time, her mother would probably already have left, and she couldn't recall why her father would suddenly have been in a good mood. The black-and-white picture didn't show any sign of fading: the contrast was still sharp, and the skirt worn by the little girl shone white in the sunshine. However, Siu Shue could no longer remember what the skirt's actual color had been and even found it impossible to recognize the location. From then on, until his death, her father had never again taken a photo of her.

Then there was the last one, taken a year ago. It was dark, the two people indistinct under a light by the roadside. They stood next to each other, both with their hands on their hips and smiling for no particular reason. The images of the figures had overlapped because of the long exposure. That evening, Wing Chiu had mentioned to Siu Shue his long-standing fascination with photography and talked about the way the grains on the negative are imprinted with the refraction of specific light rays onto a specific substance: they are the vestiges left by the caresses of the hand of time.

"It's a pity it's so late and there's not enough light," Siu Shue had said.

"As long as there's enough time, there's enough light," Wing Chiu replied. With that, he went back home to fetch his camera. It was a manual-focus FM2 and quite outmoded; the lens had a bit of mold on it, and the light meter was broken. Under the street light, Wing Chiu set the aperture to maximum and the shutter to B mode, and so the two of them had posed motionless in front of the camera, standing still for a long time.

Wing Chiu and Siu Shue had been introduced by friends and had seen each other a few times. Neither of them liked to spend time shopping or going out to eat, drink, and party, being more interested in talking about matters of no immediate practical use. Wing Chiu was ten years older than Siu Shue and had an ordinary sort of career, but he was fond of odd and unrelated bits of information about things such as clocks and watches, insects, herbal medicines, and martial arts. Siu Shue only liked reading, so the others regarded her as a loner and claimed that was the reason she'd had no experience of love. After some time, Wing Chiu suddenly stopped phoning Siu Shue, so their relationship came to an end for no apparent reason; Siu Shue assumed it was because he disliked her. Later, when Siu Shue had graduated, she stayed on working at the university library, so her social circle was small, and she had few dates. Her colleague Tsung Yin expressed interest in her several times, and since she thought he seemed like a good person, she eventually accepted.

Siu Shue asked Tsung Yin for a disk with the photos of them and opened it on her computer back home, intending to use Photoshop in secret to restore her actual appearance. However, she wasn't very good at this, and the more she fiddled with it, the worse it looked. In the middle of all this the phone rang. It turned out to be Wing Chiu. To Siu Shue, who was feeling confused and upset, it wasn't very clear what he actually meant to say. It seemed as if he was explaining why he hadn't kept in touch the previous year, but he also sounded like a distant acquaintance casually talking about how things had been recently.

"If you've got time to go out, give me a call," Wing Chiu said as he was about to hang up. Putting down the receiver, Siu Shue found it nearly impossible to straighten her arm. When she looked at the clock, it turned out that as much as two hours had passed. Back in front of her computer, she discovered that the figure that she had cut out had disappeared. In the place she had occupied in the picture, there remained only an empty space in the outline of a person. Selecting Undo repeatedly didn't help.

Wing Chiu later on told the friends who had introduced Siu Shue to him that in the end she'd never called him back, and while he'd all along regarded her as a unique, wonderful girl, it was simply that he had lost his feelings for her.

52

CONVERSE LO TEC

Ever since she'd put on the pair of Converse shoes, Pat Pat had begun walking backward, but she had no idea whether that had anything to do with the shoes.

Pat Pat had always worn high-heeled sandals, knee-length skirts, and tank tops, the standard summer dress for attractive young women. One day she'd waited for Ah Tat to get off work so they could go window-shopping. Then someone in the MTR station stepped on her heel, breaking the shoe strap.

"I'd better buy a pair of running shoes," Pat Pat said.

Ah Tat didn't think it was a good idea. "What kind of clothes would you wear to go with running shoes?"

Pat Pat was set on doing it her own way and in the shop she settled on a pair of Converse canvas shoes, red with white soles, white toe caps and white stripes. Standing next to Ah Tat in his tailored trousers and leather shoes while she tried them on, she looked unsophisticated and uncouth.

"You know, Hi Tec shoes aren't popular right now, everyone's wearing Lo Tec," the shop assistant said. Pat Pat thought they were fine and very comfortable, so she paid and walked out wearing them right away.

"What's so good-looking about them!" Ah Tat was grumbling as they left the shop. That was when Pat Pat began walking backward; she couldn't help it and was even unaware of it. Believing she was turning her face away because she was angry, Ah Tat paid even less attention to her. Pat Pat couldn't see where she was going and, as they kept walking, they ended up separated. It was only after a great deal of effort that Pat Pat got back home.

Later on, Ah Tat and Pat Pat quarreled several times because of her habit of walking backward. Ah Tat thought she was doing it on purpose to give him a hard time and make him seem weird. Pat Pat didn't know how to defend herself. Walking backward, she could never keep up with Ah Tat striding ahead, so after a while she simply stopped, twisting her head around to follow him with her eyes as he disappeared into the distance.

Pat Pat gradually got used to walking backward. Along familiar routes and where there were few other pedestrians, it was no different from walking forward. She decided she might as well buy T-shirts and chinos that matched her Converses. In any case, she had almost no need to move about in her job as a ticket seller at the civic center, and there was no dress code there. Pat Pat was not unaware of the suspicious looks she got from other people, however. In the street they gave her a wide berth, and as soon as she sat down on a train or in a fast-food restaurant, the people next to her one by one slipped away.

After Ah Tat, Pat Pat went out with someone else, a young intellectual who was keen on the performing arts. Ah Hang had bought a ticket to see the same play for the fifth evening running. The audience was streaming out just as Pat Pat was getting off work. Ah Hang emerged and waited for her by the doorway. Seeing her walk backward, he assumed she was being playful and followed by her side, chatting and joking as if everything was perfectly normal. They went out together a few more times, to see a film or for a meal, Pat Pat continuing to move backward. Ah Hang walked more and more slowly until the time he waved goodbye to her outside the building where she lived; Pat Pat walked inside, watching his figure grow small. Ah Hang didn't ask Pat Pat out again after that.

The more Pat Pat wore her Converse shoes, the more worn they became, but she had thrown out all her other shoes and hadn't given any thought to buying new ones. One day, when she was having lunch on her own in a fast-food restaurant, she noticed a middle-aged woman carrying a tray in her hands and making her way backward as she looked for a seat. She seemed like a boat berthing at the shore stern first, and the manner in which she walked and turned around appeared no less purposeful and graceful than that of ordinary people. Pat Pat waited for the woman to finish her meal and leave, then got up and followed her out, walking backward. Before she had a chance to say anything, the woman smiled at her.

"So you're one of us too!" she said. "And you're so young!"

"What do you mean by 'us'?" Pat Pat asked.

"There's quite a number of us, we live all over the place, and we just press ahead."

Pat Pat still didn't understand.

"You might think of it as a kind of secret society of the spirit!"

It was only after the woman had gone away that Pat Pat realized that she'd neglected to ask if there were any connection between walking backward and Converse, nor had she thought of checking what kind of footwear the woman had been wearing.

After some time, Ah Tat gave Pat Pat a phone call out of the blue to say he missed her, and arranged to meet her in the park on Sunday. Ah Tat was wearing casual clothes and running shoes that day, and as soon as he saw Pat Pat, he began imitating her by walking backward. He'd been in training for a long time, he said, and he could race her if she didn't believe him. As they ran giggling together, Ah Tat became a little reckless and tripped over a tree root. With his feet toward the sky, his machine-like Nike Foamposites were raised high in the air.

53

HAIRPINS

Not a single one of Fei Fei's friends at the discos believed she was studying nursing. Even Ah Tin, the boyfriend she'd been dating for four years, felt that the Fei Fei who studied nursing was a different person and that the only thing the two Fei Feis had in common was that both had hairpins.

Fei Fei had already been expert at tying up her hair well before hairpins became popular again. When she was little, her mother had loved handling Fei Fei's hair, reaching a record when she braided it into twenty-one plaits. At secondary school, Fei Fei's plaits were in a new style every day, leaving her classmates feeling overwhelmed. When hairpins were on the rise later on, Fei Fei found it easier than ever to do what she knew best. Whether it was big or small hairpins, pins in rows or criss-crossing, big waves or little plaits, silvery pins or pins in a riot of colors, no one could compete with Fei Fei. On the dance floor, she tossed her head and shook her topknot all evening without her hair getting in the least bit ruffled. During her training, her hair was tucked into the student nurse cap and kept in place with the most ordinary black hairpins—nothing fancy—but she still looked prettier than the others.

People claimed that few young women nowadays were willing to enter a profession with such awful conditions as nursing, especially girls like Fei Fei. She never offered an explanation, and only a few people knew it was because her mother had died young. Finding it easy to cope with the demands of trainee nursing—and not being put off by blood and dead bodies—it was only when Fei Fei attended the men's surgical ward that she became a bit restless. Once she got off work, she underwent a total transformation, changing into fashionable clothes and using lots of hairpins to secure her hair. She twirled around with abandon when she took to the dance floor with Ah Tin. She only felt life was really good when she reached a stage of exhaustion.

Although Whiskers only spent three weeks in men's surgical, during that time Fei Fei actually committed three mistakes. Once she almost got a patient's oxygen tube and glucose tube attached the wrong way round, earning her a severe talking-to by the matron. In fact, Whiskers didn't have any whiskers, and at twenty-one he was also quite young, taking social studies at university. It was just that his name was Wyston and he hadn't got his razor with him the first couple of days after admission. Since he had stubble all over his chin, Fei Fei called him Whiskers for a joke. He'd been sent to hospital when the bus he was on had been in a traffic accident. With his broken leg in a plaster cast, he couldn't walk but lay in bed all day reading books or else writing. When he was asked what he was writing, he said poetry; he even let Fei Fei see his scribbles, which were utterly disjointed. The nurses, including Fei Fei, made fun of the poet with the injured leg. Whiskers pressed the buzzer for a bedpan one evening when Fei Fei was on night shift. To her surprise, Fei Fei felt her cheeks burning, but fortunately the light had already been turned off on the ward.

Ah Tin certainly had his own opinion about Fei Fei's trainee nursing, resenting the fact that there was always a whiff of disinfectant about her body, she was excessively particular about hygiene, and she also forced him to use a condom when they had sex. He'd told her over and over again to switch to another career, but she wouldn't let herself be persuaded. At times her work made Fei Fei so tired that she didn't want to go for a night out; all she could bring herself to do was to lie down and fall asleep. She didn't even remove her hairpins, which were all over the bed when she woke up the next day, pricking her face like stab wounds: it was very painful.

On the day he left hospital, Whiskers presented Fei Fei with a poem written on a blank medical record, with the title "Whisk and Pin." He also told Fei Fei he and his friends were publishing a poetry magazine and he would send her an issue. Fei Fei looked away and thought for a moment. Tearing out a page from her notebook, she wrote down her address, and, pulling two hairpins from her head, she used one to attach her address to Whiskers's book and the other to attach the poem to her own notebook.

In the end she never received the poetry magazine Whiskers had mentioned. Three months later, on Christmas Eve, when Fei Fei and Ah Tin went to a dance at the university, she saw Whiskers dancing slowly with a girl in his arms, his leg apparently fully recovered. When they were leaving later on, they ran into each other outside the venue, but Whiskers didn't say hello. After Fei Fei got back home, she tore out her twenty-odd hairpins. Getting up the next morning, she discovered that they'd all gone rusty overnight.

54

CUT SLEEVES

A Han-dynasty emperor is supposed to have cut off his long sleeve rather than disturb his male lover, who was lying asleep at his side on the sleeve. "Cut sleeve" has become a term referring to homosexuality. A form of dress with cut-off sleeves and cut-off trouser legs was briefly fashionable in late 1990s Hong Kong. Both the sleeves (cut off at the elbow) and the trouser legs were attached to the rest of their garments with straps.

"You know you're pretty annoying," Ah Lan said when she saw that Ah Po had imitated her by wearing a top with cut-off sleeves.

Ah Lan and Ah Po had been pupils at the same middle school, where Ah Lan was two years ahead of Ah Po. When Ah Lan was in fourth form, she hit a teacher and was expelled. The man suffered a mark from Ah Lan's pager on his forehead, and there had been blood all over his face. The incident became known to the whole school, so Ah Po knew who Ah Lan was, but Ah Lan didn't know who Ah Po was. Ah Po was in fact extremely quiet and virtually unable to make friends, so no one was ever aware of her existence.

It was three years later that Ah Po encountered Ah Lan again. In the dim light of a karaoke place, Ah Po recognized the girl with a wild mop of red curly hair as Ah Lan. At the time, a bunch of boys were plying Ah Po with alcohol and she was afraid they would pull her clothes off. Ah Lan, who happened to be working there, came in just then with drinks.

"Ah Lan, help me!" Ah Po screamed.

Not stopping to ask questions, Ah Lan pulled her away, greeted the boys by cursing them roundly, and finally hurled a beer bottle at them for good measure. That turned into big trouble, and the fighting only stopped after Ah Lan's coworkers came in to mediate. After the incident, when Ah Lan took Ah Po back home on her motorbike, she finally asked Ah Po who she was. When she learnt they were old schoolmates, Ah Lan had no recollection of Ah Po but told her she shouldn't go out to those sorts of places if she wasn't that kind of girl; this world wasn't child's play.

Not long after, Ah Po went to the karaoke box to look for Ah Lan, but they told her Ah Lan had been sacked because of the previous incident. They gave her Ah Lan's mobile number when she asked for it, but when she called her, Ah Lan lost her temper.

"What's up now, girlie?"

However, the result was that they met up again, when Ah Po invited Ah Lan out to a sushi bar. At the end of the meal, Ah Lan snatched the bill and paid. In high spirits, she took Ah Po for a trip to Stanley, riding in the evening breeze. They sat smoking on the darkened beach, stubbing their butts out in a circle in a pile of sand. Ah Lan decided on an English name for Ah Po, calling her Apple.

"In that case, you should be Orange," said Ah Po.

From then on, Apple often went out with Orange. Orange was wearing the fashionable cut-off trouser legs that were actually neither pants nor skirt but skirt above and pants below; the trouser legs were buttoned on with straps underneath a short skirt, leaving an empty space in-between and looking very seductive. Apple would imitate anything, and that would make Orange lose her temper. Sometimes when she was in a bad mood, Orange would tell Apple off, saying she wasn't bad but copied other people being bad and then got terribly scared, turning into a real crybaby and being just too much to deal with. Or Orange would frighten her by claiming she often raced her bike and was bound to break her arms and legs one day: crack! Her cut-off sleeves and cut-off trousers made it look as if this had really happened. To her dismay, Apple actually burst into tears at this, and Orange at once soothed her, holding her arms and legs tightly, the bare skin between their cut-off clothing touching in an intimate embrace.

Later, after a boy who knew Apple ran away because he owed money, the lender insisted that Apple was the boy's girlfriend and responsible for repayment of the full amount. It was not a small sum. Orange went to see the creditor and returned saying the matter had been settled, but she didn't say how. After that, Orange became reticent, barely saying a word to Apple. When Apple pitifully begged Orange not to ignore her, Orange avoided her.

"Will you only be satisfied if I break my arms and legs for you?" Orange told her in the end. "How can you demand so much from someone else?"

"What does breaking arms and legs count for?" Apple said. Grabbing Orange's motorcycle key, she rushed out, jumped on the bike, started it, and gave it full throttle.

Apple and the bike smashed against the steel barriers along the road, narrowly avoiding being run over by a truck. She was taken to hospital, and while there were no broken arms or legs, it turned out she had injured a neck bone, and there was a risk that the lower part of her body would be paralyzed. When she came to and saw Orange by her bedside, she asked why she seemed to have no arms and legs and couldn't feel them.

Orange grasped her arm. "They're there, but paralyzed," she said. "They'll get better." As she spoke, she turned her face away and finally wept. It had been many years since her eyes had felt so terribly hot.

55

—

SCARVES

The Love Generation is a Japanese television serial from 1997. One of the characters is called Uesugi Riko, and there is a magic-trick scene.

Nobody knew whether Pak Pak liked wearing scarves and therefore specialized in performing conjuring tricks with them or whether conjuring was her special skill and for that reason she always wore a scarf. In any case, Pak Pak unfailingly wore a scarf every day and was able to perform her tricks impromptu at any time.

Pak Pak deployed her scarves brilliantly; whether it was in summer or winter, on formal or casual occasions, she could always use one at social events and be in fashion. When headscarves became popular, she would tie one around her head, use it to make a ponytail, or fold it into a hood. Later on, in the autumn, when cowboy-style three-cornered bandannas came into fashion, Pak Pak excelled at this trend too. Everyone was fascinated by Pak Pak's scarves, which drew attention to her graceful neck, delicate cheeks, and erect shoulders, so that people were even more convinced that Pak Pak was an outstanding beauty.

In the daytime, Pak Pak worked in a stationery shop and performed her magic after work or on holidays. At times it was in the nature of duty: going to hospitals, old people's homes, and foster care institutions; at other times she was able to earn a lit-tle extra cash performing with her teacher to entertain at events like evening gatherings of different organizations. Some-times Pak Pak would casually do simple tricks in front of friends, but people didn't realize how extraordinary her conjur-ing skills were.

"Well, at least I'm better than Riko in *The Love Generation!*" Pak Pak said, when Ah Kwong once asked about it.

The reason Pak Pak got to know Ah Kwong also had to do with magic. He'd gone to the stationery shop where Pak Pak was working to buy a complete set of conjuring equipment, and when she asked what he was doing, he said he intended to join the magic society at his university and wanted to get in some prac-tice first. Without a word, Pak Pak took off her scarf, formed a circle by bringing the tips of her left thumb and index finger together and pushed a corner of the scarf through it. With her right hand, she pulled the corner through, unleashing a flicker-ing cloud of gold dust all over them. Ah Kwong stood and stared.

Afterward, Ah Kwong often went to the stationery shop to see Pak Pak, begging her to teach him conjuring. He also let slip that he was in fact doing it to pursue a female student in the magic society. At first she was unwilling to help, saying he was deceiving the girl and acting in bad faith, but in the end she taught him a few card tricks as well as a little mind reading and fortune-telling. At regular intervals, Ah Kwong reported his progress to Pak Pak: for instance, the girl's reaction to the tricks, whether they'd had meals together, what films they'd been to see, when they'd held hands, his feelings when kissing her for the first time, and so forth. Pak Pak didn't mind, listening and at the same time pulling at a corner of her scarf.

One day, when a customer had left an urgent photocopying job at the stationery shop, the boss had to leave early to go to a dinner party, leaving Pak Pak alone on an extra shift. When someone outside banged at the roll-up door, she opened it to have a look, and there was Ah Kwong, all red in the face, carrying beer and saying the female student had broken off with him. Pak Pak let him sit down in the shop, where he kept talking to himself while she carried on with the copying job, the machine's light beam passing across her face again and again. When the work was done, Pak Pak turned around and asked if it was all right if she performed a magic trick for him. Ah Kwong nodded in a confused sort of way, so Pak Pak loosened the red paisley scarf around her neck and tied it over his eyes, ordering him not to steal a single glance.

In the middle of the night, Ah Kwong woke up to find a dark cover over his eyes. Groping at his face, he discovered the scarf over his eyes and couldn't help furtively pulling it off. In the faint light stealing inside from the shop sign, he saw himself and Pak Pak lying naked in the middle of the shop floor. Pak Pak's body was utterly beautiful, but somehow there seemed to be something missing. After a while, Pak Pak suddenly woke up.

"Kwong, why haven't you kept faith?" she asked.

From then on, Pak Pak abandoned magic but continued to wear her scarves, at times taking them off, folding them, and then tying them on again. Some people claimed Pak Pak had lost her ability to perform magic and asked her for confirmation.

"What you call magic," she said, "if you don't have faith, it doesn't exist."

56

ANIMAL PRINTS

Lan Kwai Fong is a bar, restaurant, and entertainment area
close to the central business district on Hong Kong Island.

Ku Wai Chun was Ku Wai Chun's real name, but her friends
called her Ku Chun, and that's also what her boyfriend Ah Lok
called her. The first time Ku Chun met Ah Lok was when she
bought her Persian cat Ku Ku. Ah Lok's newly opened pet shop
was near Ku Chun's home, so, on her way back from school,
when she stepped inside to have a look, she saw a Persian cat,
whiter than snow, curled up cold and lonely in a cage. She also
saw the boy in charge of the shop: he looked like a laborer and
was playing with a collie. She asked about the price of the Persian but thought it too dear and was about to leave.

"This is the auspicious beginning of a new enterprise!" the
laborer said. "What about taking it for half price?"

She hadn't expected the laborer would turn out to be the
owner. From then on, whenever Ku Chun wanted to buy cat food
or something else after school, she'd go to the pet shop, and even
if there wasn't anything she needed, she'd go there anyway, sitting down to chat and playing with the animals. And so she fell
in love with Ah Lok. Two years later, when she'd finished secondary five, she got a job as a shop assistant. She continued to
go to the pet shop after work, almost as if she were the owner's
wife. She'd kept Ku Ku, who was now four years old, quite fat,

and never made a sound, but when she wasn't asleep, she'd walk to and fro all day, looking pleased with herself. Originally Ku Chun had called her Kitty, but Ah Lok disapproved of this as being too common, so she changed the name to Ku Ku.

Four years later, after summer had passed, animal-print clothes and accessories became popular, and the furry fabrics printed with spots made the streets resemble wild-life reserves. Ku Chun bought a bracelet with tiger stripes, a hat with leopard spots, and a small handbag with cow patches. The first day she wore the tiger-stripe bracelet, she went with Ah Lok to a midnight show at the cinema. After coming out, they walked back hand in hand. Halfway, Ah Lok began to scratch himself, clawing with both hands in the darkness. When they came into the light from a convenience store, they were shocked to discover that his arms were covered in long scratches that were red and bleeding. Ah Lok thought it was because he'd become allergic to the pets at work, but he felt in as good a shape as ever when he opened the shop the next day.

Then at Halloween, Ku Chun, Ah Lok, and a big group of their friends went to Lan Kwai Fong to take part in the festivities. Ku Chun was wearing her leopard-spot hat, and after a couple of drinks in a bar, she plonked it on Ah Lok's head, the whole bunch of them making fun of him as Panther Man. However, Ah Lok felt a strange itching and soreness on his face, and when he went to the gents and looked at himself in the mirror, he saw blotches all over his face. When the others saw him emerge, they thought he'd put on ugly makeup in the festive spirit, like a lot of people there. Ku Chun felt there was something not right and took her hat off him. With no way of finding a doctor in the middle of the night, she was thinking of taking him to Accident and Emergency, but Ah Lok insisted he'd be all right if he rubbed some medicated oil on his face. Ah Lok was in fact quite all right the next day.

For Christmas, Ah Lok made reservations for himself and Ku Chun to go to a buffet restaurant, just as in the previous four years. Ku Chun wore a gray turtleneck jumper and a checked pleated skirt, her little cow-spot handbag over her arm. As she was touching up her makeup on the MTR, Ah Lok held her handbag for a little while. Afterward, she asked him how come he had one white and one black patch on his face. He said it was because of her cow-spot bag, but Ku Chun told him he was being absurd—it wasn't even real leather, and she herself felt perfectly well. As a result, they didn't even finish their meal before making their separate ways home. Ah Lok didn't sleep that night, shedding large and small patches of skin from all over his body, but once it stopped, he was back to his normal self.

Animal prints quickly went out of fashion, and people noticed that there was a different girl sitting in the pet shop in her school uniform. Ku Chun went on feeding the Persian cat Ku Ku as before but bought her cat food from a different pet shop, until one spring morning when Ku Ku passed away for no obvious reason.

57

THE PLEATED SKIRT

Love Letters is a Japanese film from 1995. It has two characters, one male and one female, both called Fujii Itsuki.

The first day Ching Siu Lai had walked into class 7A, she'd got down to Ip Ka Shue in the roll call when she got a cold response. Turning her gaze toward the boy sitting in a corner, she felt he looked rather like the haughty student Fujii Itsuki in the film *Love Letters.*

After getting her university degree, Ching Siu Lai had returned to her old secondary school to take up a teaching job. Three years on, it seemed as if she'd never left. Her old teachers had now become her colleagues but still looked upon her as one of their schoolgirls. She in turn didn't mind, only too content with her peaceful existence. Ching Siu Lai was small, pale and delicate in appearance, and also soft-spoken. If it hadn't been for the fact that she wore a suit, she would have appeared even more childish than the schoolgirls. In her first couple of years, she taught junior secondary school and had no problems. When she was about to start teaching in her third year, a colleague in charge of a year-seven class suddenly resigned, so the head teacher, having all along favored Ching Siu Lai, assigned her as a replacement. Anxious to live up to the head teacher's expectations, Ching Siu Lai worked hard preparing her lessons, but on the first day her well-laid plans were shaken by Ip Ka Shue.

Teaching class 7A went more smoothly than expected. Ching Siu Lai didn't put on airs, and most of the students liked her, but, being reserved by nature and lacking self-confidence, she always maintained a certain distance. While she was warm and friendly in class, it was rare that she adopted a more familiar manner outside the classroom. However, suddenly Ip Ka Shue broke through this safety line.

Not long after the beginning of term, Ip Ka Shue began writing messages to Ching Siu Lai. His notes were quite short, added at the end of homework or quizzes. Thinking back, Ching Siu Lai felt that if she could just have been resolute and dealt with him openly at the first occurrence, then the subsequent sequence of events would never have taken place. Learning of this class loner's private feelings, she was initially acting out of a sense of duty as a teacher when she replied. Little by little, she then found her own recollections and emotions entangled as the whole thing went beyond the scope of guidance and came closer to revealing their inner voices. The longer this went on, the more Ching Siu Lai felt she couldn't make their secret exchange public, since that would, without a doubt, amount to a betrayal of her counterpart's trust. Eventually she felt obliged to invite Ip Ka Shue out, in order to clarify their relationship. Although she'd rehearsed what she wanted to say on this over and over again—dozens of times—once they met, she wasn't able to utter a single word. Both fell into a deep silence, standing impassive by the side of a railway overpass. Then Ching Siu Lai let Ip Ka Shue pull her hand toward him.

What happened that evening was by chance observed by another pupil and reported to the head teacher. The next day, when they were called in for questioning, Ching Siu Lai was evasive and inarticulate, while Ip Ka Shue frankly confessed. Wanting to stand by Ching Siu Lai, the head teacher ruled that it was Ip Ka Shue who had forced himself on his teacher and insisted that he withdraw from the school immediately. With the matter still unresolved, the head teacher told Ching Siu Lai to go home for the time being.

Waiting for a decision, Ching Siu Lai was sitting at home staring blankly ahead when she noticed her sister's newly purchased gray skirt with accordion pleats lying on a bed. It was a popular style that autumn and winter and very much like the gray skirt of the school's uniform for girls. Not sure what impelled her, she picked it up and tried it on. Glancing in the mirror, she found her reflection strikingly similar to the year-seven schoolgirl of six years earlier. As she swung around, the pleated skirt flared, reminding her of how she'd felt when she'd run across the school's sports ground clutching a letter for one of her male classmates, a letter she'd never had the courage to hand over. That day, however, he'd been about to be expelled from the school for an infraction, and, hearing the news, she'd burst out of her classroom, rushing straight toward the school gate, her skirt flying up as her legs pushed her through the air—but it was all too late. That had been the first time, and until now the only time, that Ching Siu Lai had been in love.

Wearing the pleated skirt, Ching Siu Lai dashed out of her home and ran toward the school, silently repeating to herself, "I can still make it in time! I can still make it in time!" She ran straight ahead, past the sports ground and the staff room to the head teacher's office. Seeing Ip Ka Shue still there, she went over and took his hand.

"None of this was his fault," she said. "It was me who became fond of my student and led him astray. I willingly take full responsibility and offer my immediate resignation. Please, sir, let Ip Ka Shue remain at school and complete year seven!" When she'd finished speaking, the teachers and students in the room were dumbstruck. Ching Siu Lai and Ip Ka Shue grasped each others' hands even more tightly.

58

MIU MIU FLANNEL

Miu Wai Sze had been in a traffic accident one evening three years earlier. She had been celebrating her sixteenth birthday, and her boyfriend, Ah Kit, was taking her back home. They were in a taxi and crashed head-on into a truck on the highway. The taxi driver and Ah Kit died, and Miu Wai Sze spent two months in hospital. By the time she came out, her lower body was paralyzed, and the doctor said she would be in a wheelchair for the rest of her life. From then on, Miu Wai Sze always wore a pair of Dr. Martens shoes with black uppers and transparent rubber soles, because they had been Ah Kit's birthday present for her and had also survived the crash.

After her release from hospital, Miu Wai Sze did not go back to school, nor did she have a job. She stayed at home every day. Apart from watching television or VCD cartoons to amuse herself, as if she really found them funny, she spent her time going over everything Ah Kit had left behind, looking at each of his things in turn, and then crying over them. Her family didn't know what to do, but fortunately they were reasonably well off, so her mother stayed at home and could look after her day and night.

On a rare day when Miu Wai Sze actually wished to go out, her mother pushed her wheelchair to the park. She asked her daughter to sit there on her own while she went off to do the shopping. Miu Wai Sze didn't like the sunlight, and dragonflies were flying back and forth around her, so she pushed her wheel-chair to a shady spot under a tree. Underneath the tree she saw a young man, a few years older than she was, feeding a scruffy, emaciated cat with brown fur and white spots. The cat, on its guard, ran off when it saw Miu Wai Sze approaching. The young man looked up and peered at her, the foliage casting flickering shadows on his face. The next day Miu Wai Sze came back to watch the young man feed the cat, taking her place quietly to the side without saying anything. This went on for four days before the young man introduced himself. "I'm called Ah Kat." Pointing at the cat, he added, "This is Meow-Meow. What's your name?"

It had been a long time since Miu Wai Sze had spoken to a stranger, and she answered in a voice that didn't quite seem her own: "I'm Miu Wai Sze."

Ah Kat went to feed Meow-Meow at that time every morn-ing, rain or shine. Miu Wai Sze was always there too and little by little began to feel that there were after all some things in life that she could look forward to. Still, she didn't understand why that was so. She had no particular fondness for cats, nor was she starting to like Ah Kat; in short, it was just somewhere to go every morning. Once Ah Kat pointed at Miu Wai Sze's shoes. "Haven't you been wearing those a long time!"

Miu Wai Sze was surprised. She had thought that since her shoes never touched the ground, they would stay as good as new for a long time, but as a matter of fact they had begun to look worn just with the passage of time. Miu Wai Sze and Ah Kat spoke very little to each other; she had absolutely no idea what he did, and he didn't ask her about herself, either. When they did actually speak, it was only to say something about Meow-Meow, such as "seems it's got fatter," "it's pretty naughty," "it's jumping quite high," "it's female," "its pupils are so small," "its claws are very sharp," or "it's got a lame leg."

Summer passed. One day Ah Kat suddenly said, "I'm mov-ing away. I'm getting married." After a while he continued, "Will you come to my wedding?" He looked toward Meow-Meow, who was devouring her food, and sighed deeply. Waiting until Meow-Meow had finished eating, Ah Kat picked up a stick and hit Meow-Meow hard. The cat was so scared it leapt away but then looked back at him in confusion. He went on chasing the cat until Meow-Meow had fled so far that she disappeared without trace. As Miu Wai Sze looked on, she felt more and more bewildered, and the palms of her hands were covered in sweat.

The next day Miu Wai Sze asked her mother to take her to a shoe shop. Right away, she spotted a pair of high-heeled Miu Miu boots with gray flannel leg warmers. The shop assistant let her try them on. Making a huge effort, Miu Wai Sze pushed herself up with her arms and actually stood. Trembling and shaking, she walked toward her mother. Miu Wai Sze didn't go to Ah Kat's wedding and didn't see him again. She even began to doubt that there was such a person as Ah Kat. But she was able to walk in her Miu Mius and wore a matching new skirt. She could feel again what it was like being nineteen.

One bright day in autumn, Miu Wai Sze went for a job interview wearing her Miu Mius. On her way home, she passed the park where Ah Kat had been feeding the cat. Spotting a small pile of something brownish under the trees and bushes, she walked closer to take a look: it was the cat's dead body. It had starved to death and become a shapeless lump. Miu Wai Sze's legs collapsed and she fell down on the grass.

59

GRAY

After her discovery of the color gray, Kai Hang knew that at last she'd found a world where she belonged. In retrospect, starting from her scribbles in kindergarten, she'd never shown much interest in multicolored pencil sets, feeling unaccountably resistant to them. She stuck to ordinary lead pencils, so her drawings were murky and gray, and her hands were grubby. At first, her teachers were amused but later they became impatient. "What's that you've drawn, Lam Kai Hang? Is it a witch?" In primary school and later in secondary school, she'd had to use colors in order to get a pass in art. Gradually, she forgot her response to gray.

In the autumn of the year that Kai Hang turned twenty-five, gray outfits became fashionable. She didn't pay much attention to the trend at first, but when she went into a shop to buy some new clothes, she found that everything was gray. This didn't bother her, and she tried on a few items. When she looked into the mirror, memories of gray from her childhood flashed through her mind like old black-and-white photos. From then on, Kai Hang only bought blouses and skirts in different shades of gray, over a spectrum of more than twenty degrees of light and dark and set off by black or white, as she became aware that even gray could come in many variations and intensities. Although the streets were full of people dressed in gray, nobody was as thorough or flawless as Kai Hang.

Kai Hang worked as a bank teller in the daytime, dressed in a red uniform. After work, she changed into gray clothes and went to her black-and-white photography class. In fact, Kai Hang regarded herself as having no photographic sense and couldn't understand how cameras worked, but she wanted to know more about visual perception on the scale of black, white, and gray. After class, she would go and buy photograph albums by such people as Ansel Adams, Henri Cartier-Bresson, Eugène Atget, André Kertész, Jacques Henri Lartigue, and Yau Leung. She didn't even care when she got a fail for her homework. There was a very keen student in her class named Pak Wing, who was quite knowledgeable about photography. He often volunteered to show Kai Hang what do to, and he was always at her side on field trips, more or less grabbing her camera to take photos for her. At the end of the course, Pak Wing asked Kai Hang for her phone number and shortly afterward invited her out to take photos.

Kai Hang had not gone out on dates for two years, not because she didn't want to, but because she could never manage to make it work. She'd had four relationships before she was twenty-three, some lasting longer than others, but while all of the young men were crazy about her at the beginning, for some reason after a few dates they went cold. One of them told her straight out when they broke up that Kai Hang was too aloof, she hardly ever said a word and just about never smiled, her only hobby was to go to evening classes, and there was no fun in going out with her.

Kai Hang dressed from top to bottom in gray for her date. She didn't bring her own camera but let Pak Wing take photos of her. He shot two rolls of film in a park in front of masses of flowers in full bloom, and then they went to a Japanese café for afternoon tea. After the better part of an hour, Pak Wing went to pick up the photos from the photo shop. On the way back, he was lost in admiration at the prints, but Kai Hang was indifferent, asking only why he didn't shoot in black and white.

"Wouldn't it be a waste of your beauty if they were in black and white?" Pak Wing responded. Kai Hang's heart sank. Noticing her expression, Pak Wing said, "Cinderella should leave behind her gray world of cinders!"

"What's wrong with Cinderella's world?" Kai Hang only managed to respond.

Although she'd only dated Pak Wing a couple of times, Kai Hang invited him to her small rented room because she didn't want to waste his time. When Pak Wing showed up, he was wearing a bright yellow shirt, but at least he didn't bring a bunch of red roses. On entering, he saw that the whole room was filled with gray: gray furniture, electrical appliances, wallpaper, rugs, curtains, teacups, and even books. Kai Hang was wearing a gray dress, gray lipstick, and gray nail polish. Even her eyes were dark gray against her dazzlingly white skin. She asked Pak Wing to take a seat. "I'm not actually a good match for you," she said.

Pak Wing didn't reply. He took out a box and gave it to Kai Hang. Inside was a checked gray scarf. Next to it were also the photos he'd taken, now printed in black and white, and inserted among them was a small card on which was written "For Cinderella." Speechless, Kai Hang lowered her head and stroked the scarf. After a long pause, she wrapped the scarf around her neck, and a gray smile spread across her face.

60

THE COCKROACH

Cockroach (*Kaat-tsaat* 甲由) was a comics magazine published from 1998 to 2000 by Craig Au-yeung and Li Chi Tak. Lai Tat Tat Wing is a Hong Kong artist known for his comics. Zuni Icosahedron is an experimental theater group. Edward Lam is a stage director.

It was the evening Ho Ka got to know Hou Chi that she first saw a cockroach at the window. It was late at night and Ho Ka couldn't fall asleep, so she pushed open the window to smoke a cigarette. After a while she noticed a cockroach crouching motionless alongside the flower rack outside the window, only its antennae moving slightly. Together, it and Ho Ka looked down at the city lights from the height of the twenty-fifth floor. Ho Ka stubbed out her cigarette and ran to the kitchen to fetch a broom. She picked it up, put it down again, and went back to the window. The telephone rang. It was Hou Chi, who asked if she had gone to sleep. "There's a cockroach," answered Ho Ka.

After Ho Ka had finished work that day, she had taken the MTR back home. Sitting across from her was a young intellectual who was reading a large-format magazine. On the cover was a giant fruit tart and the two characters for "cockroach" printed as big as a fist. When Ho Ka was about to get off, the young man also rose, tucked the large volume under his arm, and deliberately stepped out in front of her. They took the same route up to the ground level, the magazine flapping this way and that. As they reached the last escalator in the station, the young man suddenly turned around. "Why are you following me?" he asked. As soon as Ho Ka had collected her thoughts, she asked in turn, "That magazine of yours, what is it?"

"*Cockroach*," the young man said complacently.

Ho Ka thought of Hou Chi as a young intellectual because he stayed up late listening to English-language songs and liked reading Lai Tat Tat Wing's comics and watching productions by Zuni Icosahedron and Edward Lam, all the while grasping either a draft of his own novel or sketches for a comic strip. Every day he felt determined to be a local up-and-coming creative artist. Ho Ka used to detest young intellectuals, regarding them as odd monstrosities, young men who were finicky in their speech and most peculiar in their manners, but Hou Chi was a little different. "Maybe it's because of the cockroach," thought Ho Ka.

Ho Ka's original name had been Ho Ka Man. When Hou Chi asked her why she was called Ho Ka, she answered, "My little brother used to call me that."

Hou Chi wasn't living at a hall of residence at the university because his family home was nearby, and from then on he often went to Ho Ka's home. He listened to CDs on her hi-fi set, used her computer to get on the net, send emails, and do ICQ instant messaging, or else he rummaged through her belongings. Ho Ka surprisingly enough put up with him, cooked for him, and stocked her entire fridge with his favorite Coca-Cola. Sometimes when he was tired, Hou Chi slept in Ho Ka's bed next to her, but he didn't go any further than that. Whenever Ho Ka woke up at night and found Hou Chi at her side, she would get up and have a cigarette at the living-room window, and each time she saw the cockroach in the same spot, crouching there and looking at the world below. Eventually, Ho Ka would go to the window every evening to make sure that the cockroach was there, almost as if this was the only way she could relax. In the daytime, the spot was empty, but that made Ho Ka feel she couldn't get rid of it; sometimes she thought it was still there, but she also feared it might pop up somewhere else. In any case, Ho Ka never mentioned the cockroach to Hou Chi.

One day, Hou Chi was looking through Ho Ka's bedside cupboard while she was taking a shower when he dug up a battered old water pistol made of transparent green plastic. In great excitement, he threw open the bathroom door, went in, loaded the pistol with water, and started shooting in all directions. Ho Ka, who was dripping wet, wrapped herself in a towel, snatched the water pistol, and told him angrily, "That's all you're good for—shooting with a water pistol. You, you're useless!"

Hou Chi stood there looking foolish, but a thought formed in his mind, and he gingerly stepped forward, putting an arm around Ho Ka's bare shoulders. For a moment Ho Ka trembled, but she still stopped him. "Let me tell you something now. This water pistol was my little brother's toy when he was a child. In those days we were still living in an old-style housing estate, and what he liked most of all was to load his water pistol with dishwashing liquid and shoot at the cockroaches in our home so they couldn't move. Then he stepped on them, squashing them. Later he became an ordinary juvenile delinquent; he was picked on, someone stepped on his throat, and he died. Just like a cockroach, he was squashed."

When she had finished, the smile on Hou Chi's face had vanished; he let go of Ho Ka and departed abruptly, without uttering a sound. He left behind on the couch two issues of the large-format *Cockroach*.

Ho Ka felt utterly weary. She put on her pajamas, went to the window, and lit a cigarette. Looking down, she saw the cockroach arriving right on time. She picked up the water pistol, aimed at the cockroach, and, with a fizzing sound, shot it out into the air. It dropped into the dark night.

61

THE COWBOY HAT

The Chinese names for 7-Up and Coca-Cola each incorporate one of the two parts that make up the name Happy in Chinese; the name translated as Dummy represents a combination of another two characters from the names of the drinks.

Happy and Ah Pan hadn't exactly been childhood friends. Ah Pan was in fact seven years older than Happy, and when she was eleven, Ah Pan had already been hired to help in Happy's father's bicycle shop. By the time Happy was eighteen, Ah Pan was twenty-five. As long as Happy could remember, Ah Pan had always worn the cowboy hat. He pulled it down, his deep-set eyes staring out from under the brim, a cigarette hanging from the corner of his mouth, looking very much like Marlboro Man.

Happy's nickname was Ah Pan's idea because she loved drinking 7-Up mixed with Coca-Cola, and he often made fun of her for drinking sugar water. Whenever Ah Pan was in a bad mood, he would call her Dummy, which was sure to make her angry. To put an end to the matter, Ah Pan had to make up by pulling his cowboy hat over her head. This trick always worked. At other times, Ah Pan never allowed Happy to handle his hat, as it was like a protective talisman to him. When he was in a good mood, he would take Happy bike riding. He showed off his skill at speeding along the outer suburban roads, bringing an air pistol to shoot at stray cats and dogs along the way.

When cowboy hats later became fashionable, Happy bought herself a white one and braided her hair into two plaits, one on each side. As soon as Ah Pan caught sight of it, he roared with laughter, clutching his sides. Suddenly he snatched the hat with one hand and hurled it down the hill. It had only been his intention to give her a fright before going to pick it up right away; he never imagined that the hat would soar away like a flying saucer and end up getting stuck on top of a tall power pole. The next day Ah Pan raced down to the pole whenever he had some free time, waiting for a strong wind to blow the hat down, but day after day he waited in vain, until a full fortnight had passed, and Happy had also been annoyed for a full fortnight. When he came back on the fifteenth day, he told Happy, "Why don't I let you take care of my hat from now on!" With both hands he put his battered old cowboy hat on her head; only then was Happy willing to smile.

Happy wore Ah Pan's cowboy hat when she went out to see her friends, and everyone agreed it looked great. Ordinarily she never let go of the hat: she would turn it over to carry things in, or she would put it in front of her nose to get a whiff of hair that was years old. Ah Pan stuck to the deal sure enough, and as the days passed, there were only two occasions when he asked Happy for the hat back, and she understood why. Ah Pan was not much interested in girls and had never been seen dating anyone. Girls who pursued him were invariably rebuffed. Nonetheless, he was more than willing to step forward for girls who were being given a hard time and sought his help. The first time he faced down some young delinquents, wearing his cowboy hat, they thought it was a great joke, but in no time each one of them was kneeling on the ground, pleading for mercy. Some said Ah Pan had never lost a fight, and Happy for one believed that was true.

The second time Ah Pan asked Happy for his hat back, she was riding her bike home from school. He stopped her, took the hat without saying a word, and went off. Since he was otherwise so calm, Happy felt something was not quite right. She made phone calls to all of his friends and eventually found out that a girl called Horlicks was being held against her will. Happy was told where the girl was, took the air pistol, and ran off. At a tea café in the old market area, she found a noisy crowd of people. Ah Pan was standing blankly in the middle. The girl called Horlicks said in a snide voice, "So that's Ah Pan, sure enough. I told you he would come. And he's wearing his cowboy hat, too!"

As soon as Happy realized how things were, she pulled out the pistol and aimed it at the girl's face. Ah Pan turned around, stupefied, and walked away. Happy followed him as the others burst out laughing behind them.

Up on the hillside, Ah Pan took over the air pistol and shot all the pellets at the power pole down below. Not a single one hit the target, so he threw the gun toward the pole as well. He took off his hat and handed it to Happy. He was about to leave when she asked, "This time, were you really keen on that Horlicks girl?"

"The hat's yours," Ah Pan replied. "I won't need it again."

Looking after him as he walked off, Happy rubbed the cowboy hat against her face, and then, with a great effort, threw it away. It happened to land on top of the same pole as before. Sitting there slightly askew on the pole, it seemed as if it were listening attentively to Happy's voice as she howled, "Idiot! Idiot!"

62

CIGNAL YOUTHC

Do Not Advance, Signal Youth! was a Japanese reality television show in which participants were given challenges and placed in difficult situations. The Japanese actor Itō Takashi and the Hong Kong DJ Tse Chiu-yan were sent to hitchhike from the Cape of Good Hope to Nordkapp. The Chinese character for Yat 逸 in Ah Yat's name is made up of two elements, which on their own mean "run" and "rabbit."

On the day the Signal Youths Chiu-yan and Itō set out from the Cape of Good Hope, Ah Yat left home. On her way out, she gave Leung Kwok Kiu a phone call: "Wait for me till I get back, all right?"

Ah Yat was eighteen and had only finished secondary school at the time she got a job at a karaoke bar in Mong Kok. Leung Kwok Kiu had gone there with his friends for a few drinks and singing. He'd left his mobile phone behind when he walked out, and it was picked up by Ah Yat. The phone rang, and Leung Kwok Kiu asked who was at the other end.

"It's Run Bunny," Ah Yat said. Leung Kwok Kiu didn't understand.

"What? Can you give me my phone back?" Ah Yat arranged to meet him at four in the morning by the Star Ferry in Tsim Sha Tsui. To thank her, Leung Kwok Kiu invited her over to McDonald's for something to eat. However, she wanted to eat outside, so they sat down in the open air by the harborside promenade to bite into a couple of cheeseburgers.

Leung Kwok Kiu pointed toward Polytechnic University in the distance. "That's where I work," he said and sighed. "Sitting here like this, it feels as if I were ten years younger!"

Leung Kwok Kiu was thirty-two; he'd married at twenty-eight and was divorced at thirty. He'd been active in the student union, worked as an administrator in a private organization, and then returned to university to study for a doctorate in sociology and teach at the same time. After he'd gone out with Ah Yat a few times, he said, "Why don't you come and live with me. You make me feel young."

"I'm not ready for that yet," she replied. "I'm just an ignorant girl."

Leung Kwok Kiu was becoming desperate. "There's so much I could teach you."

"I'm a Run Bunny," she responded.

After that, Ah Yat disappeared. At first Leung Kwok Kiu had thought she was just joking, but later on, realizing she'd been serious, he became anxious. He searched for her in all sorts of places without success. A fortnight had passed when Ah Yat phoned. He begged her to come back.

"I want to go through the whole course," she said. "I may give you a call from time to time."

He asked how she spent her days.

"I stay at different places every day, seeing lots of people and all kinds of things," she said.

"Why do we have to go through all this?" Leung Kwok Kiu sighed. "If you're saying you want marriage, I'll agree to that too." Ah Yat was silent for a moment.

"I need some means of confirming that I love you," she said.

Summer came, and Leung Kwok Kiu still didn't know Ah Yat's whereabouts. Had she gone on a trip abroad, it would have been easier to understand, but Ah Yat quite clearly remained in town, although she kept far away from anyone she knew and had no fixed abode—but why was that? Every evening, he would hang around in bars, karaoke clubs, cinemas, amusement arcades, and even the red-light districts, all in the hope of running into Ah Yat, who was perhaps leading an irregular life. As a result, he came to feel listless during the daytime; his teaching became careless, and he neglected his research. Every time Ah Yat gave him a call, he would ask where she was staying and what kind of people she was with, but she wouldn't tell him. At times she sobbed quietly, and at other times it seemed he could hear a man calling her in the background. Her phone calls almost drove Leung Kwong Kiu crazy, but later there weren't even any calls.

When autumn came, Leung Kwok Kiu happened to get talking with a friend in a bar about Ah Yat. The friend somewhat reluctantly told him that one evening he'd been in Yau Ma Tei and seen a girl resembling Ah Yat with her arm around the waist of a fair-haired man.

Leung Kwok Kiu was not surprised. "Then it's all been a fake ordeal! She's simply going to bed with a new man every night!"

Leung Kwok Kiu was spending November 14 out of sight in the library, working on his thesis, when Ah Yat suddenly called his mobile.

"It's Run Bunny," she said. "Can we meet tonight at the Star Ferry in Tsim Sha Tsui?"

Leung Kwok Kiu, however, gave her a cold reply. "Maybe not. I'm busy."

"Didn't you say you'd wait for me?" Ah Yat said.

Leung remained silent, so Ah Yat hung up. Confused and upset, Leung Kwok Kiu went wandering blindly through the busy shopping area. Passing an electrical-goods shop, he noticed a television program showing the final leg of the journey of the Signal Youths. After traveling for 290 days, Chiu-yan and Itō were at last reaching their goal in Norway. Leung Kwok Kiu cursed the stupidity of the program and walked off, not noticing that watching the program in the surrounding crowd was Ah Yat, shedding tears as she stared at the screen.

Less than six months later, Leung Kwok Kiu got his degree and was promoted to professor. At the same time, he was busy preparing for his wedding, his bride a student he'd previously supervised. No one knew whether or not Ah Yat had come back home.

63

H2O+

H2O+ Beauty was set up in 1989. Its founder claimed hydration to be the source of beautiful skin.

When Ah Pooi met Fai Yung again at the swimming pool, it was as if he'd returned to his secondary-school days. In front of his eyes was the Fai Yung, who seemed to belong to sunshine and water.

"It's been seven years. How did you recognize me?" Fai Yung asked.

"It's your swimming style, it had to be the Lam Fai Yung who was brought up in water," Ah Pooi said.

"You still remember that thing about being brought up in water?" Fai Yung said, surprised.

"You said you'd been a fish in a previous life," Ah Pooi replied.

Squinting in the sunshine, Fai Yung laughed, the water drops on her bronzed skin glistening. "That's not how it is now," she said. "I've become an aquatic plant." She immediately dived in and swam away.

Fai Yung went swimming throughout the winter. Sunshine was particularly abundant and temperatures particularly high that year, so that people had a feeling of well-being. However, Fai Yung had actually been jobless since autumn, and this happened to coincide with Ah Pooi devoting all his efforts to completing his doctoral thesis, only taking a break to swim when he felt bored. The two of them often ran into each other at the pool but didn't often talk, only passing each other again and again as they did their twenty or thirty laps. Out of the water, they lay side by side in the sun, watching the clouds; from a distance they looked like a loving couple. Later on, Fai Yung invited Ah Pooi to her home. It was a tiny flat with simple furnishings, the most eye-catching being a pot with dark-green ivy hanging in front of the window. As soon as they were inside, Fai Yung went over to water it and then turned around. "Why haven't you asked me what I've been doing these past years?" she said.

Since childhood, Fai Yung had been very good at swimming and had won quite a few prizes in interschool championships. If it hadn't been for opposition from her parents, she would soon have joined teams for international competitions. Fai Yung didn't seem to mind, and, with good school results, she easily passed the university entrance exam. Although her interest was in literature, she chose to do business administration. After graduation, she got a job at a snack-foods distributor, but her section was disbanded two years later and she lost her job. Seeing her so indifferent, Ah Pooi didn't give it much thought. "But you don't seem to have any worries in your life," he just said.

One evening later on, when Ah Pooi was going to City Hall in Central for the film festival, he ran into Fai Yung in the street. She wore a tight black dress and pale makeup, looking rather frail as she clung to the arm of a middle-aged man in a suit, seeming a different person compared to her usual self. She didn't say hello to Ah Pooi when she saw him. At the swimming pool the following day, he asked her about it.

Her hands gripped the side of the pool as she answered. "I'm a plant, living by photosynthesis in the daytime, absorbing light and carbon dioxide and emitting oxygen. At night, it's the opposite, absorbing oxygen and emitting carbon dioxide." Having said that, she let go and plunged into the water, and it was a long while before she resurfaced. When he was about to leave the

H_2O+

pool, Ah Pooi saw Fai Yung apply something green like seawater from a bottle, so he asked what it was. She stretched out her fingers and rubbed some on his face. It was strangely ice-cold.

"It's H2O+," she said.

Ah Pooi didn't understand. "Is it water?"

Ah Pooi hadn't bothered much about the way things were with Fai Yung, although once he happened to recall how he'd pursued her at school and been rebuffed, and he couldn't help laughing. He hadn't expected, however, that Fai Yung would suddenly give him a phone call one evening and come out with something odd: "Once I leave water, I'll die."

Ah Pooi had an ominous premonition and immediately rushed to Fai Yung's home. It turned out the door wasn't locked, so he entered. As soon as he turned on the light, he saw that the ivy in the pot had withered for lack of water. Startled, he burst into the bedroom and found Fai Yung lying very straight on the bed. Her face was covered with a layer of something light green, and a bottle of H2O+ marine-mineral hydrating face mask had dropped to her side. When he stretched out his hand and there seemed to be no breath coming from her nose, he was so panicked he shook her forcefully.

Fai Yung slowly began to wake up. "I died just now, Ah Pooi!" she said, breathing faintly.

Ah Pooi shook his head. "How could that be? You're all right."

"No, it's true!" she insisted. "I've split up with that man, the one you saw that time. Ever since I was little, people've thought I was particularly gifted, that I could have anything I wanted. Actually all I wanted was to get back in the water."

Ah Pooi didn't quite understand. "Which Fai Yung are you then?" he asked.

She gently pulled off the mask, revealing her familiar face, tanned the color of honey by the sun.

64

DEPSEA WATER

Dipsi had been feeling dehydrated ever since she first went to bed with Dr. Lam Singseon. It wasn't so much that she felt thirsty, it was more that her skin was dry and chapped. No matter how much water she drank, she felt like a zombie when she woke up in the morning. When she told Dr. Lam about it, he gave her an examination. He took her clothes off and patted her body, finding no problem: her skin was smooth and her flesh tender.

"My report is that it's quite the opposite," he said. Under the impression Dipsi was teasing him, he began to make love to her.

Dipsi had been working in insurance after she'd graduated, specializing in health-care planning, and had come into contact with Dr. Lam through her job. Lam Singseon was nothing like the stereotypical image of an unimaginative doctor. He was thirty-three years old, he wore his hair rather long, and he was charming and witty. He never missed any of the musicals performed by overseas troupes or the high-priced programs at the annual arts festival. His favorite novel was Milan Kundera's *The Unbearable Lightness of Being*, he listened to Kenny G, and he claimed that TVB's *Healing Hands* liberated the public image of doctors. Dipsi, however, thought he was a bit like an alchemist who could transform muck into miracles.

Dipsi did have a boyfriend, someone she'd been dating for three years. Their relationship was as solid as an iceberg in winter, and they'd planned to get married two years after graduation. However, snow melts with the onset of spring, and Dipsi broke up with him after she began her relationship with Dr. Lam. Dipsi was well aware that Dr. Lam had got a divorce two years earlier and claimed that he no longer believed in love. He also had more than two or three other lovers. Nevertheless, Dipsi moved out to be on her own in order to make it more convenient to meet Dr. Lam.

Dipsi had tried several skincare products. Applying heavy layers of H2O+ Face Oasis, which contained a marine-minerals compound, turned out to be useless. It reminded her of a novel she'd read called *The Woman in the Dunes*. Then, happening to pass a Shu Uemura store, she discovered Depsea Water, reportedly made with deep-sea water and a selection of fragrant oils. Dipsi tried the spray with the rose fragrance in a transparent pink plastic bottle. To her surprise, it felt like rain after a long drought, so she bought a bottle of each scent at one go. After she got home, she placed them in a row on the windowsill. The red, orange, yellow, green, blue, indigo, and violet bottles were like a rainbow light tube.

Dipsi had been dependent on Depsea Water ever since, spraying it on day and night, even carrying a spare in her handbag as if she were addicted to it. At first, she only sprayed it over her head, face, hands, and feet, but before long she took to spraying it over her whole body after her bath. Sometimes, when she was away from home and hadn't been able to apply moisturizer for a while, she felt as if her skin would crumble at a touch, like a dry leaf. Walking was a heart-stopping experience, for she was afraid that she might be pushed and crushed to death. She had to spray herself all over with jasmine deep-sea water before making love to Dr. Lam, which he mistakenly regarded as a kind of erotic play. Once, after they'd finished, he poured some of it out to satisfy his curiosity but concluded, "It's just cold water."

On one occasion, giving way to a sudden romantic impulse, Dr. Lam drove Dipsi to Repulse Bay at midnight. They strolled along the beach, their footsteps treading lightly on the fine sand. He told her several stories about going out diving at sea with friends.

"What does it look like under the sea?" Dipsi asked.

"The seabed in shallow water is fantastic," Lam Singseon said carelessly. "Lots of brightly colored corals and tropical fish. But the deeper you go, the darker, more dangerous, and more fearsome it gets. It's pitch-dark thousands of meters under the sea, and the fish that live there don't have eyes. They're grotesque, monsters!"

Dipsi suddenly squatted down on the beach as if she'd suffered a blow.

For some time afterward, Dr. Lam stopped seeing Dipsi. She knew that he was entangled with another woman, and it felt as if there were an open wound to her body, although no blood flowed from it. Suddenly one evening, Dr. Lam fumbled his way to Dipsi's home. He was the worse for drink (this was very unusual for him), and, to her consternation, he called out the other woman's name. Dipsi picked up a green bottle of mint deep-sea water and sprayed him ferociously. He sobered up on the spot and sat down on the floor looking baffled.

"You can get lost," Dipsi said, "it's over between us!" Shutting the door behind her, Dipsi rushed into her bedroom and tore off her clothes. One by one she grabbed the bottles of Depsea Water on the windowsill, screwed the lids off, and poured them over her head until her whole body and her bed were drenched. When she woke up the next morning, the Depsea Water had evaporated, leaving the room full of a pungent, complex smell. The multicolored empty bottles on the windowsill shifted to and fro in the morning breeze. Dipsi sneezed, releasing a flow of nasal fluid down her face.

65

THE PATAGONIA FLEECE

Sorimachi Takashi is an actor and singer who played the leading role in the popular Japanese television series *Great
Teacher Onizuka* from 1998. The Moomins are characters
from the children's books by Tove Jansson. A Japanese animated television series based on the Moomins was made in
the early 1990s. Kaneshiro Takeshi is a Taiwanese Japanese
actor and singer.

The first time Kit San saw Pok Yan was in the general-education
class on Greek mythology. As was his habit, he took a seat in the
last row, and it was only when the lecture commenced that he
noticed from behind a student with short hair sitting in the center of the first row, wearing a golden-yellow fleece jacket. Since
no one else was in the first two rows, this student was particularly conspicuous. At first, Kit San assumed it was a rather small,
skinny male, but he realized it was a girl when he saw her go up
to talk to the professor after class.

At subsequent lectures, Kit San moved forward one row at a
time, until finally, coming late for a class once, he casually sat
down in the front row, beside Pok Yan. That counted as being
acquainted, and when they sometimes came across each other
in the canteen, they would nod and say hello. To start with, they
sat quite far from each other, then came a bit closer, and eventually they were at the same table.

"It's pretty crowded," Kit San said. "Really difficult to find somewhere to sit."

Pok Yan just said "um," and it wasn't clear if she was smiling. That counted as officially having struck up a conversation.

Every time Kit San saw Pok Yan, she was dressed in her yellow quarter-zip hooded fleece jacket, matched with blue jeans and sneakers. When the weather turned cold, she wore more clothes underneath, a turtleneck or woolen jumper. It wasn't just that she had a man's haircut, she also had thick eyebrows and a high-bridged nose, a face somewhere between round and square, pale where it should be flushed and flushed where it should be pale, and an air of strength and confidence; she was rather like a scholar from a Cantonese opera dressed up in sportswear. She came and went by herself and would read classical literature sitting alone by the pond, giving an impression of much dissatisfaction with the world's mores. Sorimachi Takashi and the Moomins were names she'd never heard of, and if she were asked what she liked to do, she said reading, hiking up in the hills, and bike riding. Normally she didn't take the campus buses but walked up and down the hill. Once, when he'd missed the bus at the foot of the hill, Kit San was grumbling, but Pok Yan, who was already walking up, turned around and called out: "Why don't you get going, your feet aren't stuck in the mud, are they?"

Eventually Kit San went to buy himself a fleece jacket, but not being able to afford an L.L.Bean, he got a Patagonia one in aquamarine. When he put it on, he really felt especially warm. He also purchased a couple of books of Tang and Song poetry and spent the night copying romantic phrases from them, which resulted in a stylish little booklet. When he invited Pok Yan out for a meal, however, the conversation was all about coursework, and she didn't mention anything private. When she saw male and female students hugging one another affectionately or pretty girls in gorgeous outfits, her face would take on an expression of disgust. Squeezing the bag containing the booklet of love poetry between his fingers, Kit San never dared to bring it out and give to her. He then took to wearing his aquamarine fleece every day and going on foot, not catching the school bus even when it would have been easy to do so, without actually being conscious why he was doing this.

When Valentine's Day was approaching, Kit San's mind was at sixes and sevens, but in the end he went and bought flowers, choosing gerberas, which he thought were quite bright and cheerful. He also wrapped the poetry booklet in elegant gift paper. On the day, the weather had turned mild, and his back was sweaty by the time he'd walked to Pok Yan's hostel. Although her room was unlocked, neither Pok Yan nor her roommate, Siu Kei, were there. Pok Yan's bedsheets were plain green, while Siu Kei had sheets decorated with My Melody and a poster of Kaneshiro Takeshi on the wall. Since he was really too hot, Kit San took off his Patagonia jacket and hung it over the back of a chair. Standing in front of the window and looking out, he saw Pok Yan sitting on the lawn reading. She was wearing just a white short-sleeved T-shirt, both arms bare to the sun. Turning around, he saw her yellow fleece hanging outside a clothes cupboard; the brand was Giordano, hanging above his own aquamarine Patagonia. He stroked the soft yellow garment and then tried it on. It was very tight. He looked at himself in the mirror for a moment and saw a determined face, short hair, and a golden-yellow glow.

When Kit San left, the two fleece jackets were laid out side by side on Pok Yan's bed, while the bunch of flowers and the booklet had been left on Siu Kei's desk. Afterward, Siu Kei could often be seen on the campus bus snuggling up to Kit San. As before, Pok Yan wore her golden-yellow fleece, cradling her books as she walked uphill.

66
—

THE DUFFEL COAT

That day, as Cheung Sheung Cheuk walked along the secluded path in the small park, an empty red duffel coat swayed in front of his face. Recovering, he realized that it was Yau Ying, her skinny arms and legs propping up the heavy coat. In the dim glow of the streetlights, he could see her coat but not her. He couldn't tell if she just happened to be passing through or if she had been waiting. He watched her open her mouth to speak. "Are you on your own, sir?"

Cheung Sheung Cheuk was in the habit of staying at school until late after class, giving supplementary lessons, organizing extracurricular activities, or marking students' work. Afterward, he was sure to cut through the small park for a meal in the old quarter, and on his way he might well run into a student living nearby, but Yau Ying had left school last year and hadn't come back, so this sudden encounter startled him a little. However, he didn't refuse to go with her to a tea café. As they sat there, he didn't think she had changed much, except that she'd dyed the left side of her hair red. In the past, when she'd had emotional problems, Yau Ying had preferred to go to Cheung Sheung Cheuk rather than the school counselor. He thought it was because he never preached and instead acted like a friend, but Yau Ying said it was because of his gray hair. In fact, he was only thirty-five, and he had no idea what white hairs had to do with trust. Later, Yau Ying formed a relationship with a boy from a neighboring school. Her parents insisted it was rape and complained to the school. Cheung Sheung Cheuk was blamed, since he'd known about Yau Ying's circumstances for some time, and as a result he never talked to his students about their relationships again. Yau Ying left the school without having graduated.

Yau Ying didn't order anything to eat at the café but had some iced lemon tea. Early winter had started off cold but had then become milder, so it was just like early summer, yet Yau Ying was wearing this heavy duffel coat that she wouldn't take off even indoors.

"Aren't you hot?" asked Cheung Sheung Cheuk.

"I'm not wearing anything underneath," she replied. "Don't you believe me?" she smiled mysteriously.

Cheung Sheung Cheuk felt that Yau Ying's return was for the purpose of revenge.

From then on, Yau Ying would wait for him every day at dusk on the path. He didn't avoid her, and they would have a meal together. She always wore her bright-red duffel coat. It was long enough to reach her knees and was buttoned up from top to bottom; only her pointed face, pale fingers, and calves were not covered. Cheung Sheung Cheuk's eyes rested from time to time on the row of horn-shaped wooden toggles, and it occurred to him that these loose connections could break away at any time.

Yau Ying noticed his gaze. "I was stabbed a dozen times, from my chest to my lower belly," she said. "Do you want to take a look?"

At that point he finally remembered to ask, "How have you been living these days?"

"Like this." Yau Ying pretended to unbutton her coat.

"Why are you doing this?" he asked.

Yau Ying suddenly began to laugh. "It isn't about lust."

It was unusually muggy after they'd eaten. Cheung Sheung Cheuk rolled up his sleeves; the sides of Yau Ying's face were wet with perspiration, and a few strands of fine baby hair were sticking to her forehead. Strolling along, they happened on the path across the secluded small park. Yau Ying suddenly moved in front of Cheung Sheung Cheuk to block his way. "All right then," she said, "don't you believe me?"

"Why are you doing this?" he asked again.

"Because I don't have any money, it's all been stolen," she replied. "I had nothing when I escaped. Don't you believe me?" She looked around to make sure there was no one else there. "Give me some money," she said, "and I'll let you have a look." She put her hands on the buttons. Cheung Sheung Cheuk took out his wallet, stuffed three thousand dollars into the coat's big pocket, turned around, and walked off.

"Why are you always by yourself, Cheung Sheung Cheuk?" Yau Ying shouted behind him.

He didn't answer her and walked on. Then, not hearing any sound, he looked back, but Yau Ying was nowhere in sight. He looked up and saw a red shape hanging on a tree up the hill, swaying to and fro. He climbed up to grab it, only to find it was an empty duffel coat, heavy with three thousand dollars in its pocket.

67

LV VERNIS

LV Vernis is a calf-skin leather bag embossed with the Louis Vuitton monogram; it is glossy and comes in many colors. Kimura Takuya is a Japanese singer and actor. Fujiwara Norika is a Japanese model and actress and a former Miss Nippon. Lan Kwai Fong is a bar, restaurant, and entertainment area next to the central business district on Hong Kong Island.

"I like your plain, modest look," Lo Fai had said to Ling Mei on her first day at university. Other people, however, certainly didn't share that opinion. Although Ling Mei dressed simply in jeans and T-shirts, she invariably chose what suited her from what was currently in fashion, giving people the impression that she followed the trends. She was also very pretty, with a pale complexion and crimson lips; ever since secondary school, this had made the other pupils think she was wearing makeup, and she'd been admonished for it by the teachers a good many times, but she never defended herself in spite of not being guilty. Her fellow students at university also got the impression that Ling Mei was a girl who paid a lot of attention to her appearance.

Ling Mei felt Lo Fai understood her. They soon came to be seen as the most glamorous couple among the first-year students. That led to people believing that Ling Mei enjoyed showing off how attractive she was, and although she was subsequently labeled the department's beauty queen, it came with a certain hint of derision. Actually, Lo Fai was inordinately concerned with his own look: Japanese fashion magazines were his daily required reading, and he let his hair grow long à la Kimura Takuya. However, in the Arts Faculty, which was rather conservative in taste, everyone said Lo Fai had a style of his own.

"I like your naïve pose," Ling Mei said.

Some time later, Lo Fai threw himself into the arms of BMW from the Japanese Department. It seemed only right and proper. The girl was dressed in famous brands from top to toe and drove a BMW to school. Her father was said to have made a small fortune from a factory on the mainland making cheap handbags. One day outside the canteen, Ling Mei realized how things stood when she saw Lo Fai getting into the BMW and speeding off. Lo Fai formally proposed that they should break up while they were standing next to the swimming pool, with BMW waiting at the side. In her heart, Ling Mei couldn't blame him, as she calmly gazed at the somewhat banal Louis Vuitton Monogram leather bag hanging from BMW's shoulder.

When Ling Mei later saw a picture in a weekly of Fujiwara Norika carrying the new LV Vernis Bleecker vanity case in powder blue, she came to a decision. Among her fellow students a rumor began circulating that Ling Mei was preoccupied with money and was skipping classes every day to give lessons at cram schools. Some said they had seen her at a cosmetics shop working part-time during the day; others said she earned money helping classmates with their assignments; yet others said she'd even sold off her treasured Hello Kitty and My Melody "antiques"; and some went so far as to say that she played around with wealthy middle-aged men at night in Lan Kwai Fong. As was her wont, Ling Mei said nothing. The two or three T-shirts and jeans she wore were getting quite old, and for lunch she always had the cheapest food—or else didn't eat anything but just drank a lot of water—and she'd become quite frail.

One day, Ling Mei had put on her usual turtleneck jumper and jeans, but she was carrying a ten-thousand-dollar LV Vernis vanity case. Walking right up to Lo Fai and BMW, she opened her little powder-blue square case and took out a small pair of scissors. BMW was so frightened she dropped her entire Vivienne Westwood woven bag. Lo Fai, also dumbstruck, allowed Ling Mei to grab the long hair behind his neck, and with a whoosh she cut it off. She put the hunk of chopped hair into her case, turned around, and left. Covering the back of his head with his hands, Lo Fai cried out in distress, under the impression he'd been stabbed.

Back at her hostel, Ling Mei placed her powder-blue vanity case in the sunshine in front of the window, without opening it to look inside. The golden lock gleamed in the sunlight. Lo Fai arrived some time later, announcing he was going to break up with BMW.

"That was not my intention," Ling Mei said.

"Then why did you cut off my hair?" Lo Fai asked.

Ling Mei stretched out a hand, stroking his newly shorn hair. "I'll treasure those words," she said.

"What words?" he asked.

"Promise me something, will you: under no circumstances must you open this case," she just said.

He still didn't understand.

"Haven't you heard of Pandora's box then?" Ling Mei asked. She smiled tiredly for a moment and then lay down on her bed. Lo Fai sat beside the bed, and when he saw Ling Mei was sound asleep, he stole over and picked up the incomparably exquisite powder-blue case. Gently he flicked the metal latch open. Inside was a tuft of silver-white hair.

68

—

PANASONIC DVD

Panasonic introduced the first portable DVD players in 1998.
The DVD-L10 had a five-inch color LCD screen and stereo
speakers. They were very expensive when first released. EQ
stands for "emotional quotient" (or "emotional intelligence").
Young and Dangerous was a popular film about young triads,
with several sequels.

QQ Yan and Ching B had got to know each other at Mei Wa's
youth center. Mei Wa had originally thought Ching B might make
QQ Yan more outgoing; she certainly hadn't expected that QQ
Yan would make Ching B increasingly introverted.

QQ Yan had already become known as the film girl at the center, where she spent her time from morning to evening nestled
in the cinema, never seeing the light of day. After getting to know
Ching B, she switched to watching a portable DVD player all day
long. It was a Panasonic DVD-L10, which cost as much as seven
thousand dollars and was a present from Ching B, who had one
himself. Ching B's family counted as relatively well off, with no
worries about food and clothing, but his parents paid little attention to him. QQ Yan's home was poor, with a single parent, and
early on there had been nobody to look after her. Ever since they
had both got their DVD players, no one ever saw them doing anything other than watching DVDs. Whenever they came to the
center, they would just sit down side by side in a corner, pull up

the little 5.6-inch screens in their silvery metal cases, put in the earphones, and immerse themselves in their respective cinematic worlds, paying no attention to the people next to them making a racket playing board games. When they had finished watching, they closed their players, clasped them in their arms, and walked out together.

Mei Wa knew that QQ Yan and Ching B were in love and blamed herself a little for having encouraged them, worrying that their peculiar behavior would hamper genuine communication. When she asked them to take part in her study group on the EQ of love, QQ Yan asked, "What cue did you say? What's the cue good for!" Mei Wa was a bit annoyed but let it pass. When the meeting of the group was over, she vented her frustration to her boyfriend, Sai Wa. She said young people of today were more and more lacking in go-ahead spirit. They didn't understand how meaningful it was to experience hardship first and sweetness later; what they were after was no more than instant gratification. Sai Wa was used to listening to such words pouring out from her heart, so he just kept nodding yes.

As for QQ Yan and Ching B watching films on DVD, what it really meant was just looking at those incomparably clear lights, shadows, and colors on their screens. It didn't matter what kind of film it was: Western films, Hong Kong films, kung fu, crude and dirty films—it was all the same. They had seen nearly everything there was to see and had even watched some films five or six times. Mei Wa found it completely incomprehensible. When she asked if they thought *Titanic* was a great film or if they found *Young and Dangerous* vulgar, they didn't understand but just sat there as if they were on drugs.

QQ Yan and Ching B were not the same as other troubled teens. They didn't study, didn't work, didn't do anything that was proper, but didn't do anything bad either. It was just that they spent all day immersed in the imaginary world of the DVDs and were seriously out of touch with the real world. Mei Wa therefore dragged them off to take part in the center's barbecue outing. However, while the other boys and girls gathered around the barbecue, everyone totally relaxed and laughing, QQ Yan and Ching B withdrew under the shade of a tree and watched DVDs. Mei Wa couldn't stand it and was about to walk up to them and tell them how to behave, when she saw that QQ Yan was stamping her feet angrily. It was because her player's battery had run down when she'd only seen half her film. After she'd kicked up a fuss, Ching B lent her his own player, and her anger turned into smiles. Mei Wa stood there and sighed deeply.

After work at the center, Mei Wa also studied in the evenings. Administration and management psychology took up every spare moment of the week, and at times even Sai Wa found it difficult to see her. She thought it was fortunate that Sai Wa was busy too. He was working for an information-technology company and had just got on the right track, so she felt they ought to be patient for the time being to lay a good foundation for their future life. Sometimes when Sai Wa had a day off, he used it as an excuse to stay at home watching DVDs and didn't want to go out. Mei Wa made allowances for that. So when Sai Wa later said they had never really understood each other and that it was best to split up, Mei Wa's brain was like a DVD player that had suddenly run out of power and had no picture on its screen.

Mei Wa, unable to go to work, asked for a full month's leave. On the day she returned to the center, as soon as she stepped inside, she spotted QQ Yan and Ching B sitting together in exactly the same position as they contentedly watched their DVDs. Their faces shone with utter happiness.

69

SOUTH PARK

The TV show *South Park* was shown in Hong Kong under the same name, but it was also known in a translated version as *BadBoys FunPark*, the term adopted in this story. The names of at least two of the boys have connections with the TV series. Carboy corresponds to Cartman, and Ah Kot is Kenny; Ah Tan and Ah Kei may be Stan and Kyle. Kenny always wears an orange parka with a big hood that covers much of his face. In the first few seasons, Kenny was killed in one way or another in each episode but was mysteriously resurrected for the next episode without any explanation; Ah Kot is hacked to death by a triad gang for no good reason but then reappears.

Young Southie and the boys around her called it South Park because it was located on South Road in the public-housing estate where they lived, so that later Southie came to feel that the park was part of her own world. In reality, it was on the north side of the estate rather than the south.

Southie had lived here since she was little, when her mom used to scare her with stories that the park was a place where druggies and kidnappers hung out. Southie wasn't usually allowed out in the streets, and her mom would lock Southie and her brother in their small unit whenever she went out. Southie was fifteen years old the first time she went to South Park. That evening, her parents, as usual, had been quarreling.

Southie ran outside without making a sound and wandered about aimlessly until she happened to come to the park. Four youths whistled at her from behind the railings, but instead of quickly walking away with her head down, as was her custom, she came to a halt, looked around, and then walked through the park gate.

Southie seemed to undergo a total transformation after she began to fool around with Ah Kei, Carboy, Ah Tan, and Ah Kot. She began wearing trendy clothes and dyed her hair blond, while her school marks fell dramatically. The neighbors claimed these wayward boys had a bad influence on her. But the fact was they only started to run wild after Southie appeared, staking out the park near the housing estate as their territory so that even the druggies who used to live there moved out to avoid trouble. Since then the park had become Southie's home. One night, her father, armed with a kitchen knife, confronted the four delinquents in the park; afterward, he announced that he no longer regarded Southie as his daughter.

Southie and the wayward boys spent every night in the park under the stars and moon, the ground as their bed and the sky their blanket. When other people invaded the park, they drove them off with sticks and cudgels. Occasionally they recruited a few hangers-on, but Southie remained the only girl among them. Should the real triad gangs come by, they would slink away and disappear. During the daytime, they slept at Carboy's place, which was uninhabited. With no school and no work to pass the time, they occupied themselves with petty thievery and fraud. Later, when Southie became pregnant, she had no idea which of them was the baby's father. Ah Kei advised her to get rid of it, but Ah Tan called him an idiot; Carboy gave a light laugh as if it wasn't any of his business, and Ah Kot wouldn't say a word. Southie lay down on a park bench and gazed at the vast autumnal night sky. It seemed to her the world was big enough to embrace a child. Stroking her belly, she put an end to her thoughts.

Some time later, while Ah Kot was waiting for his friends in the park, he ran into some angry triad gangsters, who hacked him to death for no good reason. At first Ah Tan called for Ah Kot to be avenged, but afterward nothing happened, and it seemed as if no such person as Ah Kot had ever existed. One night, when they were lounging about in the park as they always did, Ah Kot walked over from the basketball court, his body upright and wearing his usual orange hooded parka. He sat down next to Southie. Everyone kept on idly chatting as if nothing had happened.

"The baby in your belly, it's mine, isn't it?" Ah Kot suddenly asked Southie.

Ah Kei stood up. "Get lost! What have you come back for?" he yelled. Ah Tan stepped forward and pulled at Ah Kot's collar so that the hood slipped down, exposing his bleeding neck. Carboy jumped up, thrust his hands into his trouser pockets, and walked toward the park entrance, humming a song.

The park was sealed off the next day, and it was said that it was being closed down and redeveloped for new public housing. The three boys didn't show up, and only Southie stood outside the park railings until late at night. For the first time, she realized how small the park was, and when she lifted her head to look around, she could see a bead of light from her home. When she returned home, her brother was sitting by himself watching an animated TV series and didn't bother to say hello. She watched the kids in the show quarreling with each other, using crude language, and their faces showing no emotion. Disgusted, she asked what he was watching.

"*BadBoys FunPark*," he answered.

She was watching the scene where Kenny, muffled in his orange parka, was trampled by a herd of cattle and died as his head was kicked off, when suddenly she felt a pain in her belly, and that night she miscarried.

70
—

DREAMCAST

The Dreamcast was a video-game console developed by Sega
and released in the late 1990s.

The first time Sai Ka walked into Pear Dream's game shop, he
saw the girl inside peeling a snow pear, the peel spiraling all the
way down to the floor so that it looked like the Dreamcast trademark. Sai Ka asked if she had Sega's newly released Dreamcast.
Slowly and deliberately, she took a bite of the glistening flesh, her
cheeks bulging, and shook her head. About to leave to make
enquiries elsewhere, Sai Ka caught sight of a brand-new, white
Dreamcast behind the counter. The *Godzilla Generations* game
that came with the console was playing on a television screen.
  "You've got one there, haven't you?" he said.
  The girl swallowed the bits of pear in her mouth. "That one's
not for sale. It's personal property."
  Sai Ka kept pestering her, so the girl pointed to the screen.
"I'll give it to you if you can beat me." Pear juice was dribbling
down to her elbows, her face and nose were round and smooth
like pears, and her skin a translucent white, so Sai Ka called her
Pear Dream.
  Sai Ka was beaten soundly at *Godzilla*. Pear Dream spurred
on the monsters to sweep across the metropolis, completely
destroying the structures of civilization with frightening speed—
all over in less than the blink of an eye. On his way home, Sai Ka

called on his old friend Ah Ko to borrow his Dreamcast for practice. He went into hard training for five consecutive evenings,
until he became delusional, and out in the streets he imagined
himself razing tall buildings to the ground. Returning to Pear
Dream's shop, he sat down to do battle. Two giant monsters
repeatedly flung themselves at each other, Sai Ka winning narrowly in the end.

"That's not good enough," Pear Dream said. "We'll have a
game of *Virtual Fighter* too, and it only counts if you win that."

Sai Ka thought he was on a roll but hadn't expected that he
would be utterly defeated after three rounds. Pear Dream smiled
for the first time. "Look at you: you've got a pretty murderous
gleam in your eye!"

Sai Ka then practiced for a whole three weeks, and it was
only when it became clear that even Ah Ko wasn't his match
that he looked up Pear Dream again. Although it was winter, the
weather was so warm that people were sweating. Pear Dream
was wearing a pale-green sleeveless turtleneck sweater, her
slender figure looking incredibly like the female animated characters in the games. Sai Ka threw himself into the game, each
move ferocious, while Pear Dream showed no change in her
demeanor: she was completely still except for her moving fingers and flashing eyes. To start with, Sai Ka was close behind
her, but then Pear Dream stretched her lead slightly and followed up by beating Sai Ka.

She rose to smoke a cigarette. Neither annoyed nor smiling,
she handed a CD to Sai Ka. "Let's have one more contest. If you
win this, it's yours."

Sai Ka went home but put *Sonic Adventure* aside and didn't
bother to practice. It was less than a full week before he went to
see Pear Dream again. He had begun to feel that practicing hard
had nothing to do with winning or losing. This time Pear Dream
was eating green grapes and invited him to sit down and help
himself.

Feeling a bit tense, Sai Ka asked, "If you let me take the Dreamcast, won't that mean you won't have one yourself?"

Pear Dream shrugged. "What does it matter? Sooner or later everything goes out of date."

In silence, they carried on eating grapes, taking it particularly slowly. All the time Sai Ka was thinking of saying, "Actually it doesn't matter to me at all," but every time he'd eaten a grape, he waited to say it until he'd had another, and in the end he didn't say anything at all. They played *Sonic Adventure* for a long, long time, neither of them wishing either to win or to lose. As Sai Ka eventually found it impossible to contain himself; the supersonic hedgehog sped across the fantastic landscape of the city, much as in the demo of the game. Out of control, he passed through the train station, the square, the shopping streets, the casino, the amusement park, and the highways, until he charged right through to the magnificent fastness of the magic world, the Land of Phantasmagoria.

When Sai Ka was taking away the Dreamcast, Pear Dream asked, "So will you be coming back again?"

Sai Ka thought for a moment. "There will always be a new game or console coming out, won't there?" he asked.

Back home, he got talking to Ah Ko, who said, "There's no such thing as a Land of Phantasmagoria in *Sonic Adventure*." That seemed very strange to Sai Ka, so he went back to ask Pear Dream, but her shop was nowhere to be seen. In its place stood a fashion store called Land of Phantasmagoria. Its shop window displayed clothes by Agnès b., Hysteric Glamour, and Miu Miu, lace-up shoes, leopard-spot waist bags, gray woolen skirts, checked pleated skirts, and long twill skirts with camouflage patterns . . .

71
_

TUMB RAIDER III

Tomb Raider III: Adventures of Lara Croft is a video game released in 1998 for PlayStation and Microsoft Windows. Lara Croft hunts for four stones carved from a meteorite that fell to earth in Antarctica millions of years ago. These artifacts are hidden in different locations: India, London, Nevada, and the South Pacific. The Peak on Hong Kong Island is a popular tourist spot.

Because Andrew seemed so weak that he might be blown away by a gust of wind, his colleagues dragged him off to a fitness center after work. Faced with a great heap of exercise equipment, he had no idea where to start, so he asked for a personal trainer. It turned out to be a woman, who demonstrated a few exercises for him in an offhand way. Rather incautiously, Andrew did a few clean-and-jerk movements and then collapsed, his face scarlet.

"You really look like Lara Croft, you know, the character in *Tomb Raider*," he said, panting.

The men at the fitness center called her Lala. Some said it was because they looked down on female personal trainers, who they thought were fit to teach girls aerobics at most, and so they gave her a nickname that sounded like the Chinese word for cheerleader. In fact, there weren't many men with Lala's abilities. It wasn't just the fitness equipment she could handle—she was also among the top ten in the triathlon every year. For that reason, some people spread the story that, because of having been dumped by a man, she had on impulse thrown herself into fitness training as a way to numb her feelings, thus spoiling the natural gentle beauty of her female form. Lala had done nothing to refute that. She had also been pursued by quite a few members of the fitness center who either thought of themselves as powerfully muscled or who were quite well-off. None had been successful, and rumor had it that Lala possessed a secret weapon for dealing with men.

So when Andrew began pestering Lala, everyone laughed at him for being silly, expecting to see him succumb to the female robot's merciless iron fists. It came as quite a surprise when Lala said, "If you play *Tomb Raider III*, you can go out with me whenever you complete the levels of one game location."

Andrew didn't find it preposterous and did indeed go out and buy the game. In the past, he'd only watched it and now he'd got himself a new version. The game was initially hard to learn: Lara just walked around in circles in the Indian jungle, returning where she'd started out and always ending up ambushed and dead.

After Andrew had got through the first location, Lala really did keep her promise and went out with him, only to go for a race around the Peak. Andrew became short of breath after running for less than ten minutes, but Lala had breakfast with him afterward, and that was some compensation. For his second location in the game, Andrew chose London's historic buildings. Although he was still getting trapped in wretched fights, Lara seemed to be coming to a tacit agreement with him. His next get-together with Lala involved cycling from Tai Po to Luk Keng along a winding road going up and down, and Andrew very nearly crashed into a pond. Never one to countenance defeat, he pressed on to the third location, and after one week had Lara traversing the state of Nevada. Afterward, he met Lala at the swimming pool and swam until he had cramps in his arms and legs, while Lala moved like a dolphin, shuttling back and forth in the pool for two thousand meters. Pulling off her swimming goggles, she saw Andrew hoisting himself up to the edge of the pool, shivering with cold. In the fourth location, Lara landed on a small South Pacific island, where she fought a bloody battle with the natives. What he got from that was a chance to go hiking with Lala on a pleasantly mild winter day. That day, Lala was wearing an army-green tank top and shorts. She looked exactly like Lara straight out of *Tomb Raider*, the only things missing being a long plait, pneumatic bust, and guns hanging from her thighs. Climbing up a hillside, Andrew slipped and fell, but luckily Lala caught him just in time. He was extremely agitated, but Lala was frowning, and it wasn't clear if the sunlight was too strong or if it was for some other reason.

Later, Andrew invited Lala to his home, saying he'd like her to watch him play the last stage of the game. He started with the first location, really merging with Lara, and fought his way forward with great skill until finally reaching the fifth location, Antarctica. Using the four artifacts he'd previously captured, he solved the mystery. Just as he was leaping up jubilantly, he noticed Lala's eyes redden and became alarmed.

"Let me tell you my secret," she said. "Do you know why I go to the gym? Four years ago, the man I was in love with died on the treadmill from a sudden heart attack. From then on, I started with fitness training, swimming, running, hiking, because that was what he used to do. In this way, I felt he was still alive and even living in my body, merging with myself. You are the first person I've told about this!"

When she'd finished talking, Lala got up to leave, but Andrew hurriedly grabbed her by the arm.

"I've been through the fifth location. Why don't you stay a while? I've solved the mysteries, I'm a tomb raider!"

Lala lightly brushed him aside. "Don't forget I am still Lara Croft," she said. Taking two steps back, she lowered her hands to her thighs and made as if to pull out her guns, pointed them at Andrew, opened her mouth, and said, "Bang! Bang!"

Everything at once went black before his eyes, his legs turned to jelly, and he fell down.

72

CHARP MINIDICC PLAYCR

MiniDiscs were a type of magneto-optical discs with digitized audio that were developed by Sony but also licensed to other manufacturers, such as Sharp, and marketed from 1992 on. They were for a while very popular in Japan but were later outcompeted by MP3 players.

When Yuet Poon saw that Beanpole had bought a Panasonic SJ-MJ70 portable MiniDisc player, claimed to be the world's smallest and lightest player with the longest playing time, she shouted that she wanted one of her own.

"Is there any other one better?" Beanpole asked.

"Yours can't record sound," said Yuet Poon and bought herself the newly released Sharp MD-J821. The silver case and the black case faced off as equals.

"You listen to yours and I listen to mine. That's not much fun," Yuet Poon said afterward. "I'll record things for you."

To start with, Yuet Poon just recorded some of the local pop music she liked, and even though Beanpole was in the habit of listening to English-language songs, he gracefully accepted her choices. One day, Yuet Poon gave Beanpole a disk that she'd just copied. He put it into the player, but all he could hear was some background noise. Then came Yuet Poon's voice, saying, "This is maybe our last moment!" He took off his earphones and asked Yuet Poon what she had just said. Only then did he realize that it was the sentimental conversation from when they had parted at the station two days earlier.

"From now on," Yuet Poon said, "I'm going to record everything that's said when we are together, so we can savor it later."

Beanpole was a technician at a telecommunications company and often worked the night shift, while Yuet Poon was a journalist at a weekly magazine; she too was used to spending all night getting manuscripts ready. It wasn't easy for the two of them to meet. They only went out together once a week, and usually that meant seizing the opportunity to have breakfast after finishing work. By then, they had stored up so much to say that it was as if all that was in their hearts and minds came gushing out. In the beginning, Yuet Poon's recordings were just made for fun, or for a moment's distraction and the novelty. Sometimes she repeatedly mocked the silly things he said; at other times she would listen again and again to the sweet things he'd said. Beanpole didn't mind any of this and tirelessly kept on buying new disks for Yuet Poon.

Once, they took advantage of a holiday to go bike riding along Tolo Harbor. Halfway through their trip, Yuet Poon had used up her disks. Coming to a halt at the side of the path, she lost her temper. "Today's such a special occasion," she said. "I can't bear to think I can't record it."

Beanpole thought she was putting on a show. He realized, however, that it was serious when he saw her angry, inflamed expression. Getting on his bike right away, he raced back to Sha Tin town center to buy some more disks. When he came back three-quarters of an hour later, he found Yuet Poon waiting for him on the embankment, holding her bike steady. and facing the wind, her hair blown across her face. He hurriedly inserted a new disk and started recording. He gave Yuet Poon a big hug and lovingly told her how sorry he was. She'd been frozen stiff from the wind but now felt so grateful that she suddenly burst into tears. Afterward, when they listened to the recordings of that day again, it was only that part that was really clearly audible; the rest was just the sound of the wind.

Eventually things got to the point where they were almost unable to speak unless the MD player was on. Even when it was quite clear that the machine had started recording, they still worried that they hadn't enough disks and might use up their batteries, or that the sound quality wouldn't be good enough, checking it over and over again, leaving no time for other conversation. Beanpole became alert to the danger in this situation and told Yuet Poon that it was time they broke with rigid convention.

"Yes, could we for instance record something that will be engraved in our hearts?" Yuet Poon went on to say.

Beanpole took three days' leave to go for a trip to Lantau with Yuet Poon. He also reserved a hotel room, thinking that it would be nicer than a cheap holiday flat. They had never spent such a long time together before, and Yuet Poon was greatly excited.

"This will charge us with enough energy for a whole year," she exclaimed. The first evening, they took showers in turn and timidly climbed into the double bed. They embraced for a moment. "Let's record it," Yuet Poon said. "This is our first time."

Beanpole nodded and checked the disk in the Sharp MD player. There were only thirty minutes left.

"Should be enough," Yuet Poon said, blushing. "And we've got more, forty-nine disks!"

With the player running, they fumbled awkwardly at first, but everything turned out more satisfying than they could have imagined. They uttered little cries of pleasure and came to a perfect end, reaching orgasm together. Before the lingering warmth had subsided, Yuet Poon remembered to have a look at the MD player only to discover that it had stopped for lack of power. They rummaged through their luggage, but they had brought neither batteries nor a charger. They were not even sure whether the disk in the machine had recorded anything. The two of them sat naked on opposite sides of the bed, and between them was a great stillness; it seemed as if there were a dark shadow, humming.

73

BURBERRYS BLUE LABEL

When Yuet Yan introduced Lam Foon Tung to Yip Poon Ha, she made a show of the coincidence in their names. "Ha means summer and Tung means winter: it's a match made in heaven!" More to the point, as Yip Poon Ha was aware, both of their personal names referred to plants used in traditional Chinese medicine to treat coughs. "Does Miss Lam's father also practice Chinese medicine?" he asked.

Lam Foon Tung laughed and made a slight cough into her fist. The Burberrys trench coat that she was holding over her arm, its checked, off-white lining exposed, was dipping to the ground.

Yip Poon Ha had intended to pursue Yuet Yan, but she already had a boyfriend. Yuet Yan thought Yip Poon Ha was a steady, honest person, so she told him she had a good friend who was twenty-nine years old, was nice looking, and had a good character. She was the right age to get married—just a little too quiet—and it wouldn't hurt going out with her for a while. Yip Poon Ha agreed. He hadn't had any great expectations, but to his surprise they got along quite well on their first meeting (although who knows whether their names had anything to do with it). Soon enough, Yip Poon Ha asked Lam Foon Tung out by herself. She didn't refuse but showed no great interest either.

That year, winter hardly deserved its name. Every time Yip Poon Ha met Lam Foon Tung, she would be carrying the Burberrys over her arm, but he never saw her actually wear it. They did nothing more than having meals or watching movies together, all very proper and correct. Once, Yip Poon Ha tried to liven up their routine by taking a ferry to Cheung Chau. As always, Lam Foon Tung carried her Burberrys over her arm. She leaned against the railing on the ferry deck, shaking her head in the wind to lift the hair off her lips. Yip Poon Ha reached out to brush it away. After they went ashore, he relieved her of her coat, taking the opportunity to hold her free hand. It was very cold and felt numb, so he rubbed it. Lam Foon Tung looked up at him, her usually pallid face flushing red and looking very pretty.

Yip Poon Ha felt everything was going smoothly, except that he wasn't keen on the Burberrys. Once, adopting a casual air, he asked Lam Foon Tung why she always carried the trench coat. She smiled and said there was no special reason. Straightening her thin, cream-colored jumper, she walked along the street bathed in sunshine, apparently in much higher spirits than usual. *Perhaps the time will come when she doesn't need the coat anymore*, Yip Poon Ha thought to himself.

However, the expression on Lam Foon Tung's face was usually in contrast to the sunny weather. Sometimes she would be racked with dry coughs, as if she was trying to throw up whatever was inside her empty body. Looking at her in a panic, Yip Poon Ha was unable to help and could only think of asking if she had seen a doctor, but she insisted that she was all right. One time, when Lam Foon Tung went to the ladies', Yip Poon Ha searched the Burberrys inside out but he was unable to discover anything other than that it was made in Britain. Later, he went to ask Yuet Yan about Lam Foon Tung's past.

"There's nothing to tell, seriously. Her life has been quite dull. She's never had a real romance, even though she's nearly thirty, so no wonder she's a bit unused to it. It's up to you now."

Thinking that Lam Foon Tung must have a special predilection for Burberrys, Yip Poon Ha bought her a Burberrys Blue Label carry bag, the latest model in black nylon with diagonal checks at the bottom and a zip top. They'd made an appointment to catch a performance at the arts festival, but the Observatory predicted that a cold front was about to arrive that night. However, the bright sunshine in the morning made Yip Poon Ha doubt the forecast, so he was only wearing his ordinary jacket. When they met, Lam Foon Tung accepted the gift, thanked him, and carefully rewrapped the bag.

As they emerged from the Cultural Center, a gust of cold wind drove everyone to shrink back, crying out in alarm. A light rain began to fall, and the night was enveloped in a fine mist. A rosy flush flooded Lam Foon Tung's cheeks, and her eyes gleamed with an unusual brilliance. She lifted up the Burberrys trench coat and ran out into the rain while she was still putting it on. She opened her arms and spun around with her face upturned. The breath issuing from her mouth turned into an orange vapor in the light of the street lamps. Yip Poon Ha noticed that the coat reached below her knees and its sleeves came over her fingertips, so that it seemed as if a huge figure was enfolding her. He was left standing under the porch, holding the Blue Label bag in his arms.

74

MP3

Chara is a Japanese pop singer who sang the theme tune "Swallowtail Butterfly" of the 1996 film with the same name. *Bounce Ko Gals* is a Japanese film from 1997 about schoolgirls engaging in "compensated dating" with older men. *Over Time* was a television drama from 1999; its theme tune, "At Light Speed," was performed by the Brilliant Green, a Japanese rock band.

That evening, Yue Ka Lok waited for Pok Pok to get off work in order to give her a MiniDisc with a recording of Chara singing the theme tune of *Swallowtail Butterfly*. Pok Pok asked if he had to go home right away. They bought beer at a 7-Eleven and sat on a stone bench in the park. Pok Pok told Yue Ka Lok that her wish was to go to Japan to study and also to watch sumo wrestling. Yue Ka Lok didn't understand why anyone would want to watch sumo, and Pok Pok wasn't clear about it either.

As Pok Pok was talking, she jumped up and shouted "Come on!" at Yue Ka Lok. Pok Pok wasn't fat, and that evening she was wearing a loose-fitting skirt, but all the same she struck a great pose stretching out her arms and standing with her feet wide apart. Yue Ka Lok rushed at her, and the two of them pushed ferociously against each other with their shoulders. Losing their balance, both fell to the ground. Yue Ka Lok got up and looked to see if Pok Pok had hurt herself, but Pok Pok just rolled over and over and over and laughed her head off. That was the first time Pok Pok had told Yue Ka Lok of her private thoughts, and it was also the only time they had such an intimate encounter.

Yue Ka Lok worked in a CD shop in the shopping center, and Pok Pok was a waitress in the restaurant next door serving Japanese-style Western food. One day Pok Pok, in her uniform, had run across to the CD shop to see if they had the soundtrack of *Bounce Ko Gals*. While Yue Ka Lok searched for it, she rummaged around rather like a student frantically revising for exams, turning from one book to another. Yue Ka Lok asked her if she would like to listen to the CD. She listened to the beginnings of ten songs and then looked impatiently at her watch, glanced at the price label on the CD case, and walked out in some embarrassment.

When Pok Pok passed Yue Ka Lok's shop the next morning on her way to work, he came out and pressed a MiniDisc into her hand. "Copied it for you. You got a MiniDisc player?" he said. "You like watching Japanese movies?" he added.

Pok Pok hadn't asked anything of Yue Ka Lok. She was quite stingy when it came to food and drink and was reluctant to buy the CDs she liked so much. Yue Ka Lok didn't understand why. In any case, he continued to record songs for her, all of them Japanese, and he would give them to her on her way to and from work. He didn't say anything about it except that it was easy for him to do it, and he would play them in the shop anyway. Pok Pok at first felt a little wary, but then she got used to it and stopped worrying. That was how it was until the evening when she had played at sumo with Yue Ka Lok. Back at home, she developed a headache that lasted all night. It then occurred to her that she'd never asked Yue Ka Lok anything about himself, and she felt she'd been very selfish.

After that, Pok Pok began to chat with Yue Ka Lok when she had some free time. She discovered that he was becoming fond of her, but she felt there were some things she couldn't share with him. Their colleagues in the CD shop and the Japanese restaurant spread the word that they were dating, but they both refused to confirm or deny the rumors. Later on, when Pok Pok's MiniDisc player broke down, she sensed that it was now time to put a stop to the recordings.

"But you've got a cassette recorder at home, haven't you?" he responded.

For a while, Yue Ka Lok was passing cassette tapes over to her, and then one day he gave her a CD and an MP3 player. "These are MP3s I recorded from the net," he said. "One CD can hold a hundred songs."

Pok Pok looked intently at the CD as if she wanted to read the music and lyrics of all one hundred songs, but the round mirrorlike surface only showed her own reflection. "Promise me this is the last time," she said abruptly, with an expression somewhere between smiling and not smiling.

Yue Ka Lok didn't understand.

"This is the last time," Pok Pok repeated. When she got home, Pok Pok didn't listen to the CD. Instead, she held it in her hand, gazing at the reflection of the lamplight flashing from its surface. The next day, she resigned from her job and informed Yue Ka Lok she was leaving.

As it turned out, Pok Pok didn't go to Japan. The company where her father worked went bankrupt, and her family hadn't enough money to pay the mortgage. Pok Pok took out the more than hundred thousand dollars that she had saved for studying overseas, uttered not a word about it, and went out to look for a new job.

One day, while Pok Pok was doing some mobile sales promotion for computer software, she went back to the old shopping center, where she saw Yue Ka Lok having lunch with a girl who worked in a nearby fashion store. After lunch, Pok Pok went into the CD shop and picked up a single of the *Over Time* theme tune by the Brilliant Green. Yue Ka Lok was a bit startled and said he would give it to her as a present.

She laughed. "Didn't I say the other one was the last time!"

Yue Ka Lok also smiled and nodded as he accepted her payment.

75

MIFFY

Nijntje is a little rabbit appearing in picture books by Dick Bruna. In English she is called Miffy. Bruna sued Sanrio, the creators of Hello Kitty, claiming copyright infringement. The two characters are drawn in a similar style, but while Hello Kitty has no mouth, Miffy has a mouth in the form of an X. In the Chinese calendar, each year is linked to an animal that is part of a repeating cycle of twelve. For example, a person born in the Year of the Rabbit will also have their twelfth, twenty-fourth, thirty-sixth birthday, and so on, in the Year of the Rabbit. According to Hong Kong folk belief, it is unlucky to get married in the year of one's birth animal.

Starting from the summer vacation in the year she turned nineteen and went to university, Mei Mai no longer opened her mouth to speak. She also carried a Miffy bunny in her bag all the time, but no one knew anything about the connection between these two events.

The reason that Mei Mai never spoke was not that she was ill or had any physical impairment. At first, her worried parents took her to many specialist doctors, but all of them reported she was in excellent health. Her parents then turned on her, angry at her for being a troublemaker and deliberately upsetting her mother and father. Finding it impossible to say a word, Mei Mai instead doubled her efforts to be a good daughter. In time, her family got used to her not speaking, and everyday communication was not a problem.

The reason that Mei Mai wouldn't open her mouth wasn't because of any mental problems either. Her boyfriend, Siu Wai, who started his university studies at the same time as Mei Mai, was the first to discover that she had stopped speaking. At that point he thought he'd upset her by doing something wrong, making her so angry that she wanted nothing to do with him. However, he was confused, because she was still being very nice to him. Then, convinced that she must be hiding a secret, he asked questions about her past. Not long after, Siu Wai and Mei Mai began to grow apart, but before they finally split up, Siu Wai made one last attempt.

"Mei Mai," he said, obviously in great distress, "if only you'd be willing to speak, then we wouldn't end up separating!"

"But there is really nothing to say!" Mei Mai wrote on a piece of paper, but it was too late. Siu Wai had already walked away.

Although Mei Mai no longer held spoken conversations with others, it wasn't because she was resentful or wanted to protest. Nevertheless, no one could understand what was going on, in particular her teachers at university. When they realized that Mei Mai wouldn't utter a word in class when her name was called, they concluded that she was either exceptionally obstreperous or else supremely stupid. However, Mei Mai's written work was excellent, and her teachers didn't know how to handle her. A male philosophy student, greatly admiring her unbending silence, believed she was deliberately challenging authority. After class he dragged Mei Mai away to hold forth on Foucault and deconstruction. Mei Mai didn't understand much but just went on nodding and smiling. The besotted philosophy student started to pursue her, but, after a few weeks, he ran out of things to say and found it hard to persist.

The reason that Mei Mai remained silent without uttering a word was not that she dreaded noise or the clamor of voices. She still listened to pop music, went out dancing, and even joined her friends at karaoke, sitting at the side and laughing with everyone. At the disco, she got to know Ram, a rather indolent character. He could never be bothered to say more than a few words anyway and felt Mei Mai was a terrific match. The two of them often sat idly by the harborside until dawn, sharing cigarettes and never asking any personal questions. However, Ram wasn't very good at reading and found writing even more of a burden. Mei Mai wrote him a note with the single word "Farewell." He found no reason to object.

It was not at all the case that Mei Mai had no wish to express herself, and she was actually quite diligent with writing letters and email, so she kept in close touch with her former classmates after graduation. However, since she didn't speak, she bombed in interviews and couldn't get a job. Instead she did some odd translation jobs at home. During this time, she exchanged frequent messages with a young, open-minded professor who had previously taught her linguistics, and later on they started to see each other and go on dates. He was very patient in communicating with her by writing in a way that was both lively and learned. They were quickly on very friendly terms and were soon in love. The professor then proposed marriage to Mei Mai, and her parents felt as if a great burden had been lifted from their shoulders, no matter that she had been born in the Year of the Rabbit and was now twenty-four, so it was the Year of the Rabbit again—that was just superstition. One day, the professor surreptitiously took out Mei Mai's Miffy from her handbag and fondled the doll that had been inseparable from her. Then he thought he would be clever and try to cure Mei Mai's loss of speech. With a pair of scissors he cut off the two black lines sewn onto Miffy to form her X-shaped mouth. When Mei Mai discovered this, she burst into bitter tears. Opening her mouth, she spoke: "I bought this Miffy in the summer of the year I started at university. I just happened to see her in a shop in the street. I wanted to buy her, so I bought her. And then about me not speaking, that was just because I thought that's how I liked to be, that's all. Can't you even understand that? How can we still be together now?"

In the end Mei Mai still married her professor and turned into a loudmouth who never stopped talking. It seems the Miffy bunny in her heart had left, never to return.

76

DEVON AOKI

Devon Aoki is an American fashion model partly of Japanese descent.

Freckles Pan came across the Max Factor advertisement in a magazine, a big face filling up the entire page. It was covered in freckles, the eyes small and pointing upward, the eyebrows very thin, the nose small, and the mouth turned down at both ends. The round face was divided into quarters, each with light makeup applied in four different shades. When she saw it, Freckles Pan suddenly felt now was the time for counterattack. As a child, she'd had lots of freckles, but she also had a slender, graceful body and was quite good at ballet, so her mother used to put makeup on her face, and Freckles Pan would compete with fair-faced girls for that day. Freckles Pan then took part in a selection for a role in *Swan Lake*, making her mind up not to use cosmetics. As soon as she stepped on stage, the judges were startled, and in the end she failed to be selected. Freckles Pan didn't explain to her mother what had happened but ran off to tell a boy who was in the same ballet class. Seeing Freckles Pan without makeup for the first time, he stared at her, stunned.

"Do you like freckles?" she asked.

* * *

Small-Nose Pei and High-Nose Mui were classroom adversaries. In terms of school marks, Small-Nose Pei was just a notch above High-Nose Mui, but there was unanimous agreement that in appearance the girls were as different as night and day. So even though Small-Nose Pei was the first to get on intimate terms with Wing Wai, High-Nose Mui easily snatched him away. His results were about the same as those of Small-Nose Pei, and he was also captain of the school football team. However, he was a fool when it came to emotional relationships, unaware of who were his friends and who his enemies. Some time later, he was knocked on the bridge of his nose at a football match, and the bleeding wouldn't stop. He was afraid his nose had been flattened and hid in the locker room for a long time. Once he emerged, he walked over to Small-Nose Pei.

"I'm so sorry, Small-Nose Pei," he said to her. "Forgive me."

"How's your nose?" Small-Nose Pei said, however.

From an early age, Small-Eyes Mei had been ridiculed and called Dimwit by her classmates. As she grew up, they became a bit more polite, and she was given the name Small-Eyes Mei. Even though her eyes were small, her eyesight was excellent, and she felt destined to study optometry. After finishing her studies, she helped out with eye examinations and fitting spectacles. Usually she wore sunglasses whenever she went out, and because her straight hair was so long and soft, people she passed in the street would stare at her. Small-Eyes Mei had had two boyfriends in the past, but they had transferred their affections to other girls with big eyes. Small-Eyes Mei concluded it was due to fate. The third boyfriend, Ah Leung, came in to have glasses fitted. During the eye examination, when Small-Eyes Mei leant close to him to check his pupils, he suddenly said, "Your eyes are really big."

When they were kissing later on, he would also say the same thing: "Your eyes are really big."

Once people started talking about them, they agreed that Droopy-Mouth Tap and Bright-Smile Fai would not have a happy future together. The corners of Droopy-Mouth Tap's mouth pointed downward. She couldn't smile, and even if she tried, there was no smile there. She wasn't much given to talking either, and from childhood on hadn't seemed very likable. Her teachers thought her rude and her schoolmates ostracized her, although in fact she never did anything bad. Her classmate Bright-Smile Fai, on the other hand, seemed unable to close his mouth, grinning broadly as he walked along, so everyone who encountered him thought he was bonkers. They were dating at age fifteen, living together at eighteen, having a baby at twenty, and it was only after the birth that they legalized their relationship by marriage. Every morning, Droopy-Mouth Tap and Bright-Smile Fai went out together to have milk tea with two fried eggs, ham, and macaroni at a tea café. Bright-Smile Fai would read the entertainment pages with a broad smile on his face, while Droopy-Mouth Tap read the local news section with her mouth pouting, neither of them saying much. Later on, they had another baby with a mouth like a horizontal line, neither smiling nor pouting.

After Wide-Face Ah Hoh had been out having dim sum with her colleagues in the admin department, she learned that Young Kam in maintenance was fond of steamed rice wrapped in lotus leaf, so she bought leaves in the wet market to make the dish herself. She made a number of them, ostensibly to invite everyone for a meal, but actually it was Young Kam's response she was interested in. After Young Kam had finished eating, he held a lotus leaf in his hand and asked where she'd been able to buy such large ones.

"They're not as big as my face," she said, holding one of them up in front of her. Young Kam laughed until his tears flowed, while Wide-Face Ah Hoh blushed, hiding behind the lotus leaf. Everyone agreed that Wide-Face Ah Hoh was so good to them, poking fun at herself to amuse everyone as she compared her own wide face to the big round leaf. Once, turning over the pages in a magazine after lunch, Young Kam came across a black-and-white Chanel advertisement featuring a model with a round flat face, like a doll.

"Looks pretty much like you!" he remarked to Wide-Face Ah Hoh.

She took a close look. "Models nowadays give you the creeps!" she said.

Young Kam pretended to make fun of her: "This is what's 'in,' you don't understand anything at all!" Wide-Face Ah Hoh knew then that her lotus-leaf rice had been effective.

77

MOTOROLA DUAL BAND

That evening, it was just as usual. After getting up from her nap after school, Mo Sheung marked homework and by eight thirty still hadn't had anything to eat. The mobile phone on her desk suddenly rang. It was some time since Mo Sheung had spoken, and when she answered the call, her voice sounded tired. She hadn't expected it to be Chung Chi. When he asked if she was feeling unwell, she quickly said no.

Chung Chi talked about having lost his job six months earlier and said that was the reason why he hadn't been in touch for so long, but it wasn't clear to Mo Sheung how those two things were connected. He went on to say he had just got a new job in an educational organization developing computer software for teaching. Mo Sheung also said a few words about how she'd been lately: the same old thing, still teaching, student results unsatisfactory, but if you put in a little bit of effort, it could still be enjoyable. Chung Chi asked if Mo Sheung had eaten, and she answered "Not yet," but there was suddenly some interference in the phone connection, so they paused for a moment. Then he said it wouldn't be a bad idea to meet up and go out next Saturday.

Mo Sheung thought for a moment and replied, "All right." She finished the call and put down her clunky old mobile. *Time to switch to one with better reception*, she thought.

Chung Chi had been the boyfriend of Mo Sheung's old classmate Siu Ming. Seeing that Mo Sheung wasn't dating anyone, the other two often asked her to go out with them. That hadn't particularly bothered Mo Sheung. She and Chung Chi didn't exactly become close friends; they just got along well enough. Later on, Siu Ming and Chung Chi had quarreled and broken up, with Mo Sheung trying to mediate. At one point she'd had a chat with Chung Chi in private without it helping much. Afterward, Mo Sheung didn't get in touch with Chung Chi again.

After agreeing to meet with Chung Chi, Mo Sheung realized Saturday was Parents' Day. Several times she was going to give him a ring to change the date, but she also thought he was bound to call her again, so she kept putting it off. Twice she heard a ringtone from her handbag out in the street, but when she got the phone out, there was nothing. When Chung Chi finally gave her a call on Friday night, Mo Sheung was feeling on edge about how to tell him, but he blurted out: "I suddenly have to go to the mainland tomorrow on business."

Mo Sheung relaxed. "That's just as well. Tomorrow is actually Parents' Day, but it wouldn't have been impossible if I'd wanted to go out." Chung Chi didn't say anything or set a new date but just hung up. Holding her mobile and pressing her lips together, Mo Sheung carried on getting her student reports ready.

After another few days, Chung Chi rang again, and from the way he talked it seemed as if he had forgotten about the previous broken appointment. He spoke at length about his new job: he was not getting along too well with his colleagues and criticized them for not being zealous about education.

"You're not like that," he remarked then. Mo Sheng did not say anything, and he asked if she was free on Friday evening.

Mo Sheung went to a Mandarin training class on Friday evenings, but she answered, "That's fine."

For the next few days, Mo Sheung thought of turning off her mobile several times and didn't even feel very much like taking calls from her family, but on second thought she found this ridiculous.

After school on Friday, Mo Sheung was returning home to change into something more casual. She was on the MTR when she got a call from Chung Chi. It was as if she'd had a foreboding when she heard him saying bluntly, "Yesterday we worked all night. I'm so tired, I'm not going out." Underground the words coming from the phone sounded coarse, dull, unfamiliar. Mo Sheung didn't attend her Mandarin class either but went straight home, spread out the homework notebooks, and carried on marking until late at night. Then she had instant noodles at her desk, finishing off the last drop of the MSG-laden soup.

At a later point, on a visit to Mo Sheung, Siu Ming was fiddling with Mo Sheung's mobile, a newly released Motorola cd928 Dual Band. She pressed the buttons until a number marked "CC" turned up in the list of contacts, with "Siu Ming" underneath. Without saying anything, Siu Ming put the mobile back on the pile of homework.

78

CHEESECAKE

Around five o'clock that day, Ah Kok was passing through Mong Kok when she saw a long line of people along the street. She asked a middle-aged woman what she was queuing to buy.

"I don't know," she said. "Seems they're saying it's a kind of cheesecake!"

Ah Kok, who was at a loose end anyway, lined up behind her. She'd been queuing for a full hour by the time she reached the shop front. She lifted her head and saw the words "Tanaka-san's Cheese Cake."

That evening Ah Kok ate a whole Tanaka's Japanese cheesecake at one go. She was thinking that she hadn't felt so satisfied in a long time when suddenly an idea occurred to her: she'd like even more people to have a taste of this delicacy. She made up her mind to give away a hundred Tanaka's cheesecakes to a hundred people she didn't know. Beginning the next day, Ah Kok went to queue up at Tanaka-san's every morning to buy two cheesecakes, one for herself and one to give someone else.

Ah Kok didn't tell her family what she was doing, but they began to mutter when they noticed that she'd spend the whole day outside and then tuck into a cheesecake when she got back. "It's been ages since she finished school, there's no job in sight, but she still wastes her money on cake!" Ah Kok stuck her tongue out and went out as usual to give away cheesecakes, feeling very content to have a purpose in her everyday life.

A cheesecake in hand, Ah Kok would seek out a suitable recipient on the street every day. Her first target was a woman wearing a suit. Going up to her, Ah Kok said she'd like to invite her to try the famous Tanaka-san's cheesecake.

"This is a sales promotion?" the woman said shrewdly. "Right, that's my line too! Do you have an insurance policy? Shall we find somewhere to sit down and talk about it?" Intimidated, Ah Kok ran away as fast as her legs would take her.

Most of the women dressed as office ladies said quite politely, "Thank you so much, but I can get one myself." Or else they would immediately look around to see whether or not a television crew was secretly filming a promotion, and ask what kind of prize they would get for eating the cheesecake. Some schoolgirls smoking in a fast-food shop threw a question back at Ah Kok: "You some kind of missionary? Awesome!" And blew smoke in her face. Once she encountered a foreigner in the street, with blond hair, wearing a white shirt and tie, and clutching a small book in his hand.

"Hello, mess, can I dalk to you?" he asked in heavily accented Cantonese. When she realized he was a Mormon, she thrust a cheesecake at his chest and ran away.

With older people it was even worse. Middle-aged women frowned and said they detested cheese.

"You eat Jap food?" asked an older man. "Isn't our Chinese food good enough for you?"

A mother, her face all smiles, told her just to leave the cheesecake with her and then turned around. "Don't eat it!" she said to her daughter. "That girl's bonkers, you know."

An old woman begging in the street didn't know what it was, and in any case had no teeth, but she greedily gulped down half of it and then threw up.

Her most successful encounter was with a man she met in Central. It was a few minutes past ten o'clock at night. He was just leaving his office, carrying a briefcase and looking for something to eat along the chilly street. He was very happy to hear Ah Kok ask him if he would like her to give him some cheese-cake. "Oh, it's this cheesecake! I kept meaning to buy some but never did, and then when I got back to the office, I couldn't leave!"

That was how Ah Kok gave away her eighty-second cheesecake.

After several unpleasant incidents, Ah Kok finally managed to give away a hundred cheesecakes. She felt she could relax now, after completing her task. That evening around dusk, she went back to Tanaka-san's, where, to her surprise, she ran into the man from Central in the queue. He was casually dressed, and when he saw Ah Kok, he smiled wryly.

"I've just lost my job!" he said. "The company's gone bank-rupt! I've finally got the time to come and buy some cheesecake!" Peering at the long line of people, he continued, "Take a look, it wouldn't be a bad idea to change my career to selling cake."

Ah Kok actually became so excited she jumped up and down. "Great!" she shouted. "Let me know when you're set up so I can be a customer!" she said.

"Don't just buy one, come and give me a hand selling them," he replied. He bought two cheesecakes and gave one to Ah Kok. At the street corner he waved at her, holding the cake box in his hand, and walked away. Ah Kok wanted to call after him but didn't.

When Ah Kok went home, she flipped through some maga-zines with recipes for Japanese-style cheesecake, pondering what would be needed to open a shop. Resting her chin on her hand, she wondered, "Will he still go to Tanaka-san's tomorrow?"

79

PALMPILOT

After Lei Mei had bought her PalmPilot personal digital assistant, she entered all her urgent company business into the device, conscientiously putting everything in its proper place and saying farewell to her old notebooks. Going through her schedule one day after work, she discovered she had a meeting that evening but couldn't remember whom she'd agreed to see. At the appointed time she arrived at the specified restaurant, but, looking around in all directions, she saw no one she recognized. As she was beginning to feel quite perplexed, she spotted her colleague Kin Ping coming in. Both of them were a bit startled and weren't sure what to say. While she was unable to recall when she might have agreed to meet Kin Ping, she was also afraid of having forgotten about it.

"You're, er, late," she said.

"So, er, sorry," Kin Ping replied.

Afterward, Lei Mei continued to discover reminders of other engagements of unknown provenance on her PalmPilot, and every time she arrived at the designated place, she always encountered Kin Ping. It made Lei Mei suspect she was suffering from partial amnesia, but when she caught sight of him, it didn't seem to matter—everything seemed perfectly natural. After dinner the sixth time they met like this, Lei Mei returned from a trip to the ladies' to see Kin Ping in the distance handling her PalmPilot. All of a sudden she woke up to what was going on.

"So it was you who did that to my PDA all along!" she rebuked him. "That's how it is!"

Kin Ping looked all innocent. "Can't I even look at it for a moment! You think you can blame me like this?"

Not listening, Lei Mei furiously snatched back her PalmPilot and stalked off.

After falling out with Kin Ping, Lei Mei began to be less trustful of the reminders on her PalmPilot. She often picked up the PDA stylus to check items on the screen, looking at the entries repeatedly, and the more she did so, the more it seemed as if those events had never existed. The outcome was that some work-related items were edited or deleted and some appointments ignored, so she made a lot of mistakes carrying out her duties. When she was called in by the boss, she was asked what was going on and told that she would be let go if she didn't pay more attention to what she was doing. As she walked out, feeling very frustrated, it so happened that she ran into Kin Ping. Becoming suspicious, she wondered if he'd plotted everything on purpose but couldn't entirely work out the reason.

Lei Mei had once been to a fortune-teller to have her palm read. She'd been told her fate line had many twists and turns, but the heart line offered a glimmer of hope. Because of that, she redoubled her care in making entries on the PDA, afraid of upsetting the orderliness of her work and life, but as a result she spent most of her time at work and after work making entries on it. Sometimes it seemed to her as if she were constructing the outline of a novel with intricate and complicated times, places, and people. She made changes over and over again, under a kind of delusion of forming her fate in the palm of her hand. In an effort to do everything to ensure that the data on the PDA didn't deviate from reality, she slavishly followed the arrangements recorded on the device: at the time indicated for eating, she wouldn't go for a walk in the streets; at the time indicated for watching a VCD, she wouldn't read a magazine. It was as if without the PDA she would be a ship with no navigation equipment, deviating from the set course, drifting on the vast, boundless ocean.

One evening, Lei Mei had noted down that she was to eat a sandwich after work, but when she arrived at the cafeteria, she saw Kin Ping sitting there in a corner.

"You're late," he said before she'd had a chance to get annoyed. Lei Mei found it very odd but sat down with Kin Ping and watched as he pulled out his Palm PC to show her.

"I discovered this note today: '7:00 Dinner with Lei Mei.'"

Startled, Lei Mei looked at her own PalmPilot and read: "7:00 Dinner with Kin Ping." They looked at each other in amazement.

"Did we really agree to meet?" Kin Ping enquired tentatively.

Lei Mei was deep in thought for a while. "Of course!" she suddenly said. "But we're not supposed to be here. Come on! We're taking an Outlying Islands ferry." She took Kin Ping by the hand, got up, and rushed out into the street. Her palm seemed to have a tractive force, and Kin Ping had no way of shaking himself loose.

80
—

PN ROUGE SUPLINIC

The PN brand is owned by Shiseido. Alisa Mizuki is a Japanese actress, singer, and model.

Ah Pei-Pei first applied makeup when she was eighteen, and what she'd bought was PN's Rouge Suplinic. It was a sudden decision that came about when she was sitting on the MTR leafing through a weekly magazine and saw an advertisement for PN featuring Alisa Mizuki and her sparkling, glossy lips. Ah Pei-Pei got off at Causeway Bay and went to the Shiseido counter in a Japanese department store. When she returned home that evening, her dad was able to read her lips for the first time.

Ah Pei-Pei's dad used to drive an air-conditioned bus and wear a proper uniform, regarding himself as superior to those who drove old buses with their knees pulled high and didn't bother to button their shirts. The previous year, he had swerved when a small child ran across the road but crashed into a private car in the next lane, killing a family of three. Only three of the bus passengers received minor injuries, but he himself suffered concussion and lost his hearing. The court proceedings dragged on for a long time, until there was a "not guilty" verdict, but he still suffered from a guilty conscience, regretting that he hadn't reacted more swiftly. Having lost his job, he regarded himself as useless, from then on spending his days listlessly at home, watching silent television all day long, avoiding

Ah Pei-Pei's gaze. However, that evening, when Ah Pei-Pei came home wearing lipstick, her dad actually glanced at her a couple of times, pointing at her lips. "Glassy," Ah Pei-Pei said. Her dad picked up a piece of paper and wrote: "Glassy."

Ah Pei-Pei then began to learn how to use makeup, experimenting on her own face. When her boyfriend, Ah Heem, saw her transformation, he was first greatly pleased, assuming she was making herself pretty for him and also realizing she could be really stunning. On her lips, however, Ah Pei-Pei stuck to Rouge Suplinic, which made them stay dewy and gleaming all day, but Ah Heem hardly dared touch her.

Apart from changing her appearance, Ah Pei-Pei also began to speak more at home, chattering away in front of her deaf dad. By watching her glassy lips, he could make a good guess about what she was saying. He had Ah Pei-Pei accompany him to tea houses and tea cafés, once more taking part in the social life of the neighborhood; he also followed her instructions to enroll in signing and lip-reading classes. People said Ah Pei-Pei had turned out both good and pretty, and her dad's face lit up when he could make out two- or three-tenths of what was said.

Ah Pei-Pei's dad had in fact been to university on the mainland, but after he came to Hong Kong, his qualifications weren't recognized, so he worked as a bus driver for the next twenty years. In the neighborhood, he was often called "headmaster," which Ah Pei-Pei found pretty impressive when she was little but ridiculous after she'd grown up. Because she'd lost her mom early, her dad tended to be solemn, and from an early age she didn't speak much at home. Once, in year three of primary school, she'd fallen off a swing and hurt her mouth, but her dad paid no attention to the blood dripping from her lips. Ah Pei-Pei from then on began to despise her appearance, preferring not to look in the mirror and not keeping any photos of herself other than school photos. She only remembered a wedding photo of her mom and dad, belatedly taken after they'd arrived in Hong

Kong. It was in black and white; only her mom's lips were bright red.

Ah Pei-Pei was studying makeup and at the same time working as a cosmetics salesperson. When her colleagues told her she ought to become a model, she shook her head. She seemed to have matured overnight, while her old friends were still more like girls and were drifting away. Ah Pei-Pei's dad, on the other hand, was becoming more youthful.

"This girl is quite pretty," he wrote, pointing in a joking sort of way at an advertisement with Alisa Mizuki.

One day Ah Pei-Pei went and had her hair bobbed and bought a silver-gray skirt. She applied makeup as usual with Rouge Suplinic lipstick and arranged to see Ah Heem.

"Actually I never did this for you," she told him. "It's my fault. We shouldn't be together anymore."

As Ah Heem gazed at the transparent color of her lips, it was as if her words were also transparent and he couldn't hear them. Having said her piece, Ah Pei-Pei went home. As she was about to open the door, she heard her dad speaking on the phone inside. Furious, she was on the point of bursting in to interrogate him: "Why have you deceived me?" However, biting her lip, she turned around and ran away, her high heels clattering along the corridor. When she came out of the building downstairs, she found Ah Heem waiting for her. Pulling out a handkerchief, he stepped forward and pressed it to her lips.

"What on earth have you done to your mouth?" he asked.

Ah Pei-Pei wiped herself with the back of her hand: there was blood everywhere and gleaming glass splinters.

81
—

FINAL FANTASY VIII

Final Fantasy VIII is a role-playing video game released in
1999. The female protagonist is named Rinoa. The game's
theme song, "Eyes on Me," is sung by Faye Wong.

On the evening when Anna Lei, wearing a low-cut ivory dress
with crossover straps and her long hair tumbling around her
beautiful bare shoulders, sneaked into the Easter Ball at an elite
boys' school, a couple of nice boys politely offered their services
as escorts. In the densely packed assembly hall, Anna Lei's
glance at once settled on one of the elite-school boys: tall, cool,
and actually walking toward her. He asked for a dance and held
her close, one hand around her waist, leading but not pushing,
his palm warm and soft. The hall had laser lights, which created
an illusion of fireworks, and Faye Wong's bewitching voice could
be heard over the loudspeakers.

Elite-school boys are different, sure enough, Anna Lei thought.
They're not like that hood King-Chau.

Her partner bent down to her ear and asked softly for her
name.

"Rinoa."

The moment King-Chau had met Hai-Hai, he'd had wild sex in
mind and signaled as much. Hai-Hai had nothing against that,

keen enough for him to be quite ferocious, but as time passed, she got a bit fed up, feeling it was like taking a sloppy gym class and she'd rather spend her time playing video games. She also never asked him if he liked her—she only knew that what she enjoyed most herself was the PlayStation in his home. Next she actually trained herself to do both things at the same time: when it was "game over" for King-Chau, Hai-Hai hadn't got as far as the highest level.

When reports spread that an elite-school boy and an elite-school girl had become intimate, Demon Girl led her friends to ambush the elite girl and force her into an abandoned car park. Pulling off her school uniform, the girls wrote rude words on her body with marker pens and forced her to admit her errors, swearing a bloodcurdling oath never to see the boy again. Taking out her cigarette lighter, Demon Girl set fire to the girl's underwear, although she neatly folded the school uniform.

"Just you stay obedient, and you can come and look for Demon Girl if anyone bullies you in future," she said before leaving.

She hadn't been to her old home for a long time. When she did go back, her old dad called her Ha-Ha.

"Ha-Ha, Ha-Ha," he said, "come, give your old dad a hug. Your dad hasn't held his little girl for ages!"

When Ha-Ha looked at her dad, whose diabetes had turned him into an invalid, she fired up. "Hug a shit like you!" she screamed at him.

Her dad squealed like a wounded dog. "You little bitch, you've got no feelings," he muttered. "Brought you up to be a big girl and you're fucking useless."

Ha-Ha went into the kitchen and came back with a sharp knife, intending to kill him. "You lousy old bastard, didn't you mess with me enough when I was a kid? You'd better believe I'm going to castrate you, you dirty old shit!"

The elite boy was captain of his school basketball team, never failed to change back into his school uniform after matches, was always neat and tidy, and, with little effort, got three As and five Bs in the Certificate of Education exam. As it turned out, he was brilliant at computer games and had both a PlayStation and a Dreamcast at home. When he asked Anna Lei to come up and play the newly released *Final Fantasy VIII* with him, it was romantic beyond compare, and she had almost never before been so excited; it was simply better than an orgasm and nearly made her cry out loud. The elite boy was immensely pleased with himself.

"I'm pretty bright at role-playing games. Street kids only know how to play fighting and racing games, brainless stuff, really cheap."

Anna Lei looked up admiringly at the elite boy, feeling he was really someone special. She moved close to him and kissed his arrogant eyes.

One day King-Chau gave the elite boy a sound thrashing. He looked at the boy sitting on the ground, with his hands staunching the blood from his nose. Hai-Hai was standing by protectively.

"I won't bash you too," King-Chau said to her. "If you're thinking of coming back, I might still want you."

*   *   *

Tearfully complaining to the elite boy, the elite girl said Demon Girl had humiliated her and she didn't want be part of the human race anymore. The elite boy embraced her tightly, although he felt a bit afraid of Demon Girl and her gang.

Anna Lei angrily blamed the elite boy for being so bloody useless, a single blow bringing him to his knees. With blood spurting out of his nose, the elite boy in turn asked how come she knew those hooligans.

"You're nothing like Rinoa," he sneered. "Aping other people, playing at being a lady? Ha ha!"

82
—

THE WAIST BAG

Peach-Pocket Girl was the name given to her by Ah Ng, who worked in the fast-food place. She always wore a small, skintight T-shirt and a peach-colored bag with three large pockets around her waist, hanging down in front of her hips from left to right like a skirt.

Every day, Peach-Pocket Girl arrived at the fast-food shop after midday. She invariably ordered a glass of iced milk tea, sat down in the seat in the corner, fished out a big pile of letters from the left, right, and middle pockets of her waist bag, spread them out on the table before her, and then opened and read them one after another. Whenever Ah Ng came over, pretending to be cleaning up, and looked at the girl's letters, she clutched them in her hand as if protecting something precious. Chewing a stick of gum, she stared at Ah Ng. When he asked her about them, she said, "My boyfriend writes to me, what's wrong with that?" Every day from then on, Ah Ng insisted on treating her to her iced milk tea.

Some time later, after Peach-Pocket Girl had turned up in the neighborhood, Ah Kin, the postman, discovered what she was doing. Ah Kin's attention was first caught by her peach-colored waist bag with its three bulging pockets swinging to and fro across her thighs, as if to pare down her waist. On reflection, he felt it was a bit like his own postbag, without knowing why.

He discovered later that she was stealing letters from other people's mailboxes.

Peach-Pocket Girl only stole private letters; official mail she ignored completely. The mailboxes in the old tenement buildings were for the most part not closed off from street access. They had no caretaker or metal grille in front of them, so it was possible to slip the letters out and stuff them into her waist bag (goodness only knew how many letters had been stuffed in it). When the postman Ah Kin discovered she was stealing letters, however, he didn't expose her right away, but followed her for two weeks, pursuing the swaying, peach-colored pockets full of the letters he'd dispatched.

Peach-Pocket Girl was particularly fond of reading letters sent to a boy called Ah Sum by his girlfriend in the United States. Inside, they were complete stories, so it was like reading a novel: the girl recalling what had happened from the day she and Ah Sum first became acquainted to the sorrow of their separation, followed by all kinds of reasons for them to part, and finally the inevitable appearance of a third person. She made a special point of putting the letters to Ah Sum in the middle pocket of her waist bag.

Peach-Pocket Girl was unaware that Ah Sum had become terribly worried after not having received a letter from his girlfriend for a month. Peering out from a corner of the staircase where he'd hidden himself, he saw the silhouette of someone with peach-colored pockets hanging from the waist. When the person turned and walked away, Ah Sum followed in pursuit, hoping to catch the petty thief. When he saw in the daylight that it was a young woman, he stopped, his hands falling to his sides. That evening he wrote a letter and dropped it in his mailbox.

In her catch the next day, Peach-Pocket Girl was surprised to find a letter for herself. It was addressed as follows: "For the girl with a peach-colored waist bag who steals letters." Sitting in a corner of the fast-food shop, Peach-Pocket Girl read the letter. The postman Ah Kin walked over to her. "Why do you steal letters?" he asked.

Gazing at Ah Kin, she stopped chewing her gum. "I'm looking for a subject for a novel," she replied.

"Have you found one?" he asked.

Peach-Pocket Girl, grasping the letter more and more tightly, burst into tears. Pushing this way and that, her hands involuntarily shuffled the pile of letters on the table as if drawing the prize-winning lottery ticket on television. To the side, Ah Ng had his eyes fixed on her, not noticing that the milk tea he was pouring was overflowing.

That evening, Peach-Pocket Girl went with the postman Ah Kin to deliver several hundred letters to their original recipients. When they got to Ah Sum's mailbox, she put in ten letters but kept the final letter in her waist bag. As the postman Ah Kin stood in the dark night street to see her off, his attention was fixed on the pockets flapping emptily from her waist as she walked away; he felt as relaxed as if he'd delivered the letters himself and even forgot whether she turned around to look at him. From that day on, Ah Ng never again saw Peach-Pocket Girl reading letters at the fast-food shop, and he continued to believe it was because the previous day she'd split up with her boyfriend after a row.

83

TWISTED STRANDS

Poh Kei hadn't changed her hairstyle since Ho Chik Yan's guidance in her fourth year of secondary school. Her naturally long hair reached her shoulders, and with two inches being cut every two months, that was how it was for seven years.

Poh Kei's school results had been quite good in her early years, but after her parents' divorce when she was in year four of secondary school, she was no longer in the mood for study. She had her hair permed and dyed a golden color, would hang out with a youth gang after school, and had even tried suicide. After a new guidance teacher by the name of Ho Chik Yan arrived at the school and took over her case, Poh Kei became actually quite well behaved, letting her hair grow straight and dying it coal-black again. When Ho Chik Yan's colleagues asked what was his magic formula, he just laughed and didn't say anything. It was only three years later, when Poh Kei had graduated and been accepted at the Department of Chinese at university, that they openly became lovers, but Ho Chik Yan consistently stressed that previously their relationship had just been that of teacher and student. Since they had behaved in such a strictly correct way and hadn't rushed ahead, others approved and praised them as an ideal couple.

Poh Kei never said anything about this love affair. Many boys had pursued her after she'd gone to university, but as she evaded them one after another, it gradually became known that her heart belonged to someone else, and no more complications occurred. Taking pleasure in being left in peace, and with her studies proceeding smoothly, she graduated with a first-class honors degree. Ho Chik Yan thought Poh Kei should go on to postgraduate study, and she didn't disagree, starting on a master's degree as a matter of course. They arrived at the point where they were planning marriage and getting a mortgage.

The change began with Poh Kei's braids. It was a popular new hairstyle in the spring of 1999 that was nothing like a traditional perm; instead, the hair was twisted into lots of braided strands held together and shaped with aluminum foil. Heads looked like sea urchins; shaken out, the hair became innumerable fine braids.

It was the hair stylist called Joe who egged Poh Kei into twisting her hair into these shapes. "We'll smash the shackles of convention!" he said.

Without actually giving it much thought, Poh Kei said farewell to seven years of long straight hair. Her hair done, she went to see Ho Chik Yan. For half a minute he didn't recognize Poh Kei, but once he recovered from his stupefaction, he completely lost his temper. He wanted to know why she hadn't asked him first if she wanted to change her hairstyle. Making her hair look like this, she'd turned herself into some girl out of a street gang; anything natural, true, and pure was gone. He also asked if she didn't remember how he'd helped her turn over a new leaf years ago. All along, Poh Kei listened without saying a word, waiting for Ho Chik Yan to vent his anger until he was tired.

"Then why don't we split up for a time!" she finally said.

Their friends felt Poh Kei didn't deserve it, saying she hadn't meant for this to happen, it was just that Ho Chik Yan had to be so stubborn and narrow-minded. However, in her own mind, Poh Kei had actually been well aware of what might happen. Once, Joe happened to see her on the train and came over to sit down next to her. Saying her braided hair was getting prettier the more you looked at it (and it wasn't clear if he was praising himself or Poh Kei), he noticed that her smile seemed forced and so he asked if there was something she was unhappy about. Poh Kei said it was fine, it was just that her boyfriend didn't like it.

"That's no good, no good at all!" he said at once, pulling a long face and frowning. Immediately taking Poh Kei back to his hairdressing salon, he straightened her hair again. "I won't accept payment; the important thing is you're happy with it," he said. Looking into the mirror, Poh Kei saw that her old appearance had indeed been restored, but in her heart something was not quite the same.

Seeing Poh Kei and Ho Chik Yan reconciled, everyone said they had expected it all along. Poh Kei also accepted Ho Chik Yan's opinion about giving up her study for the master's degree and instead found a job as a secondary-school teacher. Once, passing the hairdresser's, she could see Joe from a distance bending his head, absorbed in cutting a customer's hair. Then she felt her own long hair hanging down in strands, gracefully touching her shoulders, floating around her earlobes, and blown by the wind at the back of her neck. Glimpsing her reflection in a display window, she saw herself flicking fine strands of braided hair. In a sudden fright, she turned her head and quickly walked away. After that, she never set foot in that neighborhood again.

84

SUNDAY

Yue Yan and Yi Chiu had met five times altogether, each time on a Sunday for five Sundays in a row, but then they stopped seeing each other. They had got to know each other at a friend's wedding, as Yue Yan was among the "sisters" on the bride's side, and Yi Chiu was among the "brothers" on the bridegroom's side at the fetching of the bride from her home. After the groom and "brothers" had faced up to the customary challenges and battle of words with the "sisters," Yue Yan and Yi Chiu had sat down and chatted. They got along well, and confrontation turned into friendship. As everyone went their separate ways after the banquet, Yue Yan felt lost. Looking back across the street, she thought she would surely meet him again.

Afterward, the newlyweds' friends acted as intermediaries to get them together, and Yue Yan and Yi Chiu did indeed begin to see each other. Once it started, it soon became passionate. They went out together on a Sunday, and after a visit to a cultural-relics exhibition, they talked about everything under the sun, returning home in the middle of the night. The following Sunday happened to be Valentine's Day. Yi Chiu had gone to a great deal of trouble to get a small-scale reproduction of a tomb figurine of a warrior on horseback as a present for Yue Yan, but it had no special significance and seemed just a friendly gesture. They purchased film, theater, and concert tickets in advance for the next three weeks, so that they could continue to meet, and both felt quite pleased about it. The third Sunday they saw a film, but Yi Chiu fell asleep halfway through. When it came to an end, Yue Yan asked if he was too tired from work, but Yi Chiu said no. They didn't know what to do next, so the couple wandered around aimlessly outside Sha Tin Town Hall.

"We'd better get back," Yue Yan said.

The play they saw on the fourth Sunday was depressing, and the feeling lingered, so that over dinner they exchanged only a few words. On the fifth Sunday, the two of them arrived on time with their concert tickets and took their seats, but it seemed as if the symphony would never end; the longer Yue Yan sat there, the more she suffered. Afterward, the couple strolled wordlessly along the waterside outside the Cultural Center. Yue Yan kept blaming Yi Chiu for deliberately treating her coldly, but, as Confucius said, "When names are not correct, speech will not accord with them," and so she kept her thoughts to herself. Yi Chiu could tell from the look in her eyes that Yue Yan wasn't happy. Under the impression that she'd lost interest in him, he found it awkward to make a show of witty conversation. Instead he made up his mind to act like a gentleman, dull and aloof. Leaving everything vague, the couple didn't meet again.

During the weeks that she'd spent with Yi Chiu, Yue Yan had often thought of getting a mobile phone, but she'd never admitted to herself that it was to make it easy for Yi Chiu to get in touch. Having put it off for so long, when she actually got one, she was no longer angry with Yi Chiu, but it was all over between them. By then there was already someone else making phone calls to her. This man was a friend from church whom she'd known for a long time and who'd expressed some sympathy for her. Originally Yue Yan had not been interested in him, but later she suddenly accepted his attentions. The other church members expressed their approval, crowding around her, and Yue Yan thus acquired a boyfriend. Yue Yan and her boyfriend both felt that the other was very busy at work and made allowances, so that they rarely saw each other on weekdays and only met when they were assembled before the Lord at the Sunday church service. When her old friends called Yue Yan on Sunday afternoons, she was always at home.

When she'd had her mobile for three months, Yue Yan noticed that there were ads everywhere for "Sunday Independence Day," with pictures of Sun Yat-sen, Gandhi, and John F. Kennedy saying that March 1 was Independence Day. Television commercials showed what looked like Eastern European crowds at democracy rallies, furiously charging military and police lines and throwing their old handsets up in the air. When Yue Yan passed one of the Sunday Communications Company shops, she suddenly halted and asked the shop assistant what Independence Day meant.

"It just means that you can decide for yourself!" the girl said.

Yue Yan sat down and said she wanted to change her mobile provider but keep her old phone number. The assistant asked when the contract with her old provider expired.

"I signed up for two years and paid in advance, just over three thousand dollars, and it still has twenty-one months to run," she answered.

The assistant was astonished, thinking she was making a joke. "If you change your provider now, you'll lose everything you paid!" she kept repeating.

"I know, it doesn't matter," Yue Yan said.

The assistant was confused and curious. "Is your old service not so good?" she asked.

"I prefer yours," Yue-yan just said.

It was a Sunday. There was no apparent difference to Yue Yan's mobile and the number was the same as before, but she still felt it had a brand-new look to it. Coming to a resolution, she gave Yi Chiu a call and told him she would like to see him and begin all over again.

As of March 1, 1999, local mobile-phone users could continue to use their original numbers when they changed service providers.

85

A TEMPORARY TATTOO

One day after work, Loh Tat Tak and a few of his colleagues went to a restaurant serving American food. The waitresses were promoting that day's drinks specials, but he wasn't interested. It was afterward, when a waitress was placing a plate of oven-baked spareribs in front of him, that Loh Tat Tak was drawn to Little Green Fish.

Both waitresses and waiters at the restaurant wore white shirts and black trousers with blue-and-white striped aprons tied in front, and, with their sleeves rolled up, they created a casual, friendly impression. The waitress's little green fish tattoo was on the soft skin halfway up the inside of her right forearm, barely covered by her rolled-up sleeve. When she stretched out her hand to put a plate on the table, the little green fish was revealed, but it disappeared when her hand was hanging down again. From then on, Loh Tat Tak kept looking up, following the waitress with his eyes, oblivious to everything else. What he saw was a woman with her hair neatly framing her face, which was so pale that it made her shirt seem gray.

Not long after, when there was going to be a gathering of his old schoolmates, Loh Tat Tak proposed that they go to the American restaurant. As soon as he stepped inside, Loh Tat Tak sought out Little Green Fish, fearing that the seats arranged for them might be too far away from her. When the person in charge of seating showed them to the section that Little Green Fish was responsible for, Loh Tat Tak felt as if a savior dwelled in the darkness. Little Green Fish was just as attentive as previously, turning from guest to guest after the meal to ask if the food had been to their liking. They licked their lips, completely satisfied. Loh Tat Tak alone wasn't asked. Acting as if he'd dropped something, Loh lowered his head while looking sideways at Little Green Fish's right wrist. As the opening of her sleeve was briefly visible, it seemed something green flashed past his eyes. When it was time to leave, he couldn't help wondering whether she'd recognized him. His old classmates were waving goodbye and didn't notice.

From then on, Loh Tat Tak always walked past the American restaurant after work. A few times he paced back and forth outside, looking for signs of Little Green Fish in the dim light. One day, finally unable to restrain himself, he walked in and sat down on his own in the section served by Little Green Fish. As he was summoning her, he felt unsure about whether it was right to show that he recognized her. Little Green Fish, for her part, didn't suggest that he should have a drink first, so he just ordered a big serving of honey-roast pork ribs. Cutting the ribs into small pieces, he chewed slowly, mouthful by mouthful, taking ages to eat it, until finally only scattered bones were left on his plate. Then he signaled Little Green Fish over and asked if he could have one of the daily specials. She suggested a vodka cocktail in a less than warm tone of voice, but the drink made his throat burn like fire. It was only on his way home, feeling rather dizzy, that he realized he hadn't seen the green fish tattoo on her wrist this time. Then his foot slipped and he fell over at the side of the road.

Loh Tat Tak had a fever for the rest of the evening, but after work the next day he went straight back to the restaurant. It was a Friday, with lots of customers, but they managed to squeeze him into an out-of-the-way corner miles away from Little Green Fish. The waiter at his side said something to him, but he heard nothing; he just went on gazing into the distance. Little Green Fish slipped nimbly back and forth between the tables, gliding as smoothly as a block of ice. When he also noticed how she often bent down to talk to a couple of male diners, a teasing smile on her face, the previous night's vodka welled up in his mind. After suffering the whole evening, Loh Tat Tak eventually seized his opportunity when she moved over in his direction. Grasping a paper napkin, he held up a hand to signal for the bill. At first she looked around, and it was only when she saw that her coworkers were all busy that she responded. Loh Tat Tak had scribbled a few words on the napkin and took the chance to press it into her hand. Lowering her head, she peered at it, squeezed it into a ball, and put it into her trouser pocket.

Loh Tat Tak waited for two hours in a dessert shop nearby. In the end Little Green Fish did come over when she got off work. He noticed that she was wearing a pale-green turtleneck jumper with short sleeves and carrying a gray woolen coat over her right arm. She was actually quite tall.

"Why did you ask me here?" she said as she sat down. Loh Tat Tak hadn't expected her to come straight to the point, so for a moment he didn't know what to say. Little Green Fish pulled out a packet of cigarettes and lit one. Holding the cigarette in her right hand, she turned it outward, with her elbow resting on the table, so that the inside of her wrist was turned toward Loh Tat Tak. However, her milky-white, translucent skin showed no sign of the little green fish tattoo and in its place was a scar as big as a lip. She noticed how Loh Tat Tak was staring foolishly at her wrist.

"That happened when I was little and got scalded by a falling clothes iron," she said. "What's the matter with you? It's close to midnight! What is it you want?" There was a faint pattern like fishtails at the corners of her eyes and it wasn't clear whether she was smiling or what. Loh Tat Tak looked away from the scar, his gaze finding no easy resting place. All at once he was overcome by a sense of loss.

86

THE NECK POUCH

Lennie hadn't been working at the snack bar of a small cinema for very long when a girl came up to him one afternoon and asked for a can of beer. Lennie sized her up for a moment.

"Not suitable for children," he said. Opening a small transparent green plastic case that was hanging down her chest, the girl pulled out an ID card.

"See, I'm nineteen!" she said.

Looking at the card, Lennie muttered to himself: "Fong Siu Yuen?" The girl swept the card back.

"The theater doesn't sell anything alcoholic," Lennie ended up saying.

From then on, he saw Fong Siu Yuen arrive every day about three or four in the afternoon. She would buy a soft drink, Coca-Cola or 7-Up, and sit in the folding seats of the cinema lobby stretching her neck to view trailers on the big screen. She'd watch them again and again, well over a hundred times, without getting bored. In the afternoon, the cinema was as tranquil as still water, and on many occasions Lennie and Fong Siu Yuen were the only people there, she looking up at the screen and he watching her. He noticed that she usually wore a tight-fitting little tank top and cropped pants, with the funny-looking case always on her chest. It was attached by a dark-green string hanging down in a V-shape from her neck, making her throat appear particularly long. Whenever he saw her approaching, he wanted to peep into the universe inside the case, but he could only see that it was crammed with papers and other stuff, so, after a couple of glances, he pretended not to be interested.

Lennie didn't understand why Fong Siu Yuen came there every day.

"Do you want to see a film?" he asked her once. "Why don't I get you a ticket!" He pulled out his wallet and walked toward the ticket office.

"No! Don't go making trouble!" Fong Siu Yuen had yelled.

Once or twice, Lennie had asked her if she was actually waiting for somebody, but she never answered. After that, Lennie felt he might as well get tough with her.

"What's with you chasing me?" he said the next time he saw her. "No way I'd go for you! Why don't you just give up and leave me alone!" Fong Siu Yuen lowered her head without responding. On second thought, Lennie felt alarmed, wondering if somehow he'd stumbled on the truth.

Once, when Fong Siu Yuen was leaving, Lennie followed her to clear things up. Seeing Lennie behind her in the street, Fong Siu Yuen looked disgusted and told him to quit stalking her. The more Lennie thought about it, the more infuriated he became. Stepping up, he grabbed the green case and pulled it off her as he pressed her head down. He ripped open one side of the case and emptied out everything inside. What he saw were various documents and papers, ID card, passport, student's MTR card, entrance ticket for the Certificate of Education exam, follow-up appointment for a clinic, 10-percent discount ticket for a sushi bar, birth certificate, Home Return Permit, all folded very small. About to question her, he looked at her standing there, her arms hanging down, crying like a child robbed of its toys. Hastily he stuffed the things back and returned them to her.

"Look, I'm done, okay," he said. "D'you have to be like that! I haven't touched you, so don't say I've harassed you!"

After that, Fong Siu Yuen didn't go back to the cinema, and Lennie thought he had nothing more to worry about. Going out with his friends after work, he began to notice that lots of girls had a little pouch hanging from their necks. Some were made of plastic, cloth, or beads; there were long, round, and square ones; and some had press studs, zips, drawstrings, or Velcro. As soon as he saw those little pouches dangling on their chests, he would, without being aware of it, stare at them. Some girls who already knew him told him off for eyeing them up, while girls who didn't know him avoided him. There was one occasion when, in a daze, he stretched out a hand to knead a girl's round persimmon-shaped cloth pouch, feeling how soft, fresh, and tender it was; this earned him a punch from her boyfriend. Afterward, Lennie spent a long time looking around a shopping center until he found one that was exactly the same. Every day he kept it in his trouser pocket, sometimes taking it out to let it dangle for a while before hiding it away again.

Finally, one afternoon, Lennie all of a sudden glimpsed a little green case flashing by outside the cinema. Seeing Fong Siu Yuen turning away and about to leave, he stepped forward to intercept her, hurriedly pulling out the persimmon-like cloth pouch and stretching out his hand with it.

"I just wanted to give you this pouch," he said. "This one's softer, so you needn't put up with it bumping against your chest!" Fong Siu Yuen actually stopped and held out her hand for the neck pouch. She felt it.

"Cloth isn't waterproof. When it rains, the things inside will get thoroughly soaked."

Lennie thought for a moment. "Yes, that's how it is," he said.

87

CUTIE CUTE &
HORRIBLY HORRID

Lai Tat Tat Wing, born in 1971, is a Hong Kong artist known for his comics.

Rubbity-Dub began to eat incessantly after her belly had grown big.

"You're bound to give birth to a tyrannosaurus," Belle had joked. The two of them giggled a bit, then stopped talking and got stuck into the biscuits.

Belle didn't know if Rubbity-Dub's condition dated from before or after they'd met. At first she thought this question was tremendously important. Later, however, Rubbity-Dub told her, "No matter what, I'm really hoping we'll have a child that belongs to both of us."

This one can only be counted as your child, Belle thought to herself. *How could it be mine?* In any case, Belle had no intention of investigating who the man was; even Rubbity-Dub herself didn't necessarily know.

The first time Belle met Rubbity-Dub was on the MTR. People were looking at the girl in a loose-fitting brown dress on her knees next to the train door, a trickle of blood running down the inside of her calf, but nobody made any move to help. Pushing through the throng, Belle guided the girl out to rest on the platform. She was about to call for a paramedic when the girl spoke up.

"Can you take me home?"

Belle pulled off her close-fitting gray coat, letting the girl support herself on Belle's shoulder, and asked for her name.

"Rubbity-Dub. What's yours?" she said, her lips brushing Belle's earlobes.

It was only later that Belle learnt that *Rubbity-Dub & Giggle Chick* was the title of a comic book by Lai Tat Tat Wing. There were also others, with titles like *Woody Wood Stack & Middle Mid Stick* and *Bouncy Bounce Prawn & Tippity-Top Fling*, all of them Rubbity-Dub's precious possessions. Belle had leafed through these stories about freaks and monsters. Although she thought them quite boring, there was also something rather cute about them. Rubbity-Dub was working at a florist's in Central, and Belle also had a job in Central with a private agency. They took the same route to and from work, so after a while, thinking they might as well get a flat together, they rented a small place in Caine Road. With Belle wearing an attractive dress, nylon stockings, and high heels to work every day, her long legs striding among the men in their knife-edge creased trousers, Rubbity-Dub felt envious. However, noticing how Belle kept peering at her round belly, she wondered what more could she wish for. Once, when Belle's male colleague Kim had been to the florist's to order a bouquet of roses for her, she ended up with a large bunch of withered flowers and twigs. Realizing it was Rubbity-Dub's doing, she burst out laughing.

As Rubbity-Dub's belly grew bigger and bigger, Belle was getting more and more nervous. She'd become inattentive at work and pestered Rubbity-Dub about what her doctor had said. Not only that, she bought a big pile of guides to pregnancy and childbirth, pressing Rubbity-Dub every night to review them. Rubbity-Dub, however, showed no interest in them; the only thing she cared to read was Lai Tat Tat Wing's *Cutie Cute & Horribly Horrid*. Belle became despondent.

"Since you haven't bothered to teach the proper ways to the baby in your belly, you'll give birth to a monster with great lumps all over it," she said.

Rubbity-Dub only laughed. "Fine by me, just fine!" she said, gobbling up a heap of potato crisps. After that, Belle pretended the matter was of no concern to her and showed no more interest, feeling that she'd be stupid to care about this silly woman. She even thought it might be best to move out.

Belle finally agreed to go out for dinner with Kim one evening. Halfway through the meal, she got a phone call from Rubbity-Dub, who said she was in terrible pain, and Belle told Kim to drive to the hospital at top speed. They spent the whole evening fretting outside the operating theater. Seeing a doctor come out in the small hours of the morning, she asked how Rubbity-Dub and the baby were. The doctor looked baffled.

"Baby?" he said. "The patient suffered from an enlarged belly, a very odd ailment. We went ahead and operated but it was only with a lot of difficulty that we managed to get rid of all the buildup of muck. There was as much as ten or twelve pounds of rubbish!"

Belle's eyes blazed. "What are you saying?" she yelled, grabbing his collar. "You're the one that's rubbish! You lot are a bunch of quacks! Give us the baby back!"

Kim, who'd been nodding off on the bench, woke up with a fright and nearly fell on the floor.

88
—
5s

Shiseido's 5S line of skin-care products, launched in 1998, was intended for younger customers. There were five categories, known as the five senses (5S) of well-being, each with products in a broad range of colors. The 1964 martial arts film *Buddha's Palm* (*Rulai shenzhang* 如來神掌), which spawned numerous other films and comics over the years, features heroes who project deadly rays from their palms.

Ah Koko always added an "Ah" in front of the name of everyone she spoke to, so that at school she often called other pupils "Ah Girl." When her school took part in the artist-in-residence scheme and invited Fan Man Sang to teach painting, Ah Koko addressed him as "Ah Painter."

Ah Mom said that Ah Koko had always been cheeky, ever since she was a kid, and that it was their fault as parents for not bringing her up properly. Ah Dad ran a noodle stall, with Ah Mom helping out, while Ah Koko and her two Ah Brothers did their homework on the folding table next to the food stall. After finishing it off at top speed, they would scuffle with each other in the street. In this way, Ah Koko was able to continue her studies all the way to matriculation level, pass the entrance exam for the Institute of Education, and eventually teach primary school, where she was an exemplary teacher. Her family thought it a miracle. Ah Koko, however, didn't think it was anything special, because she just had PE classes, running and jumping around all day. At best it was like being an animal trainer, matching skills with the kids and being just as free of any intellectual content.

The first day Fan Man Sang came to the school, it so happened that the teacher in charge of extracurricular activities had suddenly been taken ill and was in hospital, so Ah Koko was assigned the class that was to have the painting lesson. Outside the school, she saw a man wearing black-framed glasses approaching the entrance and looking confused.

"You're Ah Painter, aren't you?" Ah Koko asked.

Fan Man Sang didn't seem like an art teacher. He instructed the students to smear paint on their hands and experience what it felt like when their palms touched the drawing paper. The children had great fun turning everything upside down, everyone like a character from *Buddha's Palm*. Ah Koko yelled at them until she was short of breath and coughing, but Fan Man Sang just smiled from the sidelines.

"Wouldn't Miss Chiu like to take part?" he asked a little later.

Once Ah Koko joined in the game, however, she found it so much fun she got completely carried away. It wasn't until she noticed the pupils had gone that she realized the class was over and only she and Ah Painter were left. When she washed her hands, she couldn't get the paint off, however hard she scrubbed.

Afterward, Ah Koko turned up to watch when Fan Man Sang came back every week and would see off the pupils after class. Fan Man Sang, however, took her on as his student, often remarking that Miss Chiu was the naughtiest student in the whole class. Once, he brought along a photo album of his own work to show to Ah Koko after class. It was a series of pictures of one girl.

"Ah Model's your girlfriend?" Ah Koko asked immediately.

Fan Man Sang was amazed. "How did you know?" he said.

"Just a feeling, you know!" Ah Koko said.

Ah Model was a dancer. Ah Koko recognized her instantly when she spotted her in the street once. She was so tall, delicate, and beautiful that Ah Koko felt herself unbearably inferior. After Ah Model had stopped at a 5S cosmetics shop and bought a multipurpose color stick, Ah Koko asked the shop assistant what it was. She was told it could be applied anywhere, eyes, face, and lips, and so she bought one without quite knowing why. Asking about the meaning of 5S, she learnt that it referred to "the five senses": energizing, purifying, calming, adoring, nurturing.

When Fan Man Sang invited her to the film festival, Ah Koko felt more unsettled than ever before, but outwardly she adopted a casual attitude.

"I'm not that good at this deep stuff, you know," she said.

It so happened that the film they went to see was from Iran, and Ah Koko did her best to follow it, until she fell asleep halfway through. After they'd come out, they went to the Regent Hotel for coffee. Ah Koko, who was wearing a T-shirt, jeans, and running shoes, found herself shrinking back and lowering her voice by half. Noticing how pink her face was, Fan Man Sang assumed she'd applied makeup, but Ah Koko hastily said the air conditioning had made the venue stuffy, something her skin was sensitive to it.

"Rough types like me aren't too keen on makeup, that sort of thing!" she said.

"Actually you have a fresh pure beauty," Fan Man Sang said. Ah Koko, realizing her face must have turned even redder, felt self-conscious and embarrassed. Later, Fan Man Sang told her his ideal job wasn't actually being a painter but running a noodle bar; Ah Koko found that even more incomprehensible. Eventually he asked her a baffling question: "Supposing I opened a noodle bar, would you come and give me a hand?"

"Teaching isn't my ideal either," she replied, somewhat beside the point.

When Fan Man Sang gave his last class, he called on Miss Chiu to be their model. While the pupils painted her as a ghost-like creature, Fan Man Sang's portrait alone made her so beautiful that Ah Koko hardly recognized herself. After that, she had no further news of Fan Man Sang. On one occasion, she took out his painting of her from the drawer and used her 5S color stick to apply makeup to the face in the picture. The more she touched it up, the more false it looked, so she simply threw it away.

89

—

DRAWSTRINGS

Miyazawa Rie is a Japanese actress, model, and singer who was known to have suffered from anorexia.

Drawstrings were popular in the spring and summer that year: they were everywhere, around the necks and lower hems of the tops, and the waists and legs of the trousers. Scarlett was in the changing room of a fashion store, trying on a pair of drawstring pants, which she pulled in until they were tight around her waist. When she looked at her flat belly in the mirror, she thought of Woody. Wearing her new pants, she walked into a lift at the shopping center only to see in the mirror that the person standing behind her was Woody.

It had been nine years since Scarlett and Woody had last seen each other, but she recognized him at a glance. Woody had been a volunteer worker at a young people's center when he was younger. One of the girls there, who was extremely clever at playing with string figures, was Scarlett. Woody was sixteen then, and Scarlett eleven, and even though the gap between them wasn't so great, it was the difference between a child and a grown-up at the time.

It wasn't clear to Woody whether Scarlett hadn't really changed or whether it was his original impression that was stuck in the past, but he felt she was still the girl who twisted strings around her fingers. Nonetheless, Scarlett would in fact already be twenty, while he himself was just twenty-five. They now belonged in the same age group, and his own girlfriend, Siu So, was only twenty-one. Somehow he found it difficult to grasp the fact that his girlfriend and the young girl were the same age.

While it wouldn't be true to say Scarlett hadn't grown taller, she'd retained her slender appearance. Her eyes, ears, nose, and the corners of her mouth were all sharply pointed, but together they resulted in an unusually harmonious beauty. Later, when Scarlett went to Woody's ice cream and yoghurt bar for something to eat, Siu So said she looked like Audrey Hepburn. Woody looked her up and down.

"I'd say she's like Miyazawa Rie after her anorexia, and you look like her before the anorexia," he said. Siu So hit him with her ice cream scoop.

Woody also found it hard to grasp that Scarlett already had a job. She handled sales promotion in Mong Kok, not far from his shop, and after this, she'd often pass by, at times with a friend, at other times on her own. Although Scarlett's friends were female, all of them were smokers. It actually made Woody feel uneasy, and it was a good thing he didn't see Scarlett smoke. He couldn't understand why he felt that way, since he and Siu So were smokers themselves. On two occasions, Scarlett brought with her a young man with dyed yellow hair, and Woody's discomfort increased. However, he didn't ask Scarlett about him.

Scarlett always wore tops and pants with drawstrings. They hung from her body, which was so thin it cast no shadow. She sat eating fruit yoghurt at the bar, her back to Woody. Her hair was piled into a bun on top of her head, exposing the scruff of her soft white neck. Woody recalled how he'd helped Scarlett in the past with extra classes after school, at times stepping aside to look at her from behind as she bent over her assignments. What she'd worn then had been a kind of strapless top with an elastic drawstring, but she hadn't pulled it tight below her shoulders, only draped it loosely around her neck. At the time, it was as if Woody's hands felt ready to stretch out, but numbness constricted his fingers. Then there was the occasion when the youth center went for a long hike. After walking half the way, Scarlett began to complain about being tired, so Woody fell back to keep her company. Unexpectedly a mist arose, so they couldn't see the fingers of their outstretched hands, and the two of them found themselves stranded halfway up the mountain. Scarlett said she was scared, so Woody untied a piece of red string with a jade pendant that he wore around his neck and tied their thumbs together at each end. Leading each other by holding on to the string, they groped their way downhill. They could feel their end of the string constantly getting tighter and then loosening, and they found it impossible to utter a word all the way down.

The day Woody told her he intended to marry Siu So, Scarlett stayed on until closing time. Siu So had something else to do and wasn't there, so Woody accompanied Scarlett on her way home. Halfway there, she said she'd like to go and sit for a while at his place. Once they'd got there, both realized what they were there for and set about doing it, as if by the most silent agreement they'd ever had between them. Although she was very thin, her body was soft and yielding, as she gently embraced Woody. Afterward, Woody felt guilty. His eyes stayed wide open the whole night, but he wasn't sure whether it was because of Siu So or because of the little girl Scarlett of the past. Feeling troubled, he got out of bed, picked up Scarlett's pants from the floor, and pulled out the drawstring from the waist. Scarlett remained fast asleep as he tied one end around her right thumb and the other around his own left thumb: it was as if they were again on the road lost in the mist. When she woke up in the morning, Scarlett cried out, rubbing her thumb that had been pulled till it hurt.

"What the hell are you doing?" she said.

"Don't you remember, Scarlett?" Woody asked her repeatedly.

Scarlett jumped up and down, pulling her pants up as the waist kept slipping down. "Remember what? Why don't you give me my string back right now!" she pressed him. "Your wife's coming to get you!"

90
—

THE THREE SKEWER BROTHERS

"The Three Dumpling Brothers" ("Dango san kyōdai" だんご 3兄弟) is a Japanese children's song about three dumplings on a skewer, which became tremendously popular in 1999. Guilian Dudu 鬼臉嘟嘟, here translated as Funnyface Tootoot, is the brand name of a kind of biscuit with faces on top. They originate in Brazil, where they are known as Trakinas, meaning "naughty child." Yoshinoya is the name of a Japanese fastfood chain with many outlets in Hong Kong.

Yosha and Funnyface Tootoot didn't really count as friends, but each was trying to find a certain kind of foodstuff, so it seemed they could understand one another.

The first time they met was outside a Mong Kok dessert shop. It was Funnyface's first day at work, and the boss had told her to stand outside in front of a stall and sell meatballs on skewers. An article cut from a weekly magazine had been laminated and put at the side, together with a homemade sign saying "The Three Skewer Brothers." Also on the sign was a photocopied picture of three meatballs on a skewer, each a round shape with eyes, a nose, and a mouth. A girl walking past in the street turned around and came back to ask Funnyface what it was she was selling. Picking up the sign, she read: "The Three Skewer Brothers." She bought a skewer and bit off a piece on the spot.

"Phooey!" she said, pulling a face. "These are cuttlefish balls!"

In the end, however, she bought five of the Three Brothers skewers, eating them as she chatted to Funnyface. She said her own name was Yosha, but Funnyface thought she said Yoshinoya. When Yosha was told Funnyface's name, she found it very strange and asked her to explain. "It's the name of a kind of biscuit," Funnyface said. "There's a silly chubby face on them."

Yosha was delighted. "Then they're just like the Three Skewer Brothers, aren't they!"

One Sunday, when Funnyface was passing a snack-food shop, she went inside to ask the sales assistant if they had the kind of biscuit called Funnyface Tootoot. To her surprise, the girl in the shop turned out to be Yosha.

"It's you!" they both shouted. Yosha said it was nearly time for her to get off work, so she left with Funnyface for a cup of tea. Funnyface told her she'd already spent two years searching everywhere for that kind of biscuit.

"Then I'll start looking for the real Three Skewer Brothers!" said Yosha.

The Three Skewer Brothers were originally characters in the song "Dango" in a Japanese TV children's program. The sales of this song exceeded three million CDs, and the opportunity was seized to release a large amount of Three Skewer Brothers merchandise. "Dango" originally referred to traditional Japanese sweet dumplings, snacks made of glutinous rice flour and stuck on skewers with powdered sugar or soy sauce. The local imitations of the Three Skewer Brothers were similar in appearance but were actually things like fish balls, meatballs, or shrimp balls. However, Yosha could count herself lucky, as more and more people were getting to know about the Three Skewer Brothers, while no one had heard of Funnyfaces.

When people asked Yosha why she was so keen on finding the true Three Skewer Brothers, she was at a loss.

"I'm sure to find them!" she'd say.

If Funnyface in turn was pressed on why she was so keen to find Funnyfaces, she'd be just as vague, shrugging and saying it wasn't important. After the occasion when they had gone out for tea, they didn't run into each other again; they just remembered what Yosha had said when they were about to part: "I'm going to save money to go to Japan for the genuine Three Skewer Brothers."

Funnyface's appearance was in no way unsightly. Her face was plump and often wore a cheerful expression, attracting quite a few customers. The three boys in a nearby shop selling running shoes even came over every day to wait for her to get off work. They called themselves the Three Skewer Brothers of Mong Kok. She would just refuse with a smile.

Late one night that summer, Yosha suddenly appeared at Funnyface's shop. Funnyface invited her to sit down and offered her some watermelon and grass-jelly ice cream. Asked whether she'd gone to Japan in the end, Yosha picked up the spoon and jabbed at the ice cream a couple of times, her lips pressed flat.

"Basically there aren't any real Three Skewer Brothers! It's all humbug!" she said.

"Three years ago, there was a boy working at a biscuit company who gave me a packet of Funnyfaces," Funnyface then said. "They had the most god-awful taste, so I threw them out. Afterward, I thought of looking for them but couldn't find them again." She picked up a bamboo stick, skewered three sticky rice-cake dumplings, coated them with shredded coconut, and handed it all over to Yosha.

"So what happened with you and the boy?" Yosha went on probing.

"Go on, have a bite! It's the Three Skewer Brothers!" was all Funnyface had to say.

91

KHΛKI

At the first class in the elementary Mandarin evening course, the teacher from Peking asked the students what color they liked. When it came to the turn of a young woman sitting in the back row, she said "khaki" in Cantonese. The teacher didn't understand. The young woman pointed to the trousers she was wearing. "Cream!" said the teacher in Mandarin, enlightened. The young woman waved her hands and shook her head, saying "no" in both Mandarin and English. It was a case of a duck quacking at a chicken, and a young man who looked like a white-collar type became impatient. Going up to the whiteboard, he wrote out the characters for "khaki" and read the word aloud in Mandarin.

From then on, Ah Mai nursed an unfavorable opinion of the young woman, who always wore khaki trousers. She always came with a young man wearing a tracksuit and always sat in the back row; the two of them were always whispering to each other during class, and they were always mispronouncing words in the oral exercises. Ah Mai, who couldn't bear their disruptive behavior, always sat in the front row. However, he was always placed in the same practice group as the young woman, so that throughout the second half of the class he couldn't avoid the indifferent expression on her face.

Ka Ka felt that she was never quite good enough at Mandarin, where she was even worse than at English. She felt she had

no gift whatsoever for languages. Going to class with her colleague Ah Nam, she couldn't help grumbling to him about irritating problems at work. Otherwise, she was so tired that her
head flopped, but the teacher thought she was nodding in agreement. Sometimes the student sitting in front in his well-pressed
suit answered questions so loudly he startled Ka Ka awake. He
was also pretty good at letting flow a stream of words in the
small group, while Ka Ka, struck dumb, dried up and tuned out.
*If you know how to talk, then don't come to the beginners' class
and mess it up for everyone else!* she thought to herself.

Ah Mai ran into her twice in the street. One time was on a
Sunday morning. Ah Mai had arranged to meet his girlfriend,
Peachy, to go window-shopping in Tsim Sha Tsui. As he was
passing through Kowloon Park, he saw the young woman coming out from the indoor sports center with seven or eight people,
male and female, clutching badminton racquets. The woman's
short hair was teased back behind her ears, her face was bright
red, and sweat was dripping from the ends of her hair. She gave
Ah Mai a glance, apparently recognizing him. While Ah Mai was
hesitating over whether or not to say hello, she turned toward
her friends and asked loudly where they should go for dim sum.
Ah Mai awkwardly raised his hand and waved. Afterward, as he
strolled along the street with Peachy, he felt distracted without quite knowing why.

Ka Ka encountered her fellow student twice in the street. One
time it was in Causeway Bay, where she'd arranged to meet an
old schoolmate to go to a sushi bar. When she was passing by
the luxury-goods shops across from Times Square, she saw him
in a display window. She was about to express surprise when a
young woman wearing a peach-colored sundress moved to his
side. Ka Ka quickly suppressed her smile and, with her head low,
pushed her way into the crowd. Eating sushi afterward, she suddenly added a lot of wasabi, and it became so hot that tears
sprang to her eyes. But she didn't understand why.

One evening, Ah Mai arrived late for the Mandarin class. There weren't any empty seats in the front row, and Ka Ka was the only person sitting in the back row, so he sat down next to her. During the small-group practice time, Ah Mai asked Ka Ka, according to the textbook, what her phone number was. She rattled off some numbers, getting the pronunciation of the Mandarin tones all wrong. Ah Mai then taught her how to recite the numbers from one to ten. After class, they discovered that they were walking the same way. Halfway along, it began to rain. Ka Ka was wearing her usual khaki trousers; Ah Mai was wearing his cream trousers. The two of them scurried along, seeking shelter where they could. As soon as they reached the entrance to the MTR station, Ah Mai hastily wiped at the rain spots on his trousers. Turning his head, he saw that a handcart pulled by a middle-aged woman had turned over in the rain, and her parcels were all muddled up. Ka Ka ran over to help her pick up the parcels and make them secure. On the train, Ah Mai said that since graduation he'd worked at a bank. "I'm a social worker at the youth center," Ka Ka said. "I'm also taking night classes to make up my degree." She gave a tired laugh.

When they were about to get off the train, Ah Mai pointed at Ka Ka's trousers. "They've got dirty," he said. "Actually, there's not much difference between cream and khaki."

"Actually, there is!" replied Ka Ka.

For the final class, Ka Ka was as usual wearing her khaki trousers, which seemed to be spotless. After class, Ah Mai asked the teacher about going up to the next level. Turning his head, he couldn't see Ka Ka. After saying goodbye to Ah Nam on the street, Ka Ka slowly made her way to the MTR station. Along the way she paused a few times, pretending to look at the shop windows.

Afterward, Ah Mai made a call to the phone number that he guessed was what Ka Ka had said in class, but no one at the other end had heard of her.

92
—

WHITE BLOUSES

The Ching Ming Festival, which falls on April 4 or 5, is marked by visiting graves. Cemeteries are frequently sited on hillsides, and the tombstones often bear a picture of the deceased. White is the color of mourning.

Ming Fa had always worn a white blouse, from the age of six. At first it was part of her primary-school uniform, which consisted of a child's white blouse and a green skirt with shoulder straps. By the time she was eleven, Ming Fa was secretly yearning to go to a secondary school where they wore dresses, but in the end she had to wear a white blouse again, together with a gray pleated skirt. After secondary five, she switched to a school of commerce, where they also wore white blouses but with short blue skirts. After leaving school, she got a job, and two years later passed the university entrance examination. However, Ming Fa still wore white blouses, and it seemed as if they'd become her natural skin color.

Ming Fa's outer garments, woolen jumpers and coats, could be any color, but next to her skin she wore nothing but white blouses. No one noticed in winter, when she was dressed in heavy clothing, but as soon as summer came, they'd become aware of Ming Fa's white blouse, always a shaft of sunlight. Whenever their crowd went hiking in the hills and had barbecues, Ming Fa would be dazzling in white, and as her blouse became drenched with sweat, it would turn semitransparent, which led to the boys nearly collapsing from heatstroke.

In the summer after Ming Fa's third year at university, everyone began wearing white blouses. They came with long sleeves, short sleeves, and no sleeves; V-necks, crew necks and upturned collars; rounded shirttails, self-edging, and drawstrings at the bottom edge; formal, funny, skimpy and irregular, in any and every style, reflecting sunlight on each other out in the street. Ming Fa had nothing at all against this but continued to wear her beloved blouses with their tight waists and long sleeves.

While Ming Fa was in primary school, her mother would help her put on her white blouse every morning, doing it up button by button, from the lowest to the topmost one at her neck, saying that getting a cold in the chest would make her cough. Later on, Ming Fa learnt to do up her blouse herself without overlooking a single button, but she still coughed, and her asthma never got any better.

Ming Fa still remembered an occasion when she'd been in secondary three and gone to a cinema after school with a boy who was two classes above her. After the film was over, they'd gone to Pizza Hut for something to eat, and the boy kept lowering his gaze. She thought he was shy. It wasn't until they were about to leave that he haltingly told her that a button on her white blouse was undone. Looking down and seeing that her bra was visible, she almost burst into tears there and then. She had nothing more to do with boys from then on.

Instead, she came under the influence of Ah Po. She sat next to her in secondary four, and at first they didn't really have much to say to each other. The white blouse Ah Po was wearing looked rather grayish; also, she'd leave her top button undone and the knot of her school tie pulled down a little below it. When Ming Fa once asked why she didn't wash her blouse, Ah Po replied that it had been washed too often; it was old and worn and had belonged to her elder sister. Ming Fa took Ah Po home with her, picked out a new white blouse from her wardrobe, and let Ah Po change into it: her whole being radiated light. Ah Po stretched out a hand, loosening Ming Fa's school tie and undoing the button at her neck.

At first Ming Fa was about to stop her. "When I was little, Mom said I might cough," she said. Then, following Ah Po's example, she opened up her blouse at the neck. Her bad cough never reappeared.

When Ming Fa no longer had to wear school uniforms, she fastened fewer and fewer buttons in her white blouses. She wore them with the top two and bottom two buttons undone, revealing her navel, and the only ones fastened were the two in the middle, barely enclosing her breasts.

It was only after a full month had passed after the year's Ching Ming Festival that Ming Fa bought some flowers and went to the cemetery. That way she avoided encountering other people. The sunlight was very bright, and as she climbed up the long slope, she was soaked with sweat, her white blouse sticking to her back. Arriving at the tomb, she saw the photo of Ah Po still in her school uniform, with her school tie pulled down. After she'd placed flowers and lit a candle, Ming Fa stood up and turned around, looking toward the vast, deep sea facing the cemetery. When a gust of sea breeze came up from the foot of the hill and lifted the hem of her blouse, Ming Fa stretched out a hand and undid a button, leaving just one fastened, right in the middle of her chest. She recalled what it was like that time when she'd been in her bedroom with Ah Po. Only one button remained. The early-summer wind opened up her white blouse, warm, caressing her whole body.

93

BALLET SHOES

Chan Wai Chiu had been an irritant to Whitey Bones since she was little. Whitey Bones made fun of her, calling her "the wee wifie," because all her life she'd been tiny and walked with dainty little steps. Whitey Bones had very pale skin and bones like logs; she'd always been the big sister in the gang of girls at the housing estate. Ordinarily, Chan Wai Chiu would not dare provoke Whitey Bones; she let the bigger girl ridicule and abuse her, keeping her head down and slipping out of the way whenever she encountered Whitey Bones. Since she'd got to know the newcomer, Ah Sing, however, Whitey Bones had begun to make trouble for her. One time, she and her gang started a fire outside Chan's door with kerosene, but when her mom found out, she gave her a good scolding. "Behave yourself, you stupid short-ass, and steer clear of people who are bigger than you." Chan Wai Chiu, it goes without saying, really lost heart.

That day, she went and bought a pair of ballet shoes with blocked toes. She immediately became several inches taller when she put them on, and when she got up, she could stand on tiptoe. Chan Wai Chiu had never studied ballet, but from then on she walked on tiptoe, and her chin seemed to lift higher. When Whitey Bones saw Chan Wai Chiu's peculiar steps, which were even higher than she could take in her three-inch heels, she thought it most unfair, grabbed a length of water pipe, and chased after her, hitting her. Chan Wai Chiu decided it was best to run away, bouncing high up on tiptoes. Whitey Bones, however, getting even more enraged, chased her until she twisted her ankle. Chan Wai Chiu sprang far into the distance, running until the toes of her shoes wore out. She only stopped when she happened to meet Ah Sing.

"You're so tall, Chan Wai Chiu!" said Ah Sing. Chan Wai Chiu smiled, letting Ah Sing support her. When she took off her worn-out shoes, she couldn't stand up; it seemed as if the bones and muscles in her feet were shattered.

Cheuk Cheuk had all along wanted to own a pair of ballet shoes, but she had never studied ballet and so felt there was no reason for buying them. Later, when ballet shoes came into fashion, she finally achieved her wish. Cheuk Cheuk took no interest in anything at school; when she went to class, she would fall asleep; her homework was always untidy, and her hair and uniform never conformed to school rules. Her teachers, at their wits' end, simply let her be. Cheuk Cheuk had no friends at school, never exchanged glances with anyone, and since she was never bullied and never bullied anyone herself, what happened in class meant nothing to her.

What no one knew was that when Cheuk Cheuk was in her first year of high school, she would often linger outside the assembly hall after class, secretly watching a fourth-form student practicing ballet inside. Cheuk Cheuk even dreamt of those slender, nimble legs and pirouetting hips. The student left the school at the end of the term, and Cheuk Cheuk stopped waiting at the school gate. Later, Cheuk Cheuk took to wearing her ballet shoes to school. The class prefect warned her about the rules, and when that had no effect, the head of the guidance team was called in. Cheuk Cheuk was ordered to take off her shoes in front of everyone. Cheuk Cheuk suddenly stood up, rose on tiptoe, and, spreading out both hands, began to pirouette, going faster and faster, so that no one could catch hold of her. She leapt onto a table, one leap followed another leap, and with the skirt of her school uniform flaring out like an umbrella, she headed for the window, whirling around, and flew out.

Ling Sau had always fancied Yi Leung in the boys' dorm, but when she saw him talking and laughing with the girl students, she dared not approach him too bluntly. She tried to find out which subjects for liberal studies he chose, but when she signed up for classes, she did not see him there. One girl in her dorm who was in the same department as he was said she could introduce them, but Ling Sau was afraid. Later, Ling Sau bought a pair of ballet shoes and wore them back to her dorm. Her roommates wondered what sneaky business she was up to, walking around without making a sound. Ling Sau didn't believe them at first, but after making repeated tests, she realized it was true. Becoming more audacious, and wearing her ballet shoes, she would secretly visit Yi Leung. She would go out late at night, drifting down the corridors like the wind, and listen surreptitiously at Yi Leung's door. When she saw him, she'd silently follow after him. Unaware of her, and thinking he was alone, he would practice speaking English to himself; Ling Sau could barely repress a smile. At the library, she would also follow closely behind to look at him. Once, she saw him hide in a corner to look at an album of nude photographs; her face went red, and her ears became hot. Ling Sau would adroitly come close and then move on, so that Yi Leung never formed any clear impression of her; he barely recognized her when he came face-to-face with her.

One day Ling Sau was eating by herself in the canteen. She saw Yi Leung at the far end take his plate and come straight toward her. He sat down opposite her and hastily lowered his head. Yi Leung concentrated on eating in big mouthfuls and did not give Ling Sau a single glance. After she'd eaten, Ling Sau, disappointed, walked back to her dorm. Seeing a stray cat asleep under a small tree, and nursing her resentment, she crept up to give it a fright. What she hadn't expected was that when she came close, the cat's ears twitched, and the vigilant animal sprang away.

94

BIRKENSTUCK

Lan lo 懶佬 means "lazy fellow"; *kan* 勤 means "diligent" or "industrious." Café de Coral is a large chain of fast-food restaurants.

That morning, Lan Lo Kan had spent the whole night playing mah-jongg at a friend's place. Eyes heavy with sleep, he returned home by way of the train station. He had just reached Nam Tin when he saw indistinctly through the light mist a short girl walking along in front. At first he didn't pay any particular attention, but as he came closer, he narrowed his eyes, realizing the girl was not wearing any shoes but wading barefooted through the puddles on the ground. "Hey, what have you been up to, losing your shoes?" Lan Lo Kan said.

"I never wear shoes when I run away!" she replied.

Even Lan Lo Kan himself didn't know why he took the girl to buy shoes, despite being tired and sleepy. When they reached the shoe shop in the shopping mall, it was too early and the shop hadn't opened yet. The girl said she was hungry. The pair of them went to the Café de Coral across the way for breakfast. Lan Lo Kan lost his appetite when he noticed the black footprints that the girl left on the floor. He went over to the counter, picked up a dozen paper tissues, and handed them to the girl. "Why don't you wipe off your feet?"

As she wiped her feet, the girl said her name was Tok Tok and asked what his name was. "So your name means you're lazy and industrious," she said, making a pun.

Tok Tok selected a pair of Birkenstock sandals in dark brown with a round toe, and Lan Lo Kan paid for them. Seeing that Tok Tok had nowhere to go, he took her back home with him. It didn't occur to him then that she would stay on. His friends told Lan Lo Kan not to be so promiscuous. Lan Lo Kan insisted that he'd never got up to anything with Tok Tok, but no one believed him, and even Lan Lo Kan felt he was being a bit stupid. With Tok Tok living at his home, whenever he looked up an old girlfriend to sleep with, he had to borrow a friend's place for the occasion. But he never wanted to touch Tok Tok—or he dared not.

Tok Tok said she'd already run away lots of times. The first time was when her divorced mom brought a man home late at night; Tok Tok was fifteen. Not stopping to put on her shoes, she'd dashed out, walking all the way from Kwun Tong to a friend's home in Cheung Sha Wan. She never returned home after that but lived with different boys. Every time that happened, she bought a new pair of shoes, and when they were worn out, she would leave them at the boy's place, depart barefoot, and then change to a new pair. She'd worn basketball shoes, high heels, platform shoes, and thigh-high boots, but never for longer than one stay. Stretched out on the sofa, she raised the Birkenstocks on her feet. "These are the most comfortable," she said. "The last ones I wore until my feet completely changed shape."

When Lan Lo Kan heard this, he changed the subject.

Lan Lo Kan saw that Tok Tok was bored with just spending her days eating and drinking at his expense, so he said, "You ought to smarten up and do some proper work." In the evening, he took her out to help him sell smuggled cigarettes in the street. Tok Tok made fun of him. "That's what you call proper work?"

They kept at it until midnight without turning a profit. A few men were sheltering underneath a kids' slide in the park, playing cards by the streetlight and moonlight. Lan Lo Kan lost more than he'd earned, got into a huff, and went off to drown his sorrows alone. After a short while, Tok Tok came up to him and nudged him in the back of his leg with the toe of her Birkenstocks. "You ought to smarten up and do some proper work," she said. It took Lan Lo Kan a few moments to realize that she was parroting his own words, and he made as if to pinch her. The pair then went on drinking for the rest of the night.

The next day, Lan Lo Kan woke up with a hangover to find that he was stretched out on the sofa at home with a terrible headache. He remembered a naked Tok Tok, her raised legs and the Birkenstocks on her feet, but he couldn't figure out if it was a dream or a drunken illusion. Getting to his feet, he noticed the pair of Birkenstocks neatly lined up by his front door. When he picked them up and looked carefully, he saw the insoles were imprinted with the shape of Tok Tok's feet. Lan Lo Kan suddenly had a premonition that something was wrong. He pulled open the door and rushed out, running along the road to the railway station. When he reached the side of the park, he saw Tok Tok in the distance, springing to and fro on the lawn. A water sprinkler was playing over the grass, drops of water falling on the shorts she was wearing. When Tok Tok saw Lan Lo Kan approaching, she laughed, pulled her soft white feet out from the mud, and then pushed them in again. Lan Lo Kan felt a sudden surge of emotion. "Tok Tok, I'm going to stop selling smuggled cigarettes."

Tok Tok looked at him, her eyes wide. "Stop selling cigarettes? I thought you said you'd stop smoking."

95

CARGO SHORTS

People thought Tsuk Tsuk's cargo shorts were certainly a mistake. Tsuk Tsuk wasn't short, but she was skinny. She always wore a white top with a frilly or shirred collar, light makeup, and her hair hanging straight down, but she combined this with mud-colored cargo shorts that were several sizes too big. Since her skin was luckily somewhat dark and she was quite lively, it made them seem not all that inappropriate.

Tsuk Tsuk enjoyed her daily walks, expending a great deal of energy on them, and anyone she wanted to catch up with could forget about escaping. She had no job these days and spent her time looking everywhere for old acquaintances or getting to know new ones. For that reason, some people claimed Tsuk Tsuk must be anxious to find a boyfriend. The more enthusiastic of these people went to a lot of trouble to make introductions, and for a while there were more people lined up than she could cope with, although nobody understood exactly why. Tsuk Tsuk looked quite good; it was just that the cargo shorts were a bit odd, reaching down below her knees and so loose they looked like a skirt. They were tied rather tightly with a belt that almost gathered the fabric into pleats. That they were unsightly was just one thing; eventually, more than a few boys were also scared off because of those cargo shorts.

Ah Tang's first meeting with Tsuk Tsuk was through friends acting as go-betweens. They'd made an appointment to meet at a restaurant, and from a distance he could see a quiet, gentle girl sitting there, so his first impression was good. Ah Tang was also a polite, well-educated person, an auditor by profession and dressed in a suit and tie. After finishing the meal, their friends said they had to leave, and Ah Tang then asked Tsuk Tsuk if she'd like to go to the nine-thirty show at a cinema. It was only when they stood up that Ah Tang saw Tsuk Tsuk's workman's pants. Actually he found her outfit quite novel.

"Did you put on your brother's pants?" he teased.

Before Ah Tang, Tsuk Tsuk had given lots of boyfriends a go, for the most part just trying her luck. Two of them she'd thought were definitely acceptable, and there was no way she could have told they wouldn't measure up. One was called Skinny; he ran a second-hand fashion store. When he saw the way Tsuk Tsuk's cargo shorts hung down, he was full of praise, saying he especially admired people who had a bold dress style. He himself often went to extremes in arbitrary combinations that clashed for an aesthetic effect. He quickly became passionate about Tsuk Tsuk. One evening, after he'd closed shop, they didn't come out for a long time. The next day Tsuk Tsuk was off.

The other one's name was Prospero, and he delivered goods in a minivan, moving and lifting things. He was deeply tanned and muscular, his body reeking of sweat all day long, but Tsuk Tsuk didn't mind; she would sit in his van enjoying the breeze or help with loading and unloading like a female coolie. His fellow workers were on the point of calling her his wife. Prospero was a rough sort of man, with a filthy mouth, but he was upright and honest. It was Tsuk Tsuk who pressed him to drive his van up into the hills and loosened his belt when they got there.

Ah Tang didn't know any of this in advance. He went to the cinema a couple of times with Tsuk Tsuk, feeling neither good nor bad about it but not being impatient. Later, he asked Tsuk Tsuk why she didn't buy a pair of pants that fitted her.

"Actually the pants aren't mine," she said. Ah Tang's heart lurched and he dared not go on asking questions. The odd thing was that, from then on, it turned out he couldn't get Tsuk Tsuk's cargo shorts out of his mind: whenever he saw anything similar in the street, he felt his heart thump. Every now and then, he would go into shopping malls to search out shops selling cargo shorts, rummaging through their merchandise but not buying anything.

One evening, after seeing a film, Tsuk Tsuk went home with Ah Tang. Ah Tang thought he could foresee what was going to happen. As they came to a convenience store, he made an excuse of buying a can of Coke but also picked up a packet of condoms at the counter, his embarrassment clearly evident. Once back at home, Tsuk Tsuk took action and unfastened her belt so that the cargo shorts dropped to the floor with a swish.

"Take off your trousers then," she said to Ah Tang. As Ah Tang stared stupidly at Tsuk Tsuk's slender legs, she pushed him down on the bed and pulled off his trousers. Next she told him to lift up his legs, picked up her cargo shorts from the floor, and put them on him. Dragging him upright, she buttoned them and made him stand and turn around. She stepped aside for an assessment.

"Yes, it's you all right! You're a perfect fit, aren't you just, not too fat, not too skinny," she said. Utterly bewildered, Ah Tang was looking at the strange spectacle of himself wearing a shirt and tie on his upper body and cargo shorts below.

"So at last you've let me find you. The other time, you left the pants behind for me and went away. This time," she explained, clutching Ah Tang as if she were climbing a tree, "you have to promise not to leave me again!"

96

FLIP-FLOPS

Kitarō is a ghost boy in a manga by Mizuki Shigeru, based on 1930s' Japanese street theater and storytelling. Kitarō's hair hangs down over his left eye socket, and he wears flip-flops.

Around ten every morning, when Luckygirl Joy went to a tea café for breakfast, the woman sweeping the floor would always ask the same question: "So you're free this morning, is it night shift today?"

"Tonight I'm going out for a good time! Who bothers to work?" Joy would reply in a loud voice.

"Joy has all the luck, she's got a husband taking care of her!" the woman would say then. When Kitarō heard them, the corners of his mouth rose in a sly smile.

Luckygirl Joy sometimes came in for tea in the afternoon, making it twice in one day. She always said her husband only thought about making money, and it was terribly depressing being left on her own. Now, to have this twenty-year-old woman going on about being married—this was something Kitarō didn't believe, thinking cohabitation more likely. When everyone else talked about losing their jobs, Joy would flaunt her good fortune and be quite loud about it. Kitarō hated it when this happened. She would sit down and wave her hand at Kitarō. "Hey! A milk tea with a buttered pineapple bun. Lots of butter." Kitarō would spread a full inch of butter on the bun.

Joy stuffed it in her mouth, and the expression on her face as she gulped it down was something that made Kitarō both alarmed and keen to see.

Once Luckygirl Joy sat down, she would keep her legs wide apart, with her arms resting on the backs of the chairs on both sides, or otherwise cross one leg over the other, her foot bobbing up and down. Her toenails were painted a different color every day, but the brown flip-flops dangling from her toes always stayed the same.

Kitarō's hair hung down over half his face, so that only one eye was visible. He was in his early twenties, wore flip-flops, and had worked in the tea café all of three months, which counted as a record (and no one knew whether *that* was the work of gods or devils). When Joy arrived, they would eye each other up, chatting idly about this and that and slouching, with their arms resting on the table. At times Joy spoke freely in what seemed like flirtatious banter, but it also happened that she would flare up for no reason and turn her back on him as if outraged. Feeling put out, Kitarō would then retreat and find something to do, wiping tables or setting out sugar bowls, at the same time stealing glances under the table at her legs and the big and second toes that held the flip-flop strap. Her instep was pale, with blue veins.

Once, when Kitarō teased Joy saying they were a match made in heaven since they were both wearing flip-flops, she gave him the middle finger.

"Why don't you get lost," she said. "Don't you know anything? Mine's a famous brand, over three hundred dollars, this year's hot item. You reckon they're like your flip-flops, cheap stuff at ten dollars!" Kitarō countered with a rude expression, but when he went shopping with his girlfriend, Ah Lan, the same evening, he took her to a fashionable store and bought a pair. It was only when she put them on that he discovered that Ah Lan's feet were actually quite chubby.

After that, Kitarō often kept his distance in a corner, surreptitiously watching Joy's feet under the table but not quite daring to raise his gaze above the tabletop. Once, though, when his brain had gone all soft with watching, he looked up and saw Joy staring at him. As Joy stuck up her chin, Kitarō put down the sugar bowl he was holding and walked over to provoke her.

"What's going on, babe?" he asked.

"Can't I look at you?" Joy said with a flirtatious smile.

Kitarō screwed up his courage. "Look as much as you like! Take a good long look!" He leaned forward and pushed his face up close, the two of them glaring at each other. He touched her with his foot under the table, pushing up until one of her flip-flops fell off, and squeezed her toes tightly with his own toes. Unexpectedly, Joy gave out a sudden cry, and when people turned to see what it was, Kitarō let go of her foot and dropped down on a chair.

Joy gave an airy smile. "Why don't you go away then?" she said, and her voice seemed to tremble slightly. As they were shuffling their feet getting up, the Y-shaped strap of one of her flip-flops broke off with a pop.

"Put mine on," Kitarō said. Joy glanced at him for a moment and picked up one of his plastic slippers with her foot.

"You bastard," she said. "How come you're being nice? I'll give them back to you later." She walked off swaggering, her own flip-flops tucked under her arm. Passing the rubbish bin in the street, she threw them in. Kitarō was sitting down rubbing his bare feet.

Kitarō was late for a date with Ah Lan that evening, and when she became angry, he pulled off her flip-flops in one quick move and threw them into the shopping center's musical fountain, so that they shot into midair to the tune of Beethoven's "Ode to Joy."

Luckygirl Joy never came back to the tea café. The woman sweeping the floor said she must have found herself a job—in the end you just can't rely on a man.

97

HIROMIX

Hiromix is the pseudonym of Toshikawa Hiromi, a Japanese photographer and artist. In the second half of the 1990s, when she was around twenty, she became famous for photo books featuring her in her everyday surroundings.

Who was real and who was fake: Me or Me's Hiromix? Neither Me nor Me's Hiromix knew, and it was even more impossible to say what relation they had to Hiromix apart from the Konica Big Mini and snapshots.

The first time Me went to Ah Chai's photo shop, she opened her simple Konica Big Mini, emptying out a roll of 400-speed film. Ah Chai asked when she wanted to pick up the photos.

"How about in the next life!" she said and giggled when Ah Chai gave a start. He asked for her name.

"Me," she said.

Ah Chai became impatient, but she repeated: "Me, my name's Me!"

After Me had walked out humming a tune, the boss came over to Ah Chai. "That crazy girl coming in? She's getting a reputation around the neighborhood!"

By the time she reached twenty, Me had never said anything serious. As a child she'd asked her grandma how come she was so old and wasn't dead yet, so her grandma had a particular dislike for her, much more than for any of her other grandchildren.

Me was the fifth girl in the family, and when her mother found it hopeless trying for a son, she'd take out her anger on Me and beat her silly. Me was often left feeling confused, either laughing at whatever she saw or being very scared for no reason. At twelve she had a boyfriend and at thirteen she went to bed with a boy. She felt making love was great fun: it doesn't cost anything and when you'd had your fun, you patted your partner on the bum and walked away. Her favorite joke was to say: "I really like you."

Me's Hiromix was very self-conscious, aware that there were eyes watching her. However, it was impossible to know what she was thinking or what she was going to change into from the expression in her eyes. Me's Hiromix always looked straight at you, never avoiding your gaze. At times she could be seen tucking into a couple of eggs for breakfast, or doing something or other in the kitchen, or gulping noodles, or sipping coffee. At times she was at dance parties, or in various messy homes, at a street corner in the middle of the night, in a public toilet, at a swimming pool, in a bathtub, or in bed. Sometimes she was wearing clothes, sometimes not. The light control was quite poor, the bright bits too bright and the dark too dark. Sometimes there was a yellow tint and sometimes a blue one, either too warm or too cold. Sometimes there was a clear view of Me's Hiromix, her face and naked body, and at times there wasn't. There weren't any other people, or maybe there were but they couldn't be seen, there was only Me's Hiromix alone, facing herself.

Ah Chai had previously worked for a company that specialized in developing photos for advertising, which counted as an apprenticeship. Because of a clash of personalities, an excuse was later found to sack him, so he cast around for a job in a small shop. The first time he was developing Me's negatives, he noted that a few showed her not wearing any clothes. It gave him a bit of a shock, but he didn't let the boss know. When Me came to pick them up, she spread them out for a good look, pointing to her body in some of the photos, saying the color was too bright. Ah Chai developed those photos for her again but hid away the rejects. Then, plucking up courage, he made a whole new set of photos to keep for himself that he could study carefully as he lay in bed at night. At one point he noticed Me holding a photo book in one of the pictures and saw a girl with long hair and small eyes in this book, so he went to look for it in a shop in Mong Kok that specialized in books with pictures of sexy models. The shopkeeper gave him a Hiromix album, saying a Japanese child prodigy had taken the pictures of herself. The next time Me came to his shop, he taunted her.

"So you're aping others, playing at taking snapshots and making yourself look like them!"

To his surprise, Me's expression changed completely. Holding back her tears, she ran away without picking up her photos.

That evening, Me's Hiromix spoke to Me: "Why don't you just let me die! Don't let others look down on us!"

Early the next morning, Ah Chai saw Me walking into the shop smiling in her usual crazy way. She put down a film cartridge and left. Ah Chai saw she looked lovely in her mauve tank top, and, feeling remorseful about what he'd said the previous day, he developed her photos right away. The images that emerged were of Me naked, immersed in the bath, with blood flowing from her wrists, her eyes closed to narrow slits and raised toward the camera lens. The blood was so thick by the twenty-first picture that her body couldn't be seen. Spotting Ah Chai in tears behind the processing machine, the boss asked what was going on, so Ah Chai used the excuse that he had a bad cold. He put the photos and the negatives into a paper bag, hanging on to it all day as he stared blankly at the empty entrance to the shop. When it was time to get off work, he placed them in the drawer for photos to be collected. Back home, Ah Chai burnt every one of his photos of Me.

98

CHAPPIES

Chappies are characters of different genders, with different hairstyles, clothing, etc., but with identical bland, smiling faces. Created by the Japanese design group Groovisions in 1994, they have been used in advertising campaigns as well as produced as toys. Ikebukoro is a lively entertainment center in Tokyo; Shibuya is known for its fashion shops and nightlife.

Metrobabe split up with her boyfriend for the sake of going to Japan to study. Living in Tokyo for a year, she spent her days at school and her evenings working, rushing back and forth with barely any time even for a visit to Shibuya. One evening, at the Ikebukoro metro station, she saw a poster about the release of a Chappie CD with an array of female cartoon figures. After pausing in front of it for a long time, Metrobabe went to buy a paper cutter, but when she returned shortly afterward, someone had run off with the poster.

Blankie was always smiling: it was the only facial expression she could manage. When her teachers scolded her, she smiled, and when her boyfriend got annoyed with her, she smiled, making him even angrier. Blankie also kept smiling when they broke up. Once, when she'd been indecently assaulted, she went to a police station. Asked for her name, she smiled, saying: "A Chappie wouldn't cry, no way!"

When Squareface was little, she was fond of playing with paper dolls, dressing them by fastening flat clothes on the flat dolls, but what puzzled her was that the undressed girls were always wearing discreet white panties. The first time she made love with a boyfriend, she'd had white panties on. "You're like a Chappie that's got no clothes on," her boyfriend had said.

Lookalike was sorting out pictures of herself. She spread several dozen different kinds on the table: school photos, ID photos, photo stickers. Taking up a sheet of drawing paper, she stuck the pictures all over it, making a wall of faces, and gave it to her boyfriend as a present. The boyfriend then drew a cartoon in imitation and gave it to Lookalike as a birthday present. At a glance, it looked exactly the same as a magazine picture of a group of Chappies.

Since childhood, Dolly had been unable to perceive three-dimensional space. To her eyes, all things looked like flat surfaces, but as she was used to it, it didn't cause any great problems. It was only when it came to learning photography that she had no way of understanding the meaning of depth of field. Dolly had all along believed herself to be a flat, two-dimensional person. This meant her boyfriend couldn't hug her, and was even less able to penetrate her when they made love. He could only kiss her, just as she would kiss a Chappie in secret.

Topsy's boyfriend was a programmer who worked with computer animation. He immersed himself in designing virtual girls, inventing lovingly detailed three-dimensional figures on a flat plane. Topsy didn't think anything of it at first, feeling that the shading and curves of their skin and muscles were absurdly exaggerated. Later, when she sensed that her boyfriend was showing less and less interest in her own body, she decided to leave him. She drew a picture of a thin, flat girl on a piece of paper and stuck it on his computer monitor, writing: "A Chappie's a good girl."

Babyface would each week bring an illustration of a Chappie to her hairdresser with instructions to create a new hairstyle and dye her hair in a new color according to the model in the picture. The hairdresser had the skill to cut it so it had a two-dimensional look. Every time after getting a new hairstyle, Babyface would go to a photo booth to take a photograph of herself, compiling an album so she could recall the sensation of her hairdresser's fingers.

What Pastyface liked most of all was to cut out pictures of Chappie heads. If she hadn't got a lot to cut out, she'd make her own—they were actually very easy to draw. Then she would leaf through old photo albums and stick Chappie heads on her own face everywhere. In the last album, which had pictures of her and her boyfriend posing together while they were traveling in Europe, she still pasted Chappies on them as before. In job applications later on, she used Chappie heads for recent photos and also pasted them onto her ID and student cards. When she sat her final exams and the invigilators checked her student ID, they didn't say a word.

When Copycat was studying design at technical college, her secret love for a male teacher was unrequited, and she lost all desire to study. Close to despair, she was flicking through some Japanese magazines when she came across Chappie dolls, designed by Groovisions. They had large eyes, thin eyebrows, and upturned mouths; vast numbers of them had the same face but endlessly varied hairstyles, clothing, and adornments. And so she copied them. The male teacher called her in for questioning. "Copying or not copying, it's all the same, isn't it?" she said. "We were all Chappies in the first place, there's no escaping that."

Ever since she was little, Ellie had become used to people telling her that she resembled other people. When they said she looked like a good person, she was happy, but when they said she looked like a bad person, she took it to heart. Then, when she'd grown up, the boys who went after her would say that she was good-looking and somehow familiar, but when they were about to split up with her, they'd say they didn't feel there was any difference between her and other girls. Eventually, she thought she might as well forestall a boy she'd just got to know. "I'm actually like a Chappie," she said. "What's a Chappie?" asked the boy.

99

MADE IN HONG KONG

This sketch has some of the plot elements of a well-known Hong Kong film of the same name, made in 1997 and directed by the independent filmmaker Fruit Chan. However, the sketch is more low-key; the characters are not as tragic as the ones in the film. The girl's name in the story, translated here as Berry, literally means fruit, an echo of the film director's name. The film begins with a schoolgirl committing suicide by jumping from a roof, but Berry's attempt at suicide is feeble. The main character in the film is a boy called Mid-Autumn, the name of a major Chinese festival. Berry gives her boyfriend, Dragon, the nickname Double-Nine, referring to the date of the Chongyang festival in autumn, during which people visit the graves of their relatives; Wang Chongyang is also the name of a Taoist master who appears as a character in martial-arts fiction. Debt collecting by gangsters is a recurring theme in the film, and also occurs in the story. In the film, Mid-Autumn, who wears colorful shirts and wraparound yellow-tinted glasses, commits suicide by shooting himself on his girlfriend's tomb in Wo Hop Shek cemetery.

Berry wasn't really intending to commit suicide, but when her teacher found out that she'd forged her parent's signature on her report card, he not only recorded a demerit but also humiliated her in class. So when she passed by the railway line, she was seized by an impulse to jump onto the track. Dragon, who happened to be walking by, saw a girl in school uniform clambering over the fence and shouted at her to stop, asking what she was doing.

"What's it to you if I kill myself?" she replied.

"You'll delay the trains if you jump on the track to kill yourself, and it'll make a huge mess all over the place," he said angrily. "There's nothing more disgusting than people who don't have a public spirit!"

Berry noticed that his shirt was unbuttoned, revealing a green dragon tattoo on his chest, and she assumed he was a triad member. She wondered how he could talk about "public spirit," and then found the whole thing so funny she burst out laughing. That made him furious. "First you shout and then you laugh! Are you making fun of me, kiddo?" She saw he was carting a box of stuff and asked him if he was a deliveryman. He said he had his own business and, with an air of mystery, took a VCD out of a paper bag and gave it to Berry. "Watch this," he said. He asked her where she lived.

"Hong Lok Yuen, in Tai Po," she answered.

Luxury flats, thought Dragon, but he didn't say anything.

Without having planned it, Berry became Dragon's girlfriend, visiting him at his stall in Mong Kok, where she could borrow any pirated VCD she wanted, since the cost was so low anyway. When she grabbed a pile of popular Japanese TV soaps, Dragon scolded her for being such a fan of Japanese things. He tossed a VCD with the title *Made in Hong Kong* at her, saying it was a new release and had apparently won some kind of film award. Berry couldn't see any movie stars in the cast and asked what it was about.

"How should I know?" he answered. "You'll find out when you watch it."

Berry went back home and watched all the Japanese soaps, without stopping to eat or sleep, before bothering to watch *Made in Hong Kong.* She found it hard to follow, but her tears flowed when she saw one of the young gang members, nicknamed Mid-Autumn, go to Wo Hop Shek cemetery and commit suicide in front of Apple's grave toward the end of the film. The rather ordinary-looking actor who played Mid-Autumn in the movie, Sam Lee, was praised as a member of the new generation of stylish men by a weekly magazine. His hair was disheveled, and he wore colorful shirts a size too small for him and wraparound sunglasses with tinted lenses. Berry bought a pair of yellow sunglasses in the same style for Dragon. He said they were pretty cool and wore them every day, which made Berry very happy. She also gave Dragon a nickname, Double-Nine, but this did not sit well with him at all; he had always called himself Lucky Dragon and used to say that it was very auspicious, but Double-Nine might doom him to an early death. And anyway, he was not in the same class as the heroic Double-Nine Wang from martial-arts fiction. When Berry asked him to go with her to Wo Hop Shek, he became even more convinced that her brain was fried.

When Berry asked Dragon whether he could get her a gun, for some reason he flew into a rage. "Killing people isn't a game. You're an idiot, you're beyond help. Even if your family is rich, you can't get away with murder."

Berry became so angry at this that she broke it off with him, and when she got home, she threw all his VCDs into the bin. Then she went out to buy a replica toy revolver, like the one Mid-Autumn used in the movie, seeking that passionate, desperate sense of killing others and yourself on impulse.

Not long after, it was reported on the news that customs had uncovered a pirate VCD factory in Wo Hop Shek and started to close down the shops that sold large quantities of pirated VCDs. Berry began to worry about Dragon. She went to the Mong Kok electronics market, but the place was deserted. Then she called him on his mobile phone and his pager but couldn't reach him on either. After having searched everywhere for about a week, she found him one evening eating fish balls in front of a cinema. When he saw her, Dragon grinned, took her hand, and walked beside her. He told her the shop had closed down and he owed someone a large amount of money, so he'd had to go into hiding to save her from being dragged into it. Unfortunately, as they walked along, they ran into three youths claiming to be triads, who were out collecting debts for the boss. Their mouths trembled, and there was little flesh on their bones, so Berry pulled out the fake gun, and Dragon grabbed it for himself. Pointing to a couple of alleyways, he yelled something at the youths, who scattered like rats. When he realized that the gun was a fake, he rapped Berry on the head. "There's nothing real in this world," he said despondently.

They went to buy a copy of *Made in Hong Kong*, a legal one, but when they put it into the player, there was no picture on the screen. They spent all night trying to adjust it, with no idea whether it was the player that was broken or there was a problem with the VCD. Dragon got so angry he took the fake gun and shot wildly at the player. The gun emptied without causing any damage, but a stray pellet hit Berry's left eye, hurting so much that her tears flowed.

Weatherhead Books on Asia

Weatherhead East Asian Institute, Columbia University

Literature

David Der-wei Wang, Editor

Ye Zhaoyan, *Nanjing 1937: A Love Story*, translated by Michael Berry (2003)
Oda Makoto, *The Breaking Jewel*, translated by Donald Keene (2003)
Han Shaogong, *A Dictionary of Maqiao*, translated by Julia Lovell (2003)
Takahashi Takako, *Lonely Woman*, translated by Maryellen Toman Mori (2004)
Chen Ran, *A Private Life*, translated by John Howard-Gibbon (2004)
Eileen Chang, *Written on Water*, translated by Andrew F. Jones (2004)
Writing Women in Modern China: The Revolutionary Years, 1936–1976, edited
    by Amy D. Dooling (2005)
Han Bangqing, *The Sing-song Girls of Shanghai*, first translated by Eileen Chang,
    revised and edited by Eva Hung (2005)
Loud Sparrows: Contemporary Chinese Short-Shorts, translated and edited
    by Aili Mu, Julie Chiu, and Howard Goldblatt (2006)
Hiratsuka Raichō, *In the Beginning, Woman Was the Sun*, translated
    by Teruko Craig (2006)
Zhu Wen, *I Love Dollars and Other Stories of China*, translated by Julia Lovell
    (2007)
Kim Sowŏl, *Azaleas: A Book of Poems*, translated by David McCann (2007)
Wang Anyi, *The Song of Everlasting Sorrow: A Novel of Shanghai*, translated
    by Michael Berry with Susan Chan Egan (2008)
Ch'oe Yun, *There a Petal Silently Falls: Three Stories by Ch'oe Yun*, translated
    by Bruce and Ju-Chan Fulton (2008)
Inoue Yasushi, *The Blue Wolf: A Novel of the Life of Chinggis Khan*, translated
    by Joshua A. Fogel (2009)
Anonymous, *Courtesans and Opium: Romantic Illusions of the Fool of Yangzhou*,
    translated by Patrick Hanan (2009)
Cao Naiqian, *There's Nothing I Can Do When I Think of You Late at Night*,
    translated by John Balcom (2009)
Park Wan-suh, *Who Ate Up All the Shinga? An Autobiographical Novel*, translated
    by Yu Young-nan and Stephen J. Epstein (2009)
Yi T'aejun, *Eastern Sentiments*, translated by Janet Poole (2009)
Hwang Sunwŏn, *Lost Souls: Stories*, translated by Bruce and Ju-Chan Fulton (2009)
Kim Sŏk-pŏm, *The Curious Tale of Mandogi's Ghost*, translated by Cindi Textor
    (2010)
The Columbia Anthology of Modern Chinese Drama, edited by Xiaomei Chen (2011)
Qian Zhongshu, *Humans, Beasts, and Ghosts: Stories and Essays*, edited by
    Christopher G. Rea, translated by Dennis T. Hu, Nathan K. Mao, Yiran Mao,
    Christopher G. Rea, and Philip F. Williams (2011)
Dung Kai-cheung, *Atlas: The Archaeology of an Imaginary City*, translated
    by Dung Kai-cheung, Anders Hansson, and Bonnie S. McDougall (2012)
O Chŏnghŭi, *River of Fire and Other Stories*, translated by Bruce and Ju-Chan
    Fulton (2012)
Endō Shūsaku, *Kiku's Prayer: A Novel*, translated by Van Gessel (2013)
Li Rui, *Trees Without Wind: A Novel*, translated by John Balcom (2013)
Abe Kōbō, *The Frontier Within: Essays by Abe Kōbō*, edited, translated, and with an
    introduction by Richard F. Calichman (2013)

Zhu Wen, *The Matchmaker, the Apprentice, and the Football Fan: More Stories of China*, translated by Julia Lovell (2013)

The Columbia Anthology of Modern Chinese Drama, Abridged Edition, edited by Xiaomei Chen (2013)

Natsume Sōseki, *Light and Dark*, translated by John Nathan (2013)

Seirai Yūichi, *Ground Zero, Nagasaki: Stories*, translated by Paul Warham (2015)

Hideo Furukawa, *Horses, Horses, in the End the Light Remains Pure: A Tale That Begins with Fukushima*, translated by Doug Slaymaker with Akiko Takenaka (2016)

Abe Kōbō, *Beasts Head for Home: A Novel*, translated by Richard F. Calichman (2017)

Yi Mun-yol, *Meeting with My Brother: A Novella*, translated by Heinz Insu Fenkl with Yoosup Chang (2017)

Ch'ae Manshik, *Sunset: A Ch'ae Manshik Reader*, edited and translated by Bruce and Ju-Chan Fulton (2017)

Tanizaki Jun'ichiro, *In Black and White: A Novel*, translated by Phyllis I. Lyons (2018)

Yi T'aejun, *Dust and Other Stories*, translated by Janet Poole (2018)

Tsering Döndrup, *The Handsome Monk and Other Stories*, translated by Christopher Peacock (2019)

Kimura Yūsuke, *Sacred Cesium Ground and Isa's Deluge: Two Novellas of Japan's 3/11 Disaster*, translated by Doug Slaymaker (2019)

Wang Anyi, *Fu Ping: A Novel*, translated by Howard Goldblatt (2019)

Paek Nam-nyong, *Friend: A Novel from North Korea*, translated by Immanuel Kim (2020)

Endō Shūsaku, *Sachiko: A Novel*, translated by Van Gessel (2020)

Jun'ichirō Tanizaki, *Longing and Other Stories*, translated by Anthony H. Chambers and Paul McCarthy (2022)

History, Society, and Culture
Carol Gluck, Editor

Takeuchi Yoshimi, *What Is Modernity? Writings of Takeuchi Yoshimi*, edited and translated, with an introduction, by Richard F. Calichman (2005)

Contemporary Japanese Thought, edited and translated by Richard F. Calichman (2005)

Overcoming Modernity, edited and translated by Richard F. Calichman (2008)

Natsume Sōseki, *Theory of Literature and Other Critical Writings*, edited and translated by Michael Bourdaghs, Atsuko Ueda, and Joseph A. Murphy (2009)

Kojin Karatani, *History and Repetition*, edited by Seiji M. Lippit (2012)

The Birth of Chinese Feminism: Essential Texts in Transnational Theory, edited by Lydia H. Liu, Rebecca E. Karl, and Dorothy Ko (2013)

Yoshiaki Yoshimi, *Grassroots Fascism: The War Experience of the Japanese People*, translated by Ethan Mark (2015)